DARK THIRST

After the kiss, I buried my face in his neck. I nipped him at first, savoring the moment, my low moans echoed by his. Then when my teeth grew longer and sharper, I could hold back no longer. I bit him brutally, tapping the artery and was rewarded by the flow of his blood: hot, salty, and bitter. He shuddered violently and fought to push me away, but his resistance was futile. Finally his struggles ceased and his body grew limp as I continued to draw on him, gently now, almost tenderly. I drank a long time, slowly, relishing the feel of my own body being replenished. Then I withdrew.

Arising from the couch, I caught sight of myself in the mirror. No longer pale and haggard, my skin glowed with life and my eyes shone, victorious and demonic. A few drops of blood were trickling down my chin. I wiped them away with the back of my hand as I turned away from my reflection.

Books in the Vampire Legacy series by
Karen E. Taylor

BLOOD SECRETS
BITTER BLOOD
BLOOD TIES
BLOOD OF MY BLOOD

Published by Pinnacle Books

THE
VAMPIRE LEGACY

BLOOD
SECRETS
KAREN E. TAYLOR

PINNACLE BOOKS
Kensington Publishing Corp.
http://www.pinnaclebooks.com

PINNACLE BOOKS are published by

Kensington Publishing Corp.
850 Third Avenue
New York, NY 10022

All Kensington Titles, Imprints, and Distributed Lines are available at special quantity discounts for bulk purchases for sales promotions, premiums, fund-raising, educational, or institutional use. Special book excerpts or customized printings can also be created to fit specific needs. For details, write or phone the office of the Kensington special sales manager: Kensington Publishing Corp., 850 Third Avenue, New York, NY 10022, attn: Special Sales Department, Phone: 1-800-221-2647.

Pinnacle and the P logo Reg. U.S. Pat. & TM Off.

First Printing: January, 1994
First Pinnacle Printing: September, 2000

Printed in the United States of America
10 9 8 7 6 5 4 3

Dedicated in loving memory to my mother, Leona Gallagher, who must be pleased to know that her many attempts to encourage a creative spirit finally paid off.

ACKNOWLEDGMENTS

So many people helped with the completion of BLOOD SECRETS that it's hard to mention them all, but I'll try. Thank you to Cherry, my agent, and John, my editor at Zebra; to Cheri, Elise, John, Pam and Randy for their proofreading talents and continuity checks; to Lori, my favorite writer/hair stylist; to the ladies of the neighborhood (Debbie, Debi, Karen, Kristi and Pauline) because they asked for more; to Ed and Celeste, whose suggestions and criticisms always went down easily with rum and Coke; to my father, Will, my brothers, Dave and Larry, and Dave's wife, Candy, for their loving support; to my children, Brian and Geoffrey, for (sometimes) being quiet at the appropriate moments; and most especially thank you to Pete, for being there, for doing the laundry and for keeping me in line.

Chapter 1

I stood at the window, staring at the late-night streets. All too soon there would be those first tentative walkers, anonymously muffled against the chilled morning air. They would be joined by others, growing bolder and more confident in their destinations. I thought myself thankful I would not have to join them.

I turned and surveyed the room. The remains of the work of the last month lay strewn around the suite: discarded papers and sketches, emptied wine bottles and brimming ashtrays. "God, what a wreck," I said aloud. The echo of my voice, in a room that had been so long silent, startled me. For the past month, I had lived on room service, solitude and my work.

The final results of this feverish month were neatly stacked and labeled for my secretary, Gwen, to pick up in the morning. Gwen was anxious to see the new summer line; her enthusiasm was almost overwhelming. It was her wide-eyed approach to life that caused me to hire her. All city people must have seemed odd to her then. In our initial contact I must have appeared as one of them—powerful, polished and no less eccentric or inapproachable. If after ten years she realized my lifestyle was more bizarre than most, she let no condemnation of it affect our friendship.

The answering machine light beckoned me, but I decided that the phone messages could wait until after I showered and slept. It was far too long since I had attended to personal needs, so immersed was I in my designs. I laughed to myself about how

I would appear to the fashion world at this moment. Disheveled and unkempt, I couldn't be that same person known for her elegant and romantic fashions, her fastidious attention to details. "You're old enough to know better," I addressed my mirrored image and appraised the damage done as I removed my jeans and shirt. I distrusted mirrors; one of my greatest fears, especially after one of my extended work periods, was that I would fade away to nothing. I was pleased to find that I was not as insubstantial as I felt; I was perhaps thinner and paler than usual, but still very much alive. I turned out the light, removed my contact lenses and stepped into the shower.

Some light filtered into the room from the hall, just enough so that I could see small tufts of steam rising. A hot shower had always been an almost religious experience for me; I enjoyed the feel of the water flowing over my body, relaxing, caressing and renewing. A new twist, in these later years, was the almost pitch blackness of the bathroom, a condition once made necessary by my extremely light-sensitive eyes. Now with new and improved contacts, I could shower in the light, but I had found the combination of darkness and water so intimate and sensuous that I could not bear to violate their union.

Afterward, I wrapped myself in a towel and prepared the suite for my sleep. The outer rooms would need to be left single-locked only, so that the hotel staff could get in. Whoever has tomorrow's shift will have quite a job, I thought to myself, remembering the condition of the room, but shrugged the guilt away knowing that sleep was what I needed most.

Picking up my lenses from the bathroom, I entered the bedroom and triple locked the door behind me. Only I had a complete set of three keys in my possession; the hotel had one of them, Gwen had a second and Max had the third. Privacy in sleep is essential to me. I closed the blinds, pulled the heavy drapes shut and crawled into bed. It was almost sunrise.

"Please, God, no dreams," I prayed. I felt my body relax, and I slept.

My slumber was burdened by interruptions that day; I felt,

rather than heard, the sounds of life all around me. The cursing of the maid cleaning the outer rooms, Gwen's tentative knock and entry, the rustling of pages and her call of "sleep well," as she left, the traffic from outside and the elevator bell farther down the hall, even the insistent whirr of the telephone answering machine; all these noises filtered into my sleeping consciousness. I wondered if people in a coma felt this way, semi-aware of life continuing around them, but powerless to make a response. I envisioned myself, lying on my back on the bed, eyes wide open yet seeing nothing, seemingly dead. A moment of panic ensued; if I should die, how long would it take to be discovered? Almost as soon as the thought entered my head, I dismissed it. I was not dead, and although there was a time when I desired death, it would not come now.

Eventually the sounds ceased and sleep came, magically deep. When I finally awoke, I perceived that the sun had already set. The noise from outside seemed sharper and more distinct; the smell of the air crisp and cold. The alarm clock read 6:30 P.M. I stretched, yawned and listened to the wind buffeting the windows. As I listened, I became aware of my growing hunger. Once recognized, it threatened to overwhelm me, an engulfing need that must be met soon. It had been too long, I knew. I needed music and talk, a drink, a man. I would find all these things at Max's.

Unlocking the bedroom door, I went into the bathroom. In the medicine cabinet, I found another pair of lenses, dark amber, as close to my original eye color as could be found. They would be fine for tonight, enough to shield my eyes from headlights and barlights. My needs urgently prodded me as I washed, brushed my teeth and applied my makeup. My hair, snarled from the day's sleep, took longer to comb than I wished. The blood in my veins pounded the count of each endless second. It took no time to choose my clothes; I knew what it would be. "Black leather." I smiled to myself. "For Max."

Before I called the doorman to arrange for a cab, I checked the mirror. The black leather jeans were supple and tight, like a second skin, but the lace blouse softened the effect. I wore high heels to enhance my height of 5'3"—I liked to look people in the eyes. My hair, a deep auburn, almost mahogany, curled around my face and fell below my shoulders. My skin was pale, almost translucent, but the makeup helped to disguise this pallor. One final critical glance in the mirror told me that I looked good, even better than I should. I removed my coat from the closet, the one I called my wolf coat—the fur was shaggy and coarse and the color was a shadowy gray. It was a huge fashion success for me last season. I put it on and went for the phone.

I was surprised that when I picked it up there was someone already on the other end. "Yes?" I said, my voice rough and my manner abrupt.

"Deirdre, where have you been? I've been trying to reach you for weeks. What's the use of that damn answering machine if you never listen to the tape?"

"Sorry, Max," I said indulgently. "I've been working."

"Your obsession with your work will kill you one day. I know you haven't been taking care of yourself. Get over here now and I'll fix you up. But hurry, we close early tonight. It's Thanksgiving, you know."

I didn't know. "I'm calling the cab now," I said, hanging up and then dialing the doorman.

He greeted me as I got off the elevator. "Miss Griffin, the cab will be here in a few minutes. I'd advise you to wait in the lobby as it's a very cold night."

I didn't mind the cold, but I smiled my acceptance at his suggestion. The smile was all the encouragement he needed. "You've not been out for a while. Are you well?" He had perfected the obsequious manner, courteous yet subservient, and the hotel patrons tipped him well.

I was no exception. In fact, I had become even more generous with the staff since I began hearing the whispers about me. Innuendos and speculative comments about aspects of my life had begun to filter through partially closed doors. This always made me nervous, almost paranoid, so I tipped well. I discovered that people would be unlikely to ask questions or turn on you if you did. "Never bite the hand that feeds you," I murmured to myself.

"Miss Griffin?" he questioned. "Are you okay?"

"Yes, I'm sorry, Frank, I was thinking of something else. I'm fine. I've just been working too hard."

The cab pulled up to the front door; he ushered me outside and into the backseat. I thanked Frank and instructed the driver, "The Ballroom, please."

Over ten years ago, Max had purchased a small nightclub in midtown. He had christened it the "Ballroom of Romance" and had retained me to provide the decor. Thrilled at the prospect of leaving a bad situation, I jumped at the chance. We decided on a Victorian approach—lace and hearts, black-and-white silk wallpaper, heavy fringe on the small lamps adorning the walls. The dance floor was surrounded by the bar and individual heart-shaped tables. It became one of the most popular clubs in town, an instant success for Max and for me. My services were suddenly very much in demand and after several years of interior design work, I was able to move into my first love, clothing. I could never quite believe my good luck, and always suspected that Max was much more involved in my initial jobs than he would admit. Over the years we had become the best of friends; he became my sole confidant and knew everything about me. His understanding of my needs and desires and his sympathy for my problems were boundless. I would have married him, but he never asked.

"Hey, lady, there's a crowd. Want to go somewhere else?" I came out of my reverie at the sound of the cabdriver's voice.

"No, thank you," I said with confidence, consulting the meter. "They're expecting me."

"Suit yourself," he said after I paid him.

There was a crowd, even on Thanksgiving. My stomach tightened with an anxious anticipation; I hoped Max had told them

I was coming. I should not have worried though, for Larry was there to greet me at the door.

"Miss Griffin, so nice to see you." He smiled, and as his handsome face lit up with that smile, I regretted my promise to Max not to fraternize with his employees.

"Thank you, Larry. It's nice to see you, too."

"We have your regular table reserved. Just follow me." He parted the crowd and I watched the way his body moved as he walked in front of me. The smell of his cologne floated back to me and I inhaled it appreciatively. Of course, Max was right; I came here too often to get involved with the help. So, although tempting, Larry was off limits.

"What a shame." I sighed as I sat at the table. Then, loudly enough to be heard over the music, I ordered my usual—a special burgundy Max kept reserved for me. I lit a cigarette while I waited, and began to watch the dancers. The dance floor was crowded with the usual types—mostly rich and bored young people anxious to show off their latest fashions and their latest lovers. Some, however, were people who had saved for months to be here this evening. I could tell who they were by their clothes and by their obvious delight at finally being here. They were continually glancing around, to find any celebrity they could. *They must be disappointed,* I thought as I looked around the club myself. Since it was Thanksgiving, the most famous and glamorous had better things to do. Still, there were a few, who like me had no family or friends with which to celebrate the occasion. *God,* I thought bitterly, *how I hate holidays.*

The band changed to a slow plaintive love song. One of Max's rules was that out of every musical set only two songs could be fast. The rest had to fit the club's theme—romance. "People come here to grope and grab," he'd told me in one of his cynical moods. "They will do things on the dance floor they would never do anywhere else but in the privacy of their own homes." He was right, of course. You could almost feel the heat exuding from the dancers. Some couples barely moved, so engrossed were they in the fit and feel of each other's bodies. Other nights

this exhibitionist behavior offended me; tonight it merely intensified my mood. Max would come through for me, and provide
a vibrant young body I could grasp and caress, while anticipat-
ing the final moment of rapture and release. I could, for a short
time, be like one of the people on the dance floor.

I jumped, startled by the hand suddenly placed on my shoulder. I spun around in my seat to find Max standing there, an
apologetic look on his face and my wine in his hand. He set the
wine on the table, and brushed the hair from my neck to deposit
a light, teasing kiss on the nape of my neck. I shuddered and he
moved away. "Please don't," I said, smiling to remove some of
the sting of the words and the shudder, "you know how ticklish
I am."

"Sorry, love. I was just thinking how lovely your neck is. You
should wear your hair up." He sat in the chair next to mine, a
challenge in his eyes. I didn't want to rehash the same old ar-
guments tonight, didn't want to get involved in the discussions
of how Max thought I should dress or style my hair, or even live
my life. I looked away and ground out my cigarette. He received
no response; my silence was answer enough.

"I know," he said, sounding chastened, "you like it that way.
Let's just drop it, shall we?" I looked up from my study of the
wine. He was dressed in a black tuxedo impeccably tailored and
correct, accentuating the lean but muscular body underneath.
His teeth were white and even, and his hands, resting on the
table, were strong. His dark hair, I knew, was becoming streaked
with gray at the temples, although his face showed no sign of
aging. It saddened me to think of Max growing old; how could
I survive without him?

"You've been away too long, Deirdre." His teasing manner
was gone and his concern for me showed on his face. "You
should stop doing this to yourself. You look ghastly. I know your
work is important, but you've got to live a little, too. If you're
not careful, you'll lose your touch. I don't think you can exist
very long as a hermit."

"No, I suppose not," I admitted to him. Sometimes, I felt that

Max knew my needs better than I did. "So, what do you have lined up for tonight?"

"A tasty little number that I think you will enjoy immensely. I'll bring him over and introduce him now." With a graceful ease, he rose from the table, hugged me briefly and left. I watched him work his way through the crowd, speaking to several people on the way. Max was a lot like me; he, too, had many acquaintances but very few friends.

I drank my wine while I waited for his return. The wait seemed long, but in reality was only a few minutes. He soon arrived, bearing two glasses of wine, followed by my partner for the evening.

"Deirdre Griffin, meet Bill Andrews." Max never showed any jealousy of the men he introduced to me. They were carefully screened by him, he knew all about their careers, their habits, their personal lives. I knew that he had spent hours behind the bar, questioning this man, delicately prying into his life. He was most likely married, or engaged, but looking for one night of excitement. Max and I both knew that no commitments would be formed; the way he set everything up ensured it. And I wanted it that way.

I smiled up at Bill. "It's nice to meet you," I purred, playing my part to the hilt. "Max has told me so much about you."

"And he told me about you, but he should have warned me how beautiful you were. I might just fall in love." The words were insincere, I knew; I had heard them all before, too many times. Suddenly I was overwhelmingly tired, sick of the entire situation, the seedy little drama acted out weekly here in the Ballroom of Romance.

"Deirdre?" Max was glaring down at me, an expression of warning on his face. "Are you feeling okay?"

I looked at the two of them standing there expectantly and suppressed my unexpected emotional reaction. "I'm fine, thank you, Max." I smiled at Bill and gestured to the chair recently vacated by Max. "Please, sit down."

As Bill did so, Max politely excused himself with a twisted smile. "Well, I've got a business to run. Enjoy yourselves."

Now that we were alone, I had no other option but to proceed as I normally would. I looked over at Bill and smiled again, hoping that my sudden disgust hadn't been too obvious. This was my life now and I could never turn back. It is too late, I admonished myself, for an attack of conscience. Too late to worry about how this evening would affect his life, his family. Too late for anything but this.

He returned my smile and I realized what a good choice Max had made for this evening; he certainly knew my taste in men. Youthful and attractive, but not devastatingly so, Bill Andrews was pleasant, unassuming and waiting for me to make the first move. I usually preferred being the predator, but tonight, for some reason beyond my understanding, I had no taste for the hunt. Maybe Max was right; I was losing my touch. I reached for another cigarette and as he lit it for me, I saw his wedding band gleam in the flame. In that instant, my heart hardened and I abandoned my rueful thoughts. He was just another bastard looking for some action. And, I thought vehemently as I gave him an appraising stare, he would get some.

He cleared his throat and pulled at his tie; my silence had unnerved him. Seeking to repair the damage, I smiled my most inviting smile and gestured toward the dance floor. "Let's have another glass of wine before we join the crowd. I hate to dance sober, don't you?" He agreed with a laugh that relaxed us both. We began to engage in the typical small talk that leads to seduction, my flattering attention to the talk of his career, his compliments on my appearance and body. By the time we finished our wine, we had moved closer together, our knees making contact under the table. His hand brushed my thigh and remained there; I could feel the heat of his touch through the leather. "Time to dance," I said provocatively, took his hand and led him to the dance floor.

Making an effort to seem slightly drunk as we began to dance, I leaned against him and he held me tightly and possessively. I made no effort to pull back from him. This was what I wanted now; it was no longer just acceptance of the inevitable. I had become intoxicated, not with the wine, but with the flesh of this man. I put my head on his shoulder so that I could better savor his aroma, the cologne he wore, the muskiness of perspiration, the acrid smell of wine on his breath. I could feel his heart pounding next to my breast, the rhythm matching my own heart and the music. As he became more aroused, he whispered in my ear, "Sweet, oh, sweet." He kept repeating it like a prayer to a goddess. His hands were caressing my back and I was trembling with the urgency of my own need.

"Come with me," I said, and he followed obediently.

The corridor outside the bar had a few secluded rooms known only to those intimately familiar with the place. I led Bill to one of these places—a lounge, seldom used, with a sturdy lock on the door and a comfortable oversized couch. The music from the band could be heard softly in the background and the bar was equipped with the burgundy I liked. I poured two glasses while he removed his jacket and loosened his tie. Sitting next to him on the sofa, I handed him his wine. He drained it in one gulp, then seemed embarrassed, so I followed suit. This was always the most awkward time, reestablishing the ardor that had developed on the dance floor. Bill was no different than the others; he seemed nervous, unsure of how to proceed.

"You know," he said, hesitating and staring at the floor, "I've never really gone in for this type of thing before. I mean, I know it's a line, but I've been a faithful husband for over five years . . ." His voice trailed away.

No, I will not lose him now, I raged inside and I cupped his face in my hands. "Bill, look at me," I ordered, and he snapped his head up, surprised at the tone of my voice. "We will not do anything here tonight that will affect your future life. I don't want your tomorrows, I just want you tonight." Our eyes made contact, and when I saw that his guilt and confusion were beginning to fade, I made my move.

"Relax," I smiled seductively, "just relax a little. I can give you an evening you'll never forget. You won't regret it, I promise." Passion began to flare again, in his eyes and in his body.

"Kiss me," I whispered, not wanting to lose the moment. He turned to me abruptly, almost violently, as if he needed the momentum to carry him past his doubts. His mouth was hot on mine, evidence of a desire almost as deep as my own. He kissed my eyelids, my ears and my neck, all the while sliding my blouse over my shoulders. I helped him out of his shirt and tie and soon we lay, naked from the waist up on the couch. He made a move to take off his trousers, but I stopped him.

"Let's take it slow," I suggested.

Lazily I caressed his shoulders and back, feeling the tensing of his muscles; his skin burned beneath my cool hands. His hands busied themselves with the unfastening of my leather jeans. I permitted this and welcomed first his hand and then his kisses in the soft curve of my stomach. He began to move back up my body, concentrating on one breast and then the other, until he again returned to my mouth.

After the kiss, I buried my face in his neck. *Now*, I thought as I heard the blood pulse in his veins. *Oh, please, now.*

I nipped him at first, savoring the moment, my low moans echoed by his. Then when my teeth grew longer and sharper, I could hold back no longer. I bit him brutally, tapping the artery and was rewarded by the flow of his blood—hot, salty and bitter. He shuddered violently and fought to push me away, but his resistance was futile. Finally his struggles ceased and his body grew limp as I continued to draw on him, gently now, almost tenderly. I drank a long time, slowly, relishing the feel of my own body being replenished, then I withdrew.

Arising from the couch, I caught sight of myself in the mirror. No longer pale and haggard, my skin glowed with life and my eyes shone, victorious and demonic. A few drops of blood were trickling down my chin; I wiped them away with the back of my hand and turned from my reflection in disgust.

Chapter 2

I knew that I had taken more blood from Bill Andrews than usual. He lay unconscious and pale. Dear God, I thought in horror, I've taken too much. He'll die. I frantically felt for his pulse, and was relieved when I found it, faint but steady. He would be weak for a few days and bear a small bruise, but he would live.

I lifted him from the couch and put his shirt back on. He was not a small man, but I am much stronger than an ordinary person, especially after feeding. I dressed myself, walked to the bar for a glass of wine and lit a cigarette.

I watched him as I smoked, waiting for a sign of his awakening. Eventually his eyelids fluttered and he looked at me, puzzled and still slightly dazed. I discovered some time ago, that people in his state were highly suggestible and, whenever possible, I used this to my advantage. I again cupped his face in my hands and made eye contact. "You don't know me," I said softly and insistently. "You had too much to drink, found this room and passed out." He nodded vacantly and I knew the suggestion would work. "You will sleep for a while, then be awake and alert when you hear a knock at the door." His eyes slowly closed and he began to snore.

I went to the door and opened it. The noise from the bar was subdued and checking my watch, I discovered that it was past closing hour. I could hear the faint clash of glasses and knew that the staff was hurriedly clearing tables so they could get home early. Bill should make his exit soon, I decided and knocked upon the door.

"Mr. Andrews?" I queried.

"Yes, that's me." He sat up and looked around. Seeing me, he smiled weakly and with no recognition in his eyes. "Sorry, I must have passed out here," he said sheepishly.

"No problem," I countered. "Max asked me to find you—we're closing now. There will be cabs waiting outside if you want one."

"Thank you, I will." He collected his tie and jacket, checked for his wallet and with a final vague smile, walked slowly down the hallway to the exit. I heard Larry say good night to him then waited until I heard the cab drive away. I collected my coat and left through a side door.

I did not need to take a cab. The cold was exhilarating and I was so full of stolen life that I wanted to walk and run and dance in the darkened streets. The night was my element. I, of all people in the city, could walk in its beauty without fear.

The next afternoon I ventured into the streets again, this time with more risk. The exposure of my flesh for just a few seconds to the sun would result in a severe burn and extreme sickness. It had happened a few times and was not an experience I cared to repeat. Still, the day was overcast and I had been rejuvenated through the feeding of last evening, and so, armed with sunglasses, gloves and a large hat to shield my face, I was relatively safe. Perversely, I enjoyed taking the risk, merely for the human feel of walking in the daylight.

As I walked I noticed that the store windows had been decorated for Christmas and I felt a wave of sadness at the season's too sudden approach. The trappings of today seemed so garish compared to those of my youth—the softly glowing candles, the handmade decorations and the warm red fire, all against a backdrop of pure white snow. There was always snow, and ebony night skies, so beautiful and icy that they could make you laugh for joy. Now all was neon and glittering, even nativity scenes seemed gaudy, embellished with flashing lights. Christmas was, for me, a dismal time made bitter by memories, parents long dead, friends aged or aging, and others, more dear, irretrievably lost. A tear slowly snaked its way down my cheek and I brushed it away impatiently; it would be blood-tinged, I knew, and would stand out angrily on my face. With the practice of all too many years, I pushed my emotions aside, replaced them with considerations of here and now.

The walk to the office was short, only five city blocks. I entered the building, showed my I.D. and signed in. Once on the elevator, I removed my gloves, hat and sunglasses; any light that would reach me now would be artificial, and my lenses were more than adequate protection. The elevator jolted to a stop on the 29th floor and opened to the glass doors of our reception area. Griffin Designs had exclusive use of the top two floors.

Gwen was talking to the receptionist as I walked in. She smiled a warm welcome, but the other woman jumped guiltily, murmured a good afternoon and immersed herself in some work behind her massive marble desk. This desk was my favorite piece of furniture, supported as it was with two large onyx statues of griffins, but it was really too decorative for my personal use, so it stood here, to impress our customers. I laughed inwardly at myself; I was no different from the doormen of the world, I just made more money.

Gwen began filling me in on the details of yesterday and today as we walked together to my office. "The pattern makers have been working all day and have some preliminaries for you to see. The fabric suppliers have been contacted and I expect the swatches by courier almost immediately. The models have been called and will be here next Friday for their fittings, and the seamstresses will report on Monday for their twelve-hour shifts. I promised the usual bonuses, okay?" She glanced at me for my approval.

"It's nice to see you, too, Gwen, only slow down a bit, please," I laughed. "Give me a chance to catch my breath."

"Sorry, Deirdre, but I just get so involved." She shrugged. "Coffee?" Knowing my answer, she filled a cup and handed it to me.

"Thanks, Gwen. Let me have ten minutes to settle in, then we can start." I walked into my office, but left the door slightly ajar. Sitting down at my desk with a happy sigh, I warmed my hands on the mug of steaming coffee. It felt good to be back here again, to be among people for reasons other than those that usually drew me to them. I lifted my briefcase to the top of the desk and began to unload its meager contents; a newspaper, a sheaf of notes and the phone answering tape I had not found the time or inclination to review. Any important calls would have come in to the office; the calls on the tape were most likely from Gwen. She often used the machine for leaving notes on items she might otherwise forget, knowing that she would ultimately be the one to review them. The other calls would be from Max. I smiled to myself; Gwen had once confessed to me that she thought that he and I had one of the most romantic relationships. She would be horrified to discover the truth of it—that Max was practically a pimp and my payment was in blood, not money. Unaware of this darker side, however, she seemed to get a vicarious pleasure in hearing his voice on the phone. I pushed the tape over to one side.

The newspaper was tempting, but I didn't succumb. Later, after working out a thousand details—fabric, color, and accessory selection, work schedules and pricing—after the office had emptied of all personnel, I would curl up and read it all, not missing one item or advertisement, saving the crossword puzzle until last. Setting the newspaper down, I turned my attention to the summer line.

Fashion is a risky business; keeping a reputation and clientele in today's variable climate is difficult. I had established Griffin Designs at a time when all others were showing tailored suits and dresses, and took a chance on more feminine clothes. It had paid off—my first show, consisting entirely of evening clothes, gowns with bustle detailing, low necklines and billowing skirts with yards of elegant, old-fashioned fabrics, received rave reviews from most of the fashion critics. I had one particular article, written at that time, framed and hanging on the wall of my office; the headline read—"Deirdre Griffin Shares Her Secrets of the Night." I think I kept it there as a reminder of my true nature, lest I get too involved in the little human world I had created for myself. Too soon, it would be ended; I had perhaps another year, maybe two before it was noticed that I hadn't changed, hadn't aged a year since my debut as a "young" designer. Then I would have to create yet another identity, pursue some other career to fill my time. How many more lives, I wondered; how many more years?

Gwen charged in, bearing a fresh pot of coffee and three pages of notes accumulated during my absence from the office. The names of clients who were patiently waiting for my personal attention to their wardrobe problems and fittings, and others who were not so patient and would have to be cajoled and flattered, all were listed and prioritized for my consideration. Gwen had, for all her faults, an organized mind and a great business sense; I trusted many of the more important details of Griffin Designs to her judgement. Some others in the office might complain of her incessant chatter, and her dressing in bargain-basement chic; I knew, however, that I could leave the office in her care for a month, and still have a viable business when I returned. I liked her talk—it filled my silence; I admired her for her unconventional approach to fashion. She was the closest I had come to having a girlfriend since my school days.

We spent the next four hours struggling over sketches and schedules, setting up appointments for the next week, and arranging the final details for our show in two weeks. Although I had established my business on evening attire, we had branched out over the years into office and casual clothes. The options for materials and accessories seemed limitless, but we finally reached the end of the list. We paused at last and became aware of the eerie quiet surrounding us; we had been so engrossed that we had not noticed the gradual cessation of noise from without.

Gwen jumped and glanced at her watch. "Oh, no," she wailed. "I'm so late and Nick will be worried. Can we finish tomorrow?"

I nodded. "We were almost through for this evening, anyway. I'll be in early. Have a good time."

"Thanks," she said, running out. "See you then." I heard the ladies' room door squeak once, then twice; she had made a hurried check on hair and makeup before meeting her fiancé. She and Nick were only recently engaged and were planning to be married in May. I had talked her into a late-evening ceremony, on the pretense that it would be more elegant, so that I could attend. Although I didn't care much for Nick, I envied her that May wedding. The elevator bell rang, and the doors thumped shut as she descended to meet a future I could never have.

I stretched and rose from the desk to make a tour of the office. I switched off all the lights on my way to lock the front door, except for the reading lamp on my desk. I would read the paper and then go to bed. I was tired suddenly; the elated feeling of last night was gone. Ordinarily, I needed to feed only once a week, but after a month's abstinence, I would have to do so four or five times over the next few weeks to regain my full strength. Tomorrow was Saturday and a good night at the Ballroom—I would feed again.

Pouring myself the last of the coffee, now lukewarm and grainy, I sat back down. I read the paper from back to front, pausing in the middle to glance at the first few crossword clues, to peruse the fashion pages then on to the real news of the front section. It held no interest for me this evening, until, while reaching into my desk for a sharpened pencil, a headline caught my eye. "Local Attorney Found Dead." The picture looked familiar, although for a moment I couldn't place it, then I read on.

"William W. Andrews was discovered lying dead on his apartment house steps early Friday morning . . ."

The pencil snapped, driving slivers of wood and lead deep

into my palm. Beads of blood, so preciously bought, dropped onto the paper, almost obscuring the words. I wiped them off gently so that I could continue to read.

". . . police have declined comment on the case, only saying that it is currently under investigation. Inside sources have indicated that foul play is suspected . . . ."

I clenched my fist, ignoring the pain in my hand. "No," I said, then louder still, "No!" until my voice reverberated in the empty building. It should not have happened; I've had many victims, but, to my knowledge, never been the deliberate cause of their death. *I can't believe it,* I thought. *There must be some mistake!* But the picture and the name were his. I looked back at the article; no further details, other than funeral arrangements, were supplied.

I got up and paced the office, pulling the small shards of pencil out of my palm and grinding them into the carpet. My mind replayed the events of last night, searching for any blame I might hold in this death.

I had fed on so many over the years; if pressed, I could not even give an accurate count. So much blood stolen through the passing years, so many bodies to sate my appetite. But none of them had suffered any lasting effects from my presence. Some may have had odd dreams or nightmares, some may have been unaccountably repulsed, or even strangely attracted, by a woman of my height and build. Perhaps they suffered headaches or dizziness for days afterward. But when my victims were left alive, they stayed alive.

Like all the others, Bill Andrews had been alive; he had gotten up and walked out of the club unaided. He should not have died, and it could not have been my fault. He could have been robbed and shot, or had a heart attack; there are so many ways that people can die. He was alive when he left, I insisted again, and there was no way that I could be connected to him or his death. I wanted desperately to talk to someone, and considered calling Max. But gradually the initial shock began to wear away and I decided that it could wait. I was just too tired.

When our offices had been constructed, a small living and sleeping area had been included. The entrance to these rooms was hidden behind draperies hanging in the rear of my office. This area was the only place I ever felt completely secure; no one knew of its existence. I would sleep there tonight.

I locked the outer door of my office and entered the secret retreat. With the closing of the inner door, a security system was armed; it would alert me to the presence of someone outside. The door itself had three sturdy bolts and these I secured. I turned on the light and glanced around; it had stayed relatively clean in my absence, as it was completely sealed off from the outside with no windows or doors other than the one, no dust could filter in. There were a few cobwebs and probably more than a few spiders but it made no difference. If there was any home for me, it was here.

The area consisted of a bedroom and bath on the upper level with a spiral staircase leading down to the living area and small kitchen. The kitchen was not really necessary but the refrigerator did hold a supply of my favorite wine. I poured a large glass for myself and sat down. The lack of windows was compensated for by a great variety of art prints and originals scattered on the walls. My favorite was a little-known Van Gogh acquired at auction many years ago for a ridiculously small sum. It was a wheat field on a sunny day, and the colors were so vibrant that I was often tempted to lay my cheek against it, as if to feel the warmth of its sun. All of the pictures were landscapes in daylight; it helped to alleviate the otherwise tomb-like atmosphere. If tradition and necessity dictated that I must dwell in a crypt, at least it was decorated to my liking.

I finished my wine and climbed the stairs. Finding a nightgown in the closet, I changed, sat on the bed and turned out the lights at the master switch on the wall behind the headboard. I removed my lenses and settled in for the night. The walls were well insulated so that sounds from within my rooms were not heard, but a mike installed outside insured that I would hear the first sounds from without. I pushed the thoughts of Bill Andrews's unfortunate death far from my mind, and prayed, as usual, for a dreamless sleep.

Chapter 3

It rained in the night, a cold November rain pounding insistently on the roof. The sound filtered into my consciousness and began to shape the dream again. I tried to fight it, to force some other into its place, but even as I fought, I knew this dream would win.

I am wearing a cotton print dress, too thin for the weather, but it accommodates my expanded waistline; I am seven months pregnant. I struggle with the voluminous skirt, now soaked at the hem, and pull my shawl closer about my shoulders. It had gotten cold and begun to rain while we were inside; he drapes his coat around me while the coachman gets our carriage. After I am settled into my seat and warmly wrapped in a wool blanket, he gives the reins a shake and we begin the long ride home. The horses are skittish, dancing sideways for a few steps before they are calmed by his steady control. He looks at me and smiles.

"We could have stayed the night. Loretta readied the spare room for us."

I snuggle against his shoulder. "I know, but I long for my own bed. And you would have been up all night, talking incessantly about the possibilities of war. It is better this way."

"I suppose so," he admits, "just so you feel fit enough for the trip."

"I am fine." A rumble of thunder interrupts the steady rhythm of the rain, the horses start and whinny, then go on. The baby kicks hard against my ribs and I make a little grunting noise.

He reaches over and with a mischievous grin, pats my stomach, proud of our unborn child. Our marriage, unlike many others of the time, is a match of love, but it had been a long ten years before the baby was conceived. At twenty-eight, many of the women think I am too old to carry a first baby full term. But we will prove them wrong, I think, my husband and I.

Our eyes meet for a second, and I read his love for me in them. I feel warm, despite the chill in the carriage, and realize that I have never felt so happy. Wanting this moment to last forever, wanting time to stop, I smile, stretch up to kiss his cheek, and recoil from the blinding glare of a flash of lightning.

There is a deafening crash, much louder than the previous thunder and a tree plummets onto the back of the carriage. With a sickening lurch, we topple over and crash to the ground. The horses rear and scream with fright, then drag us farther down the road. Eventually they slow and stop, still restive but standing now. The only sound is the stamping of their hooves, their labored breathing and the relentless downpour of rain. I try to push up on the carriage door, but the once-warming blanket is now soaked and clings tightly to my arms and legs. It is hard to distinguish my tears from the rain, but soon all sensation drains away and I faint.

On awakening, I feel a small trickle of blood flow down my face. More disturbing is the gush of warmth between my legs; my water has broken and labor has started. And he is gone. He must be here. But where? I wonder, seeing nothing but the rain, hearing nothing but the restless shuffle of the horses. I call his name and begin to cry, in pain and fright.

The carriage door opens and two strong arms reach in to ease me out. He is back, I think and sigh in relief. His embrace is comforting and I relax into it. I try to speak but he quiets me, whispering words of reassurance and love. He is kissing me, caressing me and it feels so strange, so wrong. I push away from him and peer through the rain and darkness into eyes—not his. These eyes are deep with hunger and desire, not love, and yet they seem to draw my soul from my body. His mouth finds my neck and I shudder. The tension builds in my body as he drinks; I grapple with him, pulling at his shirt and ripping it in my panic. When my teeth graze his shoulder, I bite down hard, in fear or passion or possibly both. He is startled at first, then laughs, low and cynically, as his blood washes down my throat. I am being carried away by the rapid currents of this stream; I am drowning.

I am alone, shaking and cold, lying by the side of the road. Yards behind me lies the crumpled body that had been crushed beneath the carriage. I do not recognize it, cannot seem to acknowledge the grief I should feel. My mind is filled only with the other man. As I drift into blackness, his last words, tender yet somehow bitter, echo in my mind. "If you survive, my little one, we will meet again."

The hospital walls are white and chilling. The nurses and doctors speak in rustling whispers and shake their heads in frustrated reaction to my case. With time, I come to understand that my husband is dead, the child was stillborn and there is no hope of others to follow. My own health they describe as precarious; they don't understand how I survived the ordeal. I wish I hadn't, I keep thinking before sleep comes and the walls wash into darkness once more.

I was extremely disoriented upon awakening, a combination of the dream and the dawn. I could sense the rise of the sun, although I would never again see or feel its warmth. Since the accident, my instincts had become sharpened, finely honed to those of a predator. My senses of smell, hearing and touch had intensified, and although my daytime vision was impaired, my night vision was excellent. I required little light to see. I felt deep within me the change of the seasons, the phases of the moon; my body was attuned to the earth in a way I would never have imagined.

It was this adjustment that caused me distress now; my physical being screamed danger from the dawn and even though my mind knew I was safe here, my body fought its awakening. I tossed restlessly, trying to resolve the dilemma until my body accepted the wisdom of the mind and I arose.

I took my typical shower, scalding water in utter darkness, and felt considerably restored. I dressed in clothes I found in the closet; faded jeans and a soft, comfortable oversized sweater. I towel dried my hair and pulled it back into a ponytail. It would be out of the way and I could style it later before my night at the Ballroom. I appraised my image in the mirror and thought that I looked even younger than usual. After my change, I had not aged, my body had been permanently frozen at twenty-eight. Many years ago I quit looking for gray hairs and crow's feet. "Every woman's dream come true," I scoffed at myself as I walked away.

I padded downstairs in stocking feet, found a pair of boots in the coat closet, and left my sanctuary for the office.

It was still early and there was no sign of Gwen. I was pleased because I had something special that I had designed for her in conjunction with the summer line. It was a wedding dress, patterned after a ball gown from the late 1860's. I hoped it would please her, it was unconventional enough for her taste, yet elegant and romantic. I envisioned it in ivory moire satin, with pearl and lace trim, but had included several fabric choices in the initial planning so that she could pick what she liked best. Gwen had asked me to help her shop for a gown some time ago; I knew she was hoping I could do more than that, but hadn't wanted to presume upon our friendship. I never even hinted that I would provide the dress; she would be surprised.

As I put the last touches on my final sketch, I heard someone unlock the front door. After a few seconds, I recognized the footsteps; it was Gwen switching on the lights as she came down the hall. I had been working with only the small lamp on my desk, not wanting to put in my lenses until absolutely necessary. Now I realized that in my haste, I had left them in my small apartment. I couldn't function without them in full artificial light, so I would have to return. Quietly, hurriedly, I slipped into the entrance, retrieved the contacts and paused, listening. There was no sound from without; I pushed the door open, and came through, gently closing it behind me. I breathed a sigh of relief, thinking that I had not been discovered. I could hear Gwen at the coffee machine; she always made that her first chore of the morning. I quickly inserted my contacts and went into the hall.

"Good morning." At the sound of my voice, she jumped, whirled around and dropped yesterday's coffee grounds on the floor.

"Deirdre, I didn't know you were here. Why can't you turn on the lights when you get here? How can you stand to be in this place in total darkness? It gives me the creeps to think of it. This city is full of weirdos and worse, just waiting to . . ."

"I know, Gwen. I'm sorry I startled you," I interrupted, all the while inwardly pleased that my secret was still safe. My current lifestyle was making me too complacent and trusting. It was not good. "The security here is very thorough. I don't think those weirdos you keep lecturing me about could get past the front guard. Anyway, I've not been afraid of the dark for years." I helped her clean up the mess I had caused and while the coffee was dripping, I invited her into my office. "I have something to show you, that I hope you'll like."

"Oh, Deirdre," she gushed after seeing the sketches, "it's beautiful. But . . ." She hesitated.

"But what? Don't you like it?"

"I love it, but I thought you always said you wouldn't get into a wedding line."

"I'm not, dummy, you are. Did you think I would let you walk down the aisle, wearing anyone else's dress? Just think of the scandal it would cause if you were reported wearing anything but a Griffin gown. It would be very bad for business." I was touched by her reaction, but did not want to let it show.

"Thank you so much." She practically flung herself over the desk to give me a small hug. "The gown is wonderful." Suddenly, I felt her stiffen. "Deirdre, there's someone here, behind the curtain." I could hear the tension in her whispered voice.

"Don't be silly, Gwen." I turned around and saw what had

scared her. The door that I had tried to close so quietly had not latched properly, but swung open behind the drapes. It did look a bit like a person standing there, if you didn't know what it was. Now I would have to reveal one of my best-kept secrets. Gwen was someone I trusted, yet I still felt like a fool and cursed myself for my carelessness. "Welcome to my other life." I tried to smile as I pulled back the curtain, exposing the entrance. "You didn't really believe that I slept on the office couch all those nights, did you?" I pitched my voice to sound its most reassuring and reasonable.

"No, I guess not, now that you mention it. But why the secrecy? Lots of people who work in a position like yours have this sort of arrangement." She had recovered from her fright and seemed to be enjoying my embarrassment.

"I like my privacy. Let's keep it between us two, please, I don't want the models thinking they can use it for their own personal dressing room." There was almost enough anger in my voice to stop any further discussion.

"Since it's important to you, Deirdre, my lips are sealed. But I want a guided tour someday, okay?" She was smiling, thinking, I supposed, about the midnight trysts she imagined between Max and me happening right here through the walls of our office. She wouldn't mention it to anyone, I felt sure. And it did not seem out of the ordinary to her; it probably only added to my image in her eyes.

We kept quite busy that day, working through to the late afternoon. Gwen went out to pick up some lunch at one point and, as usual, I declined. I could eat solid food on occasion, but I generally took in only liquids. It was all a poor substitute for my mainstay. Now and then, I did enjoy a rare steak; as a rule I stayed away from most other foods, especially the type Gwen would bring back for lunch. It was assumed that I followed a stringent regimen of diet and exercise and I had often been asked to share my secrets with readers of the women's magazines for whom I had granted an occasional interview. I always demurred on the question, laughing to myself at the havoc that would be created by my truthful answer. And, horribly enough, there would be people sick or obsessed enough to try to emulate my lifestyle.

The sun was setting as Gwen and I prepared to leave. We had made enough progress on the line and show to both earn a day off tomorrow. Beginning Monday, the next two weeks would probably be nonstop work and worry, so it was best to start in well rested, and, I thought to myself, well fed. I let her go ahead of me, so that I could straighten up a few things in my office and apartment. I looked at the clock and decided that I should call Max. I wanted to let him know I'd be at the club tonight; I also wanted to discuss Bill Andrews's death with him. Thoughts of the intimacies shared that night, the feel of his warm body pressed against me, juxtaposed against my vision of him now, lying cold and lifeless on a table in the morgue, had plagued me during the day. I still believed, I needed to believe, that I had nothing to do with his murder, but I wanted Max's confirmation and reassurance.

I dialed the phone and lit a cigarette while I waited for an answer. It was not long in coming.

"Good evening, and thank you for calling the Ballroom of Romance. How may I help you?"

It was Larry. I was a bit surprised because I had dialed Max's private number. "Larry, this is Deirdre Griffin. Is he in yet?"

"Hello, Miss Griffin. How are you tonight?"

"Fine, thank you. May I speak to Max?"

"Well, he's not here right at this moment. But he sort of expected you to call and asked me to give you a message." He hesitated, but I didn't feel much like being put off tonight and my irritation showed.

"Go ahead, Larry, I'm listening," I said sharply.

"I don't understand him, you know. I guess I don't understand much of what's going on." I could tell he was stalling, holding something back he didn't want to tell me.

"Larry, please, just give me his message. He can talk about whatever it is tonight, when I get there."

"But that's just it. He asked me to tell you not to come here again. He said he was very upset about what happened last night. I didn't know that anything happened last night."

I suddenly felt that he was fishing for information, that his confusion was not entirely real. "I didn't think so, either." I hoped to sound cool and unconcerned, but I began to shake inwardly. What was wrong?

"Miss Griffin," he began tentatively, "I'm sorry I was the one to tell you. But you know how insistent Max can be. He's had me sit in his office since I got here, just on the chance that you might call. I don't know what else to say, except that if he doesn't make it up with you, he's a damn fool. You're a remarkable lady, and even if he doesn't know it, there are plenty of other men around who would be thrilled to be with you. You know, I always thought that you and I could—damn, Max is coming. I've got to go now. I want to see you again. . . ."

I could hear Max's voice faintly in the background; then the phone was slammed down.

I hung up on my end. What had happened? I had no reason to doubt that Larry was telling the truth and yet, I also had no reason to think that Max would cut me cold. Unless, of course, he believed that I had killed Bill. That must be it, I thought, but he should know me better than that; he should know that even if I had, it was inadvertent. I felt betrayed. I loved Max, as much as I could feel free to love any human, and somehow had thought it was returned.

I glanced down at my hand and noticed that my cigarette had burned down to the filter. I angrily crushed it out in the ashtray. Smoking was indicative of my constant attempts to be human; it was a habit I had acquired many years ago to appear more normal, to try to fit in with the crowd. Apparently, like my relationships, it was an empty gesture. Maddened, I shredded what remained of the pack, put on my coat and left the office.

"Never again," I thought out loud on the way down in the empty elevator. "I will not rely on another. I will stay true to my nature, a hunter, a lone predator. I don't need anyone; I don't want anyone." I felt a new strength, a resolve in my very being, that was never there before. For so many years, I had been frightened, guilty and apologetic; that would end now.

As I walked out of the building and slowly made my way to the hotel, I began to make my plans. I would still feed this evening; I needed the strength, physically and psychologically. I could see now that I had lived like a pampered pet for years, Max's pet, to be thrown a morsel now and then, to be caressed and played with. Now I would reawaken my feral instincts, stalk my own prey and take what I wanted. There were many places in the city where people walked alone, where my food could be easily obtained. I was never afraid to prowl the parts of the city where the undesirable and unwanted lived. There were homeless people on park benches, people who had nothing to lose, no reason to guard against thieves, no value to anyone but me. And I would steal less from them than others had, only a little blood, something that they would gladly give for just a few dollars. Before I met Max this was how I'd lived, and I could do it again.

I spun through the entrance to the hotel, deep in my plans for the night, and nearly ran into someone waiting by the door. With surprise, I noticed it was Larry. Despite my resolve, I felt my spirits rise. Max had sent him to apologize, Larry had misunderstood his message and he wanted to set it straight. I smiled encouragingly at him, but he kept his head lowered. His expression was rueful.

"Miss Griffin?" I turned around and saw that Frank was on duty again. He looked at Larry and continued. "He said he had to speak with you, that it was important. I was just about to ask him to leave when you came in. Do you know him?" Frank always took his responsibilities as doorman and guard seriously. I had never had anyone call for me, and I imagine he found it rather unusual.

"Thank you, Frank. I do know him, it's fine." Turning to Larry, I said quietly, "Do you have time to come upstairs? I'd like to talk about this in private."

He smiled at me, too brightly, I thought. "Yes, I'd like that."

We boarded the elevator and rode silently, both staring at the lighted numbers above the door. The elevator stopped at my floor, and as we walked down the hall, I found his closeness exhilarating. Surely he was not off limits now. I imagined I could hear his heart beating, circulating the precious blood through his veins. By the time we arrived at my room, I was trembling with anticipation and nearly dropped my keys. He took them from me, and without a word, opened the door and escorted me in.

I took off my coat, walked to the bar and poured myself a drink, to steady my nerves. When I turned around, Larry was staring at me, with a look of surprise on his face. "You look so different, Miss Griffin," he said, sitting down on the couch. "Younger or something."

"Not quite the elegant lady of the night you're used to, am I?" I indicated my clothes with a gesture and made a slight curtsy. "Let's just drop the Miss Griffin, shall we? Please call me Deirdre. Can I fix you a drink?"

"I'd better not, I've got to be back to work in a bit. If Max knew I came here he'd fire me." His mouth set into a frown incongruous for his years. "And unfortunately, I need the job."

I was disappointed that he was apparently not here to apologize for Max, and yet, just the closeness of this man, this human with his aroma of blood and sweat, was enough for me to forget my hurt and concentrate on my hunger. I would have to act fast on this and satisfy my need before he had to return to the Ballroom. I knew he wanted me, I could read it on his face. It would be easy enough to seduce him, to feed on him, and then to implant the suggestion that he had spent a rather disappointing time in my bed, that his visit here was not something he'd like to repeat. I felt a rush of power, and said a thankful prayer that my first independent victim in years was so neatly delivered to my doorstep.

I moved slowly toward him. "Well, what did you want to talk about?"

"Oh, I don't know." He stood up for a minute as if to come

closer to me. I leaned forward, but he moved back, suddenly seeming uncomfortable and uneasy. Then I smiled and he relaxed, sitting down again and casually laying his arm over the back of the couch. I admired his handsome form clad in the Ballroom's uniform tuxedo. On Max the suit seemed like a second skin, on Larry, it was a cocoon from which his lean, youthful body struggled to emerge. I longed to unbutton his shirt, undress him completely and enjoy his blood. Take it slow, I advised myself. Don't scare him away.

"Are you sure you won't have a drink, Larry?"

He checked his watch. "Well, yeah, I guess a small one wouldn't hurt."

As I filled a glass for him, I was aware of his gaze following my every movement. Slowly, I walked across the room and handed him his drink.

"Thanks." He gave me a nod and took a sip. I sat down next to him and waited.

"I thought maybe you could help me out."

"And how could I do that?"

"Well, you could answer a few questions for me. I've been trying to understand what goes on with you at the Ballroom. Max has always maintained that you belonged to him; that no one at the club was to touch you. But then, he's always setting you up with other men, total strangers, some of them real sleazeballs, and you always go along with it." He looked at me, with an odd, almost pleading look, wanting answers I could never give him.

"Larry, it really is not what you think."

He gave me a sharp look. "How can you guess what I think it is? Just answer my question, what happens between you and the men he brings in? Once a week, almost like clockwork you're there, not good enough for the staff but just fine for anyone else he can drag in. And what about this Andrews guy? He's dead, did you know?" At my nod, he continued. "I thought you might. The cops were there, too, talking to everyone, looking for you."

"But I didn't have anything to do with . . ."

He didn't let me finish. "That doesn't matter," he said with a shrug. "What bothers me most is Max's reaction. When he heard, he was furious, ranting and breaking things. He doesn't even want to hear your name, and asked me to keep you away. He should know you by now! How can he turn on you like that? You, of all people, you're so beautiful and, well, he should want to protect you, worship you . . . like I do." This last was said quietly so I could not hear, but I did and looked at him intently; he stared at the floor, his cheeks flushed.

"How old are you, Larry?"

"I'll be twenty-five in January." He seemed defensive, avoiding my stare. "Not that much younger than you."

"Looks can be deceiving. I'll be thirty-six on my next birthday," I lied. I reached over to him and taking his hands in mine, made eye contact. "Take my advice, please. Don't try to get involved in any of this, not with Max or me. You'll just wind up getting hurt." I dropped my eyes but remained holding his hands. "Whatever goes on at the club"—I smiled my most convincing smile—"and even my relationship with Max, well, that is all over now. So let's not discuss it, okay?"

"But what goes on, Deirdre? What happens that's so awful you can't talk about it?"

I realized that I had perhaps underestimated him. He was young, true, but not stupid and certainly not unobservant. And unfortunately for me, not a good choice for feeding. Taking his blood now would only raise more questions in his mind, cause me more problems than it would solve. "It doesn't matter, Larry," I said with certainty, meeting his eyes with as much determination as I could muster. "All that is over. Just forget about it. Forget about it."

He stood up and shook his head briefly, confused by the forcefulness of my command. "Well, I guess I'd better get back. Thanks for the drink."

"I am glad you stopped by, Larry." I took his arm and walked him to the door. "It was so very nice of you to be concerned for me. But if you have to go, you had better go now. I would feel just terrible if I got you fired. We can get together some other time, dinner on your day off, maybe?" I didn't want to alienate him, but if I spent much more time in his presence I could lose my control. Fortunately, he seemed not to take my comments as a brush-off.

"I'd like that, Deirdre. May I call you?"

I smiled my warmest smile. "Anytime, Larry. I would be happy to talk with you again." On impulse I stretched up to kiss his cheek. He turned his head to meet that kiss, and folded me in his strong, muscular arms. His tongue probed my mouth, tentatively at first and then with more purpose, his warm hands molding the flesh of my lower back. He was so ardent that I almost relented and, regardless of the danger involved, almost sunk my sharpening teeth into his neck. As I was about to make my move, he pulled away, abruptly. Surprisingly, he was blushing.

"I'm sorry, Deirdre, I didn't want to, I mean, I'm not ready to . . . See you later." He ran from the room and down the hall as if I had bit him and was pursuing him for more. The elevator door closed and I closed my own.

I was shaking still from my unsatisfied need, when suddenly I began to laugh, sounding slightly hysterical. "It seems the great huntress may have found herself a virgin," I said to myself. "The best blood of all, so the books say, and she let him get away." I poured myself another glass of wine and as I drank it, I calmed down. In another few minutes I would leave and find myself a more appropriate victim.

Frank gave me a curious look as I left the hotel, but I ignored the questions in his eyes, and walked out into the night.

It was early evening, and there were many clusters of people pursuing their own interests—shows or dinners or drinks with friends. These could be no help to me, but not too far away were dark streets avoided by most of the city's dwellers. Gwen's weirdos walked these streets, or at least I hoped so; my conscience seldom rebuked me for feeding on these. I sniffed the air and enjoyed the stabbing sensation of cold entering my lungs. It would snow tonight, a thin white covering that would too soon be gray or black with the morning's traffic. I turned off onto a less traveled street, and began to grow uneasy; was I being followed? I looked behind me, but there was no sign of movement. I thought I could hear faint footfalls echoing my own, but when I stopped the sounds ceased, even as my own did. I brushed off the feeling; I was letting the events of the last few days influence me. There was no one there, and even if there were, I knew I could handle them. After all, I was hunting for just such a person.

Then, in the darkness ahead, I perceived a shadow against a wall. Had my night vision been less than perfect, I would have walked right by without noticing him. I heard him breathe a small sigh, his patience and silence had paid off, or so he thought.

Whether he desired my purse, my body or my life, I never had the opportunity to find out.

I walked past him, as if I did not know he was there. He came up close behind me and grabbing my arm, whirled me around. "Hey, baby," he said, and then spoke no more. I flung myself at him and fastened upon his neck. He struggled, but I drew his blood quickly and violently, quenching my dark thirst. As he grew quiescent in my arms, I fed slower, savoring each drop. It was ecstasy; it was hell; it was life. I pulled myself from him, shuddering when the withdrawal was complete. He was unconscious, but his pulse was strong, much stronger than Bill's had been last night. Ordinarily, I would have taken more, but I felt safer only taking exactly what I needed.

I left him lying where I had found him. When he came to in a few minutes, I would be gone. Chances are, he wouldn't remember the incident, and due to the darkness of the alley, he would probably not even recall my face. And I doubted that he would report the attack to anyone; after all, who would believe him?

As I turned away and began to walk back down the alley, I heard a stifled gasp coming from where he lay. There, I thought with satisfaction, he was even stronger than I thought and was already reviving. I hurried back to the more populated streets, and passing a store, peered in the window at my reflection. Other than my shining eyes, there was no telltale trace of my activity. I removed a tissue from my pocket and wiped my mouth, anyway. I fluffed my hair around my face and headed back to the hotel. I was glutted with blood and would want to sleep soon. It had been a successful hunt, I thought, and moved languidly through the streets. Snow had begun to fall; I raised my face to the night sky and felt the brush of flakes on my cheeks, like the tentative touch of a baby's hand—so beautiful, so pure, and so soon gone.

"Did you have a nice walk, Miss Griffin?" Frank asked as he greeted me at the door.

"Yes, it's a lovely evening. Good night." When I got to my room, I completed my evening rituals; the locking of the door, the pulling of the drapes. After tonight's feeding, I should sleep well and wake tomorrow, refreshed and renewed. I turned off my restless and questioning mind, fell upon the bed and slept.

Chapter 4

My sleep was disturbed by the ringing of the phone. Someone must have switched the ringer back on while cleaning the room and the unknown caller was desperately trying to avoid the answering machine. The phone would ring four times, then stop; this pattern repeated every five minutes or so. I half remembered hearing this as I slept and wondered how long it had continued. No matter, I was awake now; I had slept through the entire night and the next day. The sun was setting as I left my bed and I felt a new strength flow through my body. I had experienced this feeling many times before in my life, but it always left me in awe. I was young, strong and prepared for life. I felt like I did indeed possess the powers my kind were purported to have—flying, shape changing, dissolving into a mist—none of these seemed out of my grasp tonight. This wonder of my existence had kept me sane through my many years and lives; without it, I would have persisted in finding a way to die.

The phone rang again as I unlocked the bedroom door and entered the bathroom. I let it ring; they had been calling for a while, they would call back. I inserted my contacts, turned on the lights and sat in front of the mirror to brush my hair, which seemed electric and vibrant, with a life of its own. I could feel each stroke of the brush tingling from the roots to the ends. As I applied my makeup, I noticed that the feeding of last night had revitalized my skin; it was firm, smooth and without blemish. I felt perfected in every way, and ready to conquer the world.

As I dressed, I planned the evening. I would begin to stake out new territory, visit a few of the newer clubs that had opened. Although last night had provided satisfactory sustenance, it had not given me the contact I had grown to appreciate through years of feeding at the Ballroom. I still needed the interplay, the seduction; I wanted to ignite the spark of desire in a man's eyes. I hadn't the companionship of others like me and although I knew that at least one must exist, all I had of him were the small fragments of a dream I would like to forget.

This time when the phone rang, I answered it.

"Deirdre, don't hang up, please."

"I received your message, Max," I said coldly. "I won't be back."

"No, wait. Let me explain. You owe me that, after all these years." He sounded sincere enough, and yet I did not want to fall into the trap of trusting him again.

"Do it quickly, then, and get it over with. I have plans for this evening."

"Deirdre, love, I made a mistake. I'm only human, you know."

"And you know I'm not. Now get on with it, or let me go." I doubted he had much to say at this point.

"Look, I can't talk about this over the phone. Come and see me tonight and if I can't make a reasonable apology you have my blessing to go for my throat."

In spite of the anger, I laughed. "Too bad you didn't make that offer last night, when I really needed it. You could have saved me a bit of trouble."

He didn't laugh. "I'm truly sorry, my dear. Please come tonight. It's important."

Wearily, I agreed. "Only for a moment or two, and only because I want to hear your excuses. I'll be there."

Despite Max's attempt at reconciliation, I still wanted to pursue the plans I had been formulating. After a brief stop at the Ballroom, I would catch a cab and get a recommendation from the driver on some of the newer night spots in the city. I didn't have to feed this night, I might even be able to wait a week for my next victim, but I needed to know what alternatives I had.

I walked to the club; the snow from last night had completely disappeared and the night was bitter cold. The skies were clearer than normal and the light of the moon bathed the streets in a soft glow. I felt like I was on a holiday, somehow. I had no hunger to drive me, no needs to satisfy; tonight I could be merely human.

Larry must have been off this evening, the doorman was a stranger to me, but since it was early, and a Sunday, I had no trouble getting in. I mentioned that I was here to see Max, and he nodded. He had been expecting me, he said. Max had some urgent business that had just come up but I was to wait in his office. As I was escorted to the room, I thought that the urgent business was probably nonexistent, a ploy to throw me off balance, a chance to get me thinking about Max in familiar, comfortable surroundings. As I settled into the couch, with a glass of wine from a newly opened bottle, I struggled between anger at his self-assurance and tenderness at being completely accepted by him. He knew me so well; how could any of his ploys fail to work?

Max and I had met during the mid-60's when I had been working as the night-shift waitress at a truck stop. It had been one of the more ideal jobs for me, so many people passing through at all hours of the night, so many warm, anonymous bodies to take in the darkness.

I can remember the odors and the tastes of that time vividly: the warm fumes of gasoline filtering through the summer nights, the musty smell of marijuana that clung to the uniforms of the other waitresses, the odd and individual flavors of the blood of the drivers that passed by the truck stop regularly. Buddy had been the truck driver that night. He came through the stop once a month and always asked for me to deliver his coffee. He was dark-haired and only slightly overweight, with the plump, youthful face of a cherub. Some of the girls complained of his body odor, but he suited me just fine, and his blood had, I imagined, a sweeter flavor than most. He never complained like some others about the sharp nip I would give him during our love play and he never missed what I took.

I struggled back into my tight, pink uniform, and as I got out of his truck, he jumped out and gave me a small swat on the behind. "You serve the best coffee in the tri-state area, darlin'."

"Thank you, Buddy." My eyes danced as I reached up to kiss him. I adjusted his collar to hide the fang marks on his neck.

"Go easy on the hickies next time, honey. The last one you gave me lasted two weeks and the missus got suspicious." He was smiling as he said it, proud, I thought, of our monthly liaisons.

"I just can't control myself around you, Buddy." I gave him another kiss, this one on the cheek and watched as he got back into the cab. "Drive carefully, and see you next month."

I watched him drive away and looked at my watch. It was time for me to go off shift. I would sleep well this night.

I stopped off to deposit half of Buddy's tip in the cash register. As I walked out, Max walked in; our eyes met as we passed in the doorway. Just for that one second, I was overwhelmed with a sense of unity, a recognition of a soul within that could speak to mine. Then he blinked, the feeling faded and we went our separate ways. I thought about him as I drove to the isolated trailer in which I made my home; thought about the many years spent in a fruitless search, trying to discover someone who could share in my life, allay in some way the dark loneliness within which I existed. No spark had ever flared, until now. Not for the first time, I cursed the ill chance that made me what I was. If I could have endured the sunlight, I might have been able to stay and cultivate a relationship with this man. I was sure that, like all the others, he would be gone by tomorrow night.

When I arrived at work the next evening, however, he was waiting outside the door, and softly called my name. I smiled broadly for the mere joy of his presence.

"How did you know my name?" I asked curiously.

His voice was deep and cultured and seemed to caress my ears. "Well, for one thing, I asked your friends about you last night. And it's written as plain as day on your uniform." He chuckled a little at my expense, but somehow I didn't mind.

"Yes, I guess it is." I glanced at the name embroidered on the cheap dress, embarrassed because I had forgotten it was there. In reality, it was no more my name than any of the others I had carried over the years. But here, at a tiny truck stop in Kansas, I was known as Diane Gleason. "But," I said with a smile, "your name isn't."

"I'm Max," he said briefly. "Max Hunter." Then after a small pause, "Do you think you could get tonight off? I'll only be in town for a few more days, and I'd like to get to know you."

One of the oldest lines in the book, I thought, but it didn't matter. He seemed so perfect.

I went into the diner and got permission to take the night off. Since I usually had nothing else to do, I had covered for the other waitresses more than a few times; now they could return the favor. Besides, Max had made quite an impression on them last night, and they were happy to oblige when I promised a detailed report on him the next day.

He drove me to my trailer so that I could change my clothes. I half expected him to make his move then, but he waited politely in the car until I came out, dressed in jeans and a black suede shirt, fringed and strewn with sequins. It was one of my favorite garments, but I seldom had a chance to wear it. I caught his admiring glance as I got into the car and felt that the long evenings cutting and stitching had all been worth it.

"You have a good eye for clothes, Diane. That's very attractive." He reached over, to touch the material, I thought, but instead he stroked my cheek gently, moving his fingers softly to the base of my neck. A sweet chill ran through me and I moved toward him, waiting for his next caress. It didn't come. Instead he pulled away, leaving me confused and disappointed.

"Where shall we go?" he asked innocently, as if the contact had not been made.

I laughed at his question. "There isn't much open after dark around here, but just keep driving. We can find something to do eventually, I'm sure." He ignored the innuendo and did as I suggested.

We drove around most of the night, stopping at a few bars, or private clubs as the law liked to call them, along the way. Mostly we talked and laughed, sharing stories of our lives and our hopes for the future. He was traveling across the country from California to the east coast, I found out, and hoped to open a restaurant or club if he could get the financing. He thought that I was something of a gypsy, moving from town to town, never staying more than a few years in any one place.

"How can you ever establish a home for yourself that way, Diane Gleason?" He was still making fun of the name on my uniform and we laughed, as if it were the funniest joke ever told. I found him charming and attractive, so different from the men I met at the truck stop, and began to wonder if I could make a mate of him. Shortly before dawn, he brought me back to the trailer, and after making arrangements to meet the next evening, kissed me quickly, his lips hard and demanding on mine.

"Would you like to come in?" I asked breathlessly.

"You are beautiful, Diane, and so alive. Who would ever have thought . . ." His voice trailed off as he buried his mouth in my hair.

"Thought what, Max?"

He held me at arm's length and looked at me intently, then smiled. "That I could find a girl like you in a place like this." He kissed me once more and let me go. "I've got to go, now. Till tomorrow." He got into his car and sped away.

"Till tomorrow," I repeated as I entered my trailer.

The sun was rising as I pulled the drapes and laid down on my bed. Long after I should have been asleep, I thought about Max and the evening we had spent. Formulating plans for converting him into a creature like me, I tried to remember the procedure from the countless books I had read. My own transformation was hazy, veiled in a disturbing dream, and so could offer no solution. I fell asleep composing the words to my proposal. I would offer him endless youth and life; he and I could be united forever.

We spent the next few nights together. I took a week's vacation from work, something I hadn't done in the past two years. We must have put hundreds of miles on his car, doing nothing but driving and talking. Just being with Max made me feel more human than I had in years; I was young and vibrant again, the long lonely times finally behind me. On our last night together, we found a deserted country road, miles away from everything. We lay in a field, staring at the night sky. Thinking how I wanted to preserve the moment forever, the silence, the stars and his presence, I sighed, almost involuntarily.

"I have to leave tomorrow," he said abruptly; his words were a brutal interruption of the quiet night. "There's no way around it."

Something in the tone of his voice angered me, a detachment, and coldness I had never heard before. "Well, you needn't sound so damned happy about it," I snarled at him. "I knew you would only be here for a while. You owe me nothing."

"On the contrary, my love, I owe you a lot. You've renewed me, taken me away from my own selfish pursuits, made me feel that life may be worth living, after all. But even at that, I have to leave." The words were properly sincere, but the voice was that of a stranger. "You could come with me, I suppose, but I have never been able to sustain a lasting relationship with anyone before; I care too much about you to give you less than you deserve. It's better to end things right now."

I studied his profile in the moonlight, trying to etch it into my memory as I considered his words. The proposal I had rehearsed night after night would not come; I was too proud, too unsure of him. I could take him by force, change him as I had been changed, perhaps, but I wanted a willing partner, someone who could move gracefully into my existence. That partner would not be him. My perception of him as eternal companion began to fade, replaced by the vision of his face in twenty or thirty years, aging and grayed. Max would become one with all the others, those whom I touched and those who had touched me, only to be claimed by their final lover—death—while I lived on. With that thought, I let go of him, reluctantly, yet completely, condemning him to his fate and me to mine.

"Hell, Max," I said quietly and tenderly, "in the whole scheme of eternity, it can hardly matter."

"Ah, eternity," he said, giving a low laugh. "What must eternity be like?"

"Terrible," I said as our eyes met, "yet beautiful when filled with times like this."

We turned to each other then and made love in the cool night air. It seemed a bitter union, desperate and futile. Mentally we had both accepted the inevitable separation; physically we clung to each other in a desperate attempt to postpone the parting. We were joined in an animal mating; instinct took over, leaving no room for intellect or emotion. We were merely two bodies, taking from each other, insatiable yet dispassionate. In the final moments when our lovemaking grew frantic, our peak very near, I realized that I had been crying for some time, a silent outpouring of blood-tinged tears, flowing down my face, soaking my hair and the dark earth beneath me.

When it was over, we drove in silence back to my trailer. Max came in for the first and last time, and lay down on my narrow bed as I prepared for sleep. I drew the drapes, slowly undressed and crawled in beside him.

"Max," I said and could say no more.

"Hush, my little love, sleep now." He crooned and rocked me; I relaxed and slept in his arms like a child.

When I awoke the next evening, he was gone. He left a printed card on the pillow with his address. Almost as an afterthought, the words "Love, Max" were scrawled in red ink.

I could not cry, all my tears had been shed during our lovemaking. I dressed and returned to the life I had led before we met.

We had kept in touch over the years—Christmas cards from him and change of address notices from me. When my luck ran out in a small southern town, where a persistent sheriff had grown too curious about my nocturnal activities, Max had answered my distress call with a plane ticket, a new life and a new identity. After I arrived in Manhattan, I had offered him no explanations and he had asked no questions.

I broke down one night about three years later and confessed to him the horrors of my life. Max needed little convincing, he had already observed some of my more telling habits: that I never went out into full sunlight, never consumed solid food, how weekly I would choose a man from the dance floor of the Ballroom and return from the encounter revitalized and strengthened. He was curious, not frightened, and his only stipulation to belief was that I allow him to observe a feeding. When this had been done, he laughingly admitted that I either was a vampire or gave an amazingly convincing imitation of one. It was at this point that he began screening potential victims and directing them my way. I accepted his assistance out of the love I still felt for him. But even with my confession, or perhaps because of it, our relationship never progressed further than friendship. It was almost as if that one night of love had never happened.

A loud knock on the door interrupted my thoughts and I was jolted back into the present. "Come in," I called softly, wondering why Max would knock. When the door opened, my question was answered. A stranger stood there looking rather ill at ease, and yet oddly sure of himself. He was not the normal type that frequented the club, he looked older than most of the patrons, probably in his late forties. He was tall, fair and well built, but rather nondescript, I thought, until my gaze rested on his face. He had a strong, hawklike nose and eyes bluer and more intense than any I had ever seen. *A tough customer,* I thought to myself as I rose from the couch to greet him.

"Hello, you must be looking for Max. He should be here in a few minutes. Sit down and I'll see if I can find him for you."

"Actually," he said slowly and deliberately, looking me up and down in an appraising manner, "I've already seen him. It's you I want to see, if you're Deirdre Griffin. I was told you'd be here."

"Business or pleasure?" I asked him, smiling my most seductive smile. As a peace offering from Max, he was not really my type, nor was he necessary tonight, but it was a nice gesture. "How can I help you, Mr. . . . ?"

"Detective Mitchell Greer, Miss Griffin. And most definitely business." He gave me a stern look and flashed his badge briefly. "I'd like to ask you a few questions about Thursday night and one of the customers here. I believe you were acquainted with him." He settled commandingly into the chair behind Max's desk, leaving me with two obvious options. I could remain standing before him like a schoolgirl called to the principal's office or I could sit in one of the side chairs like a prospective employee to be interviewed and grilled. I liked neither of these options, so I walked to the bar and poured myself another drink, mostly to steady my now shaking hands. I lounged against the bar and waited for him to continue.

"Bill Andrews, did you know him?" he asked, all the while studying my face with those incredible eyes.

I saw no reason not to tell most of what had occurred. There was, I felt, still no way that I could be connected to his death. No one, especially not this man, could believe in what I am. And perhaps, if I were subtle enough in my prying, I could discover the true cause of Bill's death, and salve my conscience.

"Yes, Detective Greer, I met him here that night. We drank and danced, as I remember. Then he took a taxi home; he had overindulged a bit. I read about his death in the paper the next day."

He seemed surprised at the openness of my answer. "And just

how well did you know him, Miss Griffin? I suppose he was a regular here."

"No, he had never been here before, to my knowledge. I can't even imagine how you knew he'd been here at all."

He reached into his pocket and pulled out a pack of matches. "He had these in his coat. His wife said that he didn't smoke, and that they had never been here together, so we assumed he had been here that night and met someone. An employee here said that you and Bill were together, and Max Hunter confirmed that the two of you had left the dance floor together." He smugly put the matches back into his pocket.

Max? I thought. *Why would he willingly give my name to someone in a situation like this? He of all people knew that one night in jail, or one day, could easily kill me.* I tried to keep the anger at bay, but when I spoke, my response was scornful and more a reaction to Max than to this man. "I guess that is an example of brilliant investigative work. Nice job, Detective." I bared my teeth in more of a grimace than a smile.

Astonishingly, he smiled back, a disarming sort of smile that made him look years younger. "Well," he admitted sheepishly, "it's not exactly brilliant, but it gave us the only lead we have. To be perfectly honest, we can't really discover much of a motive in this case and we were hoping to find one here."

I softened a bit toward him, and then realized that that was probably his intention. "I really wish I could help you," I said stiffly, "but I'm afraid that I am just as puzzled as you. I did not know him very well, we had only just met that evening, you see. He did not seem to be the sort that would be involved in anything that would result in his death."

"He also didn't seem the sort that would be involved with someone like you. But apparently he was. You and he were reported to have slipped away to some back room here at the club. Would you mind explaining what transpired between the two of you?" His smile had gone and he was again an uncompromising inquisitor.

"I do not care for the tone of your voice or the implications you seem to be making, Detective. Someone here should be able to back up my statement that he took a taxi home, alone. In view of that fact, I can't see that what happened between the two of us is any of your business."

He gave me another of his sharp, appraising stares. "It is my business when what happens is against the law."

"And exactly what are the charges? Drinking? Dancing without a license? Corrupting the morals of an attorney?"

"Miss Griffin, this is not a joke. While certainly not as serious as some crime, prostitution is still against the law. And it's my job to enforce that law. You'll find that I take my job very seriously."

I must have stared at him in shock for a few seconds. Prostitution? And all the while I thought he was questioning me for the murder of Bill Andrews. I began to laugh, softly at first, then loudly and for a long time. "I'll have to thank you for this, Detective, when I recover," I said between bursts of laughter. "I haven't been so amused for a long time."

He seemed confused by my outburst, then a shy smile brushed his face. "Another great piece of investigative work, huh? The evidence seemed so overwhelming, you coming here so often, meeting so many men. Well, it just didn't look right."

I guessed this was as close as he would get to an apology and I was so relieved at not being suspected in the murder of Bill Andrews that I let him off the hook.

"Trust me," I said still smiling, "my morals may not be impeccable, but I do not take money in return for my favors." Not in this lifetime, anyway, I added silently. "For one thing, I don't need to."

He looked at me in puzzlement, so I went on. "In my business I make a profit of around seven figures a year. I own Griffin Designs." When his confused expression did not clear, I explained further. "I'm a fashion designer, women's clothes. You must be a confirmed bachelor not to have heard of me."

"Divorced, actually," he admitted reluctantly. "I'm sorry I misunderstood; it's been a long day and I'm very tired."

"Well, then, if there's nothing else I can help you with . . ."

The phone rang and he answered it without hesitation. I found myself admiring his forcefulness—here in Max's office where the furniture, I knew, cost more than he would make in a year, he was at ease and in command. Mitchell Greer was not a man easily intimidated or impressed by the trappings of wealth.

"Yes, this is Greer," he said. "What's up?" As he listened intently to the caller, all traces of amusement vanished from his face. "Another one? Where?" he questioned. Then, "Who was it? That's strange, otherwise it matches the m.o. pretty well." He ran his fingers in a tired gesture through his hair. "I'll be over as soon as I finish up here." He hung up the phone with a bang.

"I'm sorry I was so unreasonable with you, Miss Griffin, but this case has me bothered. After all my years on the force, I've still never quite gotten used to the violence." He gave me a wan little smile. "Thank you for your time tonight. Send me a bill if you want, I enjoyed your company."

I was more concerned with his telephone conversation, than his attempt at humor. "Can you tell me what is happening? I live in the area and if there is a maniac roaming the streets, I would like to be prepared." My eyes searched out his, made contact and held him there, hesitant and undecided about how much he should reveal. Had he been just slightly more forceful he might have been able to avoid my questions.

"I shouldn't really say anything, but I can't see what harm it would do. There's been another murder, but it doesn't seem to match, somehow. This one was a prostitute that frequents the area—there must be a connection somewhere but I just can't see it. It's just so odd, that they both died the same way."

"Can you tell me"—my eyes were locked on his—"can you tell me how they died?"

"Damnedest thing I've ever seen," he admitted, pulling away from my gaze and walking slowly to the door, "no signs of violence, no large wounds, but every drop of blood was drained from the bodies."

I felt a surge of excitement, and lowered my eyes to hide it from him, but he was not looking at me.

"Good night, Miss Griffin." He closed the door softly behind him.

I sank to the couch in amazement. Finally, after all these years, here was a sign of another of my kind—in the same city, the same area in which I operated. While I might have been responsible for the death of Bill Andrews, however improbable it seemed, I knew nothing of the girl. No, it had to be someone else like me and I would find them.

Plans began to race through my mind furiously; could I investigate the murders myself without becoming too obvious about my interest? I knew from past experiences that it didn't pay to get too deeply involved with the law—maybe Max could. . . .

Max—in my reaction to the information supplied by Detective Greer I had forgotten about Max and his recent role in the investigation. What game was he playing? Did he feel pressured to put me under suspicion to protect the club? To protect his reputation? Would it be bad for business if people were afraid to come to the Ballroom, due to too many murders in the neighborhood?

At that moment the door opened again and Max entered. "Deirdre," he called tentatively, "are you still here?"

"Afraid that Greer took me in for the murder of Bill Andrews, Max?" Suddenly I was angry, totally enraged, out of control. Before I knew I had moved, I was across the room, slamming the door and grasping his shoulders in a grip designed to hurt. I dug my nails in and felt the material shred beneath my fingers. "You bastard, Max. You knew he'd be here; you set me up for this. Why else would you have called me, pleading with me to see you tonight? Greer needed a murderer and you delivered one to him. Well, it didn't work, he doesn't suspect me."

He flinched and I realized I had drawn blood. I could feel its warmth oozing onto my fingertips, the thought that I had gone too far with him intensified my anger. "I could kill you very easily right now. Unfortunately, I would be a serious suspect in that murder." As I pushed him away I noticed a gleam in his eyes. I walked to the door, trying to calm myself, wondering at the deepness of my rage. I didn't want him dead, just frightened and in my control. In a gesture designed to unnerve him, I proceeded to lick the traces of his blood from my hands. He watched me, with a look of fascination on his face. Then, to my surprise, he turned his back to me, took off his jacket and began to unbutton his shirt.

"Care to finish what you started, my dear?" He turned around and I saw deep ruts in his shoulders, each surrounded with drops of congealing blood. I turned my head away in answer, disgusted at my behavior. "No? Well, then, let me just clean up a bit and we'll talk about it all." I looked at him again and saw that he had wiped the blood from his arms with his shirt. He discarded both the shirt and jacket into the wastebasket and went to the closet behind his desk to get new clothes.

"No, Max," I said desperately, anxious to leave him. The taste of his blood lingered in my mouth, the smell of his blood in the air. "There's been enough talk for one night. I must go now." I left the room and closed the door behind me. Leaning up against it, I tried to catch my breath. What was happening? I wondered, how could I lose control so quickly? If he had shown the slightest trace of fear I would have been on him in seconds, my teeth imbedded tightly in his neck. I recalled the gratifying feel of his torn flesh beneath my fingers and shivered.

"Damn," I swore softly, then hurried down the hall toward the exit, to put as much distance between us as possible. Soon I was running, as if pursued by all the demons of my past and present. The doorman hailed a taxi and I rode into the comfort of the night.

Chapter 5

The roses began to arrive at my office on Monday afternoon, bouquets of massive, deep-red blooms overwhelming in their fragrance and their beauty. Every day that week another arrangement was delivered, each one more spectacular than the previous. No cards were included but I knew who had sent them. They all had Max's signature, a single pure-black rose embedded amid the profusion of red. He had once, in an uncharacteristic, poetic mood, referred to me as a "rose clad in black." The mood had passed quickly and soon he was his cynical self, but the epithet had remained. Ever since, any gift or message he sent was accompanied by a black rose. He was, I knew, seeking forgiveness and a reconciliation. The first I could grant, given time. But the second seemed to be a risky venture. The passion and anger that he had inspired frightened me, more than I cared to admit even to myself. Yet, as the week went on, and the flowers continued to arrive, I began to soften toward him, the emotions I felt subsided. Perhaps I had misjudged him; he really had not had a chance to explain, maybe I did owe him that chance.

In actuality, I spent very little time worrying about Max and our relationship. Even the thought that there might be another of my kind prowling the city was pushed into the back of my mind. The week proved to be as busy as I had expected and I immersed myself in the work. I could lose my identity in the designs, following and coaxing the ideas and drawings into something with texture, something with a tangible beauty. By Friday evening, when my office was overflowing with flowers, all delicately displayed in tall alabaster vases, a similar array of colors decorated the rack of finished garments in the dressing rooms.

The show was now only a week away and we had made great progress. I worked like one obsessed and had expected no less of my employees. With the prospect of a free weekend ahead of them, they had matched my long hours with few complaints and were now tired but relieved that the rush was behind us. The tasks that remained for the next week were the final fittings, some accessorizing, and the staging of the show itself, mostly work for Gwen, myself and a few of our top seamstresses.

When everyone else had left the building, Gwen entered my office bearing two cups of coffee, one so diluted with sugar and cream it lost all resemblance to its origin, and for me, one black and steaming. I took it from her appreciatively and gestured to one of the office chairs. She flopped down with a sigh.

"Tired?" I questioned, needlessly, for even in the dim light I could see the dark circles beneath her eyes.

"Tired doesn't even come close to describing it, Deirdre. I don't think I could move from this chair, even if the building were on fire. But you, you still look as good as you did first thing Monday morning. Come to think of it, you still look like you did almost ten years ago. However do you manage it?" Her tired eyes squinted at me.

"Clean living, Gwen," I joked. "I don't eat junk and I work like a dog. It's the Protestant work ethic, you know."

"Whatever it is, it sure works for you. I feel like I've aged twenty years in the past five days. I had an argument with Nick about it; he wanted to go out tonight, but if I let him see me like this, the wedding would be off."

"You're such an ass, Gwen; he loves you very much, tired or not. Go home, take a hot bath, chill a bottle of wine and invite him to your place. You can spend the entire weekend in bed if you're so tired."

"Deirdre, if I didn't know better I'd think you were jealous. Don't you and Max have plans? I just assumed that with all these flowers you two had something special going on."

"I hate to disappoint you, but there is nothing between Max and me, there never really was. Part of my secret is having no serious involvement with anybody." I smiled indulgently at her. "But you are already involved, so my advice comes too late. Go home, Gwen, and have a nice time."

She rose slowly from the chair and was walking to the door, when the intercom on my desk buzzed. We jumped in unison, having both supposed the office was empty. I answered and the front desk receptionist's voice filled the office.

"Miss Griffin, I'm sorry to bother you. I just came back upstairs to get something and found someone here waiting for you. Should I send him back?"

"I'll be right out to get him," Gwen broke in. She turned to me. "Nothing happening, huh? Finally I get to meet the great Max." With no trace of her professed exhaustion, she rushed out of the office and down the hall.

Unlike Gwen, I was not so sure that the visitor was Max. He had never before made any attempt to see me outside of the confines of the club, yet, given the precarious course our relationship had taken, he would have a better chance of making his explanations in person. Perhaps it was logical for him to make his appearance tonight.

I didn't have long to ponder the question, for I could hear Gwen's chattering approach my office.

"You're not anything like I pictured you, but it's nice to meet you. I'm sure Deirdre will be thrilled to see you. She's so maddeningly private about her life, she never even told me you'd be stopping here tonight. But I knew something was up, when all those beautiful flowers started to arrive. Here we are." She was so excited about the visitor as she escorted him into my office, I felt it was cruel to disillusion her but it was necessary.

"Gwen," I said as sharply as a slap and watched the smile fade from her face, "meet Detective Mitchell Greer."

"Oh, God, I'm so embarrassed." She flushed a bright red. "I'm sorry, Detective, I thought you were someone else."

"Obviously," he said with a kind smile, "but thank you for the greeting, anyway. People seldom meet me with such enthusiasm."

"No, I bet they don't," she started, then blushed more deeply. "I mean, or I didn't mean . . . oh, shit . . ."

"Gwen," I said reassuringly, "you're tired. Just go home, I'll see you later." With a muffled good night, she scurried through the door and we were left alone.

I cleared my throat. "Your visit is such a surprise to Gwen and me. I have very few friends and none ever come here to the office. She just jumped to conclusions about who you are. I apologize if she embarrassed you." I knew it sounded as if I were babbling, but it seemed a good way to cover the nervousness I felt in his presence. "We were just about to leave for the night; had you come a few minutes later you would have found an empty office." I sat down behind my desk and began to restlessly shuffle papers around. "Sit down, please, and let me know how I can help you."

He glanced around the office for a few seconds. "Thank you," he said, sitting down, then abruptly, "Who died?"

I stiffened at his question, until I saw he was studying the flowers. "It is a bit excessive, isn't it?" I said with a small laugh, but supplied no further information. "Now, I hate to be rude, but it has been a long week and I am very tired. Can we get on with it?"

"Get on with it?"

"Yes, get on with it. Ask me your questions and then let me get out of here."

"Well," he began with infuriating slowness, "there is one very important question I'd like you to answer. Are you hungry?"

"Hungry?" What was he getting at? "Actually, I have been so busy this week, I can hardly remember my last meal. So, now that you mention it, yes, I am very hungry Why do you ask?"

His line of questioning worried me; there was no way for him to know of my habits and yet he was so unnerving. I rose from the desk and walked across the room to the flowers. Absently, I plucked a few of the drooping blooms, showering the credenza with a flood of scarlet petals.

He began to laugh. "No wonder you have so few friends, Miss Griffin. Don't you recognize a dinner invitation when you get one?" His face was lit with a mischievous smile and I could see that he was enjoying the situation.

His grin was infectious and I found myself smiling back. "Actually, I get very few dinner invitations and accept even fewer, so I never know how to react to them." I hesitated for a while; if this was a friendly gesture on his part, it would do no harm. If it was part of his investigation, still I could get more details on the progress of the case from him than from anyone else. He could be an invaluable help in tracking the murderer for me. "Yes," I replied at last, "I would like to have dinner with you. And since I assume you are not on official business, please call me Deirdre."

"Fine, if you'll drop the detective and call me Mitch. What would you like to eat? I know a place not far from here that's wonderful. Nothing fancy, but they serve good steaks and some seafood." He looked at me for my approval.

"A nice rare steak would be great for me. Just let me freshen up a bit and we can go."

As we rode the elevator, I wondered what on earth had possessed me to accept the invitation. There was something about Mitch that intrigued me, but I was hardly in any position to begin or pursue a relationship with anyone. And my idea of a dinner date hardly coincided with his. But as the doors opened into the lobby and I met his eyes and matched his smile, I felt strangely content with the situation.

A car was parked at the curb, a rather dingy sedan of indeterminate color, but unmistakably his, as the placard in the window proudly proclaimed "Official Police Business."

"Business?" I questioned, giving him a sidelong glance as he opened the door.

"Well, no . . . I forgot to take it out of the window. Besides," he said wryly, tossing the sign into the backseat, "it was easier than finding a parking spot."

"Not above the law are you, Detective? While it may not be as serious a crime as some, illegal parking is still . . ." I mimicked the tone he took at our last meeting and he laughed, a nice honest sound.

"Okay, okay, let's drop it. To be perfectly truthful, I did start out on police business. It seemed a good idea to verify your identity, so I did some checking before I came up to your office."

"Did I check out satisfactorily?" I inquired, trying to establish a casual tone.

"Most definitely," he asserted. "You are Deirdre Griffin, genius designer: hardworking, successful, ambitious and extremely wealthy." He maneuvered his car carefully into the early evening traffic, then gave me a shrewd glance. "And there may have been a few more adjectives used that I left out."

"I assume they were not all complimentary. Who provided you with this wealth of information?"

He glanced at me briefly, then gave a small shrug. "The usual sorts of informants: doormen, security guards, landlords and, uh, the editors of several fashion publications."

"Who, no doubt, were more than happy to supply you with all the details of my criminal activities. So, with what shall I be charged?" I felt secure in the knowledge that none of the mentioned persons could have anything incriminating to say about me.

"Other than asking an exorbitant amount for your clothes, and getting it—nothing, I'm happy to report." His voice lost all traces of humor. "Still I find it interesting that very little of your private life is known to anyone."

"Why should it be known?" I could hear the anger creeping into my voice. "It is private, after all."

"Don't get me wrong, I didn't mean to offend you. It's just that . . ." He hesitated for a second, considering his words. "You seem to live your life like a phantom, touching no one, leaving no impact on those around you. You hardly seem real."

"I'm real enough," I murmured, thinking myself a fool for accepting this date. He was too perceptive, too keen and I felt as if I were walking along a steep cliff merely by being with him. I glanced at him as he concentrated grimly on his driving. We sat in an uneasy silence; I turned my attention to the lights of the city flowing past the window.

I barely noticed when we stopped at the curb, until he reached over and gently touched my arm. "Deirdre," he said softly, pausing again to collect his thoughts. "I'm sorry. Don't be mad." He turned to look at me, his face seemed expressionless in the dark car. "I guess I just find it hard to believe that someone like you, with everything going for you—looks, talent, wealth—hasn't ever been married or pursued a serious relationship. It doesn't add up."

"I was married, once." My voice sounded small and lost. "He died." I looked out the window, trying to shake the fear and sadness. "I never talk about it."

"Oh, God," he began. "I'm . . ."

"Forget it," I interrupted. "I'm starving. Let's get that steak you promised. And please don't apologize anymore tonight."

"Fine with me; let's go." He opened the door and came around to escort me out of the car. We walked down the dimly lit street to the restaurant, his arm comfortingly draped across my shoulders.

"Do you really enjoy that bloody mess of a meal?" I jumped guiltily at the question. Mitch was grinning broadly and pointing to my dinner plate. "You could send it back to the kitchen and have it cooked, you know."

I looked down and saw the small piece of remaining steak sitting amid a pool of red fluid that even the most dedicated gourmand would hesitate to call "au jus."

"It is cooked," I protested. "Well, anyway, it's warm. Have some, you might enjoy it." I offered it, and laughed at his grimace. "I should think, Detective, that with your job you would be better accustomed to the sight of blood."

"Blood, yes. But not to the sight of someone making a meal of it." I caught my breath, but he went on happily, not noticing. "You really should have had the fettucini, it's much healthier. All this garlic is good for the digestion."

I crinkled my nose in distaste. "My digestion is just fine, thank you." I pushed my plate aside and poured myself another glass of wine. The waiter came to clear the table and offer coffee and dessert. The restaurant had been crowded when we entered, but was now empty except for us and an elderly couple who had just been seated. When the waiter returned with pie for Mitch, coffee for us both, and the tab was paid, we were left virtually alone.

"Thank you for the dinner," I said sincerely. "It was nice of you to ask me."

"My pleasure," he said. He reached across the table and took my hand. "Next time, I'll pick some place a little fancier."

"This place is just fine. I didn't expect fancy," I said noncommittally. There would be no next time. He was human, not someone I could afford to get involved with. Still, I felt a twinge of sadness about using him to track the other. I had discovered over dinner that I liked Mitch, and thought that I would miss his sharp eyes and dry humor when it was all over. I inadvertently sighed at my own thoughts.

"Do you want to go?" he asked solicitously. "It's not late and I have tomorrow off for a change. I thought maybe we could go somewhere and talk, or just drive around, or . . ."

"Go to your place?" I finished the thought with a smile.

"Well, now that you mention it, yes." He still had hold of my hand and pulled me up from my seat with a boyish eagerness.

I did not resist, but allowed him to steer me out of the restaurant and into the car.

As it turned out, Mitch's apartment was no more than three blocks from my hotel. He lived in an area midway between the exclusiveness of where I lived, worked and fed, and the terrible poverty on the other side. Undoubtedly I had passed this street in my search for a victim less than a week ago. I must have given him a doubtful look as we exited the car; he was quick to reassure me. "It may look like no-man's land, but it's really quite nice and relatively safe. Besides, you're in the protection of one of the city's finest, remember?"

"I was just surprised at how close we actually live to one another." Clasping my arm in his, we walked up the steps to his building, a rather typical, nondescript stone structure.

"So near and yet so far, right?" he joked. "I know where you live. My brilliant investigative work again, remember? I only hope you don't feel too far below your league." He was still smiling, but I noticed a look of doubt enter his eyes.

"Now that is just plain silly, Mitch. I may be rich now, but I came from very humble beginnings and have had my share of hard knocks, believe me." I moved closer to him as we climbed the few stairs to the entrance.

When he opened the door on his apartment, I discovered a small place, tastefully decorated and painstakingly neat. The walls were lined with bookshelves on all sides, crowded with an amazingly diverse selection of books. A complete set of Shakespeare stood next to a row of cheap detective novels, science fiction mingled with astronomy and pure science volumes, legal textbooks competed with famous erotic works. He watched as I studied this array. "I read a lot," he said casually. "Can I get you a drink?" He was heading toward a small kitchenette, while removing his tie and loosening his collar.

"Wine, if you have some, please," I replied, settling into what looked like his reading chair. Several books were stacked on the small end table and I perused his current reading material.

"Cabernet, okay?" he called from the kitchen.

"That would be wonderful." I picked up a small volume of poetry on the top of the pile. It opened of itself to a dog-eared page and a marked passage. I read it softly to myself.

In the desert
I saw a creature, naked, bestial,
Who, squatting upon the ground,
Held his heart in his hands,
And ate of it.
I said: "Is it good, friend?"
"It is bitter—bitter," he answered;
"But I like it
Because it is bitter,
And because it is my heart."

I laid it back on the table, and in doing so jostled the stack. On the bottom was an obviously new copy of a book extremely familiar to me. I pulled it from the table and held it in my hands; the price tag, still intact, did nothing to obscure the title, which flashed at me in blood-red letters, *The Annotated Dracula.* As I hurriedly replaced it, my pulse racing, Mitch returned with the wine and glasses.

"Not my normal nightly reading," he said, pouring us each a glass of wine, "but I must admit I found it rather fascinating. Have you read it?"

"Yes, some time ago," I admitted, "but surely this sort of thing is completely ridiculous. You can't think that the recent murders were actually committed by a vampire." The dreaded word, that I tried to avoid even in my own thoughts, seemed to hang heavy in the air. The voice that said it sounded high-pitched and slightly hysterical.

He looked at me with the intense gaze that so unnerved me. Every instinct cried out that this man is a danger—strike, Deirdre, it urged. Strike, kill and flee. The blood thirst, which no amount of rare steak could assuage, welled up within me. I will take him, I thought, without mercy, as an enraged wolf will take even an armed man, savage and quick. I moved in his direction, feeling my teeth enlarge, scenting the blood beating in his veins. I saw myself reflected, wild and feral, in his eyes; somewhere within me, a voice called for caution, but I ignored it. God, how I wanted this man's blood.

Then, thankfully, he dropped his eyes and began to laugh. "You're really spooked by this, aren't you?" he said, still laughing. "No, of course I don't think we have a real vampire on the loose. But we may have someone who *thinks* that he is. I just didn't think it would hurt to bone up a little on the legends, just in case I could find something that might trip our man up."

"And you think it's a man?" I rose from the chair and walked to the window, trying to compose myself.

"We're not entirely sure, of course. But it seems unlikely that it's a woman. Both victims were tough, each in their own way. Andrews worked out quite frequently, and the girl had street smarts, a real scrapper. I just can't see a woman being able to subdue either one of them long enough to drain their blood."

"How was the blood drained?" My voice sounded casual again, curious but not too eager. I had managed to submerge my desires, for the moment, and turned away from the window and sat down again.

"We don't really know yet; a syringe perhaps. Although our 'vampire' "—I cringed at the word—"was cautious enough to leave the obligatory bruises and fang marks on their necks. But that could be easily faked, I suppose. Pathology is working on it."

I made a sort of noncommittal grunt and he gave me an appraising glance. "You know, I didn't bring you here to discuss police business." He offered me a glass of wine and I accepted it, gratified to notice that my hand was steady.

"Why did you bring me here, Mitch? To be perfectly honest, you seem to be above pursuing a one-night stand and you've already discovered that I'm not the type to sustain a relationship." I felt betrayed by the situation that forced me to remember and echo the hurtful words once said to me in a dark field, under a clear night sky. Regardless of what could be assumed from my seemingly promiscuous behavior every week at the club, I had not made love without feeding since the night I heard similar words issue from Max. I was not even sure that I could perform sexually now *without* the taking of blood. A silence fell over us as I occupied myself with draining my glass and refilling it. His wine had not been touched.

"You sure don't pull any punches, do you?" His voice sounded harsh, but his eyes were kind. "I think you give yourself too little credit and me too much. But let's just say that I brought you here because you're the first woman I've reacted to since the divorce and I wanted to prolong our evening." He turned and went to a small stereo system on one of his bookcases. "Would you like to dance?" he asked with a shy smile.

"That I can do," I said and as I entered his arms and we merged with the music, all awkwardness vanished. The thoughts of guilt and deceit, death and blood all fell from me, leaving me with only a body that enjoyed the rhythmic closeness of another and a mind that relished the thought that the neck so warm above my mouth need never be violated by my hunger.

The night sped by, occupied as we were with dance and conversation. A bond had begun to grow between us, incongruous as it seemed. Mitch, I discovered, was a complex and fascinating person. His natural reticence dissolved with the wine we drank, and he told me of his private life. He talked of his earlier aspirations of a career in law, and how that was abandoned due to the financial aspects of an unexpected pregnancy. "I was thrilled with the baby," he explained, "and I didn't mind leaving school for him." Two years ago, his wife filed for divorce. "She said she was tired of struggling with the problems of being a policeman's wife, tired of waiting for the late-night call to say I'd been killed or injured." They'd had no other children but the son, Chris. Mitch's eyes shown with a quiet pride when he spoke of him. "He'll graduate from law school this summer," he said with a rueful grin, "so the cycle will be complete." They kept in touch by phone and letters and occasional visits. "I'd like you to meet him next time he comes in; he'd really think old dad hit the big time."

"Have you?" I asked, getting up from the couch and making a half-hearted attempt to tidy up the wineglasses and bottles that had accumulated during the evening.

"Who knows? Stranger things have happened." He smiled at me as I went into the kitchen.

Once there, I glanced at the clock and saw it was nearly six. "God, Mitch," I called to him, "how did it get so late? I've really got to go."

"Stay and watch the sunrise with me?" He came up behind me and rested his chin on my shoulder. His voice was soft and scratchy in my ear. "I'd like to see the sunlight in your hair."

"I can't, Mitch. You may have the day off tomorrow, or I should say today, but I have details to take care of that can't wait. I stayed too long as it is, and although it has been a lovely evening . . ." I could not remember what time sun-up was, but I knew it was close. I had to leave soon.

"I've had too much wine to drive you, but at least let me walk you back to your hotel." He moved to get his coat.

"That would be nice," I said, considering the situation, "but let's make it the office, instead. I can catch a few hours sleep on the couch until Gwen gets in. It's only a few more blocks, can you stagger that far?"

He laughed. "I imagine so, if you can."

"Never fear, Detective. I can drink a lot more than I have tonight and still find my way home in the dark." I moved toward the door and he followed.

On the streets we walked arm-in-arm, silent once more, but no longer uneasy with each other. The sky was dark and cloudy with no sign of the impending dawn, but I could feel my body's warnings begin. I quickened my step involuntarily and he looked at me questioningly.

"In a hurry?" he asked abruptly.

"Yes," I answered simply and we were quiet once more until we were within a block of the office.

"God damn it, Deirdre, slow down, will you?" He pulled my arm sharply as we stood at a corner. "I have some questions to ask you."

I winced from his tight grip and he lightened it a bit, but still kept hold as if he thought I would run away. "Can't it wait, Mitch? I have to get some sleep soon or I'll drop."

"No, it can't wait. It's important."

"Isn't it a little late to be discussing police business, Mitch? I can't think what else would be so critical that it didn't come up earlier." My fear of the approaching sunrise forced me to speak sharply.

"Don't be so damned jumpy, not everything I do or say is connected with my job. I'm a man, too, and I want some answers." His eyes searched mine and held them for a second, then fell away to study the empty street.

He paused for a long time, avoiding my gaze. I waited as patiently as was possible for me.

Hurriedly, he blurted it out. "Who sent the flowers?"

"What?" I could hardly make the connection.

"The flowers that were overflowing in your office. Who sent them?"

"Max."

"That's it. Just Max?"

"Yes, Mitch, he sent the flowers. What else do you want me to say?"

"Why?"

I sighed before I answered. "We had an argument and they were his way of trying to apologize. That's all." I could feel the precious minutes before dawn ticking away.

"Who did Gwen think I was when I came in last night." He met my eyes again for a while before looking away.

"I suppose she thought you were Max. Look, Mitch. I can't see where all this is leading, but I really do have to go."

"This is where it's leading," he said and pulled me to him

roughly. His lips met mine with a hunger and urgency so deep, I began to realize what my victims must feel with my kiss. As when we had danced earlier that evening, I responded to him without thought for my condition. It had been more years than I cared to remember since I had been kissed like this by someone I liked, someone I had no intention of feeding upon.

He broke away first and we were both breathless and shaken. "I'm sorry, Deirdre," he said, studying my face. "You can be so damn contrary at times. All I wanted to know was, who's the competition?"

"After that kiss, you should know you have none." I put my hands up and caressed his face. It was stubbly. "But"—I laughed—"you need a shave and I need some sleep. Can we go now?"

"Certainly," he said, extending his arm. We slowly walked the last block to my office building and entered the lobby. The security guard nodded to us, he was a regular and recognized me. He gave Mitch a sleepy look, then returned to his paper.

Suddenly I felt awkward again, like a school girl, until Mitch gathered me into his arms. It was a brief kiss, for we both could feel the guard's surprise and interest.

"Can I see you tomorrow?"

"I don't know," I said honestly. "Call me later and we'll talk. Good night." I gave his cheek one final caress and went to the elevator.

"Good night," he said softly and walked out the door. Before the elevator began its rise, I could see the street already lightening with the dawn.

Chapter 6

While my own personal library was not nearly as extensive as Mitch's, it was interesting to note that we possessed at least two books in common. One was a small volume of Stephen Crane's poetry, with the same page and passage marked. Another was *The Annotated Dracula*. I also possessed a much older copy of the original text of *Dracula* by Bram Stoker. In my mind, I referred to these as my survival manual; the poetry to keep me sane and the other to keep me alive.

When I had awakened in my hospital bed following the accident, I had no actual knowledge of what had occurred. I knew, merely, that I had lived and that all I loved had perished. My mind was filled with odd desires and visions, but the medical profession at the time was not concerned with mental soundness. They healed my body to the best of their abilities and sent me back into the world.

I returned to an empty house, the house in which I had been born, and four years later, in which my mother died giving birth to a still-born boy. It had always been filled with light and love, but now seemed too dark, too lifeless. It had never been empty before; I had shared it with my father, who with his exuberance and joy made it into a home. When I married it was to this house we returned after our wedding trip; so that even with my father's peaceful death two years later, I had not been alone.

I found I could not sleep through the night; I would rise within an hour of retiring to pace and stalk the empty rooms until, close to dawn, I would fall into bed and sleep through most of the next morning and afternoon. The smell and taste of food were repugnant to me; I had always been slender, but four weeks following my release from the hospital, the mourning clothes I had worn for my father's death hung on me like meal sacks, without the aid of heavy corsets. My face grew gaunt; my moods black and despairing. I would sit in the rocking chair in the parlor, hugging my emaciated arms to myself, humming odd bits of lullabies and popular songs.

One morning, too tired to climb the stairs, I remained huddled in the darkened parlor. I knew I would die if I stayed in that chair, and I wanted death to come, waited impatiently for its arrival. But my vigil was interrupted by a knock on the door.

"Go away," I tried to call out, but discovered that my voice was scratchy and hoarse with disuse. My visitor opened the door and entered, giving a gasp of surprise at what she probably supposed was my corpse. I turned my head to her and gave her a skeletal grin. "Good morning, Mrs. Blake," I croaked, "so nice of you to call. How are you today?"

She had been carrying parcels, direct from the market, which she dropped, scattering their contents on the hallway floor.

"Oh, my poor dear." She came rushing to me, and crushed me in a bosomy embrace. "I had no idea you would be so . . . well, you look so. . . . Honey, when I walked in I just thought you were dead." She held me out at arms' length and clucked her disapproval. "Hasn't anyone besides me stopped to see you, to take care of you?"

"I think people did knock. I just never answered the door and they didn't come in." Her presence began to revive me, warm me; she was so alive.

"Well, never let it be said that I let a closed door keep me from doing my Christian duty." She began to bustle around the room, neatening and straightening.

I suppressed a giggle at the accurate summation of her personality. "Daddy always said you were a good . . ."

"Hush, child," she interrupted, peering at me with watery

blue eyes. "Your daddy always said I was an interfering old busybody. And maybe he was right, but I can't just sit here and let you waste away, if only for your mother's sake. Now, have you seen the doctor?"

I shook my head. "He can't help me, just let me die."

"I'll do no such thing and I won't hear any more talk of dying. Now, we'll get you cleaned up and dressed and off to the doctor."

She half carried me up the stairs, bathed me and dressed me as if I were a child. I succumbed to her attentions and let myself be coddled and comforted. It was such a joy for me to hear a human voice again, and Mrs. Blake provided a more than adequate amount of talk.

As she helped me back down the stairs, I stumbled and fell, face forward into her neck. "Oh, Mrs. Blake," I whispered, half fainting, "your perfume is wonderful."

"Perfume? Bah! What call would an old biddy like me have for wearing perfume? While you're at it, have that doctor check your nose, too."

We reached the bottom of the stairs and she realized that the parcels she had carried in were still strewn on the floor. "Let me just put these away for now. When we get back, I'll make you a nice supper." She gathered everything and went into the kitchen, returning with a look of disapproval. "I can see no cooking's been done in that room for a month of Sundays. You need some looking after, that's a fact."

"Thank you, Mrs. Blake," I said meekly and allowed her to hurry me to the doctor's office under bleak, overcast skies.

After a thorough examination, I sat in a cold, uncomfortable leather chair awaiting his verdict. He sat across the desk, fingertips touching, and tapped his two forefingers against his lips. "I can't find anything physically wrong with you, other than the fact that you are close to starvation. My advice to you is go home, eat a good dinner and try to start your life over. You can't grieve forever." He gave me a patronizing smile and pushed his chair back. "Have the dreams stopped?"

"Dreams? What dreams?" I said confusedly. "I don't remember any dreams."

"It's probably just as well. You had some rather terrible dreams while you were in the hospital, brought on, I believe, by the shock of the accident. If you can't remember, then you must be getting over it." He got up from the desk and stood over me. "Now, Dorothy, I want to talk to you, not as a doctor, but as one of your father's friends. This part of the country is no place for a woman without a man to protect her, especially now, with the whole place in an uproar over the coming war. You should give some thought to marrying again. No, certainly not right away," he amended, seeing the shock his words caused, "but later on. You're relatively young and attractive; that, plus the money your father left you, makes you eminently marriageable. In fact, I have a nephew in Lawrence, a widower with four children who could use a wife of your breeding and background. Why don't I talk to him and see what can be arranged."

"Thank you, Doctor." I looked away from him, trying to hide my distaste at the suggestion. I had no desire to be married to a stranger, raising some other woman's children when I could have none of my own. But I deferred to him as was appropriate for the times.

"That's a good girl." He patted my arm in a fatherly gesture, seeming well pleased with himself. "Now go home and eat something. Come back in a month or so and we'll see how you're getting along." He escorted me out of the office.

Mrs. Blake babbled indignantly all the way home. "I know his nephew, my dear. Already balding and round about the middle. His wife died in childbirth, you know, delivering their fourth baby in as many years. Shameful, the way some people carry on. And telling you to go home and eat; why I could have told you the same thing and saved us all the time. Oh, no," she cried suddenly, interrupting herself, "speaking of time, I promised Francis I'd meet her at the church this afternoon. We're setting up for the social tomorrow night. I guess if you need me, I could stay on a bit, but you know how Francis is. Oh, dear, I'd never hear the end of it."

"I'll be fine, Mrs. Blake, don't worry about me. In fact, after this walk I feel a great deal better." I lied about this—the sun was burning my eyes and skin and I felt weaker than before. But I had had enough company for the day and longed for my solitude again. "Don't keep Francis waiting, she'll never forget it." I smiled at her wearily and my words seemed to reassure her.

"If you're sure you'll be fine . . . now, mind you, cook up some of that good food I left you. There's a roast, some new potatoes and some milk to mash them with."

"Thank you." Impulsively, I gave her a small hug.

"There, there, child. It will all come out right, just you see. I'll be over tomorrow to see how you are." She saw me to my front door, then hurried away, bewailing her lateness.

I dutifully went into the kitchen and began to make preparations for my dinner. I put on a pot of water to boil the potatoes and turned my attention to the meat. It had sat while we were gone, and as I unwrapped the butcher paper, my nose was assailed with the odor of blood and meat, slightly gamy, but still good. Suddenly I was ravenously hungry. I couldn't wait for the roast to cook in its entirety, but decided to cut a slice for pan frying. In my haste with the knife, I nicked the tip of my finger and put it into my mouth to suck the wound.

The first taste of my own blood almost knocked me senseless, but I continued to draw on the small cut until it was dry. Disappointed, I picked up the knife to cut myself again, until I saw the half-carved roast still on the table. This should suit me, I thought to myself as I picked it up and brought it to my mouth. I bit into the meat and pulled what blood I could from it. When the juices were all drained, I was left with a grayish husk, which I nevertheless devoured, tearing it with my teeth, teeth that suddenly felt odd, too large for my mouth. They interfered with my chewing of the raw meat. I discarded what was left of the roast, mostly fat and gristle, and went in search of a mirror to look at my teeth.

I don't know what I expected to see in the mirror but what I saw surprised me. There was no demon, no shadowy image, only my face staring back at me. But this was not the face I wore that morning. It was blood spattered from my struggle with the roast, but through the blood I could see that the gauntness had gone, the hollows beneath my eyes had been filled, and my skin had regained some of its normal coloring. I pulled my upper lip back to examine my teeth; the canines seemed longer, sharper and I felt them cautiously. Then even as I watched, they seemed to diminish back to their normal size. I shook my head to dispel the image and whispered softly.

"God, what is happening to me?"

I thought back to my pregnancy and remembered the odd whims and cravings that went with that period of my life. This, also, I rationalized, was probably no more than a passing phase, something that would not continue. And, though mentally confused, I realized that for the first time in over a month, I felt physically well. The severe lassitude had gone, replaced by such a wonderful feeling of wellness and wholeness. I attacked the household chores with a fervor I had seldom felt before, and when I collapsed into my bed shortly before dawn, the house was fit for viewing by a thousand Mrs. Blakes.

Unfortunately, the bizarre meal of that day and the shock of health and activity that followed had an adverse effect on my sleep. I began to dream, slow, winding dreams that carried me far down the corridor of my life.

I walk down a hallway. It is dark with many doors on each side. I slowly open the doors, one by one. I enter a room which contains the coffin of my mother; I know it to be hers because I am so small, I have to be lifted to see her face, pale and lifeless. I run from the room into another, to find my father, lying in his bed, motionless. He is dead, too, I know and I touch his cheek in a soft farewell before I leave. The next door I open carefully, knowing who is here. This coffin is sealed, but I try to open the lid. I had been denied a last view of this face and I want to see him again. Tears stream down my face, and I struggle with the heavy wood, scratching at the casket lid to no avail. My fingernails break and bleed, blood is flowing from my hands in concert with my tears.

The odor of blood fills the room. I put my fingers up to my mouth and suck. Suddenly, I am not alone. I can see no one, but feel a breath, hot on my back, and an urgent mouth pressed to my neck. I push away and run the length of the corridor. It seems endless and I run forever, laughter pursuing me, chasing me down to the final door.

This door I open in trepidation to find a wondrous sight. I am outdoors, on a clear summer night, in a sweet-smelling field. I lie down on the grass, slightly wet but still warm from the day's sun. I admire the stars; they are bright and beautiful and seem to speak to me of peace and contentment.

"This must be heaven," I whisper, afraid to break the mood, when suddenly the sky grows dark.

An enormous black shape overwhelms the stars; it shifts its form, coalescing into the shape of a giant bird, man-sized and elegant. It hovers above me, as if in homage to my prone body, silently asking permission. I smile and stretch my arms to it; it descends upon me and I caress its wings, glossy as silk.

I feel no shame as I realize my clothes have disappeared, for it covers my naked body with a rustling sigh. It—no, he—is dark and beautiful like the night, my skin against the ebony feathers is the pale white reflection of the moon, the stars. The coming together seems as natural, as inevitable as the tides. I welcome even the pain of his penetration, giving myself entirely to this creature of the night. We are one. His beak grazes my breasts, closing upon the nipples, and I gasp. He smells of blood, a perfume so intoxicating I almost faint. But his movement within me quickens and my body responds. "Oh, God," I cry as he fills me with the blackness of the sky.

He gazes at me, with wise crow's eyes and promises future

delights, then rises from me on strong wings. There is no feeling of emptiness when he departs, just a serene acceptance of this mystery. My thighs are sticky and warm. I lie there for what seems an eternity when suddenly above the soft night noises, I hear a strange tearing sound. I turn on my side, as curious as a child to witness this new event.

The giant bird is systematically stripping the flesh from the bones of two bodies, one full-grown, the other piteously small. I want to cradle these two, bring them back to life, but I cannot move, cannot call out. I gasp and the bird stops its mutilation and turns to me, laughing. It is his laugh, the laughter of the corridor, but the face on the bird is mine. . . .

"You must kill it," I shrieked. "Kill it before it grows larger." I realized I was grasping at someone's sleeve, my head burrowing into a warm lap. I opened my eyes to see the broad, friendly face of Mrs. Blake, concern in her eyes. "Oh, it was so horrible," I began haltingly. "I didn't know. It was so beautiful, so dark, but so evil. How could I know? And I let it touch me and then it was tearing the flesh from their bones. . . ." My mind stopped in midthought. "I can't seem to remember it all, but it is important. I must try to remember."

"Now, now, dearie, it seems to me you should just forget it. It was only a bad dream, after all." She looked at me critically. "How do you feel now?"

As my fear dissipated, I relaxed and stretched, considering her question. "Actually, I feel good." There was a note of surprise in my voice; I could hardly believe my physical state. "Better than good, I feel"—I paused, searching for the right word—"I feel reborn, as if this last, terrible month has been washed away." To emphasize my words I arose from the bed and led her in a wild, whirling dance through the bedroom.

She was flushed and breathless when we finally stopped. "Well, child," she puffed, "you certainly seem fit enough. I knew a good meal and a good sleep would set you up righter than rain." She beamed at me and nodded her head, taking full credit for my recovery.

"That's right, Mrs. Blake. You can tell them all that you did it, you and that beautiful, beautiful roast you brought."

"Well, I did have the butcher cut it special for me. I brought you another just like it, I did, when I saw that you had eaten the other." At my look of shock—had she watched me eat it?—she laughed. "You see, child, I let myself in earlier, you were sleeping like a baby and I didn't like to disturb you. But I did think I could help out with the cleaning and such. You beat me to it, though, didn't you?" She didn't wait for an answer but continued. "Hard work is a good cure for what ails you. Anyway, what I meant to say was that I noticed when I was in the kitchen that you'd eaten it all. So I ran out and got another. It's cooking right now, can't you smell it?"

Now that she had called it to my attention, I could indeed smell it; the nauseating smell of roasting flesh permeated the air. I would have to get her out of here, or she would sit down with me and force me to eat every bite. My mind raced, trying to come up with an excuse for her to leave, when I thought back to our conversation yesterday.

"What time is it?" I asked.

"Oh, about half past five. You slept a good long time."

"But Mrs. Blake," I said in mock horror, "don't you have to be at church tonight?"

"Goodness, yes, I do! Seeing you put it clean out of my mind. But will you be all right? I don't want to leave, somehow. You seem good now, but yesterday"—she clucked her tongue—"well, I don't mind saying you gave me quite a scare there." She rose. "If you're sure . . ."

"I'll be fine," I said reassuringly, restraining myself from giving her a push. "Have a nice evening."

I waited no more than a minute after I heard the door shut behind her, to rush down the stairs and try to salvage what was left of the meat.

It was almost completely cooked, I discovered as I cut slice after slice, frantically looking for small patches of red flesh. I nibbled on one small piece, pink in the middle, but it tasted like clay. I opened the kitchen door and tossed it, pan and all, into the small yard. Then I opened the doors and windows wide to clear the odor and sat down on the porch steps.

The sun was setting and the autumn air growing chilly, but I did not feel the cold. I stared into the approaching night as if answers could be found there, in the darkness. Suddenly, I sensed the stealthy approach of something nearing my house. I tensed and listened, relaxing when I picked up the soft padding of paws and the quiet breathy pants. The creature slowly came into view. It was a dog, a stray by the looks of the ribs showing through its fur. I could still smell the odor of the roast in the air; it was this that had brought him so near. "You have it, dog," I said quietly. "It does me no good." He sidled past me and fell to devouring the meat savagely.

When he had finished, he looked at me questioningly, with a half-wag of his tail. "No, boy, there's no more. Come here." Surprisingly, he came right to me, and with one sniff of my opened hand, he settled in on the porch with me.

He rested his scruffy chin on my knee and I scratched his pointed ears. "It's a strange world, dog," I confided to him, "where a mongrel like you can eat a fine meal, while I have to go hungry."

He gazed at me with trusting eyes and his tail thumped with a hollow sound on the wooden porch planks. I began to cry, silent tears streaming coldly down my cheeks in the night air. He hunched over close to me, offering what comfort he could and I buried my face in his soft fur. Instinctively, without thought, I pushed aside his thick hair with my tongue and sank my teeth into his neck. He snarled softly, whined, then relaxed as I was rewarded with the thick, salty flow. I took no more than two or three swallows, when, in horror at what I had done, I jumped away from him. He stared up at me with adoring eyes and weakly wagged his tail again.

"My god," I whispered to the quiet night. "What have I become?"

I stood on the porch for a long time, staring into the darkness, searching my mind for answers to my questions. Finding none, I entered the house, softly closed the door and went upstairs to my father's room, where most of our books were kept.

My father had been an avid reader of the horror literature of the time; by the time of his death he had accumulated quite an impressive collection, from potboilers to literary classics. One of my fondest childhood memories was his reading aloud from Shelly's *Frankenstein* or from one of Poe's short stories; I can still hear his voice echoing through the house, quoting some dramatic passage. But he had other books which he would not read aloud. "Not suitable for a young lady," he would say, putting those particular books aside, not permitting me to see them. It was these forbidden books that drew me to the shelves in his old room that night.

I opened his door, with a small shiver of anticipation, remembering the dream of that afternoon. The bed was empty, of course, but all else was as it had been when he was alive. The books on the shelves were dusty, but on the top shelf I found the one I sought. Opening the book, I began to read.

"CHAPTER 1—How graves give up their dead, and how the night air hideous grows with shrieks!" . . .

I completed it that night, huddled in a corner. When I was finished, I sighed and hugged my knees to my chest. If the whole idea wasn't quite so ludicrous, I thought, it would make sense. So many things were explained: the odd hunger for blood, the sharpened teeth, the aversion to food and sunlight. I stood up and began to pace the room.

It's ridiculous, I thought again. How could such a thing happen? There had been no demon materializing; no beast-like creature perched on my window sill. I could remember nothing that could explain this situation. But with a sudden shock, I recalled the dream, the hungry mouth fastening on my neck with a terrible desire, the mocking laughter, the man-sized black evilness that claimed my body and soul in a starlit field.

"It was only a dream," I whispered, shaking with fear. "Nothing more than a dream."

I went to the window and pulled aside the heavy drapes. The sun was just beginning to rise and I looked at the lightening sky with hope and relief. "So," I said aloud, "it can't be true." But even as I said it, I felt the rays of the sun burn into my exposed skin, reddening and blistering it as I watched. I had not the courage to endure the pain; I drew the drapes shut again and collapsed, crying on the floor.

It took many months for the horrible realization of what I had become to sink into my consciousness. I defied the conventions that had been established for one of my kind. The walls of the house abounded with mirrors and crucifixes; the first infallibly reflecting my image and the latter evoking, not the loathing and fear that would be expected, but rather compassion and a yearning toward the redemption they represented. Standing at the window, I would greet the dawn until the pain of my burning flesh could not be tolerated. Upon waking the next evening, I would discover that the burns had healed, leaving no trace of their ravaging of my skin.

Some compulsions I could not deny — the sleep of the day and the call of the night, together with the taking of blood. With each dose of blood, my powers of night vision, hearing and the heightened awareness of the world surrounding me increased along with the intolerance of light, especially sunlight.

The dog continued to make his visits to my back porch once or twice a week and we fed each other, until one night he failed to come. I wondered about his absence; we had become companions of a sort and the relationship was satisfying for both of us. But my worries over the dog were soon replaced by others more pressing. The first was how to keep my bizarre transformation from Mrs. Blake; the second, more profound and unsettling. I was beginning to suspect that the blood of animals could

not completely fulfill my hunger; eventually I knew I would
have to turn to humans for my sustenance.

Mrs. Blake died of pneumonia that winter; her death solved
both of my problems. Though it was not of my doing, I deeply
regretted both her death and my feeling of relief when it occurred. She had been good to me and had helped me through
those bad months; yet her visits had become troublesome. Her
presence in a room would make me frantic with rage and lust.
I could smell the blood within her veins and it would take every
shred of control I had to keep her at a distance. She was confused at my seeming coldness toward her, which I could not
explain. And when I received word of her death, it was too late
for explanations. I could not attend her funeral, for the day was
sunny though cold and I could not risk prolonged exposure.
Instead, I visited the graveyard that evening, bearing with me
roses cut from my now overgrown garden.

The night was frosty, and the grass in the cemetery crunched
beneath my feet as I wandered, looking for her grave. When I
found it, I tenderly lay the roses on the fresh-turned earth. "Mrs.
Blake," I said softly, then, "Anna" for there was no need for
formality now. "Anna, rest well here with the others I loved." I
sat for a long time there, leaning against the adjacent headstone
and content to have the cold air dry my tears. I heard footsteps
behind me and stood up quickly. A man stood there, gaping in
astonishment at my apparent rising from the grave.

He shook off his apprehension with the help of a flask he held
clutched in his hands. "Li'l late ta come callin', ain' it, girlie?"
He slurred the words and I could tell from his appearance and
the smell on his breath that he was quite drunk. He gave me a
crooked, leering smile. " 'm closin' the gates now."

"I am sorry," I said. "I missed the funeral and just wanted to
say good-bye."

I suddenly remembered Mrs. Blake once mentioning the un-
suitableness of the new caretaker. "Oh, my dear," she had said.

"Why old Mr. Jones picked such a man, I'll never know. . . ."
Now I understood her distress; he stood in front of me, swaying
slightly in the wind. I walked past him and he lurched toward
me.

"No need ta rush off," he said, grasping my arms. "I still got
a li'l lef' in my bottle, we can say g'bye together." He gave a
little drunken laugh, his breath hot and foul in my face. "Mebbe,
we can say h'lo, too."

"No, thank you. Please let me go." I struggled with him until
he began to nuzzle my ear and my hair. My mouth fell against
his neck and time seemed suspended. I could feel the rapid beat
of his pulse against my tongue. There was no thought, no effort
that went into the bite. Suddenly, the taste of his blood was in
my mouth, tinged with alcohol, but tangy and bitter and wonderful. I could feel the liquid flowing into my body even as I
felt his pulse falter. Feeling satiated and drugged, I pulled away
from him.

His eyes fluttered open and looked on me with confusion.
"Wha' happened?" he said. "Who're you?"

"Nobody you know," I insisted. "You are drunk, go back and
sleep it off. I will close the gates."

To my surprise, he moved away from me like a sleepwalker,
shaking his head and muttering to himself. I watched him make
his way back to the small brick building that was the cemetery
office. He did not look back, he seemed to have completely
forgotten me.

Quietly, I slipped out through the front gates, closing them
behind me. A euphoria engulfed me as I walked home; the night
seemed alive to me, I felt welcomed to its darkness.

Shortly after that night, I had packed what little belongings I
cared to take. Clothing, books, letters and papers had made a
small bundle in the hallway of that empty house. I had made
arrangements with the family lawyer to sell the house and the
furnishings; he would forward those proceeds to me along with

the profits from my father's business, a trading post and general store which I had inherited after his death. I was going to make a new start, I had told him, and would let him know where to send the money when I was settled. I was excited at the prospect of a new life somewhere away from my memories, not knowing at the time that it was just the first of many trips down that corridor of rooms, filled with death and loneliness.

Chapter 7

I had spent most of the day in memory, sitting quietly, motionlessly, considering my past. As I rose from my apartment couch, I noticed that the sun had already set. With scarcely a thought for what I was doing, I went upstairs and began to dress. I decided to abandon my normal black for this evening. Instead, I pulled from the back of the wardrobe a dress I had made last year and never worn. It was a winter-white velvet, with a scoop neck and a wide, full skirt. To liven it up, I added a wide red belt and a pair of red high heels. Surveying the results in the mirror, I was pleased with my appearance. The white seemed to brighten my hair and compliment my pale skin.

I left my apartment, locked the door and entered the office. The overpowering odor of roses filled the room and I smiled when I thought about Max. It was inevitable, I supposed, that I would have to see him again. Although he had never before attended one of my shows, he had sent the card back this time with a response of yes. If he did put in an appearance, it would be better to work out our problems before that night. After all, he had really done me no harm, and was responsible for my meeting Mitch. At the thought of his name, I gave a small sigh; how ironic it was that Max should be the one to introduce me, albeit indirectly, to someone who moved me as he had over twenty years ago. This time, however, I had no delusions about the outcome of any relationship with a human, and I had no intentions of changing Mitch, or anyone else, into a creature like me. The bitterness and hatred I felt for my unknown sire were still fresh and strong, even after all these years. I had no desire to foster the same emotions in someone I loved.

I called for a cab from the office phone and headed for the elevator. As I was closing the front door, the phone began to ring. I went back in to answer it.

"Deirdre, you're still there." At the sound of Mitch's voice my heart gave a curious little jump.

"Hello, Mitch. I was just leaving."

"Well, I can't talk long, anyway. I wanted to see you tonight, but Chris came into town today. How about dinner tomorrow night?" He sounded enthusiastic, boyish.

"I don't know . . ." I began evasively.

"You have other plans?" he interrupted sharply.

"No, no, I don't." *God,* I thought, *how I hate to do this.* Not only did I genuinely care about Mitch and want to see him again, he also provided me a chance to find the other vampire in the city. But he was dangerous, curious and quick-witted, and it would be too easy to fall in love with him. I could make my own investigations into the other of my kind easier than I could afford to begin a relationship with Mitch.

"It won't work out between us, Mitch," I tried to convince him as I tried to convince myself. "There is no way that it can." I was sure that he could hear my voice wavering. "I am sorry."

"Damn it all, Deirdre, you're wrong and you know it. What we felt last night was real." He paused for a long time, then continued, softly, "Give me a chance, please. Just one more night, and then if you still feel the same, I won't bother you again. Scout's honor."

I could hear the teasing in his voice, thought of our conversations last night, how I had enjoyed his company. How in his arms I found a release from my existence, how he made me forget for a while my struggle with the lust for blood. How for a few seconds, in the pre-dawn streets of the city, I had been human again.

"Oh, what the hell. Pick me up at the hotel at eight." Even as

I said it, I knew instinctively that I had made the right decision. "But promise me, no more all-nighters. I have a busy weekend ahead of me."

"I'll be there. Oh, and Deirdre?" His voice acquired serious overtones.

"Yes?"

"You said you were on your way out. You aren't going to see Max, are you?"

I lied. "No, I am not going to see Max. Why do you ask?"

"Well, the flowers and all that. He always seems to be lurking around in the background." His voice took on a defensive note. "I can't believe he's not in the running, that's all."

"The running for what, Detective? I am not a trophy."

"Sorry, Deirdre. I guess I'm a little insecure."

"Only a little?" I snapped at him sarcastically. I could imagine the cold glint in his eyes and instantly regretted my harsh tone. "Mitch, you have no need to be," I said gently. "I . . . I will see you tomorrow. Good night."

I stood for a while after he hung up, the phone cradled against my chest. Then I hung it up quietly and went to the lobby to catch my taxi.

The streets were crowded and the traffic heavy, so I stared out the window as we slowly made our way to the Ballroom. The idea that there may have been others of my kind prowling the streets was intriguing, and I studied all the people we passed in the hopes that I would find a sign of their presence. Not that I would recognize another from their appearance; the only way I could be sure would be to see them feeding. And surely, they would guard their secret as well as I did mine, by hunting cautiously and covering all evidence of their existence. But they had not done that. With the two corpses left behind, they had left a calling card for any with the wisdom to identify the facts. I wondered at those deaths; even at my most voracious, I had never killed. I must find the other, I thought. I could learn from him; perhaps I could find in him someone that could share my life.

The answers to my questions were not found in the streets. Everyone looked normal, human and busily involved in themselves. When we stopped at a light, however, I noticed a familiar figure crossing in front of us. I hurriedly paid the driver and got out of the cab. My heels made a clacking sound on the sidewalk as I tried to reach him. Catching up with him, I gently touched his arm. He spun around and the snarl on his face changed into a smile of recognition. It seemed a genuine smile, not his customary sneer, and I knew that he had forgiven the harsh words and hasty action of our last meeting.

"Hello, Max. How have you been?" I gave him a small hug and was surprised to have it returned with fervor.

"Deirdre, I'm glad to see you." He held me out at arms' length and smiled at me again. "You look wonderful. Were you coming to see me? Or just prowling around?"

I looked up into his eyes; they were dark, fathomless. "Max, I never gave you a chance to explain about the police. I'm sorry about that. Now that I have had time to think, I realize it wasn't your fault. At the time, I felt trapped; I thought you had turned me in to protect yourself and the club."

"That would be a logical assumption on your part, my dear. After all, I suppose I could be considered an accessory to at least one of the murders, if you did them. Did you?" He had an odd expression on his face, a mixture of curiosity and indulgence, as if I were a young relative discovered in some small indiscretion.

"No, of course I didn't. And even if I did, Max, I would hardly stand here on the street discussing it." I looked up at his face, the lights of the street highlighting its sculptured lines and felt a surge of anger at his complacency, his distance. "Now you can answer a question for me. Why did you feel it was necessary to mention my name to the police in connection with Bill Andrews?"

"Deirdre, calm down. I could hardly deny it, when so many

other people at the club saw the two of you together. And," he added, justifying himself, "I did ask you to stay away for a while."

"But you begged me to come that night, knowing that the police would be there."

"I didn't know they'd be there that night; they don't really make appointments in advance, you know. And I thought that they had finished their questioning the previous night." He reached over and touched my cheek. "Besides," he added with a twisted smile, "can I help it if I just can't do without your presence? I missed you."

"Damn it, Max. It was only one night. You can quit your little game, now." I had never been able to ascertain why Max did the things he did; now was not the time to start. And since the policeman in question was Mitch, he had really done me a favor of sorts. The anger drained away and I smiled up at him. "Anyway, it doesn't really matter at this point. Shall we go?" I clasped his arm and we continued the walk to the club.

Larry stood guard at the front door and moved the crowd away so that we could enter. Max gave him a slight nod of greeting and I noticed how Larry's bright smile darkened and his fists clenched. I had not given much thought to Larry since his visit to my hotel. Now all of the anger and confusion he had expressed that night came back to me; I regretted that he had gotten involved, even remotely, in the sordid events of my life.

"Damn," I swore under my breath as Max propelled me down the hall toward his office. He lifted an eyebrow ever so slightly as he opened the door. I removed my coat and flung it over his couch while he opened a bottle of wine and poured two glasses.

He handed one to me. "You look radiant, Deirdre. Maybe it's the dress or the color? So virginal, so innocent; it should go over well with the police." He drained his glass abruptly and poured another. His face reflected his normal cynicism with a small trace of excitement.

"I thought it was time for a change, Max. No one can stay

the same forever." I settled on the couch, demurely smoothing the velvet skirt.

"Not even you, my little vampire?" He came across the room to sit beside me and draped his arm carelessly on the edge of the couch, his fingers lightly grazing my shoulders. "No," he said, shaking his head. "You have changed. You seem more confident, more at ease. As if something has finally touched you, made you aware of yourself."

A smile crossed my face and I thought of Mitch. I knew at that moment that I loved him. God help us both, I did love him and although it would go no further, I could still hold one warm time to my heart as I faced the loneliness and coldness of my unending life.

The change in my expression had not escaped Max's attention. "Ah," he said, leaning back, "it has happened then. I envy you this moment of revelation, my dear. Enjoy the exhilaration, it can make a life such as yours worthwhile, indeed." He clinked my glass in a silent toast and we sat companionably for a few minutes. Then he rose, setting his glass down, and stared down at me. "Just promise me two things, Deirdre." He continued without waiting for my response. "Stay away from Larry. He asks more questions about you than he should. You do know that he is obsessed with you, don't you?"

"I surmised that at our last meeting."

"Only at your last meeting? I have known it for years; I'm surprised you've never noticed." Max crooked an eyebrow and gave me a slight smile. "He's been working here four years now and in all that time he's never so much as looked at another woman. To be truthful, I don't think he's ever had a woman."

"I guessed that, too."

He looked at me questioningly, then continued. "According to the other employees, he spends most of his free time at the library, or someplace like it. Doing research, he says, but nobody knows why or on what."

I really didn't care to know what Larry did. "So, maybe he's a scholar. I can't see that it matters much. But you could tell me what kind of questions he asks about me."

"Where I met you, and how long ago, that sort of thing. He wanted to know your family background, whether you had ever married and how old you were."

"And you told him?"

He smiled. "Rest assured, I gave him a varnished version. Nothing that could make him more suspicious of you. But he seems to know more than he should. Watch out."

"I can't think that he would be much of a threat, but I'll steer clear of him."

"Don't underestimate him, my dear. He seems to be in a frantic state these days; I wouldn't be surprised if he might decide to follow you on one of your nightly walks. There are things he should probably not see."

I met his eyes firmly. "I said I'd stay away from him, Max. And the second promise?"

"No more dead bodies to be traced back here to the Ballroom. You may still feed here and I will continue to help, but be more careful. Neither you nor I need the hassle of police investigations."

"Oh, it wasn't all that bad." Even to myself I sounded smug.

"Don't be flippant about this," he said angrily. "You walk a dangerous line, my dear, and I don't want you to fall."

"There is no need for you to remind me of the peril." I grew angry at his continued patronizing and for once I decided not to let it alone. "I have lived with it since before you were born and, forgive me for saying so, I will do so after you are dead and buried." Even as I said the words I wanted to take them back. Instead, I reached out and touched his hand in unspoken apology.

Unexpectedly, he threw his head back and laughed. "You don't have to be afraid of mentioning my pitiful life span," he said. "I have come to terms with it." He pulled me to my feet and gave me a strong, affectionate hug. "So, then, it's agreed?

You'll be more discreet and not leave any more bodies to be traced back here?"

"I am afraid I can make no guarantee of that, Max. You see, I did not kill Bill or anyone else. I don't even know who the second victim is."

"Oh, but you do. The girl was Linda, surely you remember her—the petite blonde, worked here as a waitress. I fired her several months ago for providing, shall we say, extra services to the customers."

"Oh, my God," I exclaimed. I did, indeed, remember Linda, pretty little Linda who always had such a lost way about her. We had often sat together and talked on nights when the club was slow and I was not on the hunt. We had a common bond; I had for many years worked her profession.

"So you *do* remember her. It's not really important, you know. What difference does one less tramp make to this city?"

"How can you say that?" I was horrified at his attitude. "Linda was a nice girl, just a little misled. I liked her."

"Of course you did, my dear, just as you like all humans— food for the superior species. I told you before, it all makes no difference to me, just leave my club out of it."

"But, Max, I didn't kill them."

"If not you, then who?"

"That is what I'd like to find out. Don't you see what this whole thing means to me? Finally, I have proof that someone else like me exists. If I could find them . . ."

"You could swap stories about the old country, trade recipes, compare family trees?"

"Max, I am serious. This is important to me. I have searched so long for someone like me."

"And when you find the mystery vampire, what do you do then?"

I thought for a long time. Although for most of my life, I had been waiting for just this situation, I was psychologically un-prepared to face it. I shrugged. "I don't really know. Maybe they could answer some questions for me; how I became what I am, what the scope of my powers are, and is the process reversible?"

"The chance of finding the person who changed you is probably not very good, Deirdre. And who else would be able to answer those questions?"

"Why would the chances be so bad? I have travelled around for over a century now; this is the first indication I have had that I'm not alone in my fate. I don't exactly think the city is teeming with us; there would be more signs."

Max gave me an intense look. "And when you finally confront your creator?"

"First I will ask him why. Then I will kill him."

"I'm surprised at you. That intent makes no sense, coming from the woman who only a few seconds ago was bewailing the death of a cheap little hooker. Don't you see how unrealistic you are being?"

"Maybe I am. But that is the way I feel. And if given the chance, I will do it." I smiled at him, cynically. "I *do* promise to be careful, though, so you need not worry about me."

"Oh, I won't. Now, let's change the subject. Did you come only to see me or are you hungry?" He gave me a twisted smile and waited for my answer.

I glanced at him for a moment and then looked away. I wondered for the first time in our relationship, did he feel that I was using him? I hoped he knew me better than that. "Max, I came to make up for what went on last week. You must know that I . . ." With my realization of the love I felt for Mitch, the words I would have said blithely last week would not come. ". . . care for you deeply." I hoped that the hesitation was not noticeable. "Now that apologies have been made and accepted and we're back on familiar ground . . ." My voice trailed off and I looked at him for reassurance.

He gave me none, but walked to his desk and began to occupy himself with his silver-plated desk set, turning the letter opener over and over in his strong hands.

"Max," I asked plaintively, "what's wrong?"

"Nothing," he said. "I was just thinking—silver for were-wolves, wood for vampires."

"What on earth?"

"Forgive me, my dear. You aren't the only one who entertains morbid thoughts on occasion." His voice grew thick with emotion, but when he looked into my eyes, I was surprised at his lack of expression. "Actually, what I was really thinking was that not too long ago you would have said you loved me." Not hearing my small murmur of denial, he continued. "You have changed, you know. You are stronger, more self-sufficient than you were." He set the letter opener down and walked around the desk to hold me. "I am happy it happened. I have been hoping for this day. It's what I want most for you, for us. But I'll miss the lonely little thing you were."

Tears began to stream down my face, soaking into his coat. "Max, I do love you," I began.

"Don't waste it on me," he interrupted. "I'm a heartless bastard, as you are so fond of reminding me." I looked up at his chuckle. "Besides, you're ruining my jacket. Now tend to your makeup; I have someone I want you to meet."

From David Leigh's walk it was apparent that he had spent a long time at the bar. He and Max seemed friendly; this in itself was unusual. But, when after the introductions, Max sat down at the table to have a drink with us, it became obvious that this was not David's first visit here. They discussed sports, football mostly, while I occupied myself with watching the dance floor. Finally, just as the conversation was turning to basketball, I looked up from the dancers and gave a long, audible sigh.

"Deirdre, I'm so sorry," Max apologized. "Dave is a long-time customer, he's been coming here for years. We were just catching up a little." He rose from the table and turned to go.

"See you soon, eh, Max." Dave stood up and extended his hand.

"Count on it," Max said, shaking his hand and clapping him on the shoulder. "Oh, and watch out for Deirdre; she's a killer."

"Very funny, Max," I said dryly. "In that case, guard your neck. Now go and run your business."

With a bow and a little mock flourish of his arm, he left us alone.

"That old Max is one hell of a guy," Dave said, watching him walk out of sight.

I grinned at him. "Hell is often one of the words that come to my mind."

"I get the feeling I shouldn't ask what any of the other words are."

I nodded my head. "It's best that way."

"What was all that about killing and Max's neck?"

I shrugged. "His idea of a joke in very poor taste, I'm afraid. I would really rather not discuss it."

He smiled his agreement. "Well, then, what do you want to talk about? I get the impression that sports is not your forte."

"Tell me about yourself," I prompted him with a smile. He was an auditor from out of town, making frequent business trips and staying over here for about two weeks at a time, before moving on. He had struck up an acquaintance with Max five years ago and visited the Ballroom as often as possible. They had just hit it off, he explained, and became good friends over the years.

"I think he must know every important detail of my life. I always felt I could tell him anything, you know. And after a few drinks, I usually do." He looked over at me and laughed. "But I guess you could tell that, huh?" He took another drink of his beer. "I know a lot about you, too."

"Me?" I jumped, jostling my wineglass and spilling a few drops on the white linen cocktail napkin.

"Well," he amended, "maybe not a lot. But Max has mentioned you a number of times. Your talent, your career, your looks." At this last statement, he looked rather embarrassed. "I think I must have made a big deal out of being introduced to you. But now that it's finally happened, well, I don't know."

"Don't know what, Dave?" I asked, blotting up the drops of wine with my fingertip.

"Don't get me wrong. You are everything he said, and more. It's just that, well, I'm a big talker, in a lot of ways. I think Max must have misunderstood my intentions. I miss my wife and family while I'm on the road, and I do get lonely. But I wasn't really looking for female companionship, if you get my meaning."

"I do, indeed, Dave, and there is no need for you to be embarrassed." His confession made the whole situation easier for me. I had decided early on in our conversation not to feed on him. It didn't seem right, since he was actually a good friend of Max's. And I discovered that I actually liked Dave, not as a potential lover, but as a friend or a brother. "And, I'll be honest with you; I was not looking for any involvement, either. Although I am enjoying our conversation, you're easy to talk to. Would you like to go somewhere quieter?" The band had returned from their break and the noise was deafening.

"Fine with me, Deirdre. It does get a bit loud, doesn't it? Let me get another beer before we go."

I grabbed his hand, stopping the gesture toward our waiter. "I'll take care of that," I said, rising from the table. "We can drink from old Max's private stock. Come with me."

It must have appeared to be the same old scenario to the staff. As we made our way past the bar, I noticed quite a few knowing smiles; Max gave me a half salute as we passed by. I led the way down the hallway to the lounge area.

Once inside, Dave gave a whistle of approval. "Nice digs," he said, as he made his way to inspect the stock in the refrigerator. He selected an imported beer and settled on the couch. I sat in a chair a safe distance away; I wanted to stay as far from him as possible so that I would not be tempted to feed. It had been a week since I had taken blood and I needed it tonight. But it would not be his.

We had been talking for some time when a knock on the door

interrupted us. Because I had not planned to feed, I had not locked it. "Come in," I called. "It's open."

Larry stood hesitantly in the doorway. "Deirdre," he said, his face flushed, "there's a, uh, a phone call for you."

Dave gave a small shrug and picked up his jacket. "I've got to get going, anyway. I have an important meeting first thing tomorrow morning." He came over to me and made a move to shake my hand. "I enjoyed meeting you and hope to see you again."

I avoided his hand and stretched up to kiss his cheek. Larry stiffened and then relaxed as Dave walked to the door.

"Wait," I said to Dave and walked over to him, laying my hand on his arm. I rummaged around in my purse and came up with a small, crumpled card. "Next time you are in town, stop by my office. Bring your wife, she can pick out anything in the shop she would like."

"Thanks. I think she'd like that. Good night."

"Good night, Dave." I smiled. "You take care."

He made his exit and I looked at Larry who had stood silent during our conversation. "Well," I said sternly, "what's this about a phone call?"

He hung his head and would not meet my eyes. "There's no phone call," he admitted.

"Then why on earth did you interrupt us? That was a close friend of Max's. We were just getting acquainted. What's the problem, Larry?"

"Deirdre," he said quietly and made a step toward me. His arms hung limply at his sides; his hands clenched and un-clenched in nervousness. "I just wanted him to leave."

"Why?"

"You lied to me," he began, "when you said that all of this was over. You made me believe that you and I could be together. Then I see you and Max come in tonight like old friends. And when I took my break, all the guys were joking about it; about how, only a week after that guy was killed, you were at it again." His voice broke in anger.

"At what, Larry?" I asked softly and urgently as I stared into his eyes. "What do they say about me?"

He fidgeted under my gaze but the contact held. "They say you're Max's whore." He spat the last word at me in a defiant gesture and sat down on the couch.

I moved next to him and stroked his hair. "Larry, that is not true. I don't work for Max, nor do I belong to him. What I do, I do for myself. Can you understand that?"

"I understand, better than you think, Deirdre," he said, shaking his head. "I know you're not what you seem to the others. But I don't like them to say those things about you; it demeans you. They shouldn't be allowed to say those things; if they only knew you like I do, they wouldn't."

Max was right about Larry, I knew—he *was* obsessed with me, but I saw no harm in him. I just couldn't believe he would do anything to hurt me. "Poor kid," I whispered to myself and held him in my arms.

Eventually he pulled himself out of his despondency and raised his head. His eyes seemed to glow with strong emotion. "Don't hate me," he begged. "I love you."

"Why would I hate you?"

"Because I'm weak and inferior and I have no control . . . because I can't stop myself from . . . hating all the others."

"Jealousy is a normal reaction," I assured him. "And love and hate are strong at twenty-five. How could I hate you for being what you are?" I got up from beside him and moved to the chair I had sat in previously. "Larry, I want to be honest with you; I also want to be kind. In this situation I cannot be both. What do you want from me?"

"I want you to love me back," he said in a choked voice, sounding at least ten years younger than he was. "I want to be with you forever."

I gave him a sharp glance. "Why do you say forever? Nothing lasts forever."

Although his head was down, his eyes glinted up at me.

"That's what people say who love each other, I'll love you forever, they say. And I will."

I shook my head and mastered the impulse I had to comfort him again. It would do no good. Instead, I looked him coldly in the eye. "I can't do that, Larry. If you wanted a friend, a sister, even a one-time lover"—his eyes glittered angrily—"I could give you that. But I cannot return the gift of your love. I am sorry."

He rose slowly from the couch and squared his shoulders. Methodically, he walked to the door and reached for the knob. His hand stopped, he spun around and confronted me. "You are what they say." His voice was awful in its quietness and its rage. "No, you're worse than they say. I know what you are and who you are, Dorothy," he hissed the name at me and I recoiled. "Hell can't come too soon for you. But before that, I will get what I want." He softened a bit and reached out to stroke my cheek. "I would have been good to you. I could protect you, take care of you, give you anything you ask, give you all you require." He licked his lips. "And I know what you require. But, no, you say, you can't, you're sorry. You will be sorry one day, I'm sure." He pulled away abruptly, making his brief touch feel like a slap, and left the room.

I stood staring at the door and raised my hand to my burning cheek. "Dear God," I said in the emptiness of the room. "What does he know about me? How could he know the truth?" I had to find Max, discover exactly what he had told Larry. Maybe he had mentioned my original name, saying that I had changed it for professional reasons. Larry could know nothing about me, I rationalized, and even if he guessed at the truth, who would believe him? Unless, of course, he was the vampire doing the killing. I dismissed that idea almost as soon as I thought it; it seemed too unlikely. Surely I would feel some sort of rapport with another of my kind, some recognition, some spark would flow between us. And as for his being my transformer, that could never be. I would know him.

I gathered my belongings, and went to Max's office where I

had left my coat. I was surprised to discover his office was empty and the lights were out. I stared for awhile at his desk, then, on impulse, turned to the employee directory. Finding Larry's name, I wrote down his address and phone number, folded the paper and carefully put it into my purse. If things got too hot, if he really *did* know something, I would have to take action against him. Shuddering slightly at the thought of what action I could take, I left the office and closed the door.

Walking slowly through the bar, I studied the faces of the patrons at the tables, hoping to find Max drinking with David Leigh. They were not there. But when I questioned the bartender, he shrugged and said that Max was probably around somewhere. Did I want him paged? I nodded and turned away, pulling on my black leather gloves while surveying the tables and the dance floor.

"Miss Griffin?" The bartender beckoned me with a smirk. "No answer from Max. But if you're looking for your other friend, he left just a few minutes ago. Maybe you can catch up with him." His manner was unpleasant, sneering, and I swallowed the urge to slap him across the face.

"Thank you," I replied with a false grin, while looking him deep in the eyes. He shifted uncomfortably until I dropped my gaze. "I might just do that. Please tell Max that I need to speak with him as soon as possible. Good night."

When I got out to the street, I saw no one I knew—there was no sign of Max, Larry or David Leigh. Just as well, I decided, if I couldn't find Max; I was in no mood for conversation with anyone else. Right now, I needed to find a victim so that I could be fed and rejuvenated before I met Mitch tomorrow.

The streets were full of people: couples, singles and large groups, bundled up against the evening air, their laughter rising up in billowy puffs. It was still relatively early and a Saturday. I would need to find a less populated street. After wandering aimlessly for a while, I found myself admiring, for once, the displays in store windows. The normally angry thought of celebrating yet another Christmas was softened now by images of spending the time with Mitch. I smiled so broadly about the idea that a couple I passed were shocked into returning my smile. With a half-embarrassed nod they hurried away on their business, reminding me suddenly of my own purpose tonight. My smile died, and I walked on with more determination.

Three blocks past the club, I turned into a side street. I could sense someone's presence at the end of this alley and went forward eagerly to meet them. He was sleeping and took no notice of me as I settled down next to him, pushed the baby-fine blond hair away from his neck and fed.

When my teeth pierced his neck he stirred, moaned and went back to his fitful sleep. Not even my withdrawal awoke him. As always, when I had finished I checked his pulse and found it strong.

I turned to walk away, when I actually looked at him. What I saw was pathetic. Dressed only in ragged jeans and a lightweight shirt; he wore shoes, but no socks, and was shivering uncontrollably in his sleep. He seemed no more than fifteen or sixteen, most likely a recent runaway for he was better fed than some I had seen. He would survive the feeding, I felt sure, but the cold would kill him. Shaking my head, I took off my coat and removed the label by tearing the lining with my still-sharpened teeth. Wrapping the fur gently around him, I tucked some money into his shirt pocket. Oddly enough the warmth woke him, and he stared at me out of eyes that belied his years, eyes shadowed with fear and despair.

"You will be all right," I whispered confidently to him. He answered me with an angelic grin that almost made up for his desperate eyes. "There's a shelter just two blocks down the street." I pointed in the right direction. "Go there for tonight. I have given you some money; do you have a home to go back to?"

He nodded, getting to his feet slowly, my coat still draped around him. He made a move to take it off, but I stopped him.

"Keep it," I urged, "and get a bus ticket for home tomorrow.

Don't spend another night on the streets, please." I began to walk away.

"Lady?" he called after me and I turned back to face him. "Thank you." He smiled his choir-boy smile again. I nodded to him and watched as he went in the direction I had shown him. His walk was youthful and strong, and I was confident that the small price I had extracted from him would not matter. His blood had had no taint of drugs or alcohol; if he took my advice, he would survive this night of cold and vampirism with no more than a small mark on his neck and a warm memory of someone who had helped him recover his life.

I lingered on the streets no longer, but returned to the office. I worked on the upcoming show throughout the night and at dawn retired to my apartment. The feeding had sated me physically and I felt uplifted from my contact with the boy. I slept dreamlessly, to awaken Sunday evening, as the sun was setting.

I lay in bed for some time, savoring, as always, the feelings of youth and strength that followed a feeding. The darkness and quiet of the room enveloped me, calming the nerves tortured by the past few weeks. I wanted to lie there forever, avoiding the world outside. Next time, I thought languidly, I will choose a more peaceful life. I had accumulated enough money to make it possible, for at least a few decades, to live somewhere with no job, no commitments, no complicated relationships.

"Oh, God," I said, sitting upright in bed and reaching for my contacts. "I forgot I have to meet Mitch." I hurriedly consulted the clock; it was only a little before seven. I would have time to get back to the hotel and dress before he picked me up. I threw on some jeans and a shirt and ran down the spiral staircase. I put on my boots and searched the closet for a coat to replace the one I had given away. I put on the first one I found; it was an ankle-length black velvet cape. I seldom wore it; even for me the effect was too theatrical. It flapped annoyingly around my legs as I rushed down the hall to the elevators. I burst into the lobby, called a quick good night to the startled guard and sped to the hotel.

When I reached the front door, I was only a little breathless and was happy to see that it was just turning seven. I slowed down, and entered the revolving door.

Frank was at the desk and jumped a bit at my entrance. "Hello, Frank," I said gaily. "How have you been?"

He stared at me uncomprehendingly at first, then said, "Fine. Uh, Miss . . ."

"I really am in a hurry, Frank," I interrupted. "If someone named Greer stops in for me, send him up, please. Thanks so much." Without a pause, I headed for the elevators, when a hand on my arm stopped me. I spun around and found myself facing two uniformed policemen. "Can I help you, gentlemen?"

The taller of the two spoke. "Are you Deirdre Griffin?" At my nod he continued. "We'd like you to come with us, if you would. We have some questions to ask you concerning a recent homicide."

"Recent homicide?" I repeated stupidly. "But I have already told Detective Greer everything I knew about Bill Andrews."

"Not Andrews this time. We have a new one."

"A new one?" I felt a sudden stab of fear. Although I was not the killer, I had known the other two victims. If this third one was also known to me, it could create a very uncomfortable situation. One night in jail, followed as it would be, by the rising sun, and I would be dead; the fact that I was innocent would not matter then. I should have left town as soon as Bill Andrews died; instead, I had stayed around, playing human, and this is where it got me. "Damn," I swore softly under my breath and glanced over at Frank as if in appeal. He looked away and busied himself at the hotel register.

"That's right, Miss Griffin." The policeman gave me what I thought was a chilling smile. "And we have reason to believe you can help with identification. Come with us, please."

And although it was not the police escort I had expected that evening, I accompanied them to the station.

Chapter 8

I sat in silence in the backseat of the police car, considering my alternatives. There was not much time to plan, since the police station was only five blocks away. As the car pulled up to the curb, I cleared my throat loudly. The driver turned around.

"Yes, Miss Griffin?"

It was too dark to make sufficient eye contact, so I simply said, "What are the charges, officer?"

"You must have misunderstood, Miss Griffin," he said with a half smile. "We are not making any charges, we only want you to answer a few questions, and as I explained before, help us with an identification of the corpse, if possible."

He was toying with me, I thought, but I nodded and decided to play along. "I will be happy to cooperate in any way I can; I'm just not sure what help I can give you." I got out of the car and went with them into the station. As we entered the lobby, I turned to the nearest officer. "May I make a phone call? I have a . . . an appointment tonight; I'd like to let them know I'll be a little late. This won't take long, will it?" I looked at him for confirmation.

"It shouldn't, but you can call if you want." He gestured to a telephone across the lobby. I walked there, checked for the number in the book and turned my back on their curious stares as I dialed.

The phone rang ten times before Mitch finally answered.

"Hello." He sounded brusque, hurried.

"Hello." I did not want to say his name out loud here.

"Deirdre, I was just coming to get you. What's up?"

"I wanted to let you know that I'll be detained for a while. Something important has come up."

The tenseness in my voice did not escape his notice. "What's wrong? Where are you?"

"At the police station." From his muffled exclamation, I could tell he knew nothing about this situation. "Don't worry, they tell me it won't take long."

"What the hell is it all about? I swear I had nothing to do with this, Deirdre." He sounded confused and angry, very angry. "I'll be right there."

"No, I will be fine, just wait . . ." I had no chance to finish; he had already hung up. I said good-bye to the empty receiver for the benefit of my listeners and walked back to them.

"Shall we go?" I addressed them with more confidence than I felt.

We rode the elevator down to the basement level, and exited into a gray, dimly lit hall. I recoiled visibly as the doors opened, for my heightened senses reeled with the overwhelming reek of death and decay. God, it was foul; the smells of formaldehyde, disinfectant and rotting flesh permeated the air. Coughing and gagging in an uncontrollable reaction to this assault, I leaned against the wall in an attempt to calm my retching stomach and my mind travelled back to a time and place I never desired to visit again.

The casualties of the first battles had been worse than anyone had ever expected. Men who marched out proud and resolute returned torn and wounded, both physically and mentally. All too soon the tents set up for the injured were overcrowded; cots and blankets with the bodies of maimed and dying soldiers overflowed onto the pathways of our encampment. I remember the early days of that war as smoke-filled and alive with pain and suffering.

I had elected to take night duty in the medical tents; few of the other women wanted the task, for it was at night that the moans of the dying were loudest; during the day the sounds of battle would block most of the cries. Beginning at sunset, I would carry my lantern through the rows of men, stopping to administer what was most needed: water, food or morphine. By the time I would reach the second tent, my skirts would be soaked to the knees, sodden with muddy water and blood.

It was in the second tent that the worst odor lingered. Here we kept the most severely injured and the dying. Those men who had lost limbs were the lucky ones. Even though they might be feverish or delirious, minus an arm or a leg, they still stood the best chance of living. But the ones with the belly or groin wounds were fated to die, a horrible, clawing death that tore them apart with the pain. The smell these soldiers exuded seemed almost tangible—a mixture of bile, feces and gangrenous flesh combined with sweat and blood. Most nights I would have to stop my rounds before entering the second tent, so that I could empty my stomach. Even if there was nothing in my stomach, I would still be possessed with the uncontrollable urge to vomit. I continued on because I was needed, but I never adjusted to the odors of death.

Dimly, I became aware of the person beside me, the officer had his arm around me and was supporting me. "I'm sorry," I gasped. "It's the smell." Soon the nausea passed and I was able to stand erect and gain control over my body.

The officer shrugged apologetically. "It gets some people that way. I guess I've just gotten used to it."

The other man addressed me. "We're sorry, Miss Griffin, but this trip is necessary. Let's just get it out of the way as quickly as possible. Will you be okay?" He pulled a small vial from his pocket.

"You may put away the smelling salts, please. I promise you

I won't faint." We walked slowly down the corridor, our shadows undulating on the walls. I stopped outside the morgue door.

"Before we go in, can you tell me what to expect? Who is it?"

"We don't know, we hope you can tell us."

"Why me?"

"He had something on him that belongs to you. Are you ready to go in?" I nodded and nervously drew in a deep breath of the foul air. He pushed the door inward and turned on the lights. They led me past carts and tables, some still containing bodies, their shapes distorted by the bright light and stark white coverings. Our destination was soon reached, a small examination room in the back.

We entered and with no preliminary warning, the sheet was stripped away. The body was naked and gray, the skin waxen; and the neck was badly bruised. The fang marks were apparent, but were not mine. Even if I could have believed that I fed on this man and had forgotten, I knew that I left no such marks. They were wider than mine, coming from a larger mouth and they were torn and stretched, as if worried by an animal. But no animal left these marks. I reached out and touched a hand, it was cold and flaccid. Choking back the tears that threatened, I gently replaced the sheet over the face.

"Miss Griffin"—the officer's voice sounded soft in that brutal environment—"did you know him?"

"Yes. His name is David Leigh. I met him last night."

"We have a few more questions to ask. Would you like to go back upstairs now?"

"Yes," I nodded gratefully. "Thank you. This is all very disturbing."

He turned out the lights and closed the doors as we walked back. Waiting for the elevator, I glanced at the clock.

"We will only take just a little more of your time, Miss Griffin. Your, um, appointment won't have to wait long."

Before we got off the elevator, I discovered that my appointment was waiting in the lobby. I could hear his raised voice through the opening doors. ". . . and why wasn't I informed that you had taken me off the case. There's no need . . ."

The man he was talking to mumbled something, then fell silent as we appeared. Mitch turned around and our eyes met. I could read his concern for me underneath the anger. He came to my side and grasped my arm. "Are you okay, Deirdre?"

I smiled. "I'm fine, now, thank you."

"Can she go now, Lieutenant?"

The lieutenant looked to the officers. They shifted uneasily. "Actually, Mitch, we weren't quite done."

"Let's finish it up, then. But I want to stay with her. I trust that there are no objections."

The lieutenant shrugged, walked off and Mitch escorted me to a small room, the other officers trailed behind us. He sat down next to me, across the table from the other two. The silence grew uncomfortable until I turned to Mitch.

"Could you get me a cup of coffee or something?"

He hesitated briefly, then got to his feet and left the room. "I don't really want to cause any problems for you," I said, smiling. "Maybe we can finish this before he comes back."

They sighed their relief. "It is a bit difficult with him here," one admitted. "Just tell us what you know about this guy."

"His name was David Leigh," I repeated while one of them began to take notes. "I met him at the Ballroom of Romance last night. He's a good friend of Max's." They didn't seem to recognize the name. "Max Hunter," I prompted. "He owns the club." The one taking notes nodded and I continued. "Dave was an auditor; I don't remember for whom he worked."

"Local guy?"

"No, he was from out of town. He came to the city frequently, though. He's known Max for about five years. If you need any more personal information, you might check with him."

"When we found him his wallet was gone. Of course, that's not at all unusual; in fact, if it were still on him, that would be strange. But he had your business card in his coat pocket. Had you made plans to meet again?"

I grimaced inwardly, thinking how all this could have been avoided had I not given him my card. "No, no plans as such. I told him to bring his wife to town next time he came; I offered to have some clothes made for her."

"Why? I can't believe you make that offer to everyone you meet."

"Oh, I don't really know. I am a bit eccentric; but I liked him, he seemed like a nice guy."

"Do you know any reason someone would murder him?" I didn't hesitate.

"Quite honestly, I did not know him well enough to make that judgement. But offhand, I would say no. None of this makes any sense at all."

"One final question, Miss Griffin." He gave me an apologetic look. "You understand I have to ask this one. And I hope you understand you don't have to answer it, at least not without the advice of counsel." He hesitated, then looked directly into my eyes. "Did you kill him?"

"No, I did not."

As we held eye contact, I felt his doubt of me lessen and fade away entirely.

"One more thing, Miss Griffin," the officer taking notes interrupted, "we may need to talk with you again; don't make any plans to leave the city for a while."

"I understand. Will that be all?" At their nods of affirmation, I stood up. The door opened and Mitch walked in, bearing a tray with four cups of coffee and set it on the table. I selected a cup for myself and took a sip. "If you don't mind, I will drink mine on the way out. I do have an appointment, you know. I hope he won't mind waiting awhile; I still have to get ready." I felt sure that Mitch wouldn't want our personal relationship made common knowledge at the station. But the knowing smiles exchanged between the two officers made me think that my caution was unnecessary.

I gathered up my cloak and couldn't resist a theatrical swirl as I settled it on my shoulders. "Good evening, gentlemen."

"Wait," Mitch called as I left. "I'll walk you out." He strode beside me, we went out the front door together and onto the street. He looked around and seeing no one, gave me a brief kiss. "I'd wait forever," he whispered, "but if you're not ready in an hour . . ." I laughed at his feigned threat. He gestured for a cab and when one stopped, he helped me in. "I just want to do some checking on what's going on. And I want to get myself reinstated on the case. I won't be long." He gave me another kiss, closed the door and the cab moved away.

Upon my return to the hotel, I gave Frank a curt nod and went directly to my room. I had not been there for a week now, but it was clean and sterile for my arrival. I entered without turning on the lights, dropped my black cloak on the floor and shed the rest of my clothes on the way to the shower. I made the water hotter than usual, to wash away the reek of the morgue that still lingered about me.

I dressed with great care, selecting a forest-green sheath with a high neck and a low-cut cowl back. I wore a thin gold necklace, gold button earrings and pulled my hair up from the sides with combs; the rest of my hair rippled down my bare back. I applied my makeup carefully and tried to coax as much color into my pale complexion as possible. For a finishing touch I changed my contacts to a pair tinted deep green to complement the dress. I checked the clock and discovered that Mitch's prescribed hour had elapsed. He would arrive soon.

One hour later I still sat in the near darkness of the room. I rose from the sofa, went to the window and pulled the drapes aside. The streets were still crowded with people hurrying to their various destinations, but I saw no one familiar. A shadowy figure walked below my window; it might be Mitch, I thought, feeling a rush of anticipation. But as I watched, he passed the hotel entrance without a backward glance. It was not him. Disappointed, I closed the drapes, then went to the bar and opened a bottle of wine to kill the time, to calm my nerves as the minutes dragged. There was work on my desk that I wanted to finish sometime this weekend; I turned on the light and tried to review the plans for the show, but I could not concentrate and kept checking the clock in disbelief. I put aside my work, switched off the light and went back to the sofa, the wine and the darkness.

Sometime after midnight I abandoned all pretense that he would show. I had waited over three hours, listening for the phone, a knock on the door or even a set of approaching footsteps. I drank the last bit of wine. He wasn't coming, I decided.

"Damn him." I flung the crystal goblet against the wall, taking a perverse delight in the destruction of the delicate glass. Then I rose from the sofa and began to remove the clothing I had so carefully donned earlier in the evening. I kicked off my shoes, tossed the dress into a corner of the bedroom, removed my jewelry and the combs from my hair. Wrapping myself in a black silk robe, I found a broom and swept the broken crystal into a corner; the hotel staff could clean the rest tomorrow. Just as I was opening the next bottle of wine, and pouring another glass, the phone rang.

"Miss Griffin?" Frank's tone was uncertain.

"Hello, Frank. What can I do for you?"

"There's someone here to see you. Detective Mitchell Greer. What shall I do?" I could sense an excitement in his voice; this would probably be one of his most memorable evenings here, with policemen and detectives hauling out residents at all hours.

"You've certainly had one hell of a night, haven't you, Frank?" I spoke more sharply than I had intended to. But after having led such a secretive existence for so long, I was growing steadily more angry over the intrusions into my life.

"Excuse me?"

"Oh, damn it all, Frank, just send him up."

"If you want, Miss Griffin." He hung up the phone.

I had a few minutes before Mitch would arrive, so I mussed the covers on the neatly made bed and ruffled my hair into a mass of tangles. There was no reason to let Mitch think I had waited patiently for his arrival. Let him think I had been sleeping, that his lateness had not bothered me.

When he knocked, I closed the bedroom door and turned on the lights in the second half of the suite. I answered the door, pushing the hair out of my eyes and affecting a sleepy smile. "I'm sorry," I began. "I fell asleep. I can be ready . . ."

"Forget about it." He slammed the door, pushed past me and stalked into the room. He picked up the bottle of wine and gestured with it. "Don't you have anything stronger than this?" He rummaged around behind the bar.

"I think there may be a bottle of scotch. Try the bottom shelf."

Even before I finished speaking, he found the bottle along with a glass and some ice. He threw the cubes savagely into the glass and filled it to the top. Then he sat on the sofa and glared angrily into his drink. "Well?"

"Well, what?" I responded as angrily as he had. "You're the one who didn't show up when expected. I do not like to be stood up."

"That's not what I mean and you know it. I've got three dead bodies, two of them tied directly to you. I jeopardized over twenty years standing in the department, almost got removed from a very important homicide case, one that I now feel personally involved with. I believed you when you told me you knew nothing about Andrews's death. And I believed you when you told me you would not be seeing Max Hunter. Then I discover that you slinked off to him last night and met some unlucky chump who just happened to turn up dead with your business card in his pocket." He drained his scotch and went to the bar for another. "What will you try to make me believe next, Deirdre? That you're not involved? That it's all just a coincidence? I'm sorry, but I've been at the job for far too long to believe in coincidences." He stood at the bar, glaring at me and swirling the ice cubes in his drink.

"Mitch, I . . ."

"I wasn't done yet. Let me finish. To top it off, as if all that isn't enough, I believed in you." His voice softened now almost to a whisper. "I really thought we might have a chance together. I fell for you, hard, and I got the feeling it was returned, regardless of your promiscuous habits. And what did it all get me? Nothing but lies, from the beginning to the end. But before I leave here tonight, lady, I will get the truth from you."

I summoned what dignity I could, clasped my robe tighter around my body and pulled myself upright. "I did not lie to you, Mitch. I knew nothing about Bill Andrews's death and I know nothing about David Leigh's. Yes, it is all a coincidence, and I'm sorry that you can't believe that. There are stranger things in this world than coincidence. I want to help you, I really do, but I'm not sure what I can do."

"Well, for starters, you can explain why, although you told me you weren't going to, you went to Max's club last night. It couldn't have taken you more than ten minutes to get to where you said you weren't going."

"What is it about Max that bothers you? I have already told you that he is not a threat to you in any way. Max is an old friend, that's all."

"But you met him after you said you wouldn't."

"I ran into him on the street, Mitch. It wasn't planned or arranged. It was just by chance that I saw him at all." He gave me a sharp glance. "I know, I know, you don't believe in that, either. Give me the benefit of the doubt, Mitch. Even criminals are thought to be innocent until proven guilty."

He met my eyes finally and a small smile began to play on his face. "I guess I've been a little too rough on you tonight, huh?" He took one sip of his drink and then another. "It's just that the job is getting to me, the press is clamoring for a solution and we're no closer to that now than when Andrews died. And there's something about Max that really gets to me, his attitude, his lifestyle, something. I don't know. When I spoke to him tonight, he was polite and solicitous, but I had the feeling he was laughing at me, taunting me. And when he speaks of you, I get angry—just hearing your name on his lips—well, I can't really explain it. He talks as if he owns you, protects you, as if you were his child, or his wife."

"I am neither, Mitch. He oversteps his bounds a lot, and he interferes with things when he should stay out. But for all that, he is still my friend."

"How close a friend?"

I sighed and moved over to him. He looked up at me, his eyes locked on mine. "Mitch, there is nothing between Max and me, now. You must believe me."

"I do, but . . ."

"Jesus, Mitch, will you just drop it? I do not want to spend the rest of the evening talking about Max. Do you?"

"No, not really." He drained his drink, got up from the couch and set his glass on the bar. "Look, I know it's late, but would you like to go out for a while? Maybe we could take a walk or have dinner? Are you hungry?"

I shrugged. "Whatever you'd like, Mitch. It doesn't make any difference to me. Let me change first, though." As I walked past him on the way to the bedroom, he touched my arm and turned me around to face him.

"Deirdre, I'm sorry." He held my arms in his gently, then rubbed his hands up and down the sleeves. I felt my stomach tighten in anticipation and smiled up at him.

"It's okay, Mitch. Actually, I am flattered that you like me enough to be so jealous. Just don't mention his name again."

"I promise." He tightened his grip on me and his eyes lit with desire. I thought to myself, before his mouth came down to mine, that this night would make up for those countless others.

For what could have been seconds or years, the kiss continued. He slid his hands under my robe; they felt grainy against the soft skin of my back as he drew me closer. His arousal was evident and I arched my body into his. He held me tightly with one arm, while struggling to remove his coat with the other. He switched arms, and removing his coat entirely, exposed his shoulder holster and gun. I reached a hand up lightly to touch it.

"I don't think you will need this now, do you, Detective?"

He agreed with a smile that lit up his eyes and draped it and his shirt over the back of a chair. He reached for me again, and as I went to him, the silk robe slipped over my shoulders. I dropped my arms and let it fall.

"Deirdre," he whispered into my hair as he lowered me to the floor. "You make me crazy." I twined my arms around his neck, drew him down to me and silenced him with a kiss.

Chapter 9

We lay sated and exhausted. Mitch rolled over, leaned on one elbow and smoothed the hair from my eyes. "God," he said, his voice somewhere between a laugh and a moan. "I'm getting too old for this."

"Oh, really? I hadn't noticed."

He smiled. "No, not for that." He laughed for real this time. "I mean making love on the floor, like a couple of kids."

"I do have a bed, but you seemed so eager I hated to spoil the moment." I stood up and he followed me. He wrapped his arm around my shoulder.

"You're cold, let's get you under the covers."

I stopped in the bathroom and removed my contacts, then turned out the lights and entered the bedroom. From his breathing I could tell that Mitch was already half asleep; I could feel his body warmth emanating from the bed, could almost hear the beating of his heart. I could even smell the blood in his veins, beckoning me.

"This will be harder than I thought," I whispered to myself as I tried to slide into bed beside him without disturbing him. I settled in and he rolled toward me.

"What did you say?"

"Oh, nothing important." He rubbed his hand up and down my thigh, massaging and caressing. "Mitch," I admonished him gently, "you have to work tomorrow. Don't you think you should get some sleep?"

"As if I could, now."

I caught my breath and my body relaxed under his ministrations, but my mind raced. I had conditioned myself for many years to look at sexual play as a prelude to feeding. I felt my canines grow in anticipation and when his mouth replaced the hand on my thigh, I moaned aloud.

That sound was all the encouragement he needed. He teased and nibbled until I began to thrash and flail in arousal. When I thought I could stand no more, he plunged into me deeply.

"Jesus," I cried and he fell upon me heavily, pinning me to the bed. My mouth was resting against his shoulder, then his neck which I kissed and suckled, not biting, not yet. I couldn't let this happen, but it was happening, the hunger for blood had awakened within me and I couldn't stop. I didn't want it to stop. I flung one arm around his neck and pulled him to me tightly. I was ready, I needed only his blood.

Time stopped; all the universe seemed to be waiting for this one moment. My mouth opened as if of its own will, my head fell to the side, my teeth contacted flesh, and hot, sweet blood filled my mouth and throat. I swallowed frantically and realized from a sharp pain in my shoulder, that I had turned away from him, that I had bitten myself.

"Thank God," I whispered reverently, as orgasms overcame us and we shuddered in our pleasure.

Finally, he reached over and turned on the light. I hid my eyes with my one arm, keeping the shoulder I had bitten pressed to the bed. "Turn it off, Mitch," I complained.

"I just want to look at you," he explained. "You're so beautiful." I squinted up at him and he smiled, reaching over to touch my lips.

"Deirdre, you've got blood on your mouth." He wiped it away with his finger.

I felt myself blush, warming with embarrassment and fear. "I guess I bit myself," I said as casually as possible. "I'll probably be all puffy tomorrow."

"God, I hope so." He snuggled next to me. "That was incredible, you know?"

"I know."

He rolled onto his back and stared up at the ceiling. Comfortable silence enveloped us, and I traced a shadowy scar down the right side of his body. He jumped and laughed and took my hand. "That tickles." He raised my hand to his mouth and gently kissed my fingertips.

"Where did you get it?"

"I interfered in a knife fight."

"Did you stop it?"

"Yes."

"Good." We lay silently again and I thought he had fallen asleep. I closed my eyes with a sigh and began to drift.

His voice brought me back. "Deirdre?"

"Yes?"

"What was he like?"

"Who?"

"Your husband. The one you never talk about."

"Oh." I paused, collecting my thoughts, wondering just how much I should tell him.

He mistook my pause for a reluctance to talk. His voice was tentative, soft. "You don't have to tell me, if you don't want to. I just wanted to know what kind of man could make a woman like you close herself off from life."

"I don't mind talking about him, really. It just seems there is no point in it. I mean, he's dead and I'm alive and there's nothing I can do about it."

"He meant that much to you, then?"

"I loved him. But there are times when I can barely remember his face." I had never talked to anyone about this, not even Max. It was hard to separate his death from the awful transformation that had overtaken me at the same time. In my mind, it was all the same. "But then I have a dream that brings it all back."

"That must be awful."

I was silent again for a time. I could hardly recognize the voice as mine when I began. "I was there, when he died. I almost died myself. It was raining and the car . . . the car . . . he lost control of the car and we overturned. I don't remember too much after that." I shuddered and continued in a whisper, "But when I woke in the hospital they told me he had died." I was amazed at how much pain was in my voice, amazed at the tears I brushed away. It had been, after all, more than a century ago. "I was pregnant; I lost the baby. They said I couldn't have any more."

"I'm sorry." He looked over at me, his eyes intense with shared pain. "But I'm glad you didn't die."

I gave a small smile and touched his cheek. "I'm glad, too." I knew then I could not admit that until I had met Mitch, I still wished I *had* died, or at least had been allowed to live a human life, following the accident, to die of natural causes. Suddenly I was overcome with anger at the person who had caused my existence, the one who I, justly or not, held accountable for my life as it was. Because of him, I had lived long enough to meet and fall in love with the one person who could have replaced my dead husband. And because of him, I could never have Mitch the way I wanted to.

"Damn," I swore and punched the pillow angrily.

"What's that all about?"

"Why is life so complicated?"

"It seems good enough to me right now." I looked over at him and he was smiling. "After all, here we are, you and I. We seem to be doing just fine."

"I suppose so."

He reached over and turned out the light, then pulled me close to him and kissed me. "Deirdre." His voice was trembling. "This is probably not the right time to say this, and I don't want to scare you off, but I love you."

"As you get to know me better, Detective, you'll discover that very little in this world scares me." It wasn't true, I was frightened of him, of life, of what this relationship could mean. Then I realized a sarcastic answer was uncalled for in this situation. "Mitch," I tried to soften my reply without making the commitment I knew he wanted to hear, the one I had no right to make. "I didn't mean it like that. Why would I be scared of you? Thank you."

"My pleasure, good night." He rolled over and was asleep in what seemed seconds. I listened to his rhythmic breathing, and mouthed the words I wanted, but did not dare to say.

"I love you, Mitch."

"Deirdre, if you're there, pick up the phone, please." Through the closed bedroom door, I could hear the pleading in Gwen's voice on the answering machine. Mitch was still sleeping; I reached over and touched his hair gently, then rose from bed to take the call. She was in the midst of her frantic message when I picked up the phone and interrupted her.

"Hello, Gwen."

"Oh, Deirdre, thank God. Where have you been? Do you know what time it is? I've been so worried."

I glanced at the clock, it was after nine. I should have been at the office by 7:30 at the latest. "Sorry, Gwen. I was sleeping so soundly that I didn't hear the phone."

"I find that hard to believe; it's never happened before. What's going on?"

"Nothing is going on. I was tired, that's all." I permitted myself a small reminiscent sigh, remembering why I had been so tired. Mitch entered the room with a sheepish smile, searching for the clothes he had discarded the night before.

"Deirdre," Gwen continued. "When will you be coming in?"

"Don't open the drapes," I warned sharply as Mitch headed in that direction.

He shrugged, then went for the light switch. "Is this okay?" he asked sleepily.

"Yes, that will be fine." I braced myself against the glare. I had forgotten to put my contacts in. "No, Gwen, I wasn't talking to you."

"You have someone there with you, don't you? Who is it?" Her voice acquired the curious, voyeuristic quality it always had when she talked about my personal life.

"Never mind that. What's the weather like?"

I could visualize her confusion as clearly as if she had been in the same room with me. "The weather? Well, it's clear and sunny, a really beautiful day, and not too cold, but what has that got to do with anything?"

"Nothing, it doesn't matter. Can you handle the office today? I won't be coming in." I spoke absently as I watched Mitch pick up clothing from the floor. He had found his shorts and put them on, then came up behind me to wrap the robe around my shoulders.

"You're as cold as ice," he said quietly as he kissed my neck and wrapped his arms around my waist. I giggled softly in reaction.

"Deirdre, are you still there? What the hell is happening?"

"Nothing." Mitch's nuzzling was becoming more intense. I reached my hand back to caress his face. "Can you take care of everything for me today?"

"I guess so, but what will I tell everyone . . ."

"Tell them I'm going on a picnic." I hung up the phone.

"Picnic?" Mitch questioned as he kissed my arm and hand, easing the robe back off my shoulders. "You want to go on a picnic?"

"Not really . . ." I began, when he interrupted.

"What the hell?"

I turned my head to see what had caused his reaction. He was staring at my shoulder; it displayed the remains of a nasty bruise, greenish blue but already beginning to fade, although it had been formed only a few hours ago. "Did I do that?" He sounded horrified. "Oh, Deirdre, I'm sorry. I never meant to hurt you."

I felt myself flush; I had inflicted the wound myself, of

course, but I could not tell him that. Instead, I pulled the robe tightly around me. "No, Mitch, you didn't cause that. It's an old bruise."

He looked at me oddly. "Funny, I don't remember any bruise there last night."

"And I don't remember you paying very much attention to my shoulder." I gave him a bright smile which he returned. "Now, be a love and order us some coffee from room service." I headed for the bathroom. "I'll be just a few minutes."

The water in the shower was as hot as possible to warm my cold skin; the heat it gave would have to last as long as Mitch was there. As it cascaded over my naked body, I enjoyed its touch, but not as much as his. He had been a wonderful lover— considerate yet passionate, gentle yet urging me to newer and more violent pleasures than I had ever known. Soaping my breasts, I thought of him touching me there, his mouth and his hands on my body, a body that responded as it never had before.

I gave a small, throaty laugh when I thought of how ridiculous I was acting—almost as if I were a bride or a novice in the sexual game. Over the hundred plus years that I had lived, I had exchanged sexual favors for blood or for protection. Or, as in Max's case, as a way to try to keep someone with me. I had known more men than I could count in so many various ways— love, hate, anger and fear. I had even married and truly loved someone who also loved me. But no one, and I felt slightly disloyal to my dead husband as I thought this, had touched me as Mitch had done. With no one had I felt the excitement, the total joining of two persons, as I had with him.

I turned the shower off and stepped out of the stall. I dried and, wrapping myself in a large towel, went to the bedroom. As I dressed I examined the bruise on my shoulder; it was already yellowing with age and healing. It had to be kept secret, I thought in a panic, Mitch couldn't see that it was substantially better. I pulled on a pair of jeans and put on a tight-necked sweater. He would have to leave, as soon as possible. I could not take the chance of him finding out the truth about me—he meant too much to me for that. And I knew there would be no second chance for me, if he knew the truth. Imagining his face, his repulsion if he knew what I was and how I had to live, I shuddered. He could never know, I realized, no matter how compelled I felt to tell him, to unburden myself in confession, to throw myself into his arms and sob out my sordid, monstrous past. For a monster I was, and I must never let myself forget it.

A silent rage built up inside me and I longed to scream, to lose myself in a primitive reaction. A man that I loved was right through the door, a door that I could easily break into splinters. A body that I knew and could never forget, lived and grew old almost before my eyes. The blood that pulsed through his veins was precious because it was his. And I could never have it, never share it or his life.

I sat staring in the mirror, brushing my hair. For once I took no delight in my reflection, my eternal youthfulness. I would give it all up for one gray hair, one wrinkle, any sign that it might someday be possible to lead a normal life. If I could not have that, I would prefer that the old myths were true, that a creature such as I would have no image to mock, no daily reminder of what I had become.

"Damn." My voice was a whisper; it would not carry to the other room. Calmly, easily, I took my hand and pressed on the mirror. Harder and harder I pushed, until I felt the glass give way under my touch. I arched my hand and flexed my nails until tiny cracks began to form and spread, making soft, tingling noises that I knew only I could hear. I applied pressure until the entire surface cracked. My reflection was distorted into a thousand images, broken and malformed, lined and twisted—a portrait of the vampire.

I pulled my hand away, picked out a few specks of glass and gently sucked the blood from the wounds. Mitch could never know, I decided again with more fervor. I had to send him away.

But before that happened I would have to use him. Not for

his blood, but for his mind, his analytical sense. He had to find the other for me, and I would follow from there. I needed others of my kind, I needed to find the one who had done this to me. And I would kill him. Or he would kill me. At this time, the outcome mattered little. Only the knowledge, only the discovery. The love I felt for Mitch would have to be submerged, buried as finally as my other loves, as deeply as my humanity.

There came a gentle knock at the door and I rose quickly from my seat. "I will be right out," I called, forcing cheerfulness into my voice.

"Breakfast is here," Mitch said complacently. "Come on out—you should be as hungry as I am."

"So, where do you go from here?" I had made a show of eating a danish; in reality I had broken it into small pieces and pushed them around on my plate. Mitch had not really paid much attention to me, there was nothing wrong with his appetite. I had, however, finished the pot of coffee and called downstairs for more.

"What do you mean?"

"Where do you go on the case?"

"You don't really want to discuss that, do you? I had the feeling from the other night that it bothered you, a lot, and that you'd prefer not to know anything more about it."

I reached over and took his hand. "It's important to you, isn't it?" He nodded. "Then it is important to me. Maybe it would help to discuss it with someone who has no previous experience with this sort of situation. I could provide a fresh, new viewpoint."

He gave me a sidelong look as he finished his coffee. "I don't know, Deirdre, I shouldn't discuss police matters with you. It's not standard operating procedure."

Although I knew I could coerce him into talking, I wanted his willing cooperation. Rising from the table, I walked behind him and began to massage his shoulders and back. "I only want to help you, Mitch." My fingers kneaded his flesh, coaxing the tension from him "And remember, I have a bit of a personal involvement here; after all, I did know two of the victims."

"I remember. I don't like it, but I remember."

I said nothing, but kept the steady pressure of my hands on his back. He moaned appreciatively and rolled his head back. "Relax, my love," I crooned softly. "Just relax. Everything will be just fine."

"When you say that, I can almost believe it. But honestly, we don't know how to proceed. We have no evidence, no clues, no suspect, no blood." His voice drifted off and I hugged him to me in silence. When I heard the elevator bell ring, I put my head down and kissed his ear.

"There's our coffee, I'll be right back."

I went to the door and collected the tray. When I turned back, Mitch had gotten up and was inserting his gun into the shoulder holster. I poured more coffee in both cups and smiled over at him. "If you have to leave soon, at least help me finish this."

He accepted the offered cup and sat back down. "I don't really have to go till this afternoon. It's just"—and he indicated the weapon—"I feel naked without this, somehow."

"That's fine with me, I like you that way." I glanced at him, the blue of his eyes began to intensify with a reawakening of passion. How easily I could fall back into the delusion that ours could be a normal relationship. It must not happen. I could not allow it. So, instead of going to him and accepting his embrace, I sat down at the table across from him. "You must have some sort of clue," I said without preamble. "How could three people be murdered without any evidence about who had done it?"

"What? Are you back on that subject again?"

"I am only trying to help you. As I said before, a fresh perspective might be just what you need."

He shrugged. "You may be right, Deirdre. I don't really know what to think of all this. And neither does anyone else. Let me hear what you have to say."

My mouth twisted into a strange sort of smile. "Do you watch movies?"

"Movies? Well, sure, but I don't really see what that has to do with anything."

"I think that right now you are all at the point where the wild-eyed doctor comes bursting into the station with the facts that everyone has been ignoring."

"Those facts being?" He had a condescending look on his face that made me feel resentful of his calm, predictable world. I hardened myself to his response; perhaps unfairly, I decided that here was a man who could look an unpleasant fact in the eyes and still deny its existence. I was wasting my time, thinking I could use him to track down the vampire. But for the sake of the love we had shared, and for my own selfish motives, I said what I needed to say.

"The fact that modern man is too stubborn and obstinent, ignorant of anything outside his self-centered definition of the world. The fact that myths and fables might all have a core of truth, however they have been distorted over the centuries. And the fact that what you may be dealing with is, indeed, a supernatural being, or at least a superhuman species, about which you know nothing."

He searched my face for a long time, trying, I thought, to find some trace of humor. There was none. His mouth twitched as if he was controlling a smile or a laugh. I poured myself another cup of coffee, my eyes never leaving his. Then the ridiculousness of the situation caught up with me. I was right about the movies, it was the doctor who should bring forth the theory; never once had a vampire tried to convince the authorities of her existence. It didn't play right, it didn't feel right. I gave a weak smile at the thought of my foolishness. "It was only a thought, Mitch, just an idea that I thought might open you up to a new way of looking at the murders."

Even with my smile, he didn't laugh. "You really believe this, don't you?"

"I do, Mitch."

"I don't suppose you have great-grandparents that came from Romania, do you?"

"Of course not."

"I do." He looked embarrassed to make the confession.

"You do?"

"Yeah, but don't tell anyone I admitted that. I'm already the butt of too many jokes at the station for my dedicated involvement in this case."

"Then you agree with me?" I couldn't quite believe it.

Finally he laughed. Oddly enough, I did not resent it; it had no ridicule in it, just the good-natured sound of two people enjoying a rather inane joke. "Now wait a minute, I didn't say I believed you. I don't, but I'm not as narrow-minded as you seem to think. It makes perfect sense to assume that our murderer believes himself a vampire; in this case, that belief is enough to make it true. I have three bloodless bodies and one madman responsible. The fact that he doesn't fly through the window in the shape of a bat, or that he doesn't live forever, really makes no difference. In his mind, he *is* a vampire. Therefore, I go to find a vampire." He smiled wearily. "That's why everyone at the station is having a heyday at my expense. But that's also why I will solve this case."

"Oh." I got up from the table and walked to the window. Through the glass I could hear the city sounds below, feel the warmth of the winter sun and wondered what Mitch would think if I pulled the drapes aside, how he would explain the irrefutable facts when I began to smoulder before his eyes. Would he think that it was only my belief that I was a vampire that caused my death?

"Deirdre?"

At his quiet question, I turned around. He had put his coat on and moved to the door.

"Let's go." He smiled and held out his hand. "I know a perfect place for that picnic you said you wanted to go on."

"I don't want to go on a picnic."

"But you said . . ."

"I just wanted Gwen to quit pressing me on when I would be in at the office. I don't want to go anywhere."

"Fine by me." He moved toward me and reached an arm around my waist. "We'll just stay in. I have two hours before I'm due at work." He pulled me closer and began to kiss me; I pushed him away gently.

"Mitch." I felt his magnetic draw on me, wanting nothing more than to spend another two hours in his embrace, but I needed sleep, and I needed to protect myself from his inquisitive nature. And with every second spent in his presence I felt the urge to feed grow stronger, even though I had fed only two nights ago. "I'd like you to leave now." The tone of my voice was cold and commanding.

He looked at me with shock. "Why? I thought that you and I could spend some more time together. I love you, and I suspect you love me, too, although you're too stubborn to admit it."

"I'm afraid that you may have just jumped to one conclusion too many. I never said I loved you."

"But last night was so good, so wonderful between us, I just assumed that . . ."

"You assumed that because we had a wonderful night of sex, that I would swoon into your arms at the next opportunity? It was wonderful, I admit, and I would like to see you again, soon. Just not today. Call me later in the week and we'll talk."

"The hell we will." His eyes flashed angrily and I knew I had gone too far. "There's nothing to talk about, really. I confused you with someone who had a heart and feelings. Now I see that you were using me for what you use all men for."

I smiled sadly, he would never know how wrong he was about that. "Mitch," I started to explain, "I'm sorry but I'm so tired. I need some sleep and I need to sleep alone. I want you to leave, but I do want you to come back."

"So you can lead me on again? Let me believe we might have a decent relationship and not just a one-night stand? Forget it, lady, I won't be back." He slammed the door and left. I locked it behind him, went to the bedroom and fell on the bed.

Chapter 10

When I awoke at 4:00 A.M. well rested and refreshed, I checked the machine in the hopes that there might be a message from Mitch. There were a few calls but none from him. I was not particularly surprised. It was possible, I thought, that I would never hear from him again, except perhaps in an official capacity. So be it, I thought and dressed for the office.

In the lobby, Frank was preparing to leave; I called to him and he came to my side immediately. He looked curious, I thought, and probably hoped to have some explanation of the previous evening's events.

"Yes, Miss Griffin. Is something wrong?"

"Not at all, Frank, but the mirror in my bedroom is broken. Please have it replaced before I return." I thanked him, nodded him a curt good morning and hurried out the door lest he try to catch up and walk with me.

The sky was cloudy with impending snow and the wind howled down the empty streets. Small bits of litter blew around and the cloak I was wearing whipped about my body. But it was still night; I reveled in it and felt sadly deflated when the walk ended and I arrived at the office building.

I signed in, rode up in the elevator and unlocked the doors. My footsteps echoed through the dark, empty rooms. I opened the door to my office, placed my briefcase on the desk and turned on a small light. The cloying scent of dying roses filled the air. I turned toward the credenza to dispose of them, when

I noticed a body lying motionless on the couch. A cold shock spread through me, until I heard the soft breathing and recognized the form. It was Gwen; how she came to be sleeping here in my office, I would discover later. She looked exhausted and pale, so I let her sleep and went about my work quietly. With the exception of sighs and a few sleepy murmurs, she slept soundly for the next three hours while I busied myself with the finishing details for Friday's show.

While I was discarding the dead flowers and arranging those that had survived in one of the vases, Gwen awoke and looked around in confusion. She sat straight up when she saw me. "Good morning," I said softly with a smile.

"Hi," she said groggily. "Have you been here long? I didn't hear you come in; you should've woke me up." She pushed her hair away from her face with both hands, then giggled as it fell back to cover her eyes. "Boy, I must be a mess. I guess I'd better go home and clean up, but we have so much to do. And I just don't think I can face the subway now."

"Why don't you use my rooms, Gwen? You can shower and change. Check the closet—there should be something that would fit you in there."

She beamed at me. "You mean it? Wow, that would be great. Ever since you told me about it, I've been dying to see inside. Are you sure you don't mind?"

"If I minded, I wouldn't offer, would I? You go and I'll make the coffee." I reached into a desk drawer, removed the key and opened the door.

"Thanks a lot, Deirdre. What a day we had yesterday without you. I'll fill you in when I get out." She smiled mischievously. "And I'll tell you about my weekend if you tell me about yours." With that provocative comment, she entered my apartment and closed the door.

I left the office and went to the coffeemaker, shaking my head and grinning. Gwen could be so outrageous at times; I would miss her companionship when the time finally came for me to leave. And that time was coming soon, I knew. The masquerade would not last much longer—I only hoped to have enough time to discover the other vampire before I had to leave.

I was pouring my second cup of coffee when Gwen finally emerged, dressed in a black suede skirt and white blouse. She stood and studied me for a moment, as if in expectation. I motioned for her to sit down. "Now, shall we get started?"

"You bet!" She smiled at me impishly, as she settled into her usual chair. "You go first, okay?"

"What?"

"You know, tell me about your weekend." She leaned forward in her chair. "You met someone, had someone there with you when I called Monday morning, didn't you? Tell me all about it . . . did he spend the night? Was he any good?"

I felt my face grow flushed. "Gwen, I really don't think . . ."

"Deirdre, you're blushing. I don't think I've ever seen that happen before. He must have been good."

"I really don't wish to discuss it, if you don't mind, Gwen."

"Honestly, Deirdre, you can be so Victorian at times. I thought we were friends; you can tell me about it. It won't go any further than me, I promise." She made a small crossing motion over her heart and the gesture was so childlike and endearing I couldn't resist sharing with her.

"Well, since it looks like no work will get done until I oblige that insatiable curiosity of yours, I have no choice. Yes, Gwen, I met someone and he spent the night." I leaned back in my chair and closed my eyes to recall that night. When I spoke again my voice was soft and distant. "It was wonderful, wild . . ." I said no more but clasped my arms to myself, thinking of his strong, warm body enfolded around me.

Gwen interrupted my reverie with a small sign. "Wow," she said, in a hushed voice. "I guess you'll be seeing him again. Who is he? Or is that a big secret, too?"

I opened my eyes and focused on her smiling face. "You met him Friday night."

"The cop?" Her eyes widened in disbelief.

"Believe me, I was as surprised as you are. Everything

clicked into place with him. I can't really say why. It seemed right, that's all."

"Seemed? Why the past tense?"

"I don't know, Gwen. I can't see it going any farther; we're too different." I gave a sigh of regret. "Can we drop the subject, please?"

"Sure, Deirdre. No problem. But if you like him, and I think you do, you should give it a chance. Differences can be overcome."

I laughed at her naive statement. "Not our differences, I think. You don't know the half of it. And," I interrupted her objections, "I don't want you to know. You should not be involved."

She took my reprimand good-naturedly. "Okay," she agreed. "Now it's my turn. Guess where I went Sunday night."

"Nick's place?" I questioned tentatively.

"Oh, no. We had a horrible fight Saturday." She grimaced in remembrance. "He can be so impossible at times. We're not married yet, I told him, and if he keeps up his nonsense we may never be."

"I hate to hear that, Gwen."

"Well, there's this girl he works with, he talks about her all the time. I don't have any proof, of course, but I think he's been sleeping with her. So when I confronted him, he didn't deny it. Didn't admit to it, either, but I know him well enough to know that something's up." She sniffed a little and wiped the beginnings of tears angrily from her eyes. "That son of a bitch, I deserve better than that and I told him so. He laughed and said I was welcome to try. So I did. Sunday night I got all dressed up and went out by myself. I called a cab and asked him to take me to the hottest club in town. You know, a real meat-market type. And you'll never guess where I ended up."

I felt a strange foreboding at her words. I nodded slowly and answered her. "I think I know, Gwen. You went to the Ballroom of Romance."

She was disappointed that I had guessed correctly, but did not let it dampen her enthusiasm. "Yeah, what a great place. I thought for a while I wouldn't be able to get in, it was really crowded. But I remembered you once said you went there a lot, so I mentioned your name."

"And did it help?"

"It sure did. They gave me the royal treatment; I didn't even have to buy a drink all night." She gave me a sly smile then continued, "And I met some friends of yours."

"Oh?" I glanced at the clock—soon the other employees would begin to arrive. I wished she would get on with her story. There was work to be done. And the delving into my personal life was making me extremely uncomfortable.

"Why didn't you ever mention that your Max was the owner?"

"Didn't I? I suppose it never seemed important. So, you finally met Max."

"Yeah, briefly. He came over to our table and introduced himself; he's real nice and so handsome. But he didn't stick around."

I permitted myself a small smirk. "No, Max doesn't stay very long. Who else did you meet?"

Gwen looked away dreamily and toyed with a strand of her hair. "Oh, Deirdre, he's so cute and he doesn't seem to know it. I guess he's shy or something. But after a few drinks he really loosened up. Said I was the answer to his prayers; isn't that sweet?"

I suppressed a shiver. "Who, Gwen?"

"Why, Larry, of course. I think I could really fall for him."

A warning went off in my head. "Gwen, I don't mean to presume, but I think you should stay away from Larry and the club. It is not the best place to be these days and you might get hurt." I thought of Larry and his vow of revenge. "Don't you think you should give Nick another chance? I can't believe you would give up on him so quickly."

Gwen looked at me defiantly. "I never realized you approved of Nick so much. I always had the feeling that you hated him. You wouldn't happen to be just a little jealous that I got along so well with Larry, would you?"

"Jealous of you and Larry? No, it's not that. You're free to do whatever you want. But promise me you'll be careful. Don't get involved so soon with someone you just met."

She shrugged and avoided my eyes. "Okay," she agreed reluctantly. "I'll be careful. But I'm not as inexperienced as you think. And I can't see that your advice has done you much good." She seemed to be thinking out loud and instantly regretted her comment. "Oh, I'm sorry . . . I didn't mean . . ."

I laughed a bit and the tension fell away. "Don't worry about it. After all, you are probably right. Now, can we please get to work?"

The days and nights of that week seemed endless, yet when I awoke in my office apartment early Friday afternoon I could scarcely believe that the day for which we had prepared so many months had finally arrived. The line was good, I knew, and the clothes would sell.

I showered and dressed and went into the office. Everyone had been given the day off to prepare for this evening, so when the phone rang, I picked it up and was surprised to hear Gwen's voice answering. "No, she's not in right now, may I take a message?"

As I began to put the receiver down, the caller spoke and my spirits lifted when I recognized the voice. "I've got it, Gwen, thank you." There was an awkward silence after the click that signaled Gwen's hanging up. "Hello," I said tentatively and somewhat breathlessly. "Mitch, are you still there?"

"Yeah, I'm here. Deirdre, I want to see you again." He sounded hesitant, fearful of my response. "I didn't really mean the things I said to you. I'd like a chance to start over again. Will you be home tonight?"

"Tonight is the night of the show. But we could meet afterward." I told him where the show was being held and the time it was scheduled to start. "I'll leave word at the entrance that you should be admitted."

"Thank you. And, uh, Deirdre?"

"Yes?"

"Well, I wanted to call you sooner, but I just didn't know how to approach you again. I'm really sorry for what I said. There are no excuses for it, I know that. It's just that our relationship flared so suddenly, it's overwhelming. I can't imagine where it will lead. But I do know that not a moment has gone by that I haven't thought about you."

"It is the same for me," I admitted gently. "I'll see you tonight."

I hung up the phone softly and stared at it ruefully for a few seconds. There was a knock on the door and Gwen walked in still wearing her coat.

"Surprise," she said breezily. "I know you gave me the day off, but I didn't really want to stay home. Nick keeps calling and I don't want to talk to him. I want him to sweat it out for a bit. Besides, I wanted to show you the dress I'll be wearing tonight. I hope you don't mind."

"Why would I mind? Bring it in."

"Don't have to, I'm wearing it." She pulled off her coat and stood before me awkwardly. "Do you like it?"

I gave her a long, appraising stare and motioned for her to turn around. The dress was an amazing creation—swirls of bright, primary colors, each color sewn on individually in a seemingly haphazard manner. It was sleeveless with large bows of different colors forming the straps. The low-cut bodice was formed into an empire waist, then fell straight to her knees. The back dropped to waist level and the skirt was gathered and flowing. The look was avant garde, modern; the complete opposite of the Griffin Design look.

"Gwen, it's lovely, it really is. I like it very much and it suits you, but . . ."

"But what?" she questioned petulantly.

"You know you can't wear another designer's creation to our show. It just doesn't look right."

"But it's not another designer's. Not really." She looked embarrassed, but continued. "It's mine, I made it." She sat down with a flop on the sofa. "I was hoping that you'd let me wear it, see what people think. And then maybe you would let me do a few things for the next show; you know, something light and frivolous."

"You designed it?" She heard the delight in my voice and brightened up a bit.

"Yeah. I wanted to show you that I could do more than answer the phone. Do you really like it? Can I wear it?"

"Gwen, please wear it, it's wonderful. And yes, you may do some things for the next show. I'm thrilled that you want to do that; I was going to suggest that you get more involved."

"Great!" She beamed her delight. "I was hoping that you would go for it. Thanks so much."

"Now, why don't you go home and get some rest before the show. You'll probably need it."

She rose from her chair and began to aimlessly shuffle the papers on my desk. "I guess so, but . . ."

"But what, Gwen? Is something wrong?"

"Not wrong, exactly. It's just that I don't want to stay at home. It's Nick, he's getting so forceful; I'm half afraid of what he might do. I feel safer here." She paused for a moment and then haltingly continued. "Do you, ah, I mean, could I please use your rooms for the weekend. I don't want to impose, but I really need to do some thinking and this would be the perfect place to do it. No one would bother me and Nick couldn't find me. Besides, I figured you might have other plans for the weekend; I mean, since you got a call from your policeman, I thought you'd have better things to do than hole up here all weekend."

My plans for the weekend had been exactly that. But Gwen was so earnest, I felt I couldn't refuse her.

"I would be happy to do it, Gwen. And it's no imposition. Go home and pack a few things for yourself. You can move in after the show tonight; I will leave the key in the top drawer." I gave her a wry smile. "But no wild parties."

"Deirdre, thank you. How can I ever pay you back?"

"Just get yourself back to normal. I need you alert and with your wits together first thing Monday. We will have a lot to do."

"You bet," she agreed. "See you at the show." In her usual headlong fashion, she rushed out of the office.

After she left, I checked the clock. It was still early; over four hours before sundown. Four long hours in which I was virtually confined in this place. With a sigh, I moved as aimlessly through the office as Gwen had—rearranging the chairs, picking loose threads from the carpet, restacking the papers on the desk. I fought the strong, but deadly, urge to open the heavy draperies and observe the street below. I felt trapped, hungry and restless.

"Damn," I swore softly to myself. I entered the apartment and opened a bottle of wine to fill the remaining hours.

Chapter 11

As I drank the wine, I thought about meeting Mitch this evening following the show. Although I had accepted the fact earlier in the week that I might never see him again, and even acknowledged to myself that it would be better if I did not, I still could not control the rush of excitement that filled me when I thought of him, the fluttering of my stomach when the phone rang and I would answer, hoping it was him. That the relationship was doomed to fail had no real impact on my thoughts. I wanted him, I loved him and could no more control my emotions than I could change the circumstances of my life. "Oh, what the hell," I said as I drained the last of the bottle. "I might as well enjoy it while it lasts." So I would see him and continue to see him as long as I could. With that decision reached, I felt relieved and turned my attentions to preparation for this evening.

After careful deliberation and discarding the usual graceful sweep of full skirts, I chose a gown designed for last year's line but never shown since it did not fit the Griffin image. It was a black, strapless sheath slit to mid-thigh for ease in walking. I had carefully embellished the hem and side slit with red sequins and rhinestones in a flame-like pattern. When I moved the light reflected and danced giving the impression that the dress was, indeed, on fire. As a final concession to Max, I pinned my hair up in an approximation of a Gibson Girl. I frowned at it in the mirror, wondering how long the countless pins would hold, but decided to leave it up. My shoulders looked almost white

against the black of the dress; I did not want to distract from
their marble appearance. The final adornment was a pair of
small ruby earrings and a matching necklace that had belonged
to my mother. After one final glance in the mirror, I covered it
all with my cape and went through the office and downstairs to
meet the limousine hired for the evening.

We arrived early enough to avoid the press and the public.
The show was being held in one of the most exclusive hotels in
town. Two of the ballrooms were reserved for the show itself,
one large room was to be partitioned off into small dressing
areas; a smaller area outside the ballrooms was set aside as the
reception area. I walked through this area, noticing with pleasure that all was elegant, understated and dignified. I held my
breath while opening the main doors; the preparations this week
had progressed well, but the area had still been unfinished yesterday.

I let my breath out in a relieved sigh. It was perfect, exactly
as I had envisioned it. The walls had been covered with heavy
gray paper, printed to appear as rough-hewn stones. The gilt
hands grasping candles that lined the walls were shamelessly
borrowed from Jean Cocteau; the theme of the show was one
that he himself had borrowed: "Beauty and the Beast." I thought
that I would probably lose points for originality on this initially,
but the theme was maintained throughout the show. The macabre backdrop was only one element. The models themselves
would carry the message that beauty and the grotesque were
often separated by a very thin line.

Removing my cape and draping it over my arm, I slowly
walked down one of the center aisles to approach the runway.
As I stepped on the platform, I jumped when one of the hands
moved, then laughed inwardly at my apprehension. They had
been designed to move almost imperceptibly, in sequence; the
technicians were merely making their final test. I laughed again
when I noticed that we had lost the fight with the fire marshall;
the hands held electric candles, not the real ones I had wanted
to use. I shrugged off this last problem; it was not noticeable

except here on the stage. All that mattered was that the desired mood be set.

Stepping through one of the side doors, I entered into the dressing areas, squinting against the bright lights. When my vision cleared, I made a mental count to find that all the models had arrived. Some were giggling in nervousness; others sat quietly while the last touches of makeup were applied.

"Good evening, ladies."

When they all turned to face me at my greeting, the effect was chilling. I experienced a moment of apprehension that perhaps I had gone too far. I studied the models individually; each wore a gown, characteristic of Griffin Designs with the romantic touches of lace, ruffles, satin and velvet. But each model had received an added touch, a flaw in their perfect appearance. On some it was subtle: excessively long nails coated in black lacquer or sharpened white canines peeking out from beneath blood-red lips. For others who were willing to take more of a risk, we had ordered full theatrical makeup, transforming them into various wild animals: one posed as a serpent; another, a cat; a third, a large black raven. Those who did not wish to take part, wore full or half-masks, to hint only of the grotesque beneath. The overall effect was nightmarish, almost hallucinogenic.

"Well," I addressed them slowly, "they will either love us or hate us, but this will be a show that won't be forgotten soon. I'm very pleased, thank you all." I glanced at the clock. "Forty-five minutes until the show, ladies. Good luck."

As they all turned away to complete their preparation, I motioned one model, the serpent girl, to me. "Janie, you look wonderful," I complimented her, knowing that she had planned on doing her own makeup. She smiled at me as I continued. "Have you seen Gwen anywhere in this chaos?"

She knew the rules about staying in the area prior to a show and looked away, hesitating slightly before she answered. "She's here somewhere, Miss Griffin. Should I look for her?"

"Janie, I know you two are friends, and I know she'd tell you where she was going. Save the mystery for the show and tell me where she is."

"Sorry, Miss Griffin. She sort of asked me to cover for her. You see, her date came early and she wanted to spend a little time with him alone. She's not been gone long, no more than five or ten minutes. Everything here is pretty much in control and . . ."

"Don't worry, Janie, she won't get in trouble. Where is she?"

"In the bar," Janie confessed in a lowered voice. "She should be back real soon now."

"Thank you, Janie. I'll get her." I smiled at her reassuringly. "Good luck."

I left the dressing room and returned to the platform. The hands followed me as I walked the runway. I glanced in the direction of the control booth. "Perfect, gentlemen," I called to them as I strode out of the room.

Two of the hotel staff members were stationed in the reception area and I questioned them about whether there was a back route into the bar. I did not want to meet with any of the crowd that had begun to gather in the lobby. Following the directions given, I rushed down the back hallways and cursed Gwen all the way there. The only good thing in all this, I thought, was that it seemed to represent a reconciliation with Nick. I didn't think she would have asked anyone else to attend. And while I did not like him much, I far preferred her keeping company with Nick than with Larry or anyone else she would find at the Ballroom of Romance. There were too many unanswered questions concerning Larry. I didn't trust him, not with Gwen.

When I entered the bar, I saw her immediately. Her bright swirls of color stood out from the primarily dark evening attire of the other clientele. She was sitting facing the door engrossed in conversation with someone I immediately assumed to be Nick, from the possessive way his arm encircled her shoulders. I approached them and she glanced at me in surprise. "Oh, hi," she said, not meeting my eyes.

"Gwen, I hate to interrupt your reunion but we really do have to get the show started. You and Nick can get cozy afterward . . ." I stopped abruptly as he turned around. Of course it wasn't Nick. His build and hair color were similar but I should not have been fooled. I suppose I saw what I had wanted to see.

"Hello, Larry." I smiled to cover my broken composure, the skin crawled at the base of my neck and I repressed a shiver, remembering his disclosures at our last meeting. "How nice of you to come this evening."

He rose slowly and looked me up and down, leeringly. "Deirdre, what a pleasant surprise. We were just talking about you, weren't we, Gwen?" He nodded at her briefly then turned his attention back to me. "You look beautiful, as usual. Who's the lucky man tonight?" His voice was calm and pleasant, but the sneer on his face distorted and twisted the words. I looked quickly at Gwen, but she did not seem to notice as she stood up awkwardly and began to collect her coat and purse.

"We really need to leave, Gwen. Nice to see you again, Larry." I turned and walked out of the bar.

Gwen caught up with me a few seconds later, breathless and apologetic. "I'm sorry, Deirdre. I know I should have stayed with the others. But when he sent the message that he was here, I wanted to see him for a bit. Everything was going fine, with the show, I mean, and I didn't think a few minutes away would hurt. He's just so nice." When I made no reply, she continued, "It won't happen again, I promise."

I stopped abruptly and turned to her. "Gwen," I said softly, looking into her eager face. "I don't begrudge you a few minutes to yourself, I really don't. God knows, I give you precious little time to pursue your personal affairs. And I do not want to interfere with your life or your choices. But before you get more deeply involved with Larry, you and I need to talk. Do you two have plans after the show?" She nodded and tried to look away, but I grasped her chin and turned her face toward me. "Cancel them," I ordered peremptorily. "I do not want you to see him again until we talk about this. Please listen to me on this, it is very important. You must not see him again." She nodded again, this time her eyes were locked on mine. I hoped the command would take.

I released my hold on her and she swayed as she stood, still dazed. Then she relaxed and shook her head briefly as she stared bewildered around her. "What are we doing hanging around here? Let's get going," she said, beginning to move down the hall, "or they'll start without us."

The show went well. The macabre treatment was tolerated by most, enjoyed by some and the designs, the most important part after all, were well received. Following the show, those with invitations remained behind for a small reception. Although I normally hated these affairs, I forced myself to attend and exchange pleasantries with my guests. After talking to a succession of nameless faces, accepting compliments and answering questions, I went to claim a glass of wine. Unfortunately, at the bar, I was cornered by a writer for a prominent women's publication. She wanted to discuss the social and psychological ramifications of the fashion industry. I smiled and nodded and managed to make the proper replies, all the while searching for the easiest way to excuse myself from her company. She provided the perfect opportunity by asking about Gwen, who had been given credit in the program for being both my assistant and co-designer. "Have you never met Gwen?" I questioned. "You really must meet, she is a wonderful help and I couldn't function without her. I'll find her and send her over."

I looked around and saw Gwen deep in conversation with someone in the far corner. I weaved through the crowd, nodding and smiling and arrived in time to hear a familiar voice quietly advising her, "Don't forget what I have told you, my dear. It's very important."

"Hello, Max." I gave him an apologetic smile for the interruption. "May I borrow Gwen for a moment?" He nodded his agreement and I pulled her to one side. "Gwen, here's your chance to earn your large bonus."

"Huh?" I wondered how many glasses of wine she had drunk. "What large bonus?"

"The one you will get for helping me out." I explained the situation and she agreed readily. "Tell her anything you like, but keep her talking and away from me. Thank you." I gave her hand a small squeeze and sent her on her way. This was a situation she would have to learn how to handle in the future.

Max drew up closely beside me. "You look elegant, Deirdre. So, you finally decided to wear your hair up. It's very becoming."

"Just for you, Max. And I see that you have finally found someone else on whom to bestow your fatherly advice." I gestured in Gwen's direction.

"She's a sweet thing, Deirdre. I was merely offering my opinion on her present choice of company. You know she has been seeing Larry, don't you?"

"He isn't still here, is he?" I glanced around the room.

"No, he's not."

"Good. I tried to warn her away earlier, but I'm not sure that she listened."

"Perhaps she'll take my advice more seriously than yours."

"I also have a problem with Larry; what exactly did you tell him about me?"

He looked at me and smiled. "I told you, my dear, a brief, varnished story. I told him where you were from initially and what your name was before you changed it to Deirdre Griffin."

I was instantly relieved and laughed. "Thank God, Max. I thought he knew everything, since he called me Dorothy. I don't mind telling you I had a few rough moments worrying over it."

"Not surprising." He moved closer to me. "But you know I, of all people, would never betray you."

"Do I?"

"Of course you do. Now, enough of that topic. Don't you want to know what I thought of your show?" He smiled mockingly.

"I don't know, do I?"

"You should, my love." He reached over and began to toy with a strand of hair that had escaped the pins. His breath was warm in my ear and I suppressed my shudder. "What a revelation for you to make. It was wild and exotic and, if I may say so, extremely arousing. You aimed straight for me, didn't you? Romance, with the element of danger. I'm reminded of a vast sky, a wide field and a certain young waitress . . ."

"I was not that young then, Max, and I'm certainly not now." I spoke harshly, because, as usual, his presence and his words had a disquieting effect on me.

He continued on, undaunted. "Why did we never repeat the experience? We could now, you know. I closed the club tonight in honor of your show. We could go there now, we would have the whole place to ourselves. Deirdre, Deirdre, come with me." His voice was low and urgent and so persuasive that I felt myself weakening. I, too, remembered that night so many years ago with tenderness and passion. He felt my resistance subside and pulled me closer to him. And yet, as I looked into his shining eyes and felt his hands grasp at my bare shoulders, I remembered other nights spent in loneliness and despair, feelings that had been caused in part by him, feelings he had not eased. My mind turned to the time I had spent with Mitch and I drew strength from that remembrance.

"No, Max," I said softly but sternly. "I will not go with you. It's too late for that."

I pushed him away and he stared at me, breathing heavily. "It can never be too late for us. I want you. Come with me now." His voice grew louder and we were attracting curious stares from the other guests.

"Damn you, Max. I said no."

He wrapped his hand tightly around my arm. "It would be different this time, Deirdre. I wouldn't leave you. We could be together . . ."

He was interrupted by another hand laid roughly on his arm, prying his grasp away from me.

"I think she said no, Hunter. You can proceed at the risk of harassment charges. The choice is yours."

Max gave a low laugh. "Ah, Detective Greer, I believe." He gave Mitch a quick, contemptuous glance and then looked back at me. He said, whispering so that I only could hear, "I congratulate you. Such a quick worker. The bodies are scarcely cold and already you have a staunch supporter on the force. I see that my concern for your naivete was needless." Once again his face became expressionless and inscrutable and his voice was pitched normally. "Forgive me, my dear, for my forcefulness. I'm afraid I may have had too much wine. Good night."

He quickly kissed my cheek, nodded to Mitch and walked out the door. Mitch and I stood in a small circle of silence, separated from the noise and laughter of the reception. "Thank you." I spoke quietly so as not to break the spell and lifted my hand to caress his cheek. He pulled it to him and kissed the palm.

"I hate that son of a bitch." His vehement comment was so out of place with his gentle gesture that I had to laugh. He looked at me questioningly.

"I could have handled him, but it would have been uglier and taken longer. Thank you again." I linked my arm in his and led him to the refreshments. "Would you like a glass of wine?" I asked, taking one for myself. He helped himself to a glass and a small plate of *hors d'oeuvres*.

"No dinner," he confessed sheepishly. "You look wonderful."

"Thank you. So do you." He looked elegant and only slightly out of context in his tuxedo.

He shrugged. "I figured fancy dress was required, so I rented this. Unfortunately, I was held up and got here too late to see the show. How'd you do?"

"Fine, thank you. It seems to have been a success." I smiled up at him warmly. I was so glad to see him that even this stilted conversation seemed wonderful. "I missed you, Mitch."

He seemed distant, distracted. "What? Oh, I missed you, too." He looked around at the thinning crowd. "Look, I know I just got here, but it seems the party is breaking up. Could we go somewhere else?"

"I don't see why not. I want to have a talk with Gwen before we go, though. It should only take a few minutes."

"Your secretary?"

"Yes, you remember her. You met her last week."

"Yeah, I know her. She was on her way out when I came in. I said hello but she seemed to be in a hurry."

I felt alarmed by this hasty departure. Gwen usually stayed until everyone had gone home. "Was she alone?"

He nodded. "She was when I saw her."

"Good, then she will be safe." He looked at me sharply but I offered no explanation. "Where would you like to go?"

"Anyplace other than here," he stated flatly. "Although it's a waste of a rented tux, I'd like to have some privacy." He looked deeply into my eyes and smiled for the first time this evening. I hoped that this signified an evening of more than conversation.

"Fine, I'll go get my coat. I won't be too long."

By the time I reached the dressing areas, most of the models had gone. Only a few remained, removing their makeup. I was pleased to see that one of these was Janie. I congratulated her on her performance, then inquired after Gwen. "Did she tell you why she left in such a hurry?"

Janie thought for a moment then answered, "I think she was upset about something you had said, and something, someone, I think she said his name was Max, had told her. She said she needed to get away and do some serious thinking. I reminded her of our party later on, but she said she couldn't come."

"Did she leave with anyone?"

"No, I don't think so. She said that the crowd was bothering her and she wanted to be alone. She didn't seem herself, though. We're all a little worried about her." She looked at me for reassurance.

"I'm sure she'll be fine, Janie. She's been having some trouble with Nick, you know." She nodded in agreement. "Thank you. And have a good time at the party tonight."

"Would you like to come, Miss Griffin? You'd be welcome." She looked at me slyly. "After all, we're going to send you the bill."

I smiled at her. "No, I don't think this time. I have other plans, but thank you." With a final good-bye, I walked out of the room.

I found Mitch at the food table, filling another plate. "Sorry I took so long, Mitch, but I see you made good use of the time."

"These are really good, you should have some."

I laughed at his suggestion. "No, thank you, I have to watch what I eat." I reached for his free hand and held it. "Would you like to go now, or maybe you'd rather stay here and eat?"

He looked intently at the plate and then at me as if deciding between us. "No," he said in his deliberate fashion giving me the slow smile that made my pulse race. "On second thought, these aren't all that good." Setting the plate back on the table, he took my cape from my arm and wrapped it around my shoulders. "Come on."

As we came through the hotel door, the limo driver jumped out and opened the door. Mitch looked at me in surprise.

"Well," I said, "if you would rather drive, we could send him back."

"Actually, I had to walk here tonight, that's one of the reasons why I came so late. My car is in the shop. I saw the limo when I came in so I assumed it belonged to someone rich and famous."

I gave him a contented smile. "I am, at least for now. Get in."

As we got settled, the driver turned around inquiringly and I glanced over at Mitch. "Would you like to drive around for a while?"

He shook his head. "We should, I guess. I mean, here I am, dressed for the part, with a woman like you, in a car like this, but . . ."

"I'm entirely in your hands, Detective," I teased as I curled up next to him. "Whatever you'd like is fine with me."

"I'll remember that," he replied with a suggestive smile, then leaned forward and gave the driver his address.

Chapter 12

We didn't speak much on the ride to Mitch's apartment. I sat quietly next to him, enjoying his presence. He rested his chin on my head and caressed my arm. We arrived all too soon.

After opening the door, the driver asked whether he should wait. "No, thank you," Mitch said. "I'll get her home from here." I nodded my head in agreement and he drove away.

We mounted the stairs to his apartment in silence. "Here we are," he said lamely as he opened the door and escorted me within.

"So we are." I surveyed the apartment; it was actually neater than the last time I had visited. The bookshelves were dusted and there were tread marks on the carpet left behind from a recent vacuuming. "Were you expecting company? Everything is so clean."

"I was expecting you," he said bluntly.

"Oh." I went to look at the books. "You seem to be pretty sure of me." I tried to make it sound casual, offhand, but failed.

"Why do you have to be so defensive? I only meant that I was hoping you would come." He looked away angrily.

"I'm sorry, Mitch. It has been a hell of a week and I am more than a little on edge."

"I know," he answered. "I'm a bit jumpy myself."

I gave him a shy smile. "Then why don't we start over? Your apartment looks very nice. Thank you for inviting me."

"My pleasure. Can I get you something. Some wine, maybe, or a cup of coffee?"

"Wine, please."

He went to the kitchen and I followed him. I watched him uncork a bottle and pour two glasses, noticing that his hands were shaking. "Did you say that you hadn't had any dinner?"

"It doesn't matter. I'll survive." He handed me my glass and looked at me. "Would you mind if I changed my clothes; I feel a little overdressed."

"Why would I mind? And while you're changing, I will fix you something to eat."

"You?"

I smiled at his surprise. "Yes, me. I do know how to cook, you know."

"How could anyone who looks as good as you do in that dress know how to cook?" He still looked doubtful. "And why would you want to?"

"I like to cook," I confessed, laughing, "and, what's more, I learned how from some of the best short-order cooks in the country. I may be a little rusty, but I think I can still scramble a few eggs without poisoning you. Go get changed." I half-pushed him out of the kitchen and he laughed and left.

I found a towel and wrapped it around my waist as a make-shift apron. Opening his refrigerator, I saw what I needed and started. In spite of my comments to the contrary, I had not cooked in an ordinary kitchen for more years than I wanted to count. In fact, I thought, the last time was probably shortly after the change.

The domestic tasks were strangely comforting. Beating the eggs, warming the skillet, setting a place at the table, all these brought back memories of happier times. For once I was not saddened by these thoughts but smiled contentedly and began to sing, softly at first, and then more confidently. *"Into the ward of the clean, whitewashed halls, where the dead slept and the dying lay, wounded by bayonet, saber and ball, somebody's darling was borne one day."* Mitch walked in just as I reached the chorus ". . . *Somebody's darling, somebody's pride, who'll tell his mother where her boy died."*

"Sounds good," he said appreciatively, smiling at me from the kitchen entrance. "No, don't stop, keep singing, please. It's good to hear that old song again. I haven't thought of it or even heard it for years. You know, my mother would sing it to me at bedtime, she told me that her grandmother sang it to her. But I'm sort of surprised that you know it."

"Oh," I said offhandedly. "I know a lot of songs."

"Then keep on singing."

"I couldn't, not now." I felt myself blushing. "Besides, your dinner is done." I gestured at the table. "Sit down."

I served him and after he shook salt and pepper on the eggs, he began to eat immediately and hungrily. With his second forkful he seemed to recover his manners. "Aren't you having anything?"

I lifted my glass of wine and took a sip.

"No, not that. Aren't you going to eat? I don't think I've seen you eat anything since that night we had dinner. Are you on a diet or something?"

"Yes," I smiled, enjoying my secret joke. "A very controlled diet. And I'm afraid eggs aren't on it. But I'll take one bite if it makes you happy."

"It would."

I turned around and got myself a fork from the drawer, then reached over and took a small bit from his plate and put it in my mouth. I chewed it and swallowed, trying not to gag. It caught in my throat and I began to choke. Mitch jumped up immediately, gave me a large thump on the back, stepped back and gave me an appraising glance. "You okay?"

"Fine," I said, trying to laugh. "Too much pepper."

"Sorry," he said, sitting back down. "I like it that way."

I finished my wine to wash the egg taste out of my mouth and refilled my glass. He looked up at me, with a question in his eyes, but his mouth was full and he shook his head. At that moment the phone rang, and I jumped. He motioned for me to get it.

"Hello?" The young man on the phone sounded confused, as if he had the wrong number. "Is, ah, Mitchell Greer there?"

"Yes, he is. Hold on a moment." I held the phone out to him with a smile, hoping that this would interrupt his chain of thought on my seeming inability to swallow even the simplest piece of food. "It's for you."

"No kidding." He wiped his mouth and took the receiver from me.

"Hello?" His face brightened. "Hi, Chris. Where are you calling from? Why didn't you reverse the charges?" He listened for a moment. "You're in town again? You were just here last weekend. I hope you're not neglecting your studies."

I could hear the caller's youthful laugh and voice quite clearly. "I hope I didn't interrupt anything, Dad. I didn't know you had company."

"No, no, you didn't interrupt. We, or, well, I was just having some dinner. Hold on a second." He held his hand over the receiver. "It's my son, Chris," he said. "Would you like to meet him?"

"Yes, that would be nice; he's in town?"

He nodded and went back to the phone. "Why don't you come on up?" He smiled at me and took my hand. "There's someone here I'd like you to meet."

I would have recognized Chris as Mitch's son immediately. They had the same nose, the same eyes with the same appraising manner. He shook my hand warmly then gave his father a sly wink. "You're right as usual, Dad."

"Right about what?"

Mitch looked embarrassed and gave Chris a sharp look. "Excuse him, Deirdre, he's a bit of a smart ass." But he smiled when he said it; Chris went to him and they exchanged a brief but forceful hug. "I can only guess that his studies haven't reached the part about confidentiality." Mitch gave him a playful push away and Chris smiled at me.

"Nope, they ain't teached me that yet. Besides"—and he turned to Mitch again—"I don't think Deirdre would mind knowing that you described her to me in minute detail. I thought he was exaggerating, but now that I've seen you myself . . ." He rolled his eyes and I laughed at him.

"Cut it out, kid, I'm old enough to be your mother."

"I doubt it," he said, looked at me again and dropped his joking manner. "But you're dressed to go out. I didn't mean to spoil your evening."

"We *were* out," Mitch informed him. "We had just come in."

"Then let's go out again. What would you like to do, Deirdre?"

I shrugged. "Whatever you'd like. What would you two do, if I weren't around."

Mitch laughed. "We usually hit the pool hall for a few games and beers. Not exactly your cup of tea."

"Oh, really? And how would you know about that?" I teased Mitch lightly. "Pool and beer sound good to me."

Chris looked at me in shock. "In that dress? There'd be a full-fledged riot."

"No, of course not. But I could change, if we made a stop first."

Mitch looked doubtful. "If you really want to . . ."

"I do," I insisted. "It's been awhile since I've played, but I don't imagine the game has changed."

"Shall I rack them up again, Chris?" I finished my beer and smiled over at him.

He shook his head and looked at Mitch, who gave a disgusted snort. "Not bloody likely, Deirdre. You've already skunked us six games to nothing. I have a reputation to keep up here."

"Dad really hates to lose." Chris seemed to be enjoying himself.

"You get out of here, rat, and get us another beer." Mitch

laughed as Chris left the poolroom. He moved toward me and put an arm around my waist.

"I am so sorry, Detective, have I ruined your macho image forever?"

"Are you kidding? The fact that you're the best-looking woman to ever enter this place has made my name legend."

"Be honest," I laughed. "I'm practically the only woman to ever come here." I looked over at the rest of the patrons with a small grimace; they were a pretty rough crew; the pool hall was not in the best area of town.

"You're probably right." He looked around, the crowd that had gathered while we played had disbursed, and while most went into the bar, some were still loitering by the doorway. Mitch lowered his voice so that I was the only one who could hear him. "Still I wish you had worn something a little less, well, tempting." I had dressed in my black leather jeans and an oversized sweatshirt that kept felling down over one shoulder. "Not that you don't look great, you understand. I know most of these guys and they're usually a decent lot, but every once in awhile they get a little rowdy. In a place like this, someone like you can be a time bomb."

"But I'm with you, and I can take care of myself."

"I guess so." He gave me a sharp look as I pulled at the neckline of my shirt. "Where's your bruise?"

"Bruise?" I couldn't remember at first. "Oh, that. It's gone," I said lightly. "I'm a quick healer."

"I still don't remember you having that earlier in the evening. I can't believe I would have missed it."

"Damn it, Mitch, it was dark and you were otherwise preoccupied. Next time, maybe you should take inventory beforehand." I smiled at him invitingly. "Assuming, of course, that you want a next time."

"Are you crazy?" He pulled me to him and held me tightly. "It's all I've been able to think about this week." He lifted me off the floor and kissed me. I locked my arms around his neck, enjoying the feel of his body pressed to mine. When the kiss was done, I sighed and nestled into his shoulder, my head deliberately turned away from his neck. I wanted him so desperately, not just his body, but his blood. I wondered what it would be like to take a willing victim, not someone I had stalked and hunted, but someone who wanted to give themselves totally to me.

The tingling in my gums signaled the extension of my canines and I gave a sharp intake of breath. At the same time, there was a muffled cough at the door; Mitch let me down abruptly and spun around. Chris stood there, three bottles of beer in his grasp and a wide grin on his face. He looked so much like a younger version of Mitch that I smiled back despite my embarrassment.

"Beers?" he said, holding them out like an offering to the gods.

Mitch laughed. "Carry them into the bar, son, I think we've had enough pool for one night."

We sat down at a small table toward the back of the room. We talked for a while about Chris' studies, but I was distracted by an oddly familiar figure sitting on the other end of the bar. He kept staring at us, at me in particular. Suddenly, I placed him with a sickening twist of my stomach; it was the man I'd fed on in the alley two weeks ago. Mitch had his back to him, and Chris was too involved in detailing his expectations of the law boards, so neither of them noticed. I glanced at my watch, yawned conspicuously and quickly finished my beer. Sensing my impatience, Mitch looked over at me.

"Would you like to go now?"

I nodded. "It has been a long day and I'm very tired. So if you don't mind . . ."

"Fine, but I need to make one phone call before we leave. I'll be back in a minute."

After Mitch left, Chris stood up. "It's been really nice to meet you, Deirdre." He reached out, shook my hand and gave me the Greer smile. "But I get the feeling that you two would like to be alone for a while. And I know Dad well enough to know that he wouldn't tell me to leave even if he wanted me to. So I'll do the decent thing and quit cutting in on his time." He looked at me intently then smiled again. "I'm probably way out of line for saying this, but I hope you stick around for a while. I haven't seen him this relaxed for years. You're good for him, I can tell"—he flushed slightly—"but don't you dare tell him I said so."

"I promise. Good night, Chris."

"Good night."

Chris wasn't out of the bar for more than a second when the man appeared at the table. I didn't have a chance to move before he grabbed my arm. "Hey, baby," he said in a voice that made my identification a certainty. "Don't I know you from somewhere?"

"I don't think so." I tried to brush him off but he held on.

"I'm sure we met, and not that long ago, neither." He rubbed his neck absently with a glazed look. "I couldn't never forget a babe like you."

"Excuse me, you must be mistaken."

He pulled me to him roughly. "Now I know. We had an appointment in a dark alley. You left too soon, as I remember it. Now that your friends is gone, maybe we can finish up."

"Leave me alone," I hissed at him. "Take your hands off me."

He laughed, and tried to kiss me. I looked around and noticed that no one was watching. Our conversation had been quiet and his invitation was probably nothing out of the ordinary for this place. Mitch was nowhere to be seen and I didn't want to wait for him to reappear. If it were an ordinary night, if I were on my own, I would simply accompany him to some dark place and feed on him again, this time being sure to implant the thought that he didn't know me. But I had no time for that now. Instead, I looked him full in the face and smiled. My teeth had grown and I saw a look of doubt and fear enter his eyes. "Next time a lady says no, you really should listen." I picked him up by the front of his shirt and tossed him onto the table next to us. He and the table collapsed with a loud crash and the sound of breaking bottles; by this time I was sitting down again and staring at

him, like the other customers. No one looked at me and no one
went to help him up. There was a lot of raucous laughter and
some good-natured joking about how Sammy couldn't hold his
liquor. He lay without moving and I thought for one moment
that I had killed him. Then just as Mitch was coming in to see
what all the commotion was about, he moaned and rolled over.

"What's happening," he said, as he rushed to my side. "Are
you okay, Deirdre?"

"I'm fine—he's drunk." I indicated the man rising uncertainly to his feet. "Let's get out of here."

"I'm scared, Deirdre. I guess it all boils down to that. It's been
a long time since I felt this way about anyone, and eventually
even that got hopelessly screwed up. I don't want that to happen
this time." Mitch had haltingly begun to apologize for our argument last week and I tried to console him without giving him
too much hope for a lasting relationship.

"I know, Mitch." We arrived at the door of my hotel; he held
back to allow me to go through the revolving door first. I did
not enter, but pulled him to one side, away from the entrance.
The things that needed to be said, should be said privately. "It's
been a long time for me, also. And although I do care for you,
I can't make any promises."

His eyes reflected pain, but he gave me a small grin. "I can
wait around while you make up your mind, though, can't I? Just
don't take too long with it. I'm not getting any younger."

"Who is?"

"You, for one."

"Why do you say that?" I questioned him sharply, seeing my
angry reflection in his eyes. "I'm not getting younger, either.
How could I?"

"Whoa, calm down a bit. It was a compliment. Most women
like to hear that they don't look their age." He pulled me to
him, kissed me and I responded as usual. When it was over,

he held me close. "You're a strange one Deirdre. But somehow, I like it."

"Coming up for a drink?" I moved away from him and he followed me through the door.

Once on the elevator, he kissed me again, teasingly this time. When he bit my lower lip I jumped back and wiped my mouth. He had drawn no blood. The doors opened on my floor and we entered the room.

"Help yourself." I indicated the bar and walked back to the bedroom. I set my key down and started to take off my shirt when suddenly he was behind me, his arms wrapped around my waist.

"Don't mind if I do." His voice was scratchy in my ear. I watched in the mirror as he undressed me. Each piece of clothing was removed gently and slowly until I stood naked before him. The new mirror displayed my reflection, unflawed and whole once more. Mitch and I might have been any human couple, any two lovers wrapped up in each other. My skin seemed to glow, it was so white beneath his tanned, calloused hands. He examined me, with his hands and his eyes. "Not a mark," he whispered in a voice full of awe. "You're perfect." He leaned his head on my shoulder and made a face at the mirror. "And then there's me . . ."

I turned around and unbuttoned his shirt; I could not match his unhurried pace, I wanted him so much. Two of the buttons dropped to the floor, sheered off by my sharp nails. He looked at me, smiled and carried me to the bed.

Shortly before dawn, he got up and began to dress. I lay, watching him, and he jumped when he turned around and saw that my eyes were open. "Sorry." He finished zipping his pants and came to sit next to me. "I didn't mean to wake you."

"Do you have to leave?"

"I've got to get home to change, then get to work. What are your plans for today?"

I stretched and reached a hand up to his face. The sun would be up soon, and I fought back the lethargy that dawn always caused. "I'm going to stay right here and wait for you to come back."

He laughed. "And if I don't?"

"You'll be back." My voice was low, throaty and I rubbed my head on his arm.

"Damn straight, I will." He kissed me, then stood up and smiled down at me. "You have to sew the buttons back on my shirt."

I blushed and threw a pillow at him. "Sew on your own buttons, Detective, I only remove them."

"And I'll be happy to do it, if you'll tear them off again."

"Promise." Through the heavy draperies I could feel the sunrise. "Oh, and Mitch?" I fought to keep my eyes open until he left. "Take the key with you. You can let yourself in."

He took it from the dressing table, tossed it up in the air and caught it. "See you tonight, then. Sweet dreams."

Only after the door shut and he was gone, did I realize that I had allowed myself to violate one of my most important rules. My sleep that day would be undefended by the normal locks and safeguards. But the thought brought no alarm and no fear. My eyes closed and my body relaxed. I trusted him, I loved him and I held his face in my mind as I fell into the deep crevasse of sleep.

The corridor winds endlessly, a mist rising from the floor. I walk slowly, my footsteps echoing loudly in this silent place of death. Here are the same coffins, the same loves buried out of my reach. I do not attempt to open them, not this time, but quicken my steps to reach something, someone or some answer, waiting, I know, at the end of the hall. There are more coffins now, they seem uncountable. I wonder why they are here, why I am here.

"They are the fruits of your sins, Deirdre," the voice pulses in my ears. "They died so that you might live forever."

"Who are you?" I call but my voice is lost in a loud clattering. The lids of the coffins, pummelled from within, fall to the floor, shattering into splinters.

"Look on them and rejoice. They are your children, they are your soul." I stand in horror as they rise from their caskets, surrounding me, grasping at me with sharp fingers. I know them all; I recognize the faces, the eyes, the mouths whispering, hissing, speaking all of my different names.

"Diane," a rasping voice calls to me. "How about some more coffee, darlin'?" Buddy's face is bloody and twisted into a lewd grin.

"Dorothy." A rotting soldier dressed in tattered navy rags reaches out to me. "Dorothy, it hurts bad. You can help, help me."

"I just might fall in love." Bill's voice is little more than a croak and although his body has not yet begun to decompose, his walk is choppy, uncoordinated. He lurches toward me.

"No," I scream, pushing them all away. They are weightless and fall to the floor with soft thuds. "No, I will not claim these. Their deaths are not mine." I run from them, tears clouding my vision. The door is near. I see a figure, a man, guarding it. His face is obscured and he does not speak, but dissolves into nothing as I reach him. Where he had been standing, is now a pool of blood. I kneel down, I reach into it, it is deeper than I had expected. I raise my hand to my mouth and drink; I lower my head and lap at it; I am compelled to take it all. Then it is gone and I sit back on my heels, sated and dazed. As I begin to rise, I notice a shred of fabric where the pool had been. I pick it up to wipe the blood from my face and hands. The colors are bright and swirled. "No," I scream again. "Not her, she is not dead."

"Too late, too late," the voices of the dead whisper through the air. They overwhelm me and I cannot seem to resist. They lay me down on the floor and wipe away my bloody tears with icy hands, caressing and stroking my hair and my face, warming their rotting bodies against mine. A darkness overtakes me; their soft words lull me. "Hush, hush," they say. "It's only a dream, it is all just a dream."

Chapter 13

I tried to shake off the hands gripping my shoulders. The voices changed, blended into one, deep and familiar. The words, however, were the same. ". . . it's only a dream, Deirdre. Wake up, please." I realized that these hands were warm, living flesh and the room was no longer dark. I opened my eyes hesitantly and squinted at the light. Mitch's face came into view and I threw my arms around him. He returned my embrace and held me until I stopped trembling. When I calmed down, he held me at arms' length and stared into my eyes. "Well," he said in a shaky voice, "that must have been one hell of a nightmare. Do you want to tell me about it?"

I shook my head. "In a bit, maybe. But not right now." I ran my fingers through my hair and glanced at the curtained window. "What time is it?"

He smiled. "After six. You must have slept all day; I came in around four and tried to wake you, but you were practically comatose. I have to admit, it scared me a bit. You opened your eyes and looked straight at me. But you didn't focus on me, or even acknowledge that anyone was here. You smiled, moaned and slowly closed your eyes again. It was pretty spooky. Do you always sleep so soundly?"

"Only when I am very tired. And it's your fault."

"Yeah, I remember." He was grinning boisterously, his eyes sparkled and he seemed inordinately pleased with himself. I wondered what was so amusing, until I realized that I was naked and quickly pulled the covers up around me.

"Did you have a good day?" I asked as casually as possible.

"Not too bad," he said slowly. "It was interesting, at least. Some really strange things are happening these days."

"Such as?"

"As if the murders weren't bad enough, now we've had a break-in at the local blood bank. And of course, since I'm the 'vampire' cop, I got the job."

I dropped my gaze, not wanting him to see the interest his words had caused. Breaking into a blood bank was a possibility that had always intrigued me, although I had never tried it myself. It always seemed too risky; if you got caught you would have to explain why, and probably spend time in jail. Much easier to obtain it the way I always had. Still, it was one more indication of the other's operations. Or perhaps there was more than one; how ironic it would be, after searching for over a century, to find a community living in the same city. But I didn't actually believe that theory; although I sometimes longed for companionship of my own kind, I would never want to share my hunts or my territories.

"Deirdre, you're not listening."

"What? Oh, sorry, Mitch. I was just thinking how it might all fit in."

"If you had been paying attention, you would know by now. As I was saying, we actually have a few suspects now, based mostly on the testimony of an eyewitness near the blood bank. You might be interested to know that you are acquainted with one of them."

"Who?"

"I'm not sure I should divulge that information."

"Jesus, Mitch, don't give me the policeman line on it. I want to know. It might be that I could be threatened by him, also."

"Actually, the department was afraid of just that. But I let them know that I would hold you in protective custody."

"I guess that's as good a name as any for what you've been doing," I said dryly. "Now tell me who it is."

"We're not positive, of course, and I really shouldn't tell you, but I don't see that it can hurt. It's Larry."

"Larry?" It would explain why he was so curious about my past, it might even explain his obsession with me. But somehow I just couldn't believe that he was a vampire.

"Yes, Larry Martin, the club doorman. You do remember him, don't you."

I shook my head.

"You don't remember him?"

"Of course I do, Mitch. But he is not a vampire." I was sorry as soon as the word was out of my mouth; Mitch did not believe in vampires.

He smiled but did not laugh. "Yeah, well, whatever he is, he's associated with all three of them. He was the last person seen with Andrews, knew the hooker and was reported to have quarreled with Mr. Leigh."

"What about the other suspects?"

"I'm putting my money on Martin. He has a history of instability as long as my arm; he's been in and out of institutions since he was fourteen. Based on what we've uncovered about him so far, he's one sick dude."

"Do you think I could"—I shifted uneasily and the blankets slipped away from me—"do you think I could speak with him?"

"If we had him in custody, sure." He looked at me intently. "Look, Deirdre, I can't concentrate on anything if you're like that. Get dressed," he jokingly ordered as I covered myself again, giving him a shy smile. "And come on out. I brought us some dinner."

I dressed quickly and left the bedroom. Mitch had spread the dinner he brought on the bar. It was from a variety of fast-food places. "I didn't really know what you'd want, so I brought a lot." He patted the barstool next to him. "Sit down and eat."

I laughed a bit and crossed the room. I selected a roast beef sandwich; it at least had the dubious distinction of being slightly rare and I thought I could eat enough of it to satisfy him. I pulled the meat from the bun and began to eat.

"Too bad Gwen's not here," I said after the first mouthful. "She would love the assortment. You should see some of the junk she brings in . . ." At the thought of her I grew serious, fearful at the remembrance of my dream. The abrupt change was not lost on him.

"What's the matter?"

"Oh, God, Mitch, the dream," I began disjointedly with a shiver. "She was in my dream. I didn't see her, but I knew she was in danger."

"You hinted at something like that the night of the show. Why would Gwen be in danger? What has she got to do with any of this?"

I ignored his comments and continued, thinking out loud. "She wouldn't have gone with him. I warned her and she promised not to see him again. Even Max warned her. She should be safe."

He looked at me sternly. "Who didn't she go with?"

"Larry. She met him at the club last Sunday. I'm afraid she developed a crush on him. She was with him before the show, too. But he left after that, I'm sure of it."

"How can you be so sure?" He, too, was growing concerned.

"Everyone said she left alone, even you said so. And Max said that Larry had gone, long before that."

"But you warned her, you say, to stay away from him. Would she listen?" Suddenly, his eyes narrowed in concentration. "But you had no knowledge of him being a suspect until tonight. Why would you warn her away? What the hell is going on here?"

I looked at him in confusion for a minute and shook my head to clear it. Of course he had no idea of what had occurred between Larry and me, no comprehension of the truth that seemed to hold us all entangled. "He just seemed unstable to me and I did not want her to get hurt. She'd had a fight with her fiancé, you see, and she was on the rebound. I did not like the thought of her being with Larry. Neither did Max, he said . . ."

"Spare me the thoughts of the great Max," Mitch snarled as he said the name. "Anyway, it can hardly matter. I seem to remember that Gwen lives clear across town and Larry was last seen in the area of your office. So their paths shouldn't have crossed at all."

"But she wasn't going home, Mitch. She was going to stay at my place for the weekend."

"Your place?" He smiled, not comprehending. "But we are at your place. And she's not here, so she must be at home."

Once again I had forgotten how little Mitch knew of my life. "She was staying at my apartment at the office."

"You have an apartment in your office?" He stopped for a moment. "I didn't know." He gave me a suspicious look. "But then apparently there's a lot I don't know. We'd better get over there."

We hesitated only a second, he to throw on his coat and I to put on my shoes. We rushed out of the hotel to his car, a regulation police-issue this time. "My car's still in the shop," he explained as he started the engine and turned on the siren. "I don't like to drive marked cars ordinarily, but this one'll help. Buckle up."

We sped the two blocks and pulled up in front of the building just as an ambulance was leaving. One other police car was parked at the curb. Mitch pushed through the small crowd that had gathered around the doors and we entered. As we approached the two policemen inside, I noticed that they were the same two who had questioned me last week. They both nodded at me in embarrassed recognition; one of them addressed Mitch.

"Well, Greer, I might have known you would show up. How do you manage it?"

"Never mind," he snarled at them. "What happened here? Is she okay?"

"She?" He shook his head. "We came on a call about the security guard. The guy coming on to the next shift found him slumped at his desk. Someone gave him a pretty rough knock on the head. He should be okay, though. What's this about a woman?"

Mitch gave me an angry look. "I have reason to believe that Miss Griffin's secretary is in the office. We're concerned about her safety."

The policeman shook his head again. "We checked all the floors and found nothing unusual; there were no signs anywhere of a break-in. We think it was an attempted robbery; but the guy got scared after hitting the guard and cleared out."

Mitch nodded slowly. "Mind if I check it out?"

He smiled, "No, you will, anyway. We were just about ready to leave. Want some help?"

Mitch considered this for a moment. "I might need the back-up," he conceded. "It won't take too long, I hope."

The four of us rode the elevator in silence. I noticed the few curious glances they gave first to Mitch, and then to me, but chose to ignore them. My whole body was tensed in fear and I silently urged the elevator upward. When it arrived at the top floor, I hurried out and unlocked the door. The office looked exactly as it had when I had left; there were no signs of struggle or unusual activity. I led them back to my office and when I opened the door, I saw that everything here also looked normal.

Mitch turned to me. "Well," he said curtly, "where's this apartment you told me about?"

With a doubtful look at the other policemen, I went to my desk and found that the key was gone. Gwen, of course, would have taken it in with her. Silently, I walked to the back wall and pulled aside the draperies to expose the door. "There's only one key," I said shakily, "and Gwen has it now." In what I thought was a futile gesture, I turned the knob; to my surprise the door opened easily and we walked in.

Mitch glanced around, walking quickly over to one corner of the room and retrieving a multicolored garment that was lying on the floor. "This is Gwen's, isn't it?" he asked, handing the dress to me.

I rubbed the material absently. "Yes, she was wearing it last night. Maybe she's still sleeping." As I said it, I knew it wasn't true. The apartment was too empty, too silent, to be occupied. And suddenly the smell overwhelmed me, the smell of blood and death. "Gwen," I called, my voice wavering in a hopeless attempt to deny the obvious. "Gwen, are you here? It's Deirdre." There was a note of hysteria in my voice.

Mitch walked over to me and gave my hand a quick squeeze. "She might not be here at all." How could he say that, when the odor was overpowering. "Shall I check upstairs?"

I nodded, my hand over my mouth, and he walked up the staircase. There was a long silence, an audible gasp, then he called out. "She's here." But even before he spoke, before his pause, before his quietly whispered, "fucking maniac," I knew what he had found.

I sat down on the couch, her dress crushed against my face and began to cry silently. Both of the policemen dashed up the stairs. A few seconds later one of them came back down and his face was yellow with shock. When he asked for the telephone, I gestured at the doorway. As he began to make his phone call, I rose slowly from the floor, and dropping Gwen's dress back on to the floor, I mounted the stairs.

Mitch tried to stop me from entering the loft, putting his arm around me. "You probably shouldn't see this," he said and attempted to lead me back downstairs, but I broke away and pushed past him.

I expected to see Gwen, gray and drained, like the body of David Leigh. I had imagined her as I walked up the stairs, waxen and doll-like. What I saw rocked me back, causing even me to choke back the contents of my stomach.

The room was covered in blood, the ceiling, the floor, the bed, everywhere I looked. I could smell its sweetness, turning rancid now from exposure to the air. Where it had pooled, the blood had clotted over, thickened and crusty. I must have gasped or cried out, for Mitch came to me again and tried to move me away. I ignored him and walked to the bed. I stared for a moment at the incomprehensible shape lying there; someone had pulled a sheet over it, and the center was peaked as if a tent. Danger, my mind whispered, danger, but my hand moved as if by its own volition to pull aside the sheet.

It was Gwen, her skin was heavy and solid, her small naked body pitiful, lying in the brown stain of her own blood. And emerging from her chest was a large wooden stake; her back was arched, actually raised an inch from the bed where the other end protruded. Her eyes were open and her hands tightly grasped that horrible implement of death, as if she had tried to wrench it away in her last moment of life. "Dear, sweet Jesus." I was glued to the spot; I could not take my eyes away from her.

This was something I had read about, something I had envisioned so many times. But it was worse than I had ever imagined, and it was wrong. The body should have been mine.

Pulling my gaze away from the stake, I reached over and gently stroked her tousled hair, closed her eyes and carefully pulled the sheet back over her. I looked into Mitch's eyes. I could tell he shared my grief and horror, but I did not want his comfort.

"Get him," I said, my voice stony and harsh, "you find the bastard that did this. And when you do, he's mine, do you understand? He's mine. I'll tear him apart."

Both Mitch and the other policeman looked at me in shock. "Deirdre?" Mitch softly approached and I permitted him to put his arm around me and lead me back down the stairs. "Do you want me to take you somewhere?" He helped me to the couch as if I would break in his arms. "Your hotel, maybe? Or my place? I'm afraid it'll take some time to get this all taken care of."

"No, thank you. I would like to wait, if I may." I wiped my hands over my face to remove my tears. "This was meant for me," I said to myself. "It should not have been Gwen, it was meant for me. If I had known, I could have stopped this." My voice sounded dead and emotionless.

"Deirdre"—he clasped me to him roughly—"don't do this. Don't blame yourself. It happened, there was nothing you, or anyone else could have done to stop it. How could you know? You're only human." He tightened his grip on me and gave me one brief kiss before turning away.

"How I wish that were true, Mitch," I said softly as he climbed the stairs.

The entire investigation took several hours. I sat motionless for some of the time, staring at the art on the walls. It gave me a point of focus other than the activity in the loft. But that focus was shattered when the morgue employees arrived to bundle Gwen up in a zippered plastic bag. I stood up and walked toward the kitchen. "I'll just make some coffee now, if anyone wants it." I spoke to no one in particular and no one answered, but the task enabled me to turn my back on the awkward package, that was once my friend, being carried down the stairs.

The smell of the coffee drew them to the kitchen, one by one. Disinterested and mechanical, I served them all. Mitch was the last to arrive. I fixed a cup and handed it to him. My hands were steady again and he gave me a sad smile. "You doing okay?" he asked.

"As well as can be expected, I suppose." I tried and almost succeeded in returning his smile. "Will you be much longer?"

"No, not too much. But you can help with something, if you would."

"You know I will do whatever I can, Mitch."

"We need to fingerprint you; we'll need to be able to tell your prints from the others we found up there. So we can get a positive ID."

The thoughts of leaving a permanent trace of my existence with the police department made me shiver involuntarily. But I knew I could not refuse, nor did I want to. I needed to identify the murderer, not only for revenge but for my own personal safety. I knew what Gwen's death meant. Somebody knew who and what I was. Somebody who was enjoying the game he was playing with me. Somebody who wanted more than my death. "Larry." I whispered his name with loathing.

Mitch said nothing, but sat watching me, his cup of coffee grasped between his hands.

Finally, I nodded to him. "I will allow the fingerprinting, but you may find it to be a futile gesture."

"You don't think we'll get him?"

"Oh, I am sure we will." I laughed, low and threateningly and he inadvertently drew away from me. "We will find him. But after I'm done with him there won't be enough left to identify."

"Jesus, Deirdre. I know that this has been a shock to you, it would be for anyone. Even if you didn't know her. But you can't do anything about it. Let us do our job."

I looked at him defiantly. He stood up and grabbed my arm, pulling me roughly to him. "I don't want you involved. I know she was your friend, I can even imagine how you must be feeling. But you must stay out of this; he will be taken care of, I promise you."

"Fine, Mitch. I'll play by your rules, for now. But if he gets away, or gets released on some technicality, I will track him down and I will kill him."

He stared at me in disbelief. "Deirdre, you're in shock and slightly hysterical; later on you will feel differently. You can't expect me to believe that you would be capable of . . ." His voice trailed off.

"You'd be surprised what I am capable of, Mitch." His eyes held a mixture of doubt and confusion, suspicion and fear, as if I had changed in his eyes. I found the emotions he reflected discomforting and saddening. "But then again"—and I smiled when he relaxed at my softened voice—"maybe you know me better than I think. Let's get this over with."

When all of the prints had been taken, and all of the evidence examined and photographed, the policemen left. Mitch and I sat in an amiable silence at the kitchen table, finishing the rest of the coffee. He rubbed his hand over his eyes and combed his fingers through his hair. "Tired?" I queried gently.

"I feel like I haven't had a good night's sleep for months. I didn't get much sleep last night, as you well know," he said with a good-natured leer. I blushed slightly and lowered my eyes. "And I don't think I'll get much tonight." He placed his hand over mine at the table. "Unfortunately, it won't be for the same reason."

"What else do you need to do tonight?"

"At the very least, I have to go to the station and file a few reports. We've got an APB out on Larry, but he may not turn up for a while. The lab guys will take care of the prints and the evidence. I hope that after the paperwork is done, I'll be able to go home and get some sleep."

"May I accompany you to the station?"

"That would be a good idea, since I'm supposed to have you under protective custody. Even if that weren't the case, I won't let you out of my sight until Martin is arrested."

I shivered again; the picture of Gwen impaled was imprinted on my mind. "Make it soon, Mitch."

He said nothing, just looked at me sadly.

"Can we go? I don't want to stay here any longer than necessary. I may never stay here again."

"I don't blame you," he agreed. "It is a shame, though. This place is very nice." He walked into the living room and began to turn off the lights. As he passed the wall of pictures, he stopped and surveyed them. "These are wonderful. But I don't recognize this one. I mean, I know it's a Van Gogh, but I don't believe I've ever seen this particular picture."

"You probably haven't, Mitch. I, well, it's sort of a family heirloom. We acquired it at an estate auction, quite a bargain, I was told."

"It's the original?" he exclaimed in astonishment. "You have an original Van Gogh and have the nerve to tell me it was a bargain? It must be worth a small fortune."

I shrugged. "It is, I'm sure. But the picture was bought during the Depression. Times were hard, people were anxious to recoup their losses, even if it meant selling something as precious as this." I wanted to tell him how precious it really was, how I had risked my life in the daylight to acquire it. How when I looked at it, I felt almost human again.

I had fed for five straight days prior to the auction, trying to build up my strength for the ordeal. Fortunately the day was overcast and the estate shaded with large trees. I had sat under one of these trees, swathed in yards of material. The bidding had been almost as fierce as the ravaging of the sun's rays. But I was determined to get it and get it I did. And though I lay in bed, burnt and shriveled for a week afterward until my skin finally healed, I never doubted for a minute that it had been worth the cost.

"Deirdre." I tore my gaze away from the painting to see his eyes warm with concern. "Let me get you out of here."

I nodded and accepted his support. He reached for the light switch but took one final look at the wall. "It's so beautiful," he said, as we left the room.

I couldn't lock the door—the key had been taken away with Gwen's effects; I merely adjusted the curtain to hide the entrance once again. As I did this, I realized that I would never return here, not to sleep, not even to work. Gwen's death had cruelly severed any ties I had with this place. The office would be closed and the business sold. I could leave this portion of my life now with little regret.

As we slowly walked to the elevators, I studied Mitch's profile in the near darkness. He had come to mean so much to me during the few days we had spent together. I could hardly visualize what my life would be like without him when I finally had to leave. For I would have to go, I knew, and as the elevator car began its downward journey, I sighed. He gave me a sad smile and put his arm around my shoulders, drawing me closer. I would miss Gwen desperately, though I truly believed she was in a better world. I would miss the daily grind of the fashion industry, the hectic deadlines and even the demanding clients, yet there were other ways I could fill my time. But as for leaving Mitch . . . I sighed again as the doors opened and we went to the street to his car. *Oh, God,* I thought, *leaving Mitch will be one of the hardest things I will ever do.*

Chapter 14

It was just after midnight when Mitch completed his work at the station. Then I persuaded him to return with me to the hotel to gather some of my clothes and personal effects. By the time we finally arrived at his apartment it was after one. That he was exhausted, mentally and physically, was apparent from the way he dragged up the steps, stumbled in the door and slumped on the couch. I set my case down in the hallway and sat in a chair facing him.

"What happens now?" I asked quietly, hating to disturb him.

"What?" He sat up straighter and looked at me. "Oh, I'm sorry, Deirdre. I'm absolutely beat."

"I know," I said sympathetically. "Is there any way I can help?"

"For now, no. I need to get some sleep. We've got men out looking for Larry now and all of his normal haunts are under surveillance. If he shows up, they'll let me know."

"And if he doesn't show up?" I somehow felt there was more that could be done and the question sounded sharper than I had intended. I glimpsed a flash of anger in his eyes.

"Then, tomorrow, we try to flush him out. I can't do anything else about it tonight. And neither can you." As suddenly as it arrived, the anger died and he smiled wearily. "You should get some rest, too, if you can. There will be plenty for you to do tomorrow." He walked over to me and lightly held my arms.

"Right now you can help me most by just staying here, with me. Will you be able to sleep?"

I nodded. "I think so. You go ahead. I'll be in a little later."

He gave me a lazy kiss and hug and turned to go, unbuttoning his shirt. As he walked down the hall I watched him with a tenderness that still surprised me. I wanted nothing more tonight than his presence. I would forego for a while my plans of vengeance and do as he wished. With a sigh, I picked up my suitcase and followed him.

He had discarded his clothes into a rumpled pile. After I folded each garment and draped them over a nearby chair, I quietly slid into bed next to him. He was asleep already, his breathing slow and regular. I could not get the picture of Gwen's corpse out of my mind. I replayed the night over and over, receiving no answers, no comfort. "Damn," I swore and turned over roughly. Mitch jumped in his sleep and lifted his head to regard me with sleepy eyes. "Go back to sleep," I soothed him, staring into his eyes. "Everything will be fine."

Nothing is fine, my mind raged and the promises I had made to him and to myself about not getting involved dissolved into the picture of Gwen, staked to my bed. I reached over and took his face in mine. Smiling, I strove to touch his mind with mine. "Everything is fine, Mitch," I repeated again. "Sleep now, I will be with you tonight, all night. I will not leave, I will stay with you all night. Sleep now."

He relaxed and his eyes closed. "Sleep now," he murmured. "You will be here." I released his face and he rolled over and went back to sleep. Ever so quietly, I slid from his bed, dressed in the black pants and sweater I had packed, smoothed on my black leather gloves and went out the door.

The night was glorious—clear and cold, with no moon. The streets I traveled were dark and shadowy and took me to an alley behind Larry's apartment. Easing around the corner, I saw the car stationed outside; the shadowy figure inside lit a cigarette and I could smell the rich tobacco from where I stood. I did not need the lowered hum of the radio to identify Mitch's surveillance team. But there was only one in the car and I realized that there must be two.

Where was the other one? Silently, I listened to the sounds of the night, the traffic noises, the muffled sounds from within the surrounding buildings. With an effort of will, I blocked these sounds and tuned them out. There, there he was. I heard the quiet breathing of a man standing just inside the entrance. He stamped his feet, and the scratchy sound of knit gloves rubbing together drifted back to me.

From the personnel file in Max's office I knew that Larry Martin lived on the third floor. I assessed the back walls of the building, laughing silently to myself. Too bad, I thought, too bad that I can't turn into a bat or a mist. Then I could be in and out with no one the wiser. But I thought I could manage the climb.

Somewhere in the back of my mind, a voice urged me to back off, to walk down the dark, beautiful streets and return to Mitch and the warm bed that awaited me. But I had become reckless with rage at Gwen's death, almost as if her death had set me free of the final restraints of humanity. That's not true, my mind prodded, if you care that much you are still human.

"Nevertheless," I whispered to the night sky, "I will go." I slipped off my shoes and set them at the side of the wall; I removed my gloves and put them into my pocket. A thrill of excitement, akin to the hunt and capture of a victim, enveloped me. My senses vibrated, my teeth enlarged. A severe hunger and restlessness overtook me and I began to climb, slowly at first and then with more confidence, my fingers and toes clinging tightly to the coarse surface of the bricks.

Before I knew it, I was halfway up the wall. My balance was superb and I scaled the rest of the distance effortlessly. It was a simple matter to complete the climb, find an open window and ease myself in. As my feet touched the floor, I suppressed the impulse to laugh—so easy, it was so easy.

Walking down the hall, I found his apartment. I suspect I could have identified it even had the number not matched that found in Max's personnel file; Larry's familiar odor permeated the hall directly outside the door. I put my gloves back on and rashly turned the knob, not caring if he were inside or not. The door was locked but I twisted the knob again, harder this time; the lock broke and the door opened. I looked up and down the hall before I entered—no one had seen me.

Closing the door softly behind me, I glanced around. It was empty, as I knew before I had even taken one step inside. There were only three rooms; I checked the kitchen first, grimacing as a roach ran over my bare foot. The bathroom, next; there was nothing here that would indicate his involvement. If there was any evidence, it would have to be in the main room, that served as both a sleeping and a living area. "But not for long." I bared my teeth at my reflection in the window as I passed.

His bookshelves held a large assortment of paperback books. I took a second look at these and was not really surprised to find that every one of them were vampire novels; he had them all, from the classics to the tawdry. Most of them I had read and discarded for their uselessness, but from their worn appearance I could tell that Larry had read each one thoroughly several times.

There were two stacks of books, horizontally arranged on the end of one of the shelves; the fact that they were out of line with the rest caught my eye. I moved one of the stacks and saw behind it not the wood of the case but the leather binding of a larger book. Pulling it out, I almost dropped it in shock. The cover was black, blood-red letters emblazoned the surface with the name, Dorothy Grey. My hands trembled and I longed to tear off the confining gloves, but I knew that I did not dare.

The first page held an old, worn picture, in sepia tone. A group of union soldiers, stern and unsmiling, stood around a tent. It could have been any encampment in that war, but I knew these men. Some had died in my arms, some I had even helped along their way. Looking closer, I saw myself, gaunt and glassy-eyed, peering out from within the tent. Underneath the picture Larry had written, "The first appearance of Dorothy Grey, The Angel of Death."

"Jesus, he knows." I slid down to the floor, grasping the scrapbook to my chest. "How the hell could he know?" I frantically rifled through the pages; many of my lives and identities were charted here—names, towns, occupations. Oh, he had missed some, but those he had captured were correct and completely damaging. What had he planned to do with this, I wondered, what possible purpose could it serve for him? None, now, I affirmed, for I would take it with me and burn it.

The last few pages he used as a journal, and when I read them, his purpose suddenly became clear. He was searching for eternal life; he wanted to become a vampire. Nowhere did Larry explain how he had learned the truth about me, but his aspirations were plainly expressed. His obsession with me went further than love or lust; beyond all of that, he longed to live forever, longed to walk the night, powerful and invincible. I was merely the key to his desire.

I snapped the book shut and stood up again, searching the room and finding a backpack. I unzipped it, emptied its contents onto the floor and put the book inside. As I did so, a scrap of paper fell out. On it was written simply "the blood is the life" and the address of the blood bank that had been robbed.

I let the paper lay where it had fallen. On impulse, I crossed the room and went back to the kitchen. The roaches scattered from the light as I opened the refrigerator. Inside were a dozen bags of blood, neatly labeled and stacked. I wondered if he thought that he could become a vampire simply by drinking the blood or if he were merely stockpiling in the event that I fulfilled his desires. He will never get to use them at all, I thought and removed all but two of them, and, hoping that the plastic would resist punctures, stowed them into the backpack along with the book. Then with a grim smile, I found a piece of paper and a pencil. "My dearest Larry," I wrote, "thank you for dinner. Watch for me, I will be back." I felt a deadly rush of satisfaction as I taped the note to the refrigerator door and left the apartment.

* * *

Getting back into Mitch's place was no problem, but as I quietly shut the door and set the backpack down on the floor, I realized that I would have to leave. I glanced at the clock; it was already after five, too much of the night had been lost at Larry's apartment. After checking to see that Mitch still slept, I began to make my plans. The evidence that I now possessed must never be seen, especially by him. And Larry must die. I had never killed before and the decision was anathema to me, but there would be no choice in the matter. For now, though, I had to seek safe harbor. I could not return to the hotel or to the office; Mitch would most certainly look for me there. And I could not allow myself to be found, not yet.

I walked back down the hallway and stood above Mitch's bed. The lights from the street shone in through the window and illuminated his sleeping features. "Damn it, Mitch. It would have been easier to have never met you." Even as I said it, I knew it was not true. No matter the outcome, my love for him was real and uplifting, a memory I could cherish in however many countless years I had remaining. There would be other lovers in my future, but none like him.

He rolled over and spoke. "Deirdre?" He was still half-asleep.

"I'm here, Mitch."

"Why aren't you in bed?"

"I have to go to the bathroom. Relax, go to sleep."

When he settled back in, I quietly picked up my suitcase and left the room; if I stayed any longer, I would be lost, in more ways than one.

I did stay long enough to write another note. Taking care to write in block letters so that the paper left at Larry's would not be connected, I wrote: "Mitch—although your protective custody is wonderful, I find I must get away. Please don't worry about me or try to find me. Trust me, I will stay safe and I will contact you as soon as I can. I love you."

The sky was becoming cloudy when I went back to the streets. I hurried three blocks away from Mitch's apartment and went into a convenience store to make a phone call.

"Answer it, damn it. Answer it," I urged, as the phone rang for the tenth time. Finally, on the twentieth ring, a surprisingly alert voice answered, "Yes."

"Max, thank God you're there."

"Deirdre, to what do I owe the honor? I would have thought that after our last meeting, it would be a cold day in hell before you called on me again."

"If so, then I guess Satan is skiing right now. Max, look, I really need your help."

"My help?" His voice took on a grieved tone, but I could hear the humor underlying it. "And what about the intrepid Detective Greer, his shoulders are not as broad as you thought, eh? Or maybe he discovered the truth about you and threw you out on your blood-sucking ass." I had mistaken the humor; these last words were spoken in a hiss, as if through clenched teeth, and Max never stooped to vulgarity unless angered.

"Jesus, Max. I'm serious, I need your help. Can I count on you or shall I call someone else?"

"And just whom would you call, my dear? It seems to me your options are very limited. They must be, for you to come to me."

He was right, I realized in shock as I ran through a very short list in my mind: Gwen, dead; Mitch, unapproachable; Larry, unthinkable. No, there was only Max now. There was always the option of checking into a hotel, but I needed to talk the situation over with someone. And given the circumstances, that person could only be Max. I sighed.

"Max"—there was a pleading in my voice that made me cringe—"I have backed myself into a corner and don't know how to get out. We have been friends for so many years, and I need your help. As far as the other night, well, maybe we could make amends and start over."

"An interesting concept, this starting over. But you don't need to beg, you know." There was a pause and he gave a low chuckle. "Of course you can count on me, Deirdre. Have I ever let you down before?"

I gave a small humorless laugh. "Several times that I can think of, but that doesn't matter. All I need is a safe place to sleep tomorrow. Then I'll be on my way."

"Deirdre, my love, I would be pleased to have you stay with me. When can I expect you?"

"I'll be there in ten minutes." I hung up the phone.

The Ballroom of Romance was closed and dark when I arrived. It seemed so odd, I had never seen it this way. Even before it had opened, there had been a crowd of builders and contractors working through the night. Now it had a forlorn and sinister appearance that was not in any way alleviated by opening of the front door. Max, looking extremely disheveled, shirtless and barefooted, stood in the unlit doorway, and beckoned me in.

"Did I wake you? I'm sorry, but I wouldn't have bothered you if it wasn't crucial."

He shrugged and led me back to his office. "It is never any bother for you." He began to open a bottle of my favorite wine. "Would you care for a drink?"

"Yes, why not? But first, I am very hungry."

He gave me a twisted smile. "I'm afraid I have no one available at the moment. Shall I send out? Or would you like to open my veins?"

I sat down on his couch, threw my head back and laughed. "A fair offer, I suppose, but this time I brought my own." I reached down, unzipped the backpack and held out one of the bags.

"You are getting enterprising in your old age, Deirdre. Of course, I heard about the robbery but really had no idea you were behind it." He took the bag from me and gingerly balanced it on his hand. "Theft doesn't seem your style."

"I did not rob the blood bank. Tonight I dine on the generosity of our good friend, Larry.

"Larry? What the hell is he doing with stolen blood? And you saw him; he gave that to you?"

"Not actually, no. Although he once suggested we have dinner together. So I suppose you could say I decided to take him up on the invitation. Is it my fault that he wasn't at home when I called?"

"You broke into his apartment?" Max made no attempt to hide his amusement. "Moral little Deirdre? The one who is always concerned with the right and wrong of things? Shame on you, my dear. And what would Detective . . ."

"You leave him out of it." I snarled the words and took the blood bag from his hand. "I have a very interesting story to tell you, Max. But first things first."

I walked to the bar and selected a large glass, then walked to his desk and removed a pair of scissors from the top drawer. Clipping the end of the bag, I poured the blood into the glass and held it up admiringly to the light. "To your health."

He had put on a shirt and was buttoning it, but stopped to watch intently while I drank. The amount in the bag was only slightly more than I would normally take from a living victim. It was not an unacceptable substitute, but by the time I reached the end of the glass, it was cool and thickening. Next time, I thought, it should be warmed. Still I tipped it back again to get the very last drop from the bottom of the glass, before I went to the bar to rinse it out and refill it with the wine Max had opened.

When I sat back down, he tucked in his shirt and glanced at the clock. "We have an hour or so before dawn, you are fed and my blood is safe, perhaps now you would like to tell me what's happening."

In answer I reached again into the backpack and pulled out the scrapbook. "Larry has done more than provide a meal; he has also given me this." I smiled bitterly. "At least now we know what he's been researching."

His eyebrows raised when he saw the name on the cover. "May I?" He reached his hand out and I gave the book to him.

Slowly, Max turned the pages, reading each entry completely. At some he paused and laughed, others he read intently. He spent a lot of time on one page, not reading, just staring. I leaned over to see what it was. "Diane Gleason," he said, meeting my eyes. "You were so young, then."

I gave a snort of indignation. "Young? That's the second time you have referred to me as young. At that time, you must remember, I was already a hundred years old."

"No," he said sadly. "Your whole outlook was young. You were vibrant, carefree and utterly enticing. You did what you wanted, when you wanted and everyone else be damned. You had no ties, no ambition, just an endless lust for new horizons. What happened to that spirit?"

"If I remember correctly, it got abused by many people, including you. It was you who left, without so much as a spoken good-bye."

"Are you still angry about that? You're the one who's so quick to remind me it was a long time ago. And we are still together, we are still friends, as you call it."

I got up and poured us both another glass of wine. He continued his reading, acknowledging my offer of the wine with a quick gesture to the table next to his chair. I set it down and walked over to look out the window. Neither of us spoke until I saw the sky begin to lighten with the dawn.

"Max," I began. "The sun is almost up."

"I know, my dear." He stood up and handed the scrapbook back to me. "We'll talk more about this tomorrow evening. You can sleep in the back lounge; no one will bother you, I promise." He smiled and with a gallantry strange for him, held out his arm. "Come, I'll walk you home."

He picked up my suitcase, opened the door and escorted me out, my hand lightly gripping his arm. I suddenly felt comfortable with him again, he was no threat to me. His knowledge of what I was had not impacted our relationship, perhaps it had even intensified it. True, he was not Mitch, but that was for the best. There was no place for me in Mitch's life, and all the love that I felt for him would not change me. With Max, there was still, if not the spark, then a chance that we could once again . . .

I shook my head and wondered at the direction my thoughts were taking. I love Mitch, I asserted, no matter how badly it might all turn out.

Max smiled at me as he opened the door to the lounge. It was a sensuous, knowing smile as if he had read my thoughts of him. And perhaps he did; he was perceptive enough to pick up my body language, my renewed ease in his presence.

"Well, here we are."

I walked in, placed the book on the couch and turned around. He carried my case in and put it on the floor. "Thank you, Max. It was good of you to take me in."

"Think nothing of it, Deirdre." A shadow fell over his face for only a moment before it was replaced with his usual cynical expression. "I suppose my spending the, er, day with you is out of the question?"

"I am so very tired, Max. It has been a rough night."

"Ah, well, then." His gaze fastened on my lips and he moved toward me. I expected him to grasp me and kiss me; instead, I felt his lips graze my cheek lightly. "I hope you don't mind using the couch. Sleep well." He walked out and closed the door.

I went to the window and pulled the curtains closed. They were heavy, well insulated and should provide the proper protection. Then, after locking the door, and opening the suitcase, I began to undress. The nightgown packed had been for Mitch's benefit—black silk, with a plunging neckline and a billowing skirt. I felt silly wearing it here, with no one to see it, but it was all I had.

Max had thoughtfully set out a blanket and a pillow on one corner of the couch. In spite of his earlier protests on the phone, I felt that he was probably pleased that I had turned to him. He had done his best to make me feel welcome and comfortable in what was an awkward situation for the both of us. I laughed when I remembered the time he had introduced himself as my Renfield to a confused victim. He was more than that to me, of course. I had never thought of him as my servant, but, and I wondered again about my thoughts in the hall, we could never rekindle our intimate relationship. Even if I had not met Mitch, I had to move on, I needed to move on, and there would be no place for Max in my future.

I looked at the phone hanging on the wall. How easy it would be to call Mitch and let him know that I was safe, that all was well and that I loved him. Crossing the floor, I picked up the phone and dialed his number, but hung up before it rang. You have no place for Mitch, either, I reminded myself and lay down on the couch.

Many years of practice, many years of life had taught me that no problems could be solved in sleeplessness. Once again, I cleared my mind of all thoughts, pleasant or otherwise, and fell asleep just as the sun rose.

Chapter 15

When I woke it was almost an hour to sunset. I dressed, went to the bar and opened a bottle of wine. Then I sat down and began to read Larry's scrapbook.

The hardest page to get past was the first; that Civil War photograph that I can remember being taken as vividly as if it were yesterday. Here I walked in my real life, my own time. And although I was a vampire, I did not yet think of myself as an ageless freak, a walking anachronism. It took the erosion of my soul by many years to do that, the frantic passage of time and man's progress. In this time, there was no progress, or if there was it was a slow and gentle evolution, unnoticed as days rolled one into the other. It was my era and I still ached for it.

But not for the war; although Max often laughed, saying that such a time must have been a paradise for vampires. I grew to know death, to live with it during this time, but I never gained acceptance of it. Each lost life was deeply mourned by me, who could never die.

They were young, younger than me; they were my lovers, my brothers. They would come to me for advice, to read me that long-awaited letter from a wife or mother. They would come to me in fear and dread, facing impending battles and skirmishes, and I would offer comfort where I could, with my body mostly, giving some of them the only chance they would have for a woman's love. Looking back, I am amazed that I had no qualms about this, being a woman of that time, marrying as a virgin and expecting no other man in my life than my husband. But he was gone and I was damned. And their need of me was great, so great that it often engulfed my own. The grasping hands, the suckling mouth, the young, strong bodies desperate for the touch of life on a field of death.

I gave what I could, and when they returned wounded, blood-ied and dying, I nursed them with a gentle patience. The field doctors knew that they could rely on me no matter what the situation; I had no delicacy that could be offended and strength enough for the necessary tasks.

After the first two battles, we had tents devoted to the dying and wounded. Here at night I walked, carrying a softly glowing lantern, the quiet swishing of skirts announcing my presence. For the recovering soldiers I had a smile or a soft greeting. The feverish I soothed with my cool hands and voice, sometimes reading until they fell asleep. For the dying, and it became pain-fully easy to recognize those who would not survive the night, I offered a release from pain and a slow draining into a quiet death. Angel they had called me then, even those who in passion had called me devil and witch, with their hands entangled in my hair and their bodies joined to mine.

Out of the group photographed, only one was still alive when I left. As I traveled from camp to camp, and battle to battle, I often thought of him, wondering who would comfort him, who would ease him into death. Soon each soldiers' face became blurred for me: there were so many, so many.

Damn Larry, I thought, brushing aside the tears that were flowing. I was violated, raped by his capture of my essence on these pages. His matter-of-fact captions, the cold stating of facts, names and occupations, reduced my life to nothing but blood and death. And it had been more than that, I knew. There had been friends and laughter, good times intermingled with the bad. I turned the pages and lingered over some—a newspaper photograph of night-shift steel workers during World War II, including one Doreen Gallagher; the employment records of Deborah Garrison who worked in an all-night diner, as had Diane Gleason; the police log on Dorothy Grey who made her reappearance as a prostitute in the sleepy, southern town from which Max had finally rescued her for reincarnation as Deirdre Griffin.

I had to admire Larry for his dedication to this task, even while hating him and questioning his motives. It cannot have been an easy job, tracing and tracking me through the decades. The gaps, bitterly notated by him as turning up nothing, gave me a grim laugh. Most of these were times when I went into hiding, living in some cases as an animal, dirty and homeless, occupying caves or abandoned shacks, running from my previous lives. Running, not in fear, but in regret and sadness for times and people that grew old and died. I hoped these gaps had worried him, tortured him, and stolen from him some of the satisfaction he must have felt for pinning me down so accurately.

The last page I ignored; his plans and aspirations I had already read the previous evening. I needed no reminder of the twisted mind that was trying to force me into doing something I had never done, something that I now had no wish to ever do. He would not become a vampire at my hands; I would kill or be killed before I allowed someone else to share in what he called the gift of life. For me it was nothing but a curse, an unnaturalness, a perversion of the beauty of humanity.

I closed the book, put it into my suitcase and locked it. By now the sun had set and I was free to go. Opening the door, I walked down the hall toward Max's office when suddenly I ducked into the adjoining room. From here the angry voices were audible and easy to identify.

"Okay, Hunter, I'll ask it again. Where is she?"

"And I will tell you again, Detective. If she had wanted you to know, don't you think she would have told you?"

"I know she must be here, I can feel it. I must see her, you must tell me where she is. Her life is in danger . . ."

Max laughed, long and loud. "Deirdre is perfectly capable of taking care of herself, I assure you. If you only knew how ridiculously unnecessary your protection is, you would laugh, too."

"And was it ridiculous for Gwen?"

"Gwen?" Max's questioning tone was sincere; I had not had the time to tell him about Gwen.

"Deirdre's secretary. Your psycho employee drove a stake through her heart."

"A singularly horrible way to die. But what has that got to do with Deirdre?"

Mitch's voice acquired a deadly patience as if he were speaking to a child. "Don't you understand? He means to do the same to her. He's left messages for her, taunting her, threatening her. And if he finds her she'll die, can't you see that?"

"Of course she would die, anyone would." Max was hedging now; playing this scene coolly, uncertain of what I had revealed to Mitch. "But he has to find her first, doesn't he? She is not easy to be found, if she chooses not to be."

"You don't care, do you? Deirdre tells me that you are her oldest and dearest friend, yet you would just stand by and let her be killed. How could you not care, not love her?"

"Love?" Max was angry now, his voice cold and frightening. "I knew it would come down to that, when you came here. You and all the others, mooning and slobbering over her, begging for an introduction, singing her praises, her beauty, her charm. She is beyond you, Greer, beyond all of you. And you could never keep her, never hold her to you for any more time than she wants to be held." His voice quieted and sounded now more sad than angry. "Don't you think I know that? I have lived with that fact since the day we met."

There was a long pause; then I could hear the clink of ice cubes in a glass and the pouring of a liquid. What the hell were they doing, toasting my death? Silently commemorating a woman they both loved and lost?

Mitch was the next to speak; his manner seemed different, as if over their drinks he and Max had reached some agreement. "Sorry, Hunter, I just wasn't thinking. What do you think I should do? How can I protect her if I can't find her?"

"Wait," Max advised. "Just wait. She'll return, perhaps here, perhaps at her hotel. I assure you, she won't be hurt. Larry doesn't want her dead."

"I wish I were as sure as you. If you hear from her, please let me know." Another brief pause and he continued. "Here are my numbers, at the station and at home. Call anytime."

I heard the door open and listened to Mitch's footsteps heading down the hall and out into the bar. I waited for a minute, but when they did not return I knew he was gone. I left the room and went next door to Max's office.

He was sitting at his desk and did not look up when I entered and locked the door behind me. "I trust you slept well, my dear. Your friend, Mitchell Greer, was looking for you.

"So I gathered," I said dryly. "He was quite vocal about it."

"Ah, you heard. Then I need not relate the event in all its pathos for you, do I?"

"You did quite well, Max. Never saying too much, not letting on that you knew anything about me or my whereabouts. I found your last statements quite touching."

"They were not meant for your ears, Deirdre." The usual scorn was back in his voice, and his face, when he lifted it to me, held his normal smile. "But they were at least effective in removing him from my office. I assume he's still lurking around, however, so if you don't want to meet him, be careful."

"I will."

"Does it give you pleasure, Deirdre?" He asked it with an agreeable smile, as if asking about the weather.

"What?"

"How you manage to enslave every man you meet, with a kiss or a look or a promise. Larry is now wanted for murder—a murder that your presence caused him to commit. And as for Greer, well, you've known him for less than two weeks now, already he would kill for you or die for you. I know his type, incorruptible and clean, he cannot be bribed or coerced and would never allow his personal feelings to interfere with his job. And yet you have managed to tear him down, rip through the veneer and reduce him to an almost savage state. And you pride yourself on your morals, your conscience, on how you have never taken a life. But he will love you until the day he dies and never realize that to you it was just a pleasant way to pass the time."

I stared at him in shock for a moment. "But, Max, I thought you knew." I hesitated. "I was sure you could tell."

"Tell what?"

"That I love him."

"Love, again? First Greer and now you. And where can you hope it will lead?"

"It will lead nowhere, but I can't help the way I feel. This is real, this is now. Tomorrow can take care of itself."

"Spare me the saccharin. I don't know what your plans are, but you may stay here as long as you wish. As one of your oldest and dearest friends, I could never deny you. Make yourself at home; I've got to get to work now."

"Well, damn," I said as he walked out. Nothing was turning out as I had expected.

I wanted to scream or throw something, in an effort to release the pain that Max's words had caused me. Instead, I walked over and sat at his desk, glancing at the few papers on its surface, idly flipping the directory that held names and numbers of employees, suppliers and important customers. All the time my mind was racing, considering the truth of his words.

What he failed to realize, I finally decided, was that the situation was as painful for me as for anyone else. I loved and the loss of that love would hurt me deeply, perhaps even more than it would Mitch. For he could return to his life, and as he aged, the pain would lessen, eventually ceasing with his death. I, on the other hand, carried with me every loss, every love, magnified and multiplied like the links in Marley's chain.

"Damn," I said again and jumped when the phone beside me rang.

"Ballroom of Romance," I answered, my voice surprisingly pleasant and calm.

There was a pause at the end of the line. "Hello," I said. "May I help you?"

"You know you can." My pulse jumped at his voice—here was one, at least, that gave me reason to continue for a while in this life. Or gave me hope of release.

"Larry."

"Did you get my message?"

"Yes. Did you get mine?"

"Loud and clear, Dorothy. I want to see you. I want . . ."

"I know what you want, Larry. You won't get it."

"But you will meet with me?"

"Yes."

His breathing quickened and I could feel his impatience over the line. "Tonight, midnight, in the cellar of the Ballroom."

"How charmingly melodramatic, Larry. You can expect me."

I hung up the phone. Here was the final test, I thought. Could I kill him, to protect myself and avenge a friend? Or would I allow him to take the life, that, despite my disgust and despair, I had tenaciously clung to for so many years? I checked the clock—there were four hours to wait.

Max had left the office door open, I could hear the band begin to play, the voices of the people gathered. I walked through the kitchen, pushed open service doors and stood at the end of the bar. Mitch was still there, standing by the main entrance, his eyes scanning the dancers. I felt that the next four hours could very easily be spent watching this man who had so unexpectedly come into my life, giving me one more chance to feel my humanity.

"Wine, Miss Griffin?"

I nodded absently to the bartender, never taking my eyes from Mitch's shadowy form. The band had finished playing one of my favorite songs, and I wondered how long it would take him to find me among the crowd. The bartender brought my drink; perhaps it was the movement that called his attention to me, perhaps he could sense me the way I could him. It didn't seem to matter; he had found me, and after my flight of last night, I wanted to be found. Before the night was over, I would be a murderer in fact, or dead; these last few hours were best spent with him.

Ignoring the drink before me, I crossed over to the band and whispered my request. The leader nodded and began the song again as I reached Mitch's side. I put my finger to my lips and led him to the dance floor.

"Where have you been?"

"Quiet, Mitch. I'm here now." Nestling my head against his shoulder, I closed my eyes and began to hum softly. His body relaxed and responded to mine, and we danced.

When the song was over, he held me for a time and looked down into my face and smiled. I could still see anger in his eyes, anger at my desertion of him last night, but the relief at finding me alive finally won out. He kissed me and we danced one more number before we returned to the dark corner of the bar.

"Your regular table is ready if you'd like, Miss Griffin." The bartender nodded his head toward Max who was standing at the other end of the bar, watching us with an amused expression on his face. "We weren't expecting you tonight, but now that you're here, Max says everything's on the house." He picked up my wine and a bottle of beer for Mitch and showed us to the table.

"What does he mean, not expecting you?" Mitch asked after we were seated.

"I usually call ahead to let them know I'm coming. It's always so crowded . . ."

"No, Hunter knew you were here all along. I could swear he did."

"Contrary to what you believe, Mitch, I do not report to Max or anyone. I come and go as I please. And if this is another excuse to start your usual tirade about Max, I do not want to hear it, not tonight."

"Actually, Max and I have come to an understanding."

"Oh?" I smiled wryly. "That must have been quite a task."

He looked at me and shook his head. "What I should have

said is that I have come to understand Max. He loves you, you know."

I laughed. "Max loves me? Are we talking about the same person?"

"I'm serious, Deirdre. I still don't like the guy, he still makes my skin crawl, but I have no doubt of how he feels about you. And I feel sorry for him. Almost as sorry as I feel for myself."

"Why should you feel sorry for yourself?"

"Because, oh, hell, let's just forget it, okay?"

I took a drink of my wine and dropped my eyes. "Max doesn't love me. He may have wanted you to believe he did, for whatever devious purpose he had in mind. He's like that, a manipulator, not happy unless he's pulling someone's strings. But he knows me too well to love me."

Mitch reached over and took my hand. "I love you. What on earth could make you think that if someone knows you, they couldn't love you?"

"How well do you know me, Mitch? Do you know where I was born, what my parents' names were, what I wanted to be when I grew up?"

"You know damn well you're too bloody secretive for me to know anything about you. But if you'd like to play twenty questions, I'll start. Where were you born?"

"Fort Leavenworth, Kansas."

"Your parents' names?"

"Robert and Eleanor Grey."

"Grey? Then Griffin was your husband's name?"

"No, I changed it for professional reasons."

"Well, then, Deirdre Grey, what did you want to be when you grew up?"

"A nurse. And the name is Dorothy."

"Dorothy? Okay, I can live with that."

I smiled over at him. "I really do prefer Deirdre after all this time."

"Fine with me; you don't seem much like a Dorothy, anyway.

Now, I know all that and I still love you. What can be so awful about you that I wouldn't love you?"

"Look, I'm sorry I even brought this up. It doesn't matter."

Suddenly his eyes clouded over with anger. "It does matter, and I've decided that I like this game. Let's continue, shall we? Why did you leave me last night when you knew it was important for you to stay? You did promise to stay. Where did you go and what did you do?"

"I felt trapped. I needed to walk. I told you, I'm not used to reporting in to anyone. And although I hate to say it, that includes you, also."

"But your life was in jeopardy, didn't you realize that?"

"My life is only in jeopardy in your mind, Mitch." I gave a small derisive laugh. "Larry won't hurt me. I'm perfectly capable of handling him."

"Why is everyone trying to convince me that you're Wonder Woman or something? Max said pretty much the same thing, earlier. And I will tell you what I told him. Don't you think Gwen thought the same thing? You see where it got her."

Poor Gwen, I thought sadly, in over her head and she never knew it. "Gwen was different. She was sweet, innocent and trusting. I am none of those. When I next meet Larry, I will be fully prepared to do what needs to be done."

"When you next meet Larry I will be with you. And hopefully he will be behind bars at the time."

"Then there's no need to discuss it, is there?"

He shrugged. "Let's get out of here, anyway. I don't like the thought of your being so visible and accessible."

I laughed. "Calm down, he's hardly likely to jump up from between the dancers and drive a stake through my heart right here, Mitch. This seems to be as safe to me as anywhere. But if you have to go, don't let me stop you."

"I don't have to go, I'm not on duty now. Just on alert. And if they need me, they know where I am."

I finished my wine and, as if on cue, a waiter brought me

another glass and Mitch another beer. He raised his eyebrows in disbelief. "Is service always so good?"

"For me it is. Let's dance."

Later in the evening, Max came over and sat with us for a while. It seemed odd to have Mitch relaxed around him, he even excused himself to go to the bathroom, leaving us alone. I checked the clock, there was an hour to go.

Max saw my glance. "Going somewhere, my dear?"

Hurriedly, I spoke, while studying the door for Mitch's return. "Actually, I have another appointment at twelve. It shouldn't take long, but I would prefer him not to know about it."

"And you'd like me to cover for you? Draw him away from you so that you can leave and come back, with him none the wiser?"

I nodded. "Can you?"

"Hasn't he informed you that he and I are comrades-in-arms now? It is so rarely that I get to make a friend, this duplicity could spoil our relationship." He smiled at me, enjoying my discomfort.

"Jesus, Max. You know as well as I that that's all just something you dreamed up. You and Mitch, friends?"

"Yes, well, then I will do as you ask. Will 11:45 give you enough time to get where you are going?"

"No problem."

"And where are you going? With whom are you meeting?"

"It's all very mysterious, Max," I said with an impudent grin. "Our very dear friend called for an assignation in the cellar at midnight."

"Happy hunting, Deirdre, and be careful." He rose as soon as Mitch returned and lightly kissed me on the cheek.

"What are you hunting, Deirdre?" His forehead had a little crease of worry that I hadn't noticed before.

I reached over the table, took his hand and pressed it to my face. "Why you, of course."

Chapter 16

Max had never done anything in a small way before, so it shouldn't have surprised me the lengths to which he went to fulfill my request. Promptly at 11:45 the fire alarm rang; panic began to grasp the people in the club. Mitch could not resist getting involved, to calm everyone and organize an orderly exodus from the club. I slipped up to the service doors, waited for the staff to leave and opened the door in the kitchen that led to the cellars of the Ballroom of Romance.

As I descended the steps, I took the time to unscrew the lightbulb and throw it to the floor. Its delicate shattering would have announced my presence but for the sound of the fire alarm still blaring upstairs. I had as long as the alarm continued, I knew, before Mitch would come looking for me. Make it last, I prayed when I got to the bottom of the stairway. I have things to say that I don't want him to hear.

The fact that I had never been here before was to my disadvantage, but I thought that well balanced with the lack of direct lighting. My night vision was perfect; Larry could hardly say the same. I walked down one of the rows of shelves and positioned myself up against the wall, so that I could see him enter. Then I collected my thoughts, and began to plan my method of attack.

I would try to reason with him first, I decided. If I could convince him that his quest was futile, that what he asked for was not a blessing and not a gift, then I could wipe his mind clean of any remembrance of me and what I was. I would need to draw his blood for that, so that the suggestion would go deep enough to block everything. Fine, I thought, and smiled into the darkness, my canines enlarging. He could then be turned over to the police and brought to justice for the death of Gwen. I trusted Mitch enough to know that he would be punished, perhaps even with the death penalty.

If none of that worked, I still had no doubt of my capacity to control him or overpower him. He was merely a human and I was what I was.

The alarm upstairs still continued and was, I realized, blocking any sounds I might have heard of his arrival. An uncontrollable chill possessed me. He could be here, now, and I might not know it. And what if all his posturing, all his ambitions were simply a front for his true intentions, to rid the world of a vampire? All of my plans allowed for some sort of interplay between us; what if he arrived, stake in hand and prepared for immediate murder? Could I stop him then?

In all my arrogance and complacency, the idea finally took hold; I may have made a mistake in accepting this meeting. Everything was conspiring against me, it seemed: the earsplitting alarm that took away my enhanced hearing, the fact that my opponent might know more about how to handle this situation than I.

It is not too late to run, my mind urged. I had come down early, he might not be here yet. Choking back my brief spell of panic, I took a step forward, heading toward the stairs. Under the blaring siren I could hear nothing but the low thudding of feet on the floor above. One of the thuds sounded close at hand and I shrunk back into my corner. But it was not followed by any other sound. I waited for a minute, alert and listening; all of the sounds seemed distant and non-threatening.

Now, I thought, *I can make the stairs and get Mitch.* Once Larry was in custody, I would be free. It was unlikely that any of his wild stories about me would be believed; I possessed the damaging evidence. Larry, on the other hand, was defenseless and likely to be taken for a raving lunatic, guaranteeing his incarceration for some time to come. With a breath of relief, I edged forward, listening, watching.

Suddenly the screech of the siren stopped, but it was too late for my escape. Larry had made his approach, silently and stealthily, now I felt his warm breath on the side of my neck. Whirling around, I faced him and he caught my wrists in his hands. I made no move, assessing the strength of his grip on me; he was stronger than I would have thought possible. And although I believed that I could break free should I wish to, I knew that when he held me, he could hold nothing else. No hammer, no stake.

My arsenal of weapons was always available. I smiled seductively at him, trying to meet his eyes. "Larry."

"You're early," he said in a husky voice.

"As are you." I tried to move closer to him, attempted to get my teeth on his neck, but he locked his arms and held me away from him.

"No tricks, Deirdre. I don't trust you, not yet. And I know you can do nothing to me if I don't look into your face." He moved his arm up, still gripping my hand, and stroked my cheek with his fist. "Such a lovely face, too."

"Then look at me, Larry." My voice was pitched low and urgent, a request to a lover.

"No."

I tried a different approach. "Larry, what you want, I have never done before. I don't know how to transform you; I don't even know if it is possible."

"It's possible, and you will do it."

"No, it is not a good thing. You don't want my life; it was forced on me, I had no choice. All those lonely years, Larry, you just can't visualize how horrible it can be. You're young, you have a good life ahead of you. Don't throw it away for this, it's not worth it. Believe me, I know."

His laughter echoed in the room. It sounded hollow, evil. "It's what I want. I've got nothing ahead of me now, don't you think

I know that. If you don't transform me, here and now, they will catch me and try me for murder." He laughed again and I shivered. "Then my good life consists of jail or death."

"You shouldn't have killed them, Larry. It was wrong."

"Them?" He shook my hands. "I only killed Gwen. She served her purpose well, of course, and for that I'm thankful."

"And her purpose was?"

His voice was calm, reasonable in his rationalization. "She made it possible for me to get you here, alone, with what I want."

"I would have come. You didn't need to kill her! And it did not need to be that way." I shuddered slightly and he laughed.

"But it was the most effective way of getting my message to you. Besides, let's be honest here, compared with all the others you have murdered over the years, what's one poor silly girl like Gwen?"

"I have never killed anyone."

"Never? I find that hard to believe. And I know for a fact it's not true."

"How could you?"

"You have my book. Did you wonder where that first picture came from? It's been in my family for generations, along with the story of the beautiful lady who bled and killed wounded soldiers. Always at night, always with a smile. My great-grandfather inherited the picture and the story from his father. He's the one on the far right. And I always assumed the story was embellished over the years, magnified to scare the children. But when I met you, I recognized you immediately. Then I stayed quiet, followed you, watched you. It wasn't hard to draw the conclusions I did. Or to track you over the years; all it took was belief. No one would think to look for a vampire, no one believes in you."

I made no attempt to justify my actions for him. His mind was made up and until he met my eyes or allowed me close enough to feed, I could only stand there, trapped by his strong hands.

"But I believe," he said, the tenderness of his voice at odds with the tense, violent stance of his body. "And I will be one. You must do it, take me and change me. I can fill the years for you, Deirdre. You will finally have someone who loves you, to stay with you forever."

"But . . ." I was about to say I didn't want him, could never love him. He felt my reluctance and tightened his grip on my wrists. I changed my tactics again. "But, Larry, my love, you must let me close enough to change you. I can hardly do it at arms' length."

He gave me a doubtful look, then shook his head. A lock of his hair fell over one eye and he impatiently brushed it aside, using his hand, still holding my wrist. I took advantage of the contact and stroked his hair and cheek before he dropped his arm.

"Oh, Larry. You don't understand, do you? I was only testing you, I had to make sure that your resolve was strong, your desire true. Because the whole time that you were watching me, I was watching you, wanting you, grooming you for immortality. Trust me, my love. You won't be sorry." I laughed, low and sexy, and he sighed with longing. "But you must let me get close to you. You'll like it," I purred. "It's an incredible experience. Better than love. Better than anything you can possibly imagine. I have so much to teach you, to show you. What would you like to know? Shall I tell you of the beauty of the nights, the feeling of being free and secure in a world of people who exist only to satisfy your every need? Shall I tell you of the power of life and death, the crisp touch of teeth to tender skin, the warm flow of life. Or shall I tell you of love?" My body writhed as if in remembrance. "Shall I tell you how a vampire makes love, or shall I show you?"

He said nothing, just stared down at me, still avoiding my glance. The only sign that he was weakening was the glistening of sweat on his forehead.

I turned up the heat some more. "Just imagine, Larry, your senses are heightened, your pleasure is enhanced, your endurance and strength are unimaginable to a human. You will be able to call women to you, all women, any woman you want. They will worship your perfect body with their bodies and their hands and their mouths."

His breathing was labored now, his tongue darted out to lick his lips.

"Oh, Larry, think about it. Even a single touch can drive you to a sexual frenzy that is humanly impossible. And love with another vampire, oh, Larry, I can't find words to describe it. You must let me show you, let me show you."

He said nothing, but his arms began to tremble.

"You will let me do it, won't you, Larry?" I spoke eagerly and earnestly and felt my words hit him. "You must let me do it, Larry. I can feel it now, your blood and my blood, intermeshed, blending together, as our bodies . . ." I let my voice trail off in a low moan.

His arms loosened and relaxed; I moved up to him, rubbed my body against his and he groaned. "Now," I whispered, "now," and I sunk my teeth deeply into his neck.

I was right, I realized as I let myself be carried away in the flow of his blood, it was incredible. His hardened penis pressed urgently against me, he was willingly giving himself to me, not pushing away but welcoming my bite, pulling me deeper into him. Almost, I wished I could take him with me.

Almost, except for the image of Gwen, naked with her blood spattered about my bed. Poor silly girl he had called her. I removed my bloodied mouth from him. "Bastard," I hissed; all the rage in my soul was contained in that whisper and he rocked back from the sound, even as I positioned myself for a slashing bite.

He stared at me, his eyes glazed over. Then his hand shot out, and gripped my wrists again. God, he was strong. I had read about the strength of madmen, but had never realized its truth until now. He whipped me around and pressed me up against the wall, his eyes glinting dangerously in the darkness.

"I should have known better than to trust you, Deirdre," and he reached behind him, stooping, still holding me against the wall. I struggled but his grip held. "I came prepared." And he held up a wooden stake and a mallet that he had hidden. "There are more ways than one to get your blood. I can just as easily drink it from your dying body. And although you'd be gone, I can still find other women, younger, more beautiful than you, who'd be happy to take your place."

"Larry, it doesn't work that way."

"No, I won't listen to you. It must work, it has to." He pinioned my body against the wall with his legs, placed the stake over my heart and raised the mallet.

"No," I screamed, dodging away from his strike, and heard my scream's echo from the stairs, seconds before a searing pain flashed in my shoulder. He missed, I thought, confused as the hammer dropped from his hand and the stake clattered to the ground. Then he fell, and took me with him, his legs still gripping mine. Larry was dead and his blood was flowing over me, soothing the pain in my arm.

"Oh, God, Deirdre." Mitch rushed down the stairs. "Oh, Deirdre," he cried again.

"Mitch, I'm not hurt. He's dead, just get him off of me." Quickly, Mitch rolled the body from me. I pushed my hand against the wall and stood up. My whole right side was drenched in blood, some of it mine. But I would not tell him that the hole left by the bullet that had passed through Larry would heal quickly. Too quickly for explanations.

"Jesus, look at you."

"It's okay, Mitch. I wasn't hit, all this is Larry's."

"Are you sure?"

"Of course I'm sure. Why would I lie about it?"

I took a step toward him, but my legs were trembling and I couldn't move. He came to me then, held me tightly and whispered into my hair. "I almost lost you, do you know what that would have done to me?" He lifted me up and kissed me.

"Mitch," I said when he finally released my mouth, "thank you."

"For saving your life? Gee, lady, it's all part of my job."

"No, not that. Well, for that, too. But mostly, thank you for loving me."

"Oh, that. No problem. Now let's get you out of here and cleaned up. I can take your statement later."

"Don't you have to stay here?"

"Yeah, I guess I do."

I reached up and kissed him again. "Put me in a cab; you can finish up here and then meet me back at my hotel."

I saw the doubt enter his eyes and he shook his head. "I don't know, Deirdre."

"The person you were protecting me from is there." And I pointed to Larry's body, trying to control my shudder. "I don't think he is likely to follow me, do you?"

"No, but . . ."

"And I would really like to get away from this place, not just the cellar, but the whole club. I'll wait for you at the hotel. Don't be too long."

He put his arm around my shoulder and helped me up the stairs. Only about half of the clientele remained after the fire scare. They milled around uncertainly, but when the band resumed playing, they went back to the bar or their tables. Max was nowhere in sight. On the way to the door, we passed a coat rack and Mitch removed the closest coat, wrapping it around my blood-spattered clothes.

The doorman signaled the cab and when it came, Mitch helped me in. "Are you sure you'll be okay?"

"I'll be fine. I need a shower, some rest and a chance to think." I reached into my purse and handed him my hotel key. "Let yourself in again."

As the cab drove away, I waved, but he had turned away and was walking back into the building. I watched the set of his shoulders, the determined stride and smiled to myself.

At the hotel, I got an extra key from Frank and went to my room. Shuddering at the clammy, sticky feel of the partially dried blood, I stripped off my clothes and noticed the two small holes in the right sleeve. Although I had been shot, the bullet had passed clear through. In front of the bathroom mirror, I probed the wound, tenderly at first and then with more firmness. It was clean, with no bone chips or debris; it should heal cleanly and quickly. My white skin had a rosy glow, due to the thin coating of Larry's blood and mine. I shivered when I thought how close I had come to dying and how it would have been of my own doing, as surely as if I had held the stake and raised the mallet. Had it not been for Mitch, I would have been as dead as Gwen was. But with one possible exception. Would it have been my body lying in blood on the cellar floor, the one in which I lived, the one to which Mitch had made love? Or would it have been a skeletal wreck, as all the unnatural years accumulated in minutes? Or perhaps only a small pile of dust and ash?

I shuddered again as I stepped into the shower, allowing the hot water to wash away the unclean taint of blood that covered my body. Through my folly, I had at least learned one thing— that my life was still precious to me and the next time I decided to risk it by confronting a madman, I had better come prepared with more than my ego and body to protect me.

Mitch was not long in arriving, but even so, I was ready and waiting for him. Knowing that he would have questions for me, questions that I could only in part answer truthfully, I had rehearsed my answers, my responses, as I prepared for his entrance. And of course, I realized as I applied the makeup to my pale complexion, there would be his anger to deal with, the anger that he had not expressed at the club from the sheer relief of finding me alive. But he'd had plenty of time to think since then, to wonder why I had done the things I did. He would be furious that I had attempted the meeting alone, that I had told Max, and not him, of my intentions. So I dressed in self-defense; the red silk of the caftan rustled when I walked, calling me back to more elegant days, making me, I thought, more vulnerable. But no woman of those times could have felt comfortable in such a dress—the silk was thin and, since I wore nothing underneath, it clung to my body, accenting my breasts, outlining all my curves.

I admired the result in my mirror when I heard the key turn in the lock. I hoped that my appearance would keep him sufficiently distracted; that way he might not notice that my answers were less than satisfactory. I hated the thought of deceiving him, seducing him away from his job, but I had no alternative. He must never be allowed find out the truth.

"Deirdre," he called. I was right, the anger had set in. His voice was full of it, cold and uncompromising again, like the first night we met. But what had passed between us, I hoped, would keep us together, if only for a while.

"Hello, Mitch." I came out of the bedroom and went to him. "You're earlier than I expected."

He shrugged. "There was less to do than you might think. And since you were the one involved, most of the work revolves around you. Do you feel up to answering a few questions?"

I nodded. "There's not much to tell, really. Larry called earlier that evening, and said he wanted to meet me." I sat down on the couch and smoothed the red fabric over my legs. "I, I guess it was stupid of me, but I thought I could get him to turn himself in. I never really thought he would try to hurt me, and I thought he might listen to me."

"Why didn't you tell me? Max knew about it, I suppose that's why he set off the fire alarm. And we were together the whole evening, you and I, and you gave no indication of your plans. Did you think I wouldn't help you? You knew what he was capable of, you saw what he did to Gwen, why on earth wouldn't you tell me, take me along?"

The lie I had practiced came easily to my lips. "He said"— and I allowed a tremor to creep into my voice—"he said that if I didn't meet him alone, that he would start killing everyone who knew me. I did not want to risk it, I have so few friends, and he knew about us. You might have been next."

"Damn." He ran his fingers through his hair and looked at me. "And for some strange reason, you thought you could control the situation better than I could? Jesus, Deirdre, that makes no sense at all."

"I never said it made sense. I'm just telling you what happened."

"What did he say to you? Did you talk or did he just jump out at you, brandishing his stake?"

I winced at his sarcasm. "We talked for a bit; he said that Gwen didn't matter. I was angry when I heard that, I couldn't help it. I swore at him. Then he turned on me; I didn't expect him to. And suddenly you were there and he was dead. That's all."

"And how long were you there? I seem to remember you disappeared right after the fire alarm went off. I didn't make it downstairs until about twenty minutes later."

"I waited around for him. Then when the siren went off, I thought I would just leave, come and get you. But it was too late, he was already there."

"So your conversation took about five or ten minutes?"

"I suppose so. Jesus, Mitch, I was frightened and I didn't have a stopwatch with me."

He gave me a rather grim smile that did nothing to break the tension between us. "When I got to the top of the stairs, I heard him say something about how he didn't want to listen to you. How it must work, it has to work. What was he talking about?"

I lowered my eyes. "You heard that? Well, your guess is as good as mine. He was crazy, deranged. That much should be obvious."

"Deirdre." His tone of voice was harsh; he leaned forward on his seat as if he could catch the words I wouldn't say, pull the information from my mind.

"Mitch?"

"You know," he said in a hesitant way, "I would not have expected you to be a hostile witness on this. You're holding back on me, I can tell. Why?"

"Damn it, Mitch. Don't you understand what I went through with Larry? I was almost killed, staked down like some exotic insect. And you expect me to give you a blow by blow description of everything that happened. How am I to answer for the ravings of a madman? Obviously, if I knew what motivated him, I probably would not have been there in the first place."

"Damn straight."

"All right, it was stupid to meet him. We both know that. But I was doing what I thought was the right thing. And I will be damned if I will let myself be put on trial for it. It's over now, Mitch. I'm alive, and you have Gwen's murderer. It seems to me that everyone should be happy about this; you and I and the whole damn department."

"Okay, okay." He smiled at me, a real smile this time, one that lit up his eyes. "I didn't mean to be so rough on you, but every time I think of how you set yourself up for this, how if I had just been one minute later . . . I don't like the thought of your being dead."

"Trust me, I don't like it much, either."

"No, I guess not." He stood up, reached for my hands and pulled me into a brief embrace. "I've got to get back now," he said regretfully. "There's a lot of paperwork involved in closing this one out. I suspect, given Larry's background and penchant for vampire lore, that we'll pin them all on him. We suspected him, anyway, in the original three and even though Gwen's murder doesn't match up, it's all in the same vein."

I groaned slightly at his unintended pun. He held me out and smiled at me again.

"Sorry, it's not really a joking matter. But we still have one situation to explain before we're done."

"That being?"

He looked into my eyes and held my hands. "There were fresh bite marks on Larry's neck, similar to the others but with a smaller span. But don't you worry about it, Deirdre, I'm sure there's an answer somewhere. I'll call you tomorrow. Good night."

He kissed me on the forehead and slammed the door behind him.

Chapter 17

Knowing that I would get no sleep after Mitch's last remark, I dressed and went to the office. There was work to do; not just the preparation for filling the orders from the show, but also something that I dreaded—packing up Gwen's personal items and returning them to her family. It was my responsibility, one that I could not shirk.

After I checked in with the guard, I bought a newspaper and rode the elevator alone. For once, the darkness of the rooms frightened me and I turned on all the lights as I made my way to my office. I pulled the curtains aside, and opened the door to my apartment. The room smelled heavily of disinfectant with only a slight undertone of blood. Taking a deep breath, I slowly walked up the spiral staircase to my loft bedroom. I was glad I had accepted Mitch's advice and his recommendation of a cleaning service. The sheets had been stripped away and were gone, the walls and ceiling had been sponged off, but the mattress and carpet, although damp from their cleaning, still showed the faint brown stains from Gwen's blood. I shuddered and went back down the stairs, making a mental note to get them replaced before I sold the business.

At my desk, I made a list of prospective buyers for Griffin Designs; all the thrill I had in this business had dissolved with the death of Gwen. I could not continue, did not need to continue. The money I had made in the past ten years, along with that netted from the sale, would be tucked away into some bank account with a different name for my use later on. I would be well provided for and could devote my time to the tracking of the other vampire in this city; I did not believe that Larry was responsible for Andrews and the others. Let the police postulate on how the murders were done, with their theories of syringes and pumps—I knew the truth of it. And I would find him.

But I would have to be quick. I knew that now; Mitch was too discerning and our relationship could never continue. He was sharp and intelligent, and sooner or later the proof would overwhelm his disbelief. Already he was raising questions that he should never have thought to ask. Thank God he had more sense than to believe the superstitions of his Romanian ancestors, otherwise the next time the stake was at my heart, he would be wielding the mallet, not shooting the one who was.

I laughed humorlessly; how ironic, I thought, that Mitch should be the one with the roots in the old country; I was merely a Kansas pioneer with bad luck.

Getting up from my desk with a sigh, I went down the hall and got two boxes from the storage closet, then stopped off and started a pot of coffee.

Gwen's presence was still very much alive at her desk. As I packed, I almost expected her to come bouncing down the hall, berating me for interfering with her possessions; I felt like an intruder here, more of the ghost than she would be. Oddly enough, I did not believe in ghosts; I had seen too many die in my lifetimes, none had ever returned to speak to me or to punish and torture me. They were dead and I hoped, in a better place; one that perhaps I would never attain.

There was something belittling about the two packed cartons that represented Gwen's work here. I moved them to one side, planning on delivering them later tonight at the funeral home. Gently, I pushed in her chair and whispered a good-bye.

After splashing my face with cold water in the bathroom, I filled my mug with coffee and went back into my office and closed the door. I read the paper, noting the time and place of Gwen's viewing, then continued to make notes on the work I had ahead of me. When I glanced at the clock I realized that it was only a little after three. None of the calls could be made until tomorrow morning. I was not hungry, but restless, and dawn was still four hours away. In the outer office, I pulled aside the drapes and looked out on the city. Spreading my arms, I leaned against the glass, my cheek on the window pane. The surface was cold and I could hear the slight howl of the wind. Here and there people walked, cars drove by and the sky was dark, with a small crescent moon just beginning to show. I walked out of the office, leaving the lights blazing and the doors unlocked, heedless to everything but the beckoning streets, the beckoning night.

That night I remember as being my last in that city. Perhaps it was just the last time I felt I belonged there. That night was for closing the doors of the corridor of my waking world. And I walked all the streets that for ten years I had considered my territory.

The Ballroom of Romance was dark when I passed; I envisioned Max at his desk, deep within the club, reviewing his books, totalling the receipts of tonight. I wondered if he was angry or amused at this evening's events. I was tempted to ring the night bell but thought better of it and moved on.

Around the corner, there was a small coffee shop. It was open all night and the lights were bright. Few people were inside, but outside three women lingered, looking cold and lonely in their short skirts and high heels. One of them was a friend of Linda's, I had met her once and the three of us had sat in the diner over coffee and cigarettes. She recognized me and waved, but I shook my head, turned around and headed back the other way.

As I passed the office again, I looked up. Where I had left the curtains parted a thin slot of light shone. I should go up and turn them off, I thought, but continued my walk. Not pausing at the hotel, nor acknowledging Frank's wave, I quickened my pace. Before I realized it, I was outside Mitch's apartment building. I stood in the shadows and looked up to his windows. They were dark; was he sleeping or just not home? I longed to climb

the stairs and open the door, to curl up into his arms and remain
there until dawn. Farther up the street was the alley where I had
fed on the runaway, the alley where I had surprised the man
called Sammy, and the pool hall to which Mitch, Chris and I
had gone. I looked at my watch, it was still early, just a little
after four. What the hell, I thought, I could use a drink.

Some inner sense warned me before I pushed open the door.
I peered through the window and saw Mitch—there was no
mistaking his profile and the way he sat in his chair. He was at
the table we had occupied that night, and was talking earnestly
to someone who looked familiar. I moved away, but not before
the man looked up and recognized my face as I recognized his.
Sammy stood and pointed, but I was gone before Mitch could
turn around. I pulled off my shoes and ran silently, through the
alleys and side streets, not slowing until I was back at the office.
Outside the doors, I glanced up and down the street and saw no
one. I put my shoes back on, and calmly entered the lobby. The
guard looked up and smiled at me.

"It's only you, Miss Griffin. Back so soon?"

"Yes, I'm afraid so. It's getting too cold to walk."

"You shouldn't be out by yourself, anyway. As you well know,
there's some strange goings-on around here." He hummed
slightly to himself and then went on. "I read in the paper that
they got the scum that killed Gwen. A real shame, that was, she
was a sweet girl. I was off that night; I hate to think of it. Maybe
if I'd been here that guy couldn't have got in."

"You mustn't blame yourself." I reached over and patted his
hand, wishing I could take that advice myself.

He grasped my hand. "Thank you, Miss Griffin. You get upstairs now and get warm. Your hand is as cold as ice."

I smiled at him and moved away.

"Take care, now," he called as the elevator doors closed.

The predawn hours dragged and when the staff finally arrived, their shocked expressions and reddened eyes told me that

the news of Gwen's death had made the rounds and taken its toll. At ten, overly conscious of the empty desk outside my office and the dismal pall that hung over everyone, I sent them all home with pay for the next two days. Switching all but my private phone line to the answering service, I called my attorney and outlined the plans I had to sell Griffin Designs. He tried to talk me out of it, as I knew he would.

"But, Deirdre, think of all the money you'll be losing. You built the company up from nothing and now that you are showing a good profit, you want out?"

"That's right, I want it sold. Quick and dirty. Can you handle it?"

"Well, sure we can handle it. But don't you think you should think about it? It's a pretty big step for you."

"I have thought about it. All I want is enough to live comfortably for the next ten years. And the provisional two-month stay for the employees with the new owner. Is that unreasonable?"

"No, it's a steal. I can think of several people right now who would jump at the chance. Even for much more than you're asking."

I laughed. Of course the higher we sold for, the bigger his percentage would be. "Get what you can for it, Fred. I'm fed up with the business; I just want out."

"Okay, you're the boss." He hesitated and I knew what he was going to say. "Deirdre, I was sorry to hear about Gwen. The whole thing was pretty horrible, huh?"

"Yes." My answer was curt, to forestall any discussion of the event, but I suddenly remembered that he and Gwen had dated for a while, before Nick came into the picture, and softened my response. "But they tell me, for what it's worth, that it was probably quick; that after the initial blow, she would have died instantly."

"Even so, it was horrible."

"Yes."

"Well, I guess you'll be going to the funeral home. If I don't make it, please give my condolences to her mother."

"I will, thank you. Give me a call tomorrow and let me know how everything is going on the sale."

I hung up the phone and checked to see that everyone had gone home, then locked the front door and turned out the lights.

Going back to the loft, or even the apartment was out of the question, so I curled up on the couch in my office, closed my eyes and slept.

The cab driver spoke very little English, and although he had no trouble finding the funeral home, he could not understand that I wanted him to wait. After repeated attempts to collect his fare, and my attempts to get him to stay, I finally gave in and paid him. Unceremoniously, he dumped the two cartons and me on the steps of the building. "Damn," I swore, watching as he drove away, "now how the hell am I going to get home?"

"Don't worry about it."

I turned around and jumped when I saw Mitch walking out of the door. "What the hell are you doing here?" I was shook up enough—funeral homes upset me terribly—and I didn't really want him around, looking over my shoulder, asking questions, especially after seeing him last night at the pool hall. It didn't take much imagination to recreate the story Sammy must have told him.

He gave me a suspicious glance. "Sorry, I thought you might want some company. I knew you would be here tonight, being as this is the only night viewing."

"And what is that supposed to mean?"

"Nothing." He walked past me and picked up the cartons. "Do these go inside?"

"Yes, thank you." I followed him up the steps and in the door. He put the boxes down in the corner, next to the sign that announced the names of the dead. There were four others, in addition to Gwen DeAngelis. Seeing her name there was a shock, it was so final and seemed so matter of fact. I must have stared at that sign for a long time because finally I became conscious of Mitch's hand on my arm.

I shuddered slightly and looked up at him. "I am sorry," I said in a hushed voice. "I hate these places."

"Most people do." His voice was harsh and I lowered my eyes. "Look," he said in a softer voice, but tightened his grip on my arm, "I've already been in and made my condolences. If you'd like to go alone, I'll understand and wait outside."

"That would be nice, Mitch, but you needn't wait."

"I'll wait," he said.

"But I may be a long time," I explained, hoping he would just leave. "It could be hours. In fact, I'll probably stay until closing."

"Take as much time as you like. I'll wait. We need to talk."

I looked up at his face again. It held no expression, not anger or distrust or even love and his eyes were cold. His words echoed in the empty hall like a death knell and I knew then that there was no avoiding our confrontation.

"Well, then, I'll see you later." I moved from his grip and went into the viewing room.

The first thing I noticed was the profusion of flowers and was thankful their fragrance balanced out the smell of death that was so pervading at the entrance. They also helped to alleviate the smells of life; even so, in a crowded, hot room with so many humans gathered together, I could always scent their individual odors, some sweet, some bitter, all intriguing to me. But masking it was the overpowering scent of the funeral baskets, and I thought that I could stay without losing my control.

Gwen's mother was the first person I recognized out of the sea of people. She stood guard next to the casket, a small, dark-haired woman dressed in black, worrying the beads of a crystal rosary in her hands. Mrs. DeAngelis was a woman, strong in her faith, who had already buried her husband and two sons. But Gwen had been her favorite, and I knew this death would break her heart. She looked up, our eyes met and, giving me a sad smile, called me to her.

I slipped through the other mourners and reached her, but said nothing. Instead, I hugged her against me, giving and taking comfort. Finally, she broke away and gently led me to the kneeler in front of the coffin. I knelt, my head down for a time, then lifted it to look at Gwen's face.

She looked better than I had imagined she would. The undertaker had done his job well, applying color to her bloodless skin. Her hair, I noticed with an irreverent smile, had been styled, not the way Gwen liked it, a mass of unruly curls that often hung down in her cyes, but as her mother liked it, smooth and sculptured. On the occasions I had accompanied her to her mother's house, Gwen's hair had often been the topic of heated but unmistakably loving discussions. I resisted the urge to reach out and toussle it slightly; instead, I stood up and laid my hand on her cold ones and leaned down to kiss her forehead.

A tissue was pushed surreptitiously into my hand, I used it to wipe away my tears then turned to Mrs. DeAngelis.

"I'm so sorry," I said simply, not being able to produce anything to justify this death.

"I know, my dear." She twisted the rosary in her hand again and her voice became distant. "She was a good girl, she never did anything to deserve this." Her fingers caressed the silver crucifix attached to the beads. "I know the Lord has his own reasons, but why he needed to take her now, and this way, I'll never understand." Her words were angry and drew attention from the people gathered. A young man, tall and well built, rushed to her side, giving me a dark look.

"Mother, you've been standing all day, let me get you a chair." He walked her across the room and sat her on a sofa. She was crying helplessly now, and I made a step in her direction. The man stopped me and gestured for several ladies to sit with her. When she was settled in, he came back over to me.

"Hello, Nick."

"Deirdre." There was anger in his voice, directed at me. "I'd like to talk to you outside, if you don't mind."

"But"—I looked over to where Mrs. DeAngelis sat—"I can't just leave her like that."

"Of course you can. What's it to you, anyway?" He took my arm and led me, not too gently, through the people and out of the room.

He looked around to see if we were unobserved, then hissed at me, "This is all your fault, you know."

"My fault?" I knew that it was, that Gwen would still be alive if she had not been associated with me. But how had Nick reasoned that out?

"You had no right to take her away from us, from me. I know you never liked me, never thought I was good enough for her; but I loved her and you had no right to introduce her to your friend or to interfere with our plans."

"But, Nick, I never introduced her to anyone. She met Larry on her own; I had nothing to do with that. I tried to talk her into going back to you, to try to set things straight."

"There was nothing to set straight. We were going to be married."

I looked at him intently. "That's not what she said."

He met my gaze defiantly for a minute, before his anger faded and was replaced with sorrow and guilt. "I know we had a little disagreement, but I never really expected her to go out and pick up some other guy. Why would she do that?"

"It just happened, Nick. There was nothing anyone could have done about it. And she loved you, you know that, don't you? She loved you very much."

"Did she?" He began to cry silently, with just the horrible trembling of his shoulders and his head to indicate it.

"Of course she did." I gently touched his shoulder. He didn't push me away so I wrapped both arms around him and held him tightly while he cried. I could feel the tension in his body slowly relax and when he stopped, his face, though tinged with tears, was lighter somehow.

"I'm sorry," he said, disengaging himself from my embrace, "I didn't really mean to take this out on you. I know it wasn't your fault, or mine even. I just feel so helpless without her."

"As do I, Nick. And if it is any consolation, the bastard that did this to her is dead, too. No parole, no life sentence; just a nice cold slab in the morgue. And no one deserves it more."

"Jesus," he said, in a surprised tone, "you really hate that guy."

"I would have killed him myself, if I had been able to." Perhaps it was the look on my face, or the determination in my voice, but Nick shivered slightly.

"Remind me never to get on your bad side, Deirdre." He gave a shaky little laugh. "I don't think I'd like it much."

"Probably not. Do you feel better now?"

He thought for a moment. "Yeah, I don't know why, but I do. Thanks, I wasn't able to cry before."

"Well, I think you should probably go back in now."

"Yeah, you coming?"

I shook my head. "I don't think so."

"Will you be at the funeral tomorrow?"

"No. Look, I brought some of Gwen's things from the office. They're in those boxes." I pointed. "Can you see that her mother gets them?"

"Sure. See you around?"

I smiled and kissed his cheek. "Maybe, who knows?" Nick left, and I stood for a moment, watching until he disappeared into the crowd, then walked out the door and into the fresh night air. As promised, Mitch was waiting.

"Who was that guy?"

"Guy?"

"You know, the guy you were practically necking with in the hall."

"Damn, Mitch. You've got a real problem. That was Gwen's fiancé, Nick. Didn't you meet him?"

"Oh, yeah," he said sheepishly. "I guess I did. I'm sorry, Deirdre, I wasn't thinking."

"Obviously."

My dry comment drew the first smile out of him that evening. "Let's get out of here and get something to eat."

"Okay, but I'm not very hungry; I ate before I came."

His smile disappeared. "Well, humor me, anyway. I would guess we could find something you can choke down."

I looked at him sharply, but said nothing. He opened the car door for me, closed it behind me and got in behind the wheel.

"Where to, lady?"

"Your choice, Mitch. Remember, I am humoring you tonight."

"Just see that you remember it." As I watched his unsmiling profile, he pulled the car out of the parking lot and turned onto the street, and I thought that it was going to be a long night.

Chapter 18

We went to the same restaurant he had taken me to before. We had the same waiter and ate the same meal, but the atmosphere was charged with the unspoken between us. All of my attempts at conversation were brushed off with a shrug or a one-syllable response. Eventually, I quit trying and concentrated on my steak and the second bottle of wine. Mitch had turned from a witty and exciting companion to a sullen child, and ordinarily I would have gotten up from the table and left, never to see him again. But even in the tense silence, I realized that I still loved him; enough that his anger, combined with the events of the last few days, finally reduced me to tears. I excused myself and fled to the ladies' room.

When I returned I was more composed, having reached the decision that our relationship was now at the point I had always feared. No longer would I try to salvage what we had; instead, I would cut my losses and get out. It seemed best, but when I sat back down, he looked over at me with concern on his face and love for me in his eyes once again.

"Are you okay?" he asked, and touched my hand across the table.

I pulled away and noticed the extra glass, now half empty, on the table. I picked it up, sniffed and set it back down. "Scotch, Mitch? On top of all that wine? Do you think that's wise?"

"No, but at this point I don't much care." He took another drink and looked away. "What's happening with us?"

"Us?" I laughed more shrilly than normal. "After tonight, I don't think there will be any us. You were the one who said we should talk; so here we are, let's talk. Or let's just give it up."

"But that's the problem; I don't want to give it up. When I'm away from you, I have all these doubts and questions. Nothing about you or your reaction to situations makes any sense to me. I've never seen you in the light of day, never seen you eat anything substantial. And I have heard some pretty unsavory things about you from various people." I gave him a questioning look and he continued. "But I don't really want to talk about any of that. It can all be explained, I'm sure." He glanced at me with a sheepish smile. "Nothing about you is as it seems, but when we're together, nothing else matters but you."

"You certainly have a strange way of showing it."

He shrugged. "I've been fighting you all evening, but I didn't realize it until I made you cry. I know these past few days have been rough on you, and you've taken it all pretty well, considering. I should be treating you better than this, we both know that. But everything seems so uncertain. I just don't know what to do, what to say."

"So you say nothing."

"Exactly." When he touched my hand this time, I did not pull away. I closed my eyes and began tracing the outline of his hand with my fingertips, softly touching his fingers, his close-trimmed nails and the callouses on his palm. When I reached the soft part of his wrist, he shivered and I raised his hand to my mouth and kissed it. I opened my eyes and looked him square in the face.

"Pay the bill, Mitch, and let's get out of here."

Frank was there to greet us at the door of the hotel, nodding his head in acknowledgement. "Miss Griffin. Detective Greer."

I smiled at him as I passed and he gave me a wink that seemed very out of character. When the elevator doors closed on us, I burst out laughing.

"What's so funny?"

"Frank. He winked at me."

"So?"

"So, you've ruined my reputation, Mitch. Less than a month ago I was a mysterious, unapproachable resident. All anyone knew of me was the little they read of me in the papers or magazines. They may have gossiped about me behind closed doors, but wink at me? No one would have dared. Now suddenly I am an ordinary person, carrying on a perfectly ordinary affair." I laughed again and he still looked puzzled. "I'll have to move."

The elevator doors opened and we walked down the hall. Mitch was still unamused by my predicament. "Why?" he asked, his expression petulant. "Because all of a sudden you have a personal life? It's really nothing to be ashamed of, living like an ordinary person."

"But I have never been . . . oh, never mind, it is not important." I opened the door of my room and he walked in ahead of me.

"Besides," he said, "I don't really think that what you and I have could ever be called ordinary." He took off his jacket and his gun holster and hung them over a chair, then turned around and smiled.

I stood against the locked door and lazily began to unbutton my dress. "Mitch, you have never said anything truer in your life."

He watched until I reached the bottom button and dropped the dress on the floor. Then he crossed the room, his eyes intense and blazing, took me in his arms and switched off the light.

He lay sleeping with his head pillowed on my breast, one hand lightly grazing my hip. I could not sleep, but had stayed perfectly still for what seemed hours so as not to disturb him. Eventually when he stirred and rolled over, I slipped out of bed and pulled aside the heavy drapes.

The night curled in perfect darkness, the slivered moon and

the stars were blotted out by thick clouds, rushing through the sky. Dawn was perhaps two or three hours away and I felt the night calling to me. For there, in the dark, I would find what I needed. I had drawn no blood, mine or his, when we made love, but the desire to feed had arisen strongly. To lie next to him now, with my hunger full and strong, would be a great mistake.

I turned and looked at Mitch; his skin seemed to shine faintly in the darkness. Sighing, I quietly pulled my robe from the closet put it on and gently closed the bedroom door. Once in the other room, I went to the small refrigerator under the bar, remembering an opened bottle of wine that would help alleviate, though not fully satisfy, my thirst. When I opened the door. I also saw what else I had stored there: the nine remaining bags of blood I had taken from Larry's apartment.

"Damn!" I reproached my carelessness. Mitch could have seen these, easily, had he decided he wanted a drink. Thank God he had not. Looking over my shoulder at the still-closed bedroom door, I listened carefully. Mitch's regular breathing reassured me. I stood the blood bags against the back wall, supporting and hiding them with the bottles inside, adding additional ones from the bar. I left the scotch in the front, should Mitch awaken and decide he would like to have a drink at some point in the evening. Hopefully, he wouldn't ask me why I was now storing the liquor in the refrigerator.

With my glass of wine poured, I sat down on the couch. With each sip I visualized the blood, remembered its taste and texture. My body trembled and I broke into a sweat, trapped where I sat. I could not go to the bedroom—my desire to feed was too strong now. And I could not risk using one of the bags for fear of Mitch discovering me. But, he was, after all, in a deep sleep, wasn't he? And I was practiced in stealth and silence. I should be able to feed and return to the bed and he would never know. And yet, should he awake and find me, what then?

My body made the decision for me. Getting up from the couch and opening the door, I dislodged one of the bags. The bottles clinked very faintly and I froze, but there was no accompanying noise from the bedroom, only Mitch's rhythmic, soft snoring.

Knowing that I could not drink it cold, I went into the darkened bathroom and turned on the hot water. This might wake him, but it was such an ordinary noise, it would not seem unusual. I held the blood under the faucet and the water splashed out, soaking me to the skin. Swearing under my breath, I slid out of the wet robe and pushed it into the corner of the room. When the plastic of the bag became pliable and the liquid inside seemed the right temperature, I removed it from the sink, then realized that I had brought no scissors with which to cut it, and no glass from which to drink.

I might have laughed but frustration had taken hold. I had to feed, I thought. I had to! The bag was awkward in my hands, but I held it to my mouth. The plastic was more resistant to my bite than human skin. But eventually I managed to puncture it, somewhat messily, then drank with ease.

The taking of blood, even in this fashion, is a rapturous event; I become aware of nothing more than its nourishing flow, the heat of the liquid warming my throat, my stomach, my whole body. Except for sleep, it is probably the only other moment that one of my kind is defenseless and without protection from the outside world. There is only the blood and the drinking of the blood; nothing else, at that moment, exists.

When the light flicked on and Mitch entered, I was at the peak of this experience. My eyes fastened on him, still glowing with the hunger, and it took me more than a minute to recognize his presence, to realize what had happened. My naked body was exposed in the glaring light, tiny rivulets of blood trickled from my mouth, and elsewhere there were small splashes of blood from my clumsy attempts to puncture the bag.

Mitch stared at me, his face white with shock. The half-empty bag dropped from my hands onto the white-tiled floor. Two small fountains spurted up from my fang marks, then settled down into a small spreading pool.

"I see," he said, his tone flat and emotionless. "Oh, yes, I finally see."

He walked out and closed the door behind him. I stood motionless, staring at myself in the mirror. Turning on the water again I scrubbed at my face frantically to wash away the traces of blood, then struggled into my wet robe. By the time I left the bathroom, Mitch was dressed and putting his shoulder holster back on. He did not look at me when he buttoned his jacket, nor when he crossed to the front door and kicked my discarded dress out of the way. I shivered for a moment and wrapped my arms around myself.

"What," I croaked, my voice scratchy and hoarse, "what will you do?"

Mitch looked at me at that moment, and I wished he had not. Then without a single word, he opened the door and left.

Chapter 19

For the rest of the night I sat in the darkness, shivering in my wet robe. When I felt the rising of the sun, I threw off the garment and stood naked by the window, my hand on the curtains. How I longed at that moment to open them, to see for the first time in over a hundred years the colors of dawn. I remembered the other times I had been caught by the sun's rays, the agony of burned flesh, the weeks of painful recovery. This time there would be no recovery; if I exposed myself I would not retreat, but allow the sun to burn away all traces of my life.

My hands trembled as they reached for the cords, then jerked away. They moved forward again. "Coward," I whispered. For I was afraid; not of my contemplated death, nor even the pain. That was the easy way out; that was the cowardice. No, I was frightened of where my life would lead.

With a conscious effort I turned away from the window. I would see this through, I decided, and even though I could very well be dead at the end of this day, it would not be by my own hand. Mitch would return, I was certain, for answers or justice. Or both. And I knew that if his justice meant that I must die, I would let him kill me.

Oddly enough, my mind was eased by this decision. I went to the bedroom and dressed in jeans and a shirt, nothing fancy or sexy to distract him from his purpose. I cleaned the blood from the bathroom floor; combed my hair and brushed my teeth, but applied no makeup. No need anymore to pretend to be human; no need to disguise myself. He would see me as I really was.

Halfheartedly, I began to straighten up the room. I started to make the bed, and when I picked up the pillow on which he had slept, I held it to my face. The case smelled of him and I closed my eyes for a moment and remembered the love we had shared. Then I set the pillow back down and covered it up.

When the phone rang, I was removing the liquor from the refrigerator. The sound shocked me and one of the bottles slipped from my hands and shattered on the floor. As I went to the phone, there was a pounding on the door. "So soon, Mitch?" I said softly, then picked up the phone.

"Hold on a minute, please," I said before the caller had a chance to say anything, walked across the room and unlocked the door. He was there, as I knew he would be and I motioned him in.

"Hello, Mitch, I was expecting you."

"I'll bet you were."

"Look, I've got a phone call, I'll be with you in a minute. Sit down." From the tone of my voice, he could tell nothing of my excitement or my fear. It was as if he was paying a social call and my attitude caught him off guard. He went to the couch and sat down while I returned to the phone.

"Yes?"

"Miss Griffin?" It was the daytime doorman. "There's someone on his way up to see you. I know you don't usually have visitors, but Frank said that lately you've been seeing this guy and, well, I hope it's okay."

"It's fine," I said calmly and I could hear his relieved sigh. "I was expecting him. Oh, and could you please send up some coffee and danish?"

"Right away."

I hung up the phone and turned to Mitch. "I've ordered us some breakfast. Have you eaten yet?"

"No." He gave me a strange look. "Have you?"

I shook my head. "Just coffee for me, of course. The danish is for you."

"Thank you."

"I have a mess behind the bar to clean up. Do you mind?"

"No, go ahead. We can talk when the coffee gets here. I didn't sleep real well last night and I could use the caffeine." He ran his fingers through his hair in the gesture I had learned he used when tired or confused. I smiled at him for a moment then ducked behind the bar.

"I hope you won't want a drink anytime, Mitch. It was the scotch that fell." I sopped up the liquor with a few paper towels and pushed the broken glass aside. When I stood up again, he was staring in my direction.

"So, how did you sleep?"

I laughed. "I don't sleep much at night, Mitch. I thought you had figured that out by now." There was a discreet knock at the door. "Coffee's here," I said and went to collect it. Setting the tray on the bar, I looked over at him. "Cream and sugar, right?" At his nod, I prepared a cup for him, poured one for me and settled down in a chair, facing him. He took a sip of his coffee, and I jumped up. "Did you want a roll?" I asked and moved toward the bar to get him one.

"Damn it, Deirdre, this is not a social call and you know it. Quit playing the hostess and sit down. We need to talk."

"Sorry." I sat back down, cross-legged, and took a drink of my coffee. "Now I guess you can read me my rights and get on with it."

"What? Why would I do that?"

"For the first three murders, I would guess. Even though I had nothing to do with them, I must be a prime suspect now that you know."

"I know nothing, except that you need help."

I looked at him in surprise. "Help? Why would I need help? Any help I received now would only be about a hundred years too late."

"Deirdre"—his voice was soft, reasonable—"I know that

you think you're a vampire. But there are doctors who specialize in this sort of sickness. You could take treatment and be cured of this obsession after a while."

"Obsession? Sickness?" I laughed. Even to me it sounded hollow and hysterical. "You know that I only *think* myself a vampire? Oh, Mitch, that's priceless! After last night, after everything you've discovered about me, you still won't believe."

"How could I believe it? I've spent time with you, made love to you. Damn it, even after last night, I'm still in love with you. But you're human, you're real; I can touch you, see your reflection in a mirror. Just because you're disturbed, and believe in legends and folklore, doesn't mean that I have to."

Suddenly I was angry at his lack of belief. "Ever the skeptic, aren't you, Detective? What if I could offer you proof?"

"And what sort of proof would that be? Can you change into a bat or a wolf? Dissolve into a mist? Crawl down a wall?"

"No, but I can give you proof even you cannot doubt." I got up from my seat and knelt in front of him. Taking his face in my hands, I looked into his eyes and kissed him, slowly and passionately.

He did not pull away from me, instead he held me for a moment. "What was that for?" he asked, almost smiling.

"Because you won't want anything to do with me in a few minutes. And because I love you." I gave his cheek a final caress and stood up. "Now stay there and pay attention."

He folded his arms with a smug expression and watched me. I looked around the room and saw the broken glass by the bar. I picked up a piece of it; it was long and jagged and glinted in the light. He looked alarmed and reached for his gun.

"Don't move," I commanded and he dropped his hand. "Proof number one," I said harshly. "Regenerative powers." I quickly slit both of my wrists with the glass.

"Deirdre, no!" Mitch gasped as he saw the bright blood flowing down my hands.

"No doubt, you have seen more than a few suicide cases." He was still riveted to the couch by my command but he nodded and I held my arms out to him. "These would be fatal wounds, wouldn't they, if I didn't get prompt attention?"

He looked away from me. "Let me call an ambulance, please. You didn't have to do this. Let me help you."

"Look at me," I ordered and he did. "I do not need help with this." I rubbed my wrists on the side of my jeans and held them out for his inspection again. The blood had congealed and the cuts, although obviously recent, were already healing. "Touch them," I said gently and moved toward him. He ran a trembling finger over the wounds. "By tomorrow," I said matter-of-factly, "there will only be small scars. Within a few days, there will be no sign that this ever happened." I turned my back on him and went to the window. "You see," I said bitterly, "I have tried this little trick before."

When I looked at him again, his face was ashen, the expression in his eyes bleak. "Deirdre, I'm so sorry, I had no idea . . ."

I smiled reassuringly. "It's okay, Mitch, it really is. Now, if you'll let me continue."

"No more, please," he interrupted. "I believe you."

"No, Mitch, I don't want you to have any doubts at all. We'll do this my way." I stood back and opened the heavy draperies about an inch. "Test number two," I said, taking a deep breath, "sunlight." I thrust my hand into the ray streaming into the room. It began to smoke immediately, but before the smell of burning flesh became overwhelming, I withdrew my arm and shut the drapes again. "Damn," I said, walking to him. "That really hurts."

He reached up to me and gently took my hand. "Will this heal, too?" he asked in awe as he surveyed the damage. The skin was blackened and withered in the small area that had been exposed.

"Yes, in a day or two." I pulled away from him and sat back in my chair. "Now just let me rest up a bit and we'll go for number three."

"Is that really necessary?" His voice now reflected fear and although I could not determine if he was afraid of me or for me, I could see the belief in his eyes.

I responded with a weak smile. "I had hoped it would not be. The next one is the worst of all."

After several minutes of uncomfortable silence, Mitch spoke again. "Deirdre, I hate to ask, but I have to know. What's test number three?"

"Oh, that," I said disparagingly. "It's the test of immortality."

"How can you prove that?"

"Quite simply, I take your revolver and shoot myself through the heart." I shuddered slightly and went on. "It hurts like hell, but only for a little. As long as the bullet goes clear through there are no serious complications."

He stared at me in horror, then dropped his face into his hands. The minutes ticked by, seeming like hours. I made an attempt to clear our cups, but found that my hands were shaking, so I sat back down again and studied his body for some sign of what would happen next. Eventually, he raised his head. "Oh, God," he said quietly, then wiped his eyes and looked into my face. His expression was strangely composed, his voice calm and confident, as if knowing the worst about me had strengthened him in some way. "Thank you. This explains so many things for me. And it must've been hard for you to tell me all this."

I nodded. "At least now you don't think I'm crazy. Of course, I am crazy"—I gave him a little smile—"for telling you this. I could have let you believe what you wanted to believe. But I thought that you would try to drag me off to see a doctor this morning and that would not only have killed me, it would have been a shock to your comfortable theory. So now, instead of killing me accidentally, you can be fully aware of your actions."

"Kill you? Why would I want to do that?"

I laughed again. "I can think of several reasons, offhand. I am an inhuman monster who should be exterminated. I am a damned soul who should be released. I am a drainer of blood, a leech on mankind. And then you have your three murders."

"No," he said with a sidelong glance at me. "I have four murders."

"Four? But surely Gwen doesn't count in that number? Larry should account for her death."

"No, I wasn't counting her." He gave me a curious look, partly surprise, partly relief. "You really don't know, do you?"

"Know what?"

"Last night there was another murder. Like the first three. And the time of death has been pinpointed during the time that you and I were, ah, otherwise engaged. So, even if I suspected you, which I did not, you would be free on this."

"Why don't you suspect me? I could have left quietly and come back, you never would have known."

"No." He looked at me sharply. "I would have known. Besides, you may be a, well, what you are, but you are not a killer. You have lied to me about many things, and now I know why you did. You are secretive and crafty, but I know you, maybe better than you think. You could not kill anyone, not like this. Oh, you might be capable of murder, in passion or anger, most people are, but not in cold blood and not repeatedly."

"Thank you. What will you do now?"

"Damned if I know. This is all a little hard to take. And to believe. Oh, I do believe you," he said quickly. "You don't have to give me any more proof. But all along, I've been believing that the person we wanted was deranged. Now I've learned that he may be a true vampire"—he winced as he said the word— "how on earth am I going to catch him or make anyone else believe what we are looking for?" He glanced at me in an appeal for help.

"I do not know, Mitch. If the question had arisen one month ago, I would have denied the existence of others of my kind. In all my years, I have only had proof of one other, the one who made me what I am. However, I'll be more than happy to help you any way I can."

"Why would you help? Isn't that against your code or laws or something?"

"I have no code or laws for dealing with others. I've never met anyone like me. But I want this one."

"Why?"

"Because, if he is the one who changed me, I want him dead. If not, I would like to ask him some questions. You see, I was changed into what I am by accident, I believe. I had no one to guide me, no one to teach me what I needed to know to survive. Somehow, I blundered through and lived."

"How long?" He looked at me sadly for a minute. "How old are you?"

"I was born in 1832, changed in 1860. I've stayed the same since."

He laughed. "You're over a hundred years old? I can believe a lot of things, but not that."

"Truly, Mitch." I walked into the bedroom, and retrieved Larry's scrapbook from the closet where it had been hidden. I came back and handed the book to Mitch. "My life story, or almost, as compiled by Larry Martin."

His hands shook as he took it from me. I poured myself another cup of coffee and watched him read. There were no sounds in the room but the rustle of slowly turned pages.

When he had finished, he looked over at me with regret in his eyes. "You haven't had it easy, have you? All that moving about, for fear of discovery. All the things you've seen—war, poverty, the deaths of people you've known."

"Living forever is not exactly what it is cracked up to be. But short of taking a long walk in the sunlight, there's not much I can do about it."

He rifled through the pages again, pausing with the book open to the photograph on page one. "Where did you get this?"

"The night that Gwen died, I left your place and broke into Larry's apartment."

"But it was under surveillance. No one saw you go in."

"Of course they didn't. I climbed up the back wall and went in a window." I smiled at his expression.

"But there's no way in, in the back. The fire escapes are on the sides of that building."

"I know. I climbed the back wall."

"Oh, I didn't think you could do that."

I laughed. "Actually, it was the very first time I had ever tried. It was amazingly simple. Larry wasn't there, but you know that. I found the book, borrowed some of his private stock and left."

He nodded, putting the missing pieces in place. "We found the other blood and your note. But we didn't know who it was from. We couldn't figure that one out, or how the lock on his door got broken. I guess you did that, too."

I nodded.

"But there were no prints."

"I have been dating a detective, remember? I wore gloves."

"Oh, of course, you'd been printed that night." He stared at me for a second. "And you knew he had killed Gwen, but still you went to meet him. Obviously, he knew what you were and he came prepared to kill you. I still don't understand why you didn't let me help you."

"Be reasonable, Mitch. I didn't want you to find out about me; he would have told you then and there and been happy to do it. And I really thought I could handle him. But he surprised me; he was much stronger than I would have thought."

"And the marks on his neck?"

"The bite marks are mine." I said it softly, but he shuddered, anyway. "Larry wanted me to transform him. I finally managed to convince him to let me close enough to him so that I could take his blood." Mitch's face paled and I continued quickly. "You see, when I take blood, I'm able to plant suggestions. I hoped to take enough to weaken him, and then wipe away any remembrance of me and what I am. After that was accomplished I planned to let him go; you would have caught him eventually and my secrets would have been safe."

"What went wrong?"

"Everything went wrong that night." My voice lowered. "I

discovered that I was not as invincible as I thought. It was a sobering experience."

He sat and thought for a while. Then he got up and poured himself another cup of coffee and took a danish. "Want one?" he said, holding out the plate.

"Not really, Mitch. You forget that I don't need to take food. In most cases, I can't even swallow it."

"Oh, yeah. It's easy to forget." He looked at me sheepishly. "I just can't think of you as what you are; I guess I should be frightened or horrified. And I am, a bit. But mostly, I feel sorry for you. Does that make any sense at all?"

"Perfect sense, to me. I'm still the same person I was yesterday and you and I are bonded together, to some degree."

A sudden flare of anger entered his eyes. "You mean you can control me, control my feelings?"

"No, Mitch." I walked over and took his hand in mine. "I don't control you, nor would I want to. I'm not sure that I could; you're very strong in your own right. And I haven't taken your blood."

His free hand went to his neck in a protective, involuntary gesture. He dropped it with an embarrassed look when he realized what he had done. Averting his eyes, as if in the presence of some perversion, he asked softly, "Why didn't you take any blood? Don't you have to?"

"Not always." I smiled reassuringly at him. "And I wouldn't take yours. But that first time we made love, well, do you remember the bruise on my shoulder?"

"Yeah"—the realization of the situation dawned in his eyes— "at first it wasn't there. I knew it wasn't. And then it went away much too fast."

"Exactly, and now you know why. I did that to myself. For so long, the taking of blood has been the only intimacy I've had, the only one I thought I needed. I can't fully explain the feelings I get when I'm feeding; there's the survival factor, the needs satisfied, but there is also a union with my victims, however unwilling they may be. There is a sexuality apart from sex, a power and a fulfillment"—I broke off as he dropped my hand and gave a shudder of distaste—"but you're different." A note of pleading entered my voice. "You touch a part of me that has been repressed for over twenty years. I couldn't sully that experience by taking your blood. So I turned my head, and drew my own."

"And the other times?"

"I fought the urge. I don't want to hurt you, Mitch. For what it's worth, I love you. So you're in no danger from me in that respect."

He left my side, went over to the window and peeled back the drapes slightly to look outside. Although I was out of reach of the sunlight, I instinctively jumped back. Lost in his own thoughts, Mitch took no notice and went on, quietly as if to himself. "Shit, I really can pick them, can't I? The first woman I've allowed myself to love for years and she turns out to be a . . ." His voice broke and he turned back to me with an odd pleading look in his eyes.

"You can say it, Mitch. I don't care much for the word myself, but in this case it is appropriate. And you have used it before."

"But not about you. And not for real. I don't want to say it. Jesus, I don't even want to believe it. Right now I need to get out of here, away from you. I've got a lot of thinking to do." He walked to the door.

I found I could not move toward him. "Mitch," I said in a soft, choked voice.

His name stopped him and he turned to me. Quickly, he gathered me in his arms and held me.

"I'm so sorry," I whispered.

"So am I, Deirdre." He kissed me gently and held my face between his hands. "I'll be back," he promised and walked out into the hall.

I stood against the door after he left, until I heard the elevator close and start its journey downward. Then, bearing the weight of many years, I locked the door and went into the bedroom.

Chapter 20

I slept fitfully that day, and when the phone finally woke me at three, I got up to answer it, expecting that it would be Mitch. I was disappointed to hear my attorney's voice, but he had good news for me.

"I've got a buyer."

"So soon? You sure didn't waste any time, Fred." There was a pause on the end of the line. "But you said you wanted it over quickly."

"I did. I just didn't think it would happen so soon. That's great." I tried to put enthusiasm into my voice and failed.

"The deal isn't final yet, of course, so you could still change your mind."

"No, I won't change my mind. Tell me about it."

He talked for some time, going into details that were not terribly important to me; I only half-listened to him, thinking, instead, of the conversation Mitch and I'd had that morning. He had taken it better than I thought he would, and that confused me somewhat. Maybe I had underestimated his grasp of the situation or the depth of his feeling for me. Could it be possible that he would still wish to continue our relationship, knowing what he did about me? And even at that, how long could either one of us expect it to last? I sighed and Fred was startled.

"Deirdre?"

"Hmmm?"

"You aren't even listening, are you? If you're so uninterested, why did you ask me to call you?"

"I am sorry, Fred, please continue."

"They'd like to meet over lunch, tomorrow. Can you fit that into your schedule?"

"No, lunch is out of the question. What about dinner, tonight?"

"Tonight? Jesus, Deirdre, you don't know what you're asking. It'll take us at least another four hours to get the contracts reviewed and typed. I work fast, but not that fast."

"Did they meet my two conditions?"

"You weren't listening—I knew it! Yes, they met your conditions and upped them a bit. They're very interested."

"Then get it ready for tonight. We can eat late, say around nine or nine-thirty. The office is still closed today; tomorrow when I go in I want to inform the staff of what's been done. After everything else, I don't want an office full of hysterical women, worried over the rumors of a sale. You know how fast this kind of situation gets broadcast on the gossip mill. Can you handle it?"

"Well"—he thought for a moment—"if I take everyone off what they're doing now, yes, we can probably make it."

"Great, arrange for whatever bonuses you think are necessary. And make reservations for us at The Imperial. I'll cover the bill."

"Fine with me," he said. There was a trace of a smile in his voice now.

"And bring your wife. That should make up for all the long hours I force you to work."

"I should hope so. Well, I'd better go. Are you sure you don't want to go over the details again?"

"No, I trust you. If you say it is a good deal, I can believe it. Oh, and, Fred?"

"Yeah?"

"Reserve an extra seat for dinner. I might want to bring a guest."

"You, a guest? I can't wait. You really are full of surprises these days, Deirdre. See you tonight."

I laughed to myself when I hung up the phone. Poor Fred. I guess I had given him a harder job than I should have, but I wanted that portion of my life ended as quickly as possible. There was really no sense in continuing; I didn't need the money or the hassle at this point. I felt a sudden lightening of my mood. The worst was over, things could only improve. Mitch had been told the truth, I could look him in the eyes with no dishonesty or lies. I had faced off someone who wanted me dead, and had lived through the attempt. My time would be my own again, to use any way I wished. When the other was found and dealt with, I was free to begin an entirely new life, or stay in the old for a while. That decision would depend on Mitch.

I rang the police station and found him at his desk.

"Greer speaking." His voice sounded hurried and distracted.

"Mitch, I'm sorry to bother you, but I wondered if you would be free tonight for dinner. The Imperial at nine?"

"Whew," he said, surprised at my request. "I'd better check my bank book first."

"Don't be silly; I'm paying. It's actually a business dinner but I would like you to be there, if you can make it." I suddenly realized that I was making a big assumption. Just because he didn't rant or rave this morning or attempt to kill me straight out didn't mean that he would want to see me again, ever. "I mean," and my voice was soft, less confident now, "that is, if you can stand to be with me after today."

"Hell, Deirdre, for dinner at The Imperial I'd go out with Jack the Ripper."

"That is not very funny, Mitch. If you don't want to go just say so."

He gave a small chuckle. "My, aren't we touchy today? Of course, I'll be there. Should I rent another tux?"

"That's up to you. And thank you."

"No, thank *you*. How could I turn down an offer like this?"

"No, you know what I mean. You've taken everything well."

His voice changed, soured slightly. "What choice do I have? And when do you want me to pick you up?"

"Why don't you just meet me there? I'll take a cab."

"Fine, see you at nine."

After a leisurely shower, I stood in front of my closet and tried to decide what to wear. Had my choices been limited, the choosing would have been easier. As it was, the rod was crowded with clothes for all occasions. Some were dismissed as too casual, others were too formal, or had been worn before at some other fashion-industry function. Finally, I was down to ten dresses that would be appropriate. Of these, eight were black. "Deirdre," I said to myself, "you have allowed yourself to get into a rut," and eliminated all but the remaining two. One was red; too blatant, I decided. But I hesitated over the last one. It was velvet in the same deep forest green color I had chosen to wear for Mitch the night he had shown up three hours too late. Maybe it was a bad omen. Then again, it was a color I had always loved— it had been the color that my husband had always wanted me to wear.

I pulled it from the closet, removing its protective bag, and laid it on the bed. It had been packed away with a sachet and the scent had remained fresh. Holding the fabric to my face, I sniffed deeply.

Lily of the valley—it had been my mother's favorite flower. And although she had died while I was very young, I still associated it with her. My father had tended her garden beds religiously until the day he died, keeping the roses, azaleas and lilac bushes pruned and proper, but this flower he allowed a free growth and it flourished. On a warm day in May its odor would permeate the yard and the house. Somehow it seemed appropriate to meet Mitch this evening, wrapped in the fragrance that was, to me, the scent of love and a symbol of loyalty and faithfulness.

When my makeup and hair were complete, I slipped the dress

over my head and struggled with the zipper. Then I smoothed the skirt over my legs and stood in front of the mirror. With a shock, I realized that this dress was similar to the one I had designed for Gwen's wedding—it fell off the shoulders, had a rounded bodice and pulled to the back in a small bustle. But unlike Gwen's, this dress was unadorned, with no pearls or lace, allowing the elegance of the fabric to speak for itself. I wore no jewelry, except for a small pair of emerald stud earrings and had inserted the contact lenses that matched the color of the dress.

After one final check on my appearance, I worried for a second about the ironies of fate that had caused me to clothe myself in remembered deaths, but shrugged it off and collected my cloak.

I was early in arriving at the restaurant, two hours early the maitre'd informed me with an apologetic smile.

"I am very sorry, Miss Griffin, but Mr. Carlson made the reservation for ten. I hope you will not be too inconvenienced."

"Not at all. May I wait at the bar?"

"Certainly."

I removed my cloak and gloves; he took them from me.

"I will check these for you if I may."

"Thank you." I reached into my purse and gave him a tip. "I'm expecting a Mr. Greer around nine; please see that he finds his way to me."

He nodded and I crossed the hall and entered the bar. It was brightly lit and elegantly decorated as one would expect from a restaurant of its class. But for all of that, I felt out of place and disoriented. I had spent too many nights at the Ballroom, in its comfortable darkness and ambience, to view this place as anything more than an overpriced waiting room. Still, I thought to myself with a smile, as I claimed a table from a couple leaving for their dinner, at least here I did not have to contend with sneering bartenders and overbearing owners.

The service was good, the wine list better, and soon I was securely ensconced with a bottle of burgundy of excellent vintage. After admiring the color and taking my first sip, I began to reevaluate my opinion of The Imperial. Perhaps I should begin to branch out and bring some of my business here. Of course, I wouldn't receive quite the same personal service that the Ballroom offered and would have to make contact with victims on my own. That would not be a bad thing, I thought, looking around curiously at some of the men lounging at the tables and bar. They were young and healthy and could provide amply for my needs. As I continued to glance at the prospects for future reference, I felt my mouth curve in what must have seemed a devilish smile.

Quite accidentally, my eyes made contact with an older-seeming man standing at the edge of the bar. He intercepted my smile with one of his own, and I looked down at my wine in embarrassment. You'll have to be more subtle than that, I chided myself, if you want to succeed at this game. I was severely out of practice. To further my disadvantaged feeling, when I looked back up again, he was standing at my table, smiling down at me.

"Excuse me," he said, his voice betraying a slight Germanic accent, "you are Deirdre Griffin, are you not?"

"Yes." I did not return his smile, but gave him an assessing stare. I couldn't remember ever having met him before, although it was possible that he was a former victim. I'd had many. That thought was distressing; if I had fed off this man and could not recognize him now, I had stayed in this city too long. "Do I know you?"

"No, may I join you?" Despite the coldness of my greeting, his smile did not subside.

"Actually, someone is meeting me."

"But in the meantime, a lovely lady like you should not be drinking alone." He reached over and lifted the bottle of wine, reading the label. "An excellent choice, and one of my favorites. Perhaps I should have the waiter bring another glass."

I gave him my sternest look. "Look, I hate to be rude, but I don't know you. And I am not generally in the habit of . . ."

"But of course you are not," he smoothly interrupted me. "And I am afraid that I have been having a little joke on you.

You see, we have a mutual friend. He has had the bad manners of never introducing us, so I thought that I might rectify his mistake. I am Victor Lange."

"And our mutual friend?"

"Max Hunter."

At the mention of the name, I relaxed but smiled in resignation. And I thought I would be avoiding his manipulation tonight. I gestured to the chair. "Please sit down, Mr. Lange."

"Victor, please."

As he sat the waiter came over with an empty wineglass. I was surprised at the fast service and said so.

"You must come here often. I think that waiter just read your mind."

Victor threw his head back and laughed. "Miss Griffin, you really should step out of that dive that Max runs and take in the rest of the world. Yes, I do come here often, as you say. I own the place."

"Oh." I took a drink of wine to cover my chagrin.

"But you mustn't be embarrassed. I am afraid that I did rather mislead you. Did you think I was trying to pick you up?"

"No." I looked at him again and smiled. "Well, yes, I did. I am sorry to have misunderstood."

He nodded sympathetically. "It is quite understandable. It must happen to you often."

I shrugged and finished my wine. He filled the glass for me, drained his and then stood up abruptly. "I believe this must be the gentleman you are waiting for. What will he want to drink?"

I looked up and saw the scowl on Mitch's face as he came toward us. "Scotch, on the rocks, I'm afraid."

Victor said a polite good evening to me, nodded to Mitch as he arrived at the table and left. I stood up and gave Mitch a small kiss on the cheek.

We both sat down again, and the waiter brought the scotch. "How did you know I would want this?" he asked, taking a sip.

"From the look on your face, my love." I reached over and stroked his cheek. "Bad day?"

"No, not too bad." He hesitated and frowned and I waited for the inevitable question; it was not long in coming. "Who was that?"

I laughed. "Mitch, I really hate to say it, but you are so predictable. That was Victor Lange, he owns The Imperial."

"Do you know all the restaurant owners in town? Or does it just seem that way?"

"No, I only met him this evening. He's a friend of Max's."

"Oh, Max." Instead of his usual disgruntled expression at the mention of the name, Mitch smiled. It was not entirely a pleasant smile, but it was a good sign.

"What is so funny?"

"You may not find it funny, but I got a kick out of it. Before I came here tonight, I stopped over at the Ballroom and slapped a citation and a pretty heavy fine on Hunter for setting off a false fire alarm."

"Mitch, you didn't, did you?"

"Yeah, I did."

Our eyes met and we both began to laugh simultaneously. "I'll be willing to bet the price of tonight's dinner, that he wasn't happy about it."

"Deirdre, that's got to be the biggest understatement you ever made in your life. He was livid. I wish you could've seen his face." He laughed again, thinking about it. "I'm afraid it wasn't a pretty sight."

"Too bad, you two were just starting to get along."

"Yeah, well, he canceled that out by letting you go down to his cellar alone. He's a smart son of a bitch, I'll give him that. He almost talked me out of the citation. I think he knew that it was more a personal matter than anything else."

"He'll sue you for police harassment."

"I doubt it." Mitch looked over at me and smiled. "But even if he does, it'll be worth every penny. So, who are we having dinner with tonight?"

"You mean besides Jack the Ripper?" I gave him a stern glance, but his eyes danced. He was enjoying that little insult, so I let it go, relaxed and answered his question. "My attorney and the people purchasing Griffin Designs."

"You're selling the company? Why on earth would you want to do that?"

I could not tell him the entire truth; the fact that I wanted to be unencumbered and with cash available should I decide to move on soon, I kept to myself. "Mostly it's because of Gwen. Yesterday I found that I could hardly tolerate the place. It made my skin crawl. I keep seeing her, dead and bloody, in that loft. I don't think the image will ever fade."

"But you could just move into a different building."

"Yes, I could do that. But truthfully, it is time to get out. I have been in business for ten years now—in that time most people begin to age. I have not. Fashion is a high-profile industry and although I have managed to avoid publicity more than some designers, I could not continue for too much longer without it being extremely noticeable. I just can't take many more chances than I already have."

He took a long drink of his scotch, his mouth twisted into a frown. "Then you'll be leaving town?"

"Not necessarily. If I don't have to run Griffin Designs, I can fade into anonymity again, staying another five or ten years if I wish."

"And do you want to?"

I took a deep breath and reached over to touch his hand. "That all depends on you, Mitch."

"On me?" He looked surprised and I laughed at him.

"Yes, on you." I began to say more when the waiter came to the table. "Miss Griffin, Mr. Greer, the rest of your party is here. Shall I seat you?"

Mitch stood up and moved my chair back. "Well," he said in a thoughtful manner, extending his arm to me, "I guess we can talk about that later."

Introductions were made at the table; I had never met the woman who was purchasing the company, although I had heard of her. Betsy McCain was what I considered the epitome of the modern business woman—intelligent, brassy and high-pressure. I disliked her at first sight. Conversation with her merely reinforced my initial impression.

She was accompanied by two attorneys and two assistants. With the exception of the lawyer seated to her right, they had little to add to the discussion. I felt that she had merely brought them along for a free meal. But after I realized that the purchasing price was twice what I had asked Fred to get for me, I thought she was entitled, even when all five of them ordered the most expensive items from the menu.

She, at least, made no pretense about how she planned to run Griffin Designs. "We will modernize the entire place, of course"—her eyes reflected the glitter of the candles—"and any of the employees who cannot adapt to the situation will be welcome to leave after their two months are up." I knew then that she meant to replace them all. "And the clothes themselves will have to be updated." She reached over and laid her hand on my arm. "Not that what you have on isn't a lovely dress, Deirdre"—she was practically purring at this point and I could smell the champagne heavy on her breath—"but today's woman needs clothes that represent her place in today's world."

I looked over at her. She wore a navy blue tailored suit, probably the same one she had worn to her office today. With the exception of her skirt, it was identical to the ones worn by her attorneys. She had at least made an attempt to dress it up for this evening with jewelry, gold necklaces and bracelets that clinked together harshly with every gesture she made. I smiled at her sweetly. "No, there isn't much room for romance in today's world, is there, Betsy?"

"Romance?" She snorted disdainfully. "It's a rough world out there. We need to dress like we mean business, all the time. Any woman in the marketplace should know how to go for the throat when necessary."

Mitch was in the middle of a drink of champagne and he made a small choking sound. I glanced over at him and winked, then turned back to her. "I do know what you mean, but I'm afraid I never developed much of a killer instinct over the years. Perhaps you could give me lessons sometime?"

Mitch choked again, turned it into a cough and excused himself from the table. She, of course, was oblivious to the irony of the situation.

"That would be a real pleasure, I'm sure. I could never figure how someone as young and inexperienced as you could make a profit, anyway." I was glad Mitch left before this last comment; he would probably be under the table in hysterics by now. Fred caught my eye warningly—he knew me well enough to sense my dislike and was probably worried that I might call off the deal.

"Even so," I said noncommittally, and signaled for the waiter. "More champagne, please. Now, shall we sign?"

Mitch returned after we had completed the deal. He seemed to have regained his composure, but his eyes were still laughing. I took his hand and held it for a minute; the new owner of Griffin Designs caught the gesture and leaned forward over the table with an eager smile. "So, Mr. Greer, what do you do for a living?"

"I'm a detective."

"Oh, how fascinating. Just like Mike Hammer; it must be exciting."

"Actually, I'm with the police department."

"I see," she said with a bit of a sneer in her voice. "And how on earth did you two meet?"

"Murder investigation." Everyone at the table grew silent and stared at Mitch. The waiter brought our meals; after we were all served, he spoke again. I could hear the repressed laughter in his voice. "Deirdre was my main suspect." Unconcerned, he took a bite of food and a drink of champagne. "Still is, as a matter of fact. I go with her everywhere, so that when she slips up, I can get her."

I smiled sweetly on my dinner partner again. "So, you see, Betsy, I probably don't need those lessons after all."

Fred started the laughter, and the others joined in, nervously at first then wholeheartedly. The tension dissolved and eventually even Betsy participated.

"Bravo, Deirdre. Maybe we're not as different as I thought."

Chapter 21

The new owner and her entourage left shortly after I paid the bill. We had reached an uneasy truce based on a grudging respect due to our verbal sparing. We made plans to meet the next week to tour the facility and take an inventory. She would not actually take control of Griffin Designs until the first of the year. That gave me time to start on the orders from the show, get everyone into the routine and then bow out gracefully.

Fred, his wife, Mitch and I lingered at the table with after-dinner drinks and coffee. Betsy McCain had not been out of the restaurant for more than a minute before we all began to laugh.

"Good God, Fred, where did you dig up that ghoul?" I wiped tears of amusement from my eyes.

He shrugged. "You never specified we had to sell to someone you liked. She was interested enough to double the price; I figured that was a good deal."

"And it was, of course. Sally"—I nodded toward his wife—"would you like some more coffee?"

"No," she said with a shy smile, checking her watch. "Everything was wonderful, though. Thank you so much for inviting me. But I think we'd better get going, don't you, honey?"

Fred stood up and agreed. "We promised the sitter we'd have her home by one-thirty or two at the latest. It was interesting, Deirdre." He shook hands with me and then turned to Mitch. "Nice meeting you, Greer. Maybe we should all get together sometime, without the sharks."

"You could come over for dinner some night," Sally urged. "You haven't even seen the baby."

"I would like that," I said, giving her a small hug. She smiled and they left.

Mitch and I sat back down and he poured us each another cup of coffee. "They're nice people, Fred and Sally I mean."

"Yes, did you have a good time?"

"Well, I don't know that good could describe it accurately. But as Fred said, it was interesting." His face lit up in a mischievous grin. "That Betsy is something, isn't she?"

"I am sorry about that, Mitch. I had never met her before; but her money is good."

"Did you know that when you went to the ladies' room, she moved over next to me?"

"And?"

"Well, I'll just say that she definitely lacks subtlety. I think she was hoping that maybe more than your company was up for grabs. She must have drunk more champagne by herself than all the rest of us put together." He laughed again, remembering her actions.

"Or"—I moved closer to him and put my hand gently on his leg—"maybe she just knows a good man when she sees one."

He leaned in to kiss me.

"Excuse me." The accented voice broke in on us and we jumped apart. "I don't wish to interrupt but I wanted to know if you enjoyed your meal."

"Victor, yes, thank you, everything was wonderful."

He turned to Mitch. "Mr. Greer, I am Victor Lange. I did not have a chance to meet you before." They shook hands and Mitch looked at his watch. "Deirdre, we'll have to go soon, too. Just let me make a stop first; I'll be right back."

As he walked toward the men's room, Victor apologized. "I always seem to be breaking in at the most romantic moments. I am sorry."

"Don't worry about it; this is not the place for it, anyway."

"No, but you'd be surprised what goes on, sometimes. I'm afraid I did the same to Max just the other night."

"Max?"

"Yes, and it was even more embarrassing than that. I called the young lady he was with by your name. She was like you, same height and build, but I see now that her hair was different. Yours is its natural color, is it not?" I nodded and he continued. "Hers came from a bottle, I'm sure. You see, he had described you to me and I was so sure. Quite an unfortunate incident."

"How odd." I had never known Max to be with another woman. I was not jealous, but why had he never mentioned his involvement to me?

Victor gave me a curious look, and at that moment Mitch returned. "Ready?" he asked. When I stood up, he turned to Victor and shook his hand. "Dinner was excellent, I enjoyed it very much. You live up to your reputation."

"Thank you, we try to." Victor beamed from the compliment. "But I'm afraid that our chef was very distraught with Miss Griffin here, when she refused his special garnish for the steak."

Mitch caught my eye with an amused look. "But I thought it was wonderful. It had a garlic base, didn't it?" Victor nodded. "Oh, well," he said, as he wrapped an arm around my waist, "you have to understand that Deirdre is a purist. Good night."

We stopped by the coat check room, then waited outside for the valet to bring Mitch's car around. I grabbed Mitch's arm, shook it and began to giggle.

"What?"

"A purist? And that crack about me being a prime suspect? You were wonderful. It stopped them all in their tracks." I gave him a sidelong glance. "You had a good time, didn't you?"

"Yeah," he said with a slow smile as he helped me into the car. "You know, I didn't expect to and I'm sort of surprised to admit it, but I really did."

He pulled out into traffic, stopped for a red light and turned to me. "I thought maybe we could go back to my place, that is if you're not too tired." His voice sounded tentative, unsure.

"That would be fine, Mitch. I slept some today. But what about you? Don't you have to go to the station tomorrow?"

He scowled a bit. "Today, after you called, I checked the calendar and realized that I've had only one day off since Thanksgiving. And I haven't had a decent night's sleep either, so I took tomorrow off. If they need me, they know where to find me. I plan on spending the entire day in bed." The light changed and he drove, reaching over and taking my hand in his. "But I wouldn't mind a little company."

I said nothing but smiled and tightened my grip on his hand.

When we arrived at his apartment, he took off his jacket and tie and threw them on a chair. "Get comfortable, if you'd like," he said. "I have something I want to talk about before we go to sleep."

"Did I leave any clothes here?"

"No." He frowned at me. "You packed everything up and cleared out, remember?" Then he shrugged and made an effort to smile. "But you can borrow my robe. It's on the hook on the bathroom door."

I found the green terry-cloth robe where he had said it was, carefully removed my dress and hung it on the hook. Putting on the robe, I looked at myself in the mirror. It seemed odd that although the robe covered more than the gown, I felt naked in it, somehow more vulnerable than before. Then I realized why that was; this would be the first night Mitch and I had spent together since my revelation to him of what I was. Tonight there would be no lies between us, he knew the worst of me. For the first time in so many years, I had nothing to hide and I felt defenseless. As I walked out the door, though, I caught the faint odor of the robe. It smelled like Mitch; I rubbed my cheek appreciatively on the sleeve and savored the aroma. Everything would be fine.

He was in the kitchen, making coffee. I stood silently in the entrance for a time and watched him. After a while he became aware of my presence and turned to me.

"I thought that after all that champagne, coffee would be nice. Or I could open a bottle of wine."

"Coffee is fine."

"That looks better on you than on me," he said, wiping his hands on a towel. He fixed a tray with mugs, cream and sugar. "Let's adjourn to the living room." He picked up the tray. "You bring the coffee, okay?"

I waited a minute for the water to stop dripping, then carried the pot into the other room and set it on the tray. Wordlessly, he poured our cups and fixed his, his eyes never leaving my face. I took a small sip of mine, then put it aside, waiting for him to make a move. He cleared his throat and began haltingly. "Deirdre, you must know that yesterday morning was one of the strangest times I've ever had." He stood up and began to pace, touching books, straightening a lamp shade. Finally he sat down and took his mug in his hands, but did not drink. "I've always had a conservative nature," he continued. "People kid me about it sometimes, how I won't read my horoscope or play the lottery. I don't believe in luck, coincidences or the supernatural. So what you had to tell me really shook me up. When I left I had no intention of ever seeing you again."

I looked away from him and began playing with the robe belt, wrapping it over my fingers. "But I am here," I said softly as if to myself.

He either didn't hear or ignored my interruption. "As the day went on, I began to see things differently. I started to think of you in another light. Not as a blood-crazed lunatic, but as a victim, too. I even did a little research on the areas you said you had been in over the years and found no records of murders similar to the ones we've had here. Intuitively, emotionally, I guess I knew you were innocent. But me, I needed definite proof."

I glanced up at him to see him take a drink of his coffee.

When he looked at me, I turned away. He slowly rose from his seat and sat down next to me.

"Deirdre, I want to be honest with you. It's not an easy thing."

"I know. Please go on."

"I agreed to meet you tonight with the sole purpose of talking the case over with you, enlisting your help. If what we are dealing with is a vampire, and now I must believe that it is, then your firsthand knowledge on the subject will be extremely helpful."

So that was it. I could help him solve his case and then go on my way alone. I stood up and walked away from him. "I'll help you anyway I can, Mitch. You should know that by now. But some other time; now I would like to get dressed and go home. You don't need to walk me back, I'll catch a cab." I started down the hallway.

He stopped me halfway there and backed me up against the wall, blocking my escape. "Why don't you ever let me finish?" he asked with a wry grin. "Are you always this hasty?"

"Yes, but I prefer to call it caution. And I don't usually have a problem exercising it. Let me go, Mitch." I could easily break away from him, but I wanted his concession.

He did not give it. "Deirdre, how could anyone live as long as you and still not understand other people? I thought that age was supposed to give you a certain perspective. It hasn't done you much good, has it?"

"I'm still alive, aren't I?" I snarled. "That should be good for something."

He smiled. "It is good, you know. It saved you for me."

I glanced at him, startled.

"When I thought of you, my intentions were strictly business. But when I spoke to you and saw you tonight, I realized that, despite all my plans and despite what you were, I wanted you here tonight and damn the consequences." He stepped away from me. "And now, I've finished. Do you still want to leave?"

"I never did," I said in honesty. "If I did, you wouldn't have been able to stop me."

He moved me up against the wall again, gently this time. "I knew that, Deirdre. Will you stay?"

"For a while, Mitch, gladly."

I awoke shortly after noon the next day to find Mitch, fully dressed but lying on the bed beside me. He propped himself up on one elbow, carefully considering me. "Good afternoon," he said with a gentle smile. "Did you sleep well?"

"Fine, and you?"

"Like a baby. Chris was right, you are good for me."

"Chris told you that?"

"Yeah, he called the next day. He's really quite smitten with you."

"He is a nice kid, Mitch, but don't you think he's a little young for me?"

He reached over and brushed my hair over my face with a devilish smile. "Yeah, probably, but come to think of it, Deirdre, so am I." Before I could respond, he jumped up from the bed and retrieved a paper bag that was sitting in the corner of the room. "Here," he said abruptly, "these are yours."

I looked inside to find a pair of jeans, two or three shirts, some underwear and a bra. "Thank you. Where did you get them?"

"I stopped by your hotel and picked them up for you. He reached into his pocket and handed my key back. "I hope you don't mind."

"Not at all."

"You get dressed. I have some coffee ready."

I smoothed the hair from my eyes. "Sounds good, but is it safe?"

He shot me a quizzical look. "You've drunk my coffee before and lived to tell the tale. Of course it's safe."

"No, I mean is it daylight? Are all the windows covered?"

"Oh!" he said, walking out. "I'll check." I heard him pulling drapes shut, then he called to me. "All clear, I think."

"Thank you." I dressed quickly and cautiously stepped into the living room. "This should be fine."

He was standing at the window with his back to me, his hands still on the drape cord. "It seems a shame. It's such a glorious day."

"Glorious for you, maybe, but deadly for me." His shoulders slumped a bit. "Let it be, Mitch."

He spun around, stung by my comment. "I wouldn't open them. How could you think that?"

"That's not what I mean. I know you wouldn't hurt me. But you should quit tearing yourself up over this situation. It is not worth it. I can't change, no matter how much you or I might wish it."

"But maybe you could. I've been doing research in the area for weeks since this case started. Did you know there's a recently discovered disease that they think may have caused the myths of vampirism to arise? Propheria, I think it was called." He looked at me hopefully and I hated to disillusion him.

"*Porphyria.* I know all about it, Mitch. I paid one of the researchers on the subject good money to examine me and then forget about it."

"And?"

"Sorry, my darling. They could find no trace of it in my system. They did, however, find out some facts that interested them greatly. My metabolism, my DNA structure; all sorts of details that they wanted to study." I gave a small laugh in recollection of the situation. "I had one hell of a time getting out of the office intact and with all my files."

"How did you get out?"

"Oh," I said casually, but locked my eyes on his, "I talked them into it."

He shuddered slightly as my gaze held him. "I believe it." Then he smiled at me as I dropped my stare. "You must teach me to do that, Deirdre. It would be very handy in my line of work."

"No doubt," I agreed glibly. "But I don't think it can be

taught, only acquired." I grew serious, considering the matter. "And not without great cost." An uncomfortable silence filled the room as we studied each other, both trying to fathom the other's thoughts.

"Okay, I'll drop it," he said at last. "Now, how about that coffee?"

The hours passed quickly in his company. We sat and talked about commonplace things, carefully avoiding any mention of recent events. He received several phone calls that I presumed were about the case, but made no comment on them, and I asked no questions. It was a peaceful time, unlike the frenzy of passion or anger we usually experienced. Sometimes he would reach out to me and gently stroke my hair or shoulder. I was grateful for the ordinariness of the situation. We could have been any other couple on their day off. It was a comfortable feeling, one that I fervently wished could continue.

In the early afternoon, the phone rang again. Mitch went to it with a shrug and a smile for me. He answered it, talked for a while and then hung up. When he turned back to me he was not smiling. "Nothing, we've got nothing on this case. Everywhere we turn, we come up a blank. How the hell am I supposed to solve this, when I have no witnesses, no clues, no idea of who might be doing it. At least with Larry, I had something concrete. But for this one, he could very well be made of mist, it's that hard to track him." His voice raised in frustration.

"You said last night that I could help you. What exactly do you have in mind?"

"I don't think you should get involved, not anymore. It could be dangerous for you. I keep picturing you in Gwen's place, or like the girl in the morgue."

"What girl in the morgue?"

"The one they brought in, you know, the fourth murder. There was something about her that . . ." He stopped and shuddered.

"Anyway, I think it would be best for you just to stay out of it. I can keep you safe here until everything is over."

"Mitch, you cannot keep me locked away forever. And you cannot always be around to protect me. Sooner or later I will have to feed, and should you be around, well, let's just say you could become very anemic over time. Neither of us wants that to happen."

"Well, I did bring your supplies over with me in addition to the clothes." He gave me a shy smile. "I put it in the vegetable drawer."

I laughed. "Good place for it, but that doesn't solve the problem."

"I know. Everything you're saying is true. It's just that the thought of losing you makes me crazy."

"Fine, let me help you and it will all be over sooner. I don't believe that the other vampire would harm me in any event."

"I seem to remember that that's what you said about Larry."

I smiled. "Then the odds that I am right will be better this time. Let me help, Mitch."

He finally reneged. "Actually," he admitted sheepishly, "there's really no danger to you on this. I just want you to come along with me while I talk to everyone again. Maybe there will be something you can pick up from them, recognition maybe, I don't know. But if we start now, we can finish by eight or nine, get some dinner and come back here."

"Now?" I questioned, glancing at the clock. "The sun won't set for hours. But," I said quickly seeing the disappointment on his face, "I could leave at sunset. Will that be soon enough?"

"I guess it will have to be. I don't have a choice, anyway, do I?"

"No, and neither do I." I went over to him and gently touched his arm. "Nothing of importance is likely to happen in the next few hours, considering that the person we're looking for also can't go about in daylight."

He brightened briefly. "Yeah, I guess I hadn't thought of it that way. I'm just not used to this confinement. When I want to go out, I go."

I wrapped my arms around his neck and kissed him. When I was done, I looked up at him and smiled. "We have some free time, Mitch. Do you know what I'd like to do?" I moved away from him and started backing down the hall, slowly unbuttoning my shirt. "I'd really like to have a shower." I laughed at the look on his face and tossed my shirt to him.

His face lit up with a playful grin. "I hope you don't mind sharing?"

"Not at all," I replied. "And I hope you like the water hot."

Chapter 22

When we eventually emerged from the shower, Mitch laughed. "Damn, I feel like a lobster. How can you stand it?"

I shrugged as I wrapped myself in a towel. "It warms me."

"I should hope so," he said with a wry grin, as we went to the bedroom to dress. "It damn near parboiled me."

I sat on the edge of the bed to brush my hair. "Let me do that," he said and took the brush from my hand. He knelt behind me and began to brush, slowly at first, and then with harder strokes. It felt so good that I leaned back into him, contentedly. He continued for a while, then stopped abruptly, threw the brush across the room and buried his face in the mass of hair at my neck. "Oh, Deirdre," he said, making my name into a low, passionate moan, then made a grab at the towel that covered me. He flung it to the floor and pulled me down on the bed next to him.

I looked into his eyes, so blue and intense. "I thought we had to go out," I teased him softly.

"Later," he said and kissed me.

The phone rang and he jumped from me. "Let it ring," I urged, twining my arms around his neck and pulling him back.

"Shit," he swore as he rose from me reluctantly. "I can't just let it ring. It might be important." He reached over, picked up the phone, then covered the receiver and took one more kiss before answering it. "Yeah," he said brusquely into the phone, "this had better be good."

I could hear the voice of the caller, low, urgent and somehow familiar, but did not pay attention. Instead, I occupied myself with lazily tracing the muscles in Mitch's now tense arm until he brushed me off and sat up straight.

"Look, Hunter, I thought I made the situation plain last night. She's with me now. I'll take care of her. You should just leave her alone."

"Damn," I swore quietly and Mitch gave me a sharp look. I could hear Max's cynical laugh and comment quite plainly. He, too, had raised his voice. "Calm down, Greer. I only want to talk to her. I know she's there."

Mitch put his hand over the receiver again. "It's Max," he snarled, handed me the phone and stalked out of the room.

"Damn it, Max. Your timing couldn't be worse. What do you want?"

"I spoke with Victor Lange today. He said you had dinner at the Imperial last night."

"That's right. And?"

"It was brought to my attention that I just might have some information for Greer, if he would be interested."

I looked up and Mitch was standing in the entrance of the door, glaring at the telephone. "What the hell does he want?" he said in a voice loud enough to be heard.

"Tell him what I said, Deirdre"

"I don't much care to be caught in the middle of this, Max. Why don't you just talk to Mitch, if that's what you want. Or maybe he should listen in on the extension." I wasn't sure with which one of them I was most annoyed.

"An excellent idea, Deirdre," Max agreed. "I do have something of importance to say to both of you."

"Pick up the extension, Mitch," I said, exasperated. He went to the kitchen and we maintained silence until we heard the click from the other phone.

"Now, isn't that better," Max said sarcastically. "All cozy and together again."

"Get to the point, Hunter. We have better things to do . . ."

"I'm sure you do." Max's voice was smooth, insinuating. "So I'll make it quick. I didn't wish to interrupt your afternoon. But it was important that I talk to Deirdre. When I couldn't find her at any of the usual places, I assumed she was with you." I could hear an uncharacteristic sadness in his voice. Mitch must have heard it also, because he awkwardly cleared his throat. Max continued without acknowledging him. "Be that as it may, even if she weren't there, I would have called to give you some information." Max paused and I could hear a faint tingling of ice against a glass.

"Get on with it, Hunter," Mitch said and Max laughed.

"He's so abrupt, my dear. I must admit, I don't quite understand the attraction, but it must be considerable. You don't know how lucky you are, Greer. She's been through hundreds of men since I've known her and never gone back for seconds." He laughed again.

"You bastard . . ." Mitch started.

"It doesn't matter, Mitch," I cut in. "Don't let him get to you. He does it only for the reaction. Isn't that right, Max?"

"Just so, my love. But my advice to you, Greer, is to make hay while the sun shines. Some night she'll fly away and you'll never get her back." There was still a trace of cynical laughter in his voice.

"Spare us the dramatics, Hunter. I heard them all the other night. Just get on with it."

"Fine, I won't waste your time any longer. Today in conversation with Victor Lange, I suddenly realized that I had important information on your case. If the two of you were to stop over at the club tonight, I'd be more than willing to share it."

"What exactly is going on?" Mitch sounded angry. "You gave no indication earlier that you knew anything about this. I know you have been questioned and had nothing to say. I could charge you for withholding evidence, or . . ."

"Don't threaten me, Greer. It will do you no good. Let's just say that I became aware of something of importance to you and I wanted to do my civil duty."

I laughed at that comment, coming from Max. Responsibility, civil or otherwise, was never one of his strong points.

"Deirdre, you wound me." I said nothing and he continued. "You will come, won't you? Together?"

Mitch broke in quickly. "I'll be there, Hunter. But I don't see the need to drag Deirdre into this. She'll stay here. Last time she was at your club, she was almost killed, thanks to you."

"Deirdre will come with you, won't you, my dear? Otherwise the deal is off. I'll expect you both after sundown."

"We'll be there, Max."

I hung up the phone and Mitch came back into the bedroom. "What do you suppose this is all about?" he asked me and I shook my head.

"It's hard to tell with Max. It may even be his idea of a practical joke."

"It's not funny."

"Not to you, maybe or even me. But Max is different; I don't really think he means any harm. It is just the way he is."

"You have too high an opinion of that man, Deirdre. I could believe almost anything of him. He's just too damn smooth."

"Let's not waste our time talking about Max. We'll find out soon enough what he wants. And until then"—I checked the clock—"we have about two hours before sunset. Do you think we could pick up where we left off?"

"Absolutely," he said, crossing the room and smiling the smile that lit his eyes.

Afterward, we both fell asleep and the dream found me swiftly and mercilessly.

It begins at the side of the road; I leave the carriage and the frightened horses, I step over the body there without question to follow the dark figure that beckons just out of my reach. With every step that takes me nearer to him I grow in strength, but even that is not enough. Still he moves ahead and I struggle to catch up, to match a face to that form and voice that haunt me through dreams and wakings. I am running now, wearing the green velvet dress. It is dirty and stained, the hem sodden and thick with blood and tears. It catches around my ankles and I stumble. He turns around to watch me. His laugh is as dark and unimaginable as his face.

"Come," he urges. "Hurry," he calls and the words are carried on the wind as if from a long distance away. I pull myself from the ground and follow for what seems like miles, never tiring and yet always behind. Soon he leads me down a street I recognize to a house, my house, my father's house. The air is heavy with the sweet scents of the garden but I cannot stay. I must find him.

He has entered the house, I know; the door swings slightly ajar in the wind. His footsteps echo in the upstairs hall and I ascend to meet him. The corridor is long and shadowy, but the dead are not here. "At rest," I whisper. "Have you gone to rest?" There is no answer; all is empty and hollow.

The doorway at the end stands open and I see the starlit sky, the open field. I enter and he is not there. "Show yourself," I scream defiantly, angrily and am answered with a wild rustling of wings, stirring the warm evening air. I feel his presence behind me, his breath is hot on my neck and my hair begins to raise. I do not turn around. "Are you here, then?" I ask quietly.

"I am here."

"I would see your face."

"There is no need, little one. It has been before you for years and you did not see."

"I would know who you are."

"But you know me, Deirdre. Better than any other. We are one. Why do you deny me?"

I feel the silken touch of his wing on my neck. It is smooth as before and dark. I tremble at the touch and clench my fists in anger. With his lightly deposited kiss and my ensuing shudder, there can be no doubt. For I do know him now, but as I turn around to confront him, he is already dissolving into the darkness. There is only the brief glance of confirmation: the moonlight shining off the sculptured lines of his face, the lifting of an eyebrow, the cruel twist of his mouth, a mouth that had lied and comforted, kissed and tortured, a mouth and a hunger that had killed many and destroyed me—Max's mouth, Max's hunger.

And then he is gone.

Chapter 23

I awoke alone with his name echoing angrily in my head. Mitch must have risen without waking me. I dressed quickly and walked out of the bedroom. Mitch was sitting at the kitchen table, finishing a sandwich. He looked up at me, smiled and finished swallowing. "Sleep well?"

"Fine." I stared at him for a minute, as he stood up and put his plate into the sink. When he turned around he gave me a puzzled look.

"What's wrong? You look shook up."

"Bad dream." I said simply. "Are you ready to go?"

"Yes, if you are."

We walked out of the apartment and got into his car. As he began driving, he turned to me. "Are you sure you're all right? You look like you might be getting sick or something."

"No, I'm fine." I reached over and touched his thigh gently. "Mitch," I asked casually, "what was that you said yesterday about the girl in the morgue?"

"Who?"

"You know, the fourth murder victim. Something about her disturbed you."

"Yeah, she reminded me of you. It bothered me a lot." He smiled and put his hand on top of mine. "But I'm okay now. All of that helped me realize that it didn't matter what or who you are. I knew that I still loved you, if I could get so upset about seeing the dead body of someone who just looked like you."

"In what way did she look like me?"

"Well, she was about your height, your build and her hair was almost the same color, other than that . . ." He stopped abruptly and gave me a sharp look. "Why? Is it important?"

"No, probably not." It really didn't matter at that point; I was still overwhelmed by the identity of the man in my dream. I began to think about our relationship over the years. How could I have been so blind? That first spark of recognition at the diner in Kansas should have told me. So many things since I had known him should have told me. The way he controlled and manipulated me, the way I could never stay angry about anything that he did to me, the way I always came crawling back to the sanctuary of his presence. "Damn," I whispered to myself.

"What did you say?"

"Nothing, only, do you think you could drive a little faster. I'd like to get this over with."

He looked at me questioningly, and said nothing but increased his speed as much as possible. The streets were congested with cars and pedestrians. It took us over twenty minutes to travel the remaining six blocks. The whole time I stared out the window, clenching my fists so tightly that my nails broke the surface of the skin. I opened my hands, eight perfect crescents of congealed blood marked the palms.

Mitch parked his car out front and when the doorman tried to stop him, he showed his badge. "Police business," he said and the doorman let us through. We shouldered our way through the crowd in the bar and eventually made our way to the hall that led to Max's office.

Before we reached the door, Mitch stopped in his tracks and grabbed my arms. "Deirdre, what the hell is going on here? All of a sudden, it's like you know something I don't. Care to enlighten me?" His voice was tense and nervous.

"How could he take me in so completely?" I spoke as if to myself. "All these years, and I never knew him, never knew who he was. And now, it's so obvious."

"What's obvious, Deirdre? Who are you talking about?"

I shook my head. "I've been a fool. I suppose I didn't really want to know." I broke away from Mitch and began walking again. He stood still, staring for a moment, then caught up with me as I reached Max's closed door.

I pulled him into a fierce embrace. "I love you," I said as I stretched up and kissed him, forgetful for one moment of all that waited for me, behind the door.

"And I love you, too. But this hardly seems the time or place . . ."

"There may be no time, later." I looked deeply into his eyes. "Wait here, Mitch," I pleaded. "I'll handle this by myself."

"Handle what?" he started, but the door opened.

Max stood there, elegant as usual. His features seemed more cruel, more inhuman than I could ever have imagined them. His eyes blazed as they met mine. "What a delightful surprise. You're right on time. Please come in."

I ignored him and kissed Mitch again, slowly and lingeringly. "Stay here," I said to him again when we had finished.

Max laughed. "How touching, Deirdre. But you have me all wrong. I don't intend to hurt him, not if he gives me what I want. And he will, you know. Please come in, you're both most welcome."

" 'Enter freely and of your own will?' " I quoted to him. "Don't you think that just may be a trifle melodramatic, Max?"

He smiled at me and nodded. "Perhaps it is, my little one. But at least you finally understand. That's good. Although I had wanted to reveal myself to you at my own time, when I spoke with Victor, and he told me he had informed you about my escort the other night, well, I realized that it wouldn't be long before the two of you began to put everything together on your own. And so now you know who and what I am. I'm glad; it will make everything so much easier."

Mitch looked at both of us, in confusion. "I don't understand. Would someone just tell me what is going on here?"

"Dracula welcomes Jonathan Harker to his castle," I said to

him gently. "Chapter two, I believe." Max nodded and I continued. "I thought you had done research, Mitch."

"Then," he said in disbelief, "Max is also a . . . just like you."

Max's sardonic laughter echoed in the hallway and I felt a chill run up my spine. "So you found the courage to tell him, my dear. And he still stands with you. That's good." Then he turned to Mitch. "Yes, Greer. I'm also a vampire. But you'll find that, unlike some"—and he gave me a surprisingly gentle glance—"I'm not afraid to say the word, nor to use the powers I have. But it is most inappropriate to discuss this here in the hall." He motioned us in and we obeyed.

The power he was exerting over us seemed insurmountable and when he gestured for us to sit down, we did so mechanically and without question. Mitch, I noticed briefly, was busy surveying the surroundings, but I could barely take my eyes away from Max. "You and I have a few scores to settle, Max," I said through clenched teeth. "Let Mitch go. He can't hurt you."

"Oh, but he already has. He has taken you and loved you. And made you love him. That cannot be allowed. I'd wager that he wouldn't hesitate to kill me now, if he could. Isn't that right, Greer?"

"You son of a bitch," Mitch snarled and reached into his coat for his gun. He was no match for the other's reflexes. Max moved across the room in a blur and gripped Mitch's arm, twisting until the gun dropped. Then, with a small smile at me, he continued to twist. Mitch gave a moan of pain and I could hear his bones breaking, accompanied by a wet, tearing sound. One of the bones had broken through his skin and my nostrils flared. The room was now filled with the scent of blood.

"Max!" I pleaded with him. "Please stop."

"Anything you say, my dear." Max flung him into a corner of the room as if he weighed nothing. Mitch's head hit the wall and his moaning ceased. I ran to him, searching for the pulse in his neck.

"Still alive?" Max inquired. When I nodded, he shook his

head. "He must be stronger than I thought. It makes no difference, I suppose. He can live, for now."

"So help me, Max, if you kill him . . ."

"Oh, but I won't kill him, Deirdre." He looked amused. "I wouldn't even dream of it. Once again you have misjudged me."

I managed a low, bitter laugh. "Misjudged you? No, I don't think so, Max. Underestimated, maybe. But you're capable of anything, aren't you?"

He thought for a moment. "Let's just say that I rarely fail when I set my mind to something. Besides, when one is faced with eternity, as are you and I, a few lives don't matter."

"How can you say that?" I was horrified. "That's inhuman."

"Ah, but then, isn't that the point? We are inhuman."

"Thanks to you, I am. Would you care to explain that?"

"You, I'm sad to admit, were a mistake. I never intended to turn you into a vampire. I've found over the years that women make very poor initiates. They just don't have the cruelty, the ruthlessness that is needed." He gave me a tender glance and walked gracefully to me. He took my hand and kissed it gently. "You don't, either, my love. But you had a will to survive and that carried you through. I admired you at the time for the fight you put up. I admire you now. You are one of my best creations."

I stiffened and pulled my hand away. "You have other creations? Where?"

"All over the world, I believe. I keep in touch with a few of them, still. Some are more successful than others, but none turned out quite so well nor half so beautiful as you. I have retried the experiment over the years, you know. Taken someone unwilling and forced my blood upon them. They all died, hideously with the first sunrise. But you had the instincts and the wit to survive." He moved closer to me and fastened his eyes upon me again. "When I met you at that diner in Kansas, I could hardly believe you were the same person. The fact that you had lived for so long, on your own, unguided and untaught, surprised me. Even those with the best of teachers fail and die, usually within fifty years of their transformation." He reached over to me and laid his hands on my shoulders. "But there could be no mistaking you; the blood we had shared called to me. And to you, although you did not know enough then to recognize the bond that held us together. I almost told you, the night we made love, but you weren't ready yet."

"Ready for what?" I asked and a moan interrupted us. We both looked over to the corner where Mitch lay and found him sitting up, rubbing his head with his left arm. His right arm dangled uselessly at his side. I tried to move, but Max's grip tightened.

"Ready to join with me, forever."

"I would never do that, Max. You represent everything I hate, everything our kind has been reviled for over the centuries. There is no need to kill, no hunger so great that would necessitate the death of the victim."

Max threw back his head and laughed. "Oh, Deirdre, you are so young, so innocent yet. Look at her, Greer. Is she not magnificent? The face of an angel and the kiss of a devil. A body captured and preserved at its peak of maturity and passion. Yet in vampire terms, she is still only a child, little more than an infant. She has yet to realize one-tenth of her powers, powers of the body and mind which I have bequeathed to her." He gave both Mitch and me a humorless smile, frightening in its inhumanity, then grasped my face in his hands. "And still you talk of needs and hunger as if the thirst for life could be measured in pints. There was no need, I kill simply because I can."

A faint sound from Mitch's corner interrupted him. Max turned and went to him. "I don't think you will need that radio, Greer. Give it to me."

As Max's hand neared him, Mitch clutched the unit tighter. "You won't get away with this, Hunter," he said grimly, his mouth contorted with pain. Quickly Max reached over and wrested the box from his grip. He looked down on Mitch, an expression of disdain on his face.

"Can you stop me?" he sneered derisively as he reached down and took hold of Mitch's knee. Small beads of sweat began to

form on Mitch's forehead and once again I could hear the sound
of breaking bones. He let out one labored breath as Max continued, "Are you man enough to take me, Greer?" He turned
away abruptly and began to laugh.

"Damn you, Hunter," Mitch said with a grimace. "Get on
with your story. I'd like to hear your justification for four murders."

Max laughed again, still looking down at Mitch. "Justification? Why should I need justification for any of my deeds? And
why would I provide it to such as you? I could explain to Deirdre, for she might come close to understanding. There are times,
lately, when the blood is not enough, when I need the total
quenching of life. It was not premeditated, not planned; the
deaths simply happened. At such times I have no control, but it
makes no difference."

Mitch stared at him, as did I; his total lack of shame for his
deeds appalled us. "Before you go any further," Mitch told him
in a tight, pained voice, "I must inform you that anything that
you say can be considered a confession at this point and it will
be used as such."

Max turned to me. "I begin to understand your attraction, my
dear. He is a very determined man, even when helpless. He
would do well as one of us, don't you think, Deirdre?"

I said nothing but I gasped. "But, no," Max went on, "that
would probably be unwise. And you seem to like him human,
so human he will remain." He lowered his voice, all traces of
humor vanished. "The span of his human endurance I leave up
to you."

He strode over to me, held me in his arms. His eyes were
crazed, maniacal, striving to draw me into his madness. I looked
away, but stood limp and passive in his embrace, not wanting
my struggle to inflict further torture on Mitch. "I want you,
Deirdre." He whispered to me now, an urging, demanding whisper that caused a chill to travel through my body. "I have always
wanted you. You will grow stronger, you will cast away your
petty morals. I will teach you to revel in death, as I do." His

voice was deep and passionate, his words echoed in my brain. He began to caress my back, his hands strong on my yielding flesh. "Look at me," he commanded and wrapped my hair around his hand, drawing my head back roughly. Our eyes met and I knew I was lost. Then Max kissed me, his lips burned on mine, his eyes blazed into my very soul and I thought he would never stop. I did not want him to stop. Mitch whispered my name in anguish, but I still could not take my eyes from Max.

"Soon, my little one, you will learn that human lives are worthless, next to the power we possess. The power of life eternal, savagely drained. And the power of death. That night at the club, when I said you had changed, I thought that you had finally awakened and come into the power that is yours by right." He smiled at me and I saw that his canines had grown sharper and longer. "I know now that was not the case. That you had only been in love. In love," he repeated with scorn and grasped my face roughly between his hands again. His face glowed with a fury and a love that I had never seen before. "You have no idea what that word means, until you taste what I have to offer." Somewhere in the back of my mind a voice was crying violation and rape, but I was again drawn into him against my will, and when he bent his head to drink at my neck, I welcomed his kiss.

"Ah," he said, as he withdrew his bloodied mouth. "She walks in beauty, like the night."

I caressed his cheek and smiled. He kissed me again; I could taste my own blood on his tongue and was deeply aroused. "Tell me more," I urged huskily. "About our power."

"We are gods, you and I. They can mean nothing to us; they are here for our sustenance, nothing more." He spoke insistently. "Your initiation has been delayed for too long, little one. But now your time has come. You will be my mate, my love, my passion through all eternity." He turned me in his arms to face Mitch. He was struggling to rise from the floor, to reach us, to stop us. "Look at him, Deirdre," Max commanded. "Look at your human lover. Pitiful, isn't he? You could break his neck with one blow. You could crack his spine easily, without a second thought. But we don't want him dead, not just yet, do we?" I looked at Max questioningly, I was a child in his hands. "Go to him, Deirdre. Take him, he is yours. Take all of him. I suspect he'd rather suffer his death at your hands than at mine. But just to show what a good sport I am, Greer, I will let you die in private."

Max laughed and gave me one more kiss, still holding my gaze. "Soon, my love, we will begin our life together, we will roam the earth together, the night will be ours." He closed the door softly and I walked slowly toward Mitch.

"Deirdre," he said weakly. "You have to stop him." I knelt down next to him, took his uninjured hand in mine and stroked his hair. "He's crazy, you know that. He's got you under some sort of spell, don't you realize that?"

"Don't worry, Mitch," I said. "Everything will be fine." I was startled by the expressionless tone of my voice; he heard it, too, and tried to crawl away from me. The horror on his face was terrible and yet somehow gratifying. I remembered what Max had said, that he was mine to take completely. I smiled, knowing that my canines were exposed to his view.

His face grew ashen with fear. "Deirdre." A note of pleading entered his voice. "You don't have to do this. He can't make you kill me."

"Oh, but he can, Mitch." I lifted him gently in my arms.

"Look at me, Deirdre. Really look at me." I heard him as if from a distance, but the words made no sense. The veins were throbbing in his neck, calling me, pulling me. I put my mouth on him, nuzzling and licking the skin, his scent was fear and blood.

With one final burst of strength he grabbed my chin and pulled my face up. His eyes drew me; I could read fear there, but beneath it I could see his love for me still. "I love you," he whispered and I heard the truth in his words. "And I will love you even as you do this."

I shuddered and began to lose some of the urgency of Max's words. "I love you, Mitch, and I won't hurt you. It will be painless, I promise." He shook his head weakly, the desperate grab had drained him. "If I don't," I continued in a panic, "Max will. You know that. He won't be kind."

"I don't give a damn about the pain, or even my death. But I don't want him to turn you into someone you're not. You can't be like him, Deirdre. It would kill you eventually." He looked at me again, his eyes that intense blue I so loved. Somewhere, deep inside me, his words were being heard.

"You are not afraid of me, then?"

"No," he said, never taking his eyes from mine. "I know what you are, but I am not afraid. I trust you with my life and my soul. You won't hurt me."

Tears began to stream down my face and I knew that the battle had been won, if only temporarily. "But I don't have the strength to fight him, Mitch. He's fed on me and he is strong, fortified by my blood. He's weakened my body, knowing that my mind will follow. When he returns, he'll force me to kill you or do it himself. You must leave."

He tried to smile. "I can barely sit up, Deirdre, how could I leave?" He looked at me again and shook his head. "No, there is only one way, you must take me, take my blood. Take it all if you need, my death won't matter if you can rid the world of that madman."

"No, I won't."

"You must. I want you to. It's the only way out for you. And you're all I have now. I don't want to live, knowing that he will always be there, to corrupt you, to twist you into a creature like him. You must kill him and you must take my strength to do it."

"Are you sure, my love?"

"Yes, now do it quickly, before he returns."

I kissed his mouth and slowly moved to his neck "Now, do it now," he whispered and I sank my teeth into his skin; he never even flinched, but sighed and smiled as his blood flowed into my mouth, warming and strengthening my body and my resolve.

When I had finished, I gently stroked the hair from his pale face. "Forgive me, Mitch," I whispered to him. His eyes fluttered weakly but I hoped that he would hear. "I never meant for this to happen." I kissed his cold lips and rose from the floor.

I quickly surveyed the room. It was exactly as I remembered it; how many nights had I sat here with Max, drinking and laughing? And yet how changed it was now. It had acquired a nightmarish quality and I knew that I would never be free of the dreams that had occurred here tonight: dreams of love, passion and death. "Max." I called his name aloud and it echoed around the room. "Max!" I screamed it in fury and paced around the room. I tossed a barstool at the wall to see it shatter into pieces. Picking up the largest splinter, I turned it over in my hands. It was one of the legs, about two feet long and the end that had broken was sharp and pointed. "Max!" I screamed again, knowing that he would hear. "Come and see what a god has done."

He burst through the door, and saw me, my arms hidden behind my back. His eyes took in the crumpled heap that was Mitch and lit with a devilish glow. "Good, Deirdre. You have done well. Come to me and I'll reward you. Tonight you will feed on me."

I moved toward him, slowly and sensuously. He closed the door and leaned against it. He looked at me; then loosened his tie and unbuttoned his shirt. His neck exposed, he beckoned to me. "Come to me, Deirdre," he said forcefully. "Tonight is our wedding night. I will share my essence with you once again."

I felt a moment of panic as I came closer to him—his power over me was still formidable. Had I taken Mitch in vain?

But at that second, Max closed his eyes, reached for the light switch and turned it off. His power over me was gone and I found him in the dark, as he once found me. I kissed his neck; he gave a low, passionate moan. "Put your arms around me," he said huskily. "Hold me close to you." I could feel his heart beat next to me. I placed one hand firmly on his shoulder, pinning him to the door. "Now your other arm, Deirdre. Ah, I have waited so long for this, so long for you."

"So have I, Max, although I never knew it until tonight. Thank you." I bestowed one more kiss on his neck, then his mouth. He was silent in expectation. "Now," I said quickly and he caught his breath in passion. I brought my other hand from behind my back. The stake found him quickly; I used all my borrowed strength and drove it deeply though his heart. The force of my blow lifted him from the floor and impaled him firmly on the door. He gave a choked cry and flailed his arms about in an attempt to free himself. One of them caught the switch and the lights blazed on.

The sight was horrifying: Max writhing, blood spurting from his chest, his lips foam-flecked and his face grimacing in pain and surprise. When he tried to grip the stake, to remove it, I pinioned his arms to the door. His eyes frantically searched about the room for release; finding none, they fastened upon mine. I could not fathom their expression; was it disbelief, fear or hatred? Perhaps it was even relief, or love. No matter, he held me there as compellingly as I held him. His mouth moved, but no sound emerged. Was he saying my name, pleading with me?

Tears began to flow down my face, but still I held him, and was forced to watch the life slowly drain from him. And as he died, I saw the years accumulate, not in his face or body, but in his eyes. "Dear God," I whispered softly. "How many years, how many centuries?" I loosened my grip upon him in horror at what I had taken away from him and from myself: the knowledge, the capacity to survive for so many years. He struggled no longer, but continued to draw me into his eyes. I shared his pain and despair, his triumphs and conquests; somehow I was pulled into him, deeply pulled into him and felt his power and his pain enter into my own body and soul. Mentally, I staggered back from the invasion, no longer sure that I could hold him or my resolve. No longer sure that I desired his death. But before I could loosen my hold, before I could repair the damage I had inflicted, his eyes glazed over and his mouth fell open in a ghastly grin. His bloodless lips curled back, exposing his teeth, still sharpened, startlingly white. "Deirdre," I heard his whisper in my mind. Then, as abruptly as the slamming of a door, he was gone.

I let go of his arms and they dropped limply at his sides. His body swung gently back and forth and small drops of blood ran down the length of the stake into the expanding pool at his feet. I wiped my hands on my pants and turned away.

"Is he dead?" The voice was weak but undoubtedly Mitch's. I went to where he lay.

"Yes," I said wearily. Speaking was an effort; I was tired and shaken. "He is dead." There was no happiness, no triumph in my voice, but Mitch did not notice.

"Good!" He tried to smile at me but failed. "What a night, huh?" His eyes closed once more. I walked slowly to the desk, and called for an ambulance. Then I sat down next to him and cradled his head in my arms until I heard the sirens. When they arrived, I kissed Mitch and felt for a pulse in his neck. It was there, but so faint that I could have missed it. "Please live," I urged him. "I have enough blood on my hands. I don't want yours." I rose then, carefully opening the door that still held Max impaled and lifeless, and fled into the blackness of the night without turning back.

Chapter 24

During the three weeks Mitch spent in the hospital, I completed my plans for departure. The transfer of Griffin Designs went smoothly. Other aspects took longer—the transfer of my funds to Swiss accounts, travel arrangements and living arrangements at my new destination. But by sundown, New Year's Eve, I was packed and ready to go. Most of my effects had been sent on ahead so all I had was a small travel case, plane tickets and a passport with the picture and name of a stranger. The name I could get used to—I had before; but I looked with doubt at the picture and its image in the mirror. I had cut my hair short and dyed it a deep brown, almost black. It was very chic, very modern and I hated it. But I looked sufficiently unlike Deirdre Griffin to proceed with a new life. That, I told myself again, was all that mattered.

I called the lobby and asked Frank to get a taxi for me in about half an hour. My flight would not leave for almost three hours, but I saw no need to linger. The rooms had already acquired an impersonal feeling; it was strange to consider that soon someone else would be living here. I made a final tour to make sure that I had left nothing behind. I was in the bathroom, when there was a tentative knock on the door.

"Come in, Frank," I called for I assumed he was here to get my bag. "The door is open."

"Deirdre?" The voice was not Frank's; my heart rose then fell when I realized the confrontation I had tried so hard to avoid had come.

"Mitch?" My voice was tremulous, betraying emotion best kept under control. I walked out of the bathroom and into the hall. Mitch stood, glancing around the room, taking in its emptiness and the packed bag at the door. As I entered, he looked at me in shock.

"What on earth did you do to yourself?" he questioned sharply.

Nervously, I ran my hand through my too-short hair. "Don't you like it?"

"No."

"To tell you the truth," I said with a wan smile, "I don't like it much, either. But it keeps the publicity hounds at bay. How are you?"

"Fine." He looked anything but fine. His right arm was in a cast as was his left leg. His face was unusually pale, from the loss of blood, I assumed, but his eyes were as blue and intense as ever. And at this moment they were angry and defiant. I found I could not answer his gaze; I looked away.

"Would you like to sit down?" He grunted an agreement and hobbled across the room on a cane. After he was seated, I walked over and sat facing him.

"You're leaving." It was not a question and I could not lie.

"Yes," I said simply. "It seems best that I do."

"Oh." The single word held such anger, such reproach that I choked back any words of explanation I might have made. Instead, I rose from my chair and went to look out the window. A heavy silence descended on the room. When I finally turned around he was still staring at me, but some of his anger had been replaced with resignation and sadness. I would have preferred the anger.

He began to speak hesitantly. "I thought you might like to know the outcome of the other night. I just stopped by to let you know that you'll not be questioned or held accountable in any way for Max's death."

"Thank you. I was wondering what happened after I left." My voice softened on the last word.

"I know why you left, Deirdre. And I don't blame you." He glanced over at me, and gave the nuance of a smile. "At least not too much. I spent three weeks flat on my back, rationalizing the situation, knowing that you wouldn't have left me without good reasons, knowing what those reasons were."

"Mitch, I . . ."

"And still you won't let me finish. I took the blame for Max's death, self-defense in the line of duty. Actually"—and he gave me a cold-blooded grin—"I prefer to think of it as credit, rather than blame."

"But you were so weakened, so beat up. How could they believe you had done it?"

He shrugged. "The files are full of cases of people performing under duress. It won't be investigated fully, anyway. I heard his confession. There's no family or friends to press any charges and the precinct is happy to have the case successfully solved at last."

"I am glad, Mitch, that it turned out well for you."

"There is one thing that bothers me, though." His voice softened and he looked up at me from his seat at the couch. "Why didn't you come to see me in the hospital? I thought you would do at least that for me."

"But I did come, Mitch. The first few times they wouldn't let me in. After that, I bypassed the nurses' station and came in after hours." I thought back to those dark nights when I sat by his bed, holding his hand as he tossed and turned in delirium. "You were asleep, but I was there."

He gave me a smile, genuine now. "I knew it. I knew you'd been there, it couldn't have been a dream. But when I asked the nurses they didn't know who you were and swore there had been no visitors. How'd you manage it?"

I gave a little laugh. "You shouldn't have to ask that, Mitch. I managed, that's all."

My confession relieved the tension somewhat. "You could

have come when I was awake, you know. They do have visiting hours at night."

"I know, but I wasn't sure what sort of welcome I might get. After all, you were there, in part, because of what I did to you. I was afraid you might not want to see me."

"Deirdre"—he stared at me with his blue eyes—"you're a fool. If you don't realize how I feel by now . . ." He broke off as he again considered my suitcase by the door. "But I guess you don't, since you planned on leaving without a word to me. I guess I've just been wasting my time." He sounded bitter and my heart felt torn.

"I am a fool, Mitch," I said and knelt on the floor in front of him. Reaching up, I took his left hand in mine and held it to my face. "I had no right to get involved with you, and certainly no right to fall in love with you. But I do love you and nothing can change that now. Not my leaving, not your anger."

"Then don't leave," he urged. "Stay here, Deirdre. Marry me. How can I convince you that I don't care who or what you are." He gave me a long, appraising stare then chuckled and reached over and tousled my hair. "I don't even care what you've done to yourself." He grew serious again. "All I care about is being with you. I love you. I don't doubt that you'd like to get away from here. That's fine, we could go together, start a new life for the two of us. Marry me, Deirdre," he repeated urgently. "Say yes."

I sighed and shifted my position slightly so that I could rest my head on his uninjured leg. I gave no answer, no sign of the wavering I felt. Instead, I rubbed my cheek on his knee, considering his words. We could leave together. Another plane ticket could be purchased, another passport obtained. My new home could accommodate two quite easily. I allowed myself to envision a future with Mitch, our lives shared and our loneliness abated. It was a gentle dream and I sighed with the sweetness of it.

"Deirdre," he asked, his voice low and intense, "will you?"

The phone rang and I got up to answer it without a word.

"No, Frank," I said, still gazing at Mitch. "I'm not ready now. Ask him if he'll wait a while; if not, you can call another." I gently put the phone down.

"My cab is here," I said nervously and dropped my eyes. "I don't know what to say, Mitch."

"That's an easy call," he said, smiling uncertainly. "Just say yes."

I tried to return his smile but began to cry, instead. "I can't. It wouldn't work." I saw him through a glaze of tears. "You and I both know that it wouldn't. The first few decades would be wonderful, but after that . . ." I brushed away the tears and continued. "How could I bear to see you grow older every year, knowing that I never would? How could I bear to see you sicken and die and know that I could never join you after death? And how could you endure what I need to do to survive? Your love cannot change what I am: a creature of night, doomed to prowl and hunt for my sustenance." I shook my head and repeated, "It wouldn't work."

"But there's another way," he insisted. "You say that you can't change, but I can. You could change me, turn me into a vampire. Maybe, after the other night, you already have." I read fear in his eyes when he said this, but there was also a trace of hope. "Then the decision would have been reached; it would be out of our hands. You'd marry me then, wouldn't you?"

"Yes, but you must know that's not the case, Mitch." I saw the hope fall from his eyes. "You would need to have my blood to make the change and I won't give it." I crossed the room to him and took his hand again. "You're asking me to give you something that I have always considered a curse. For so many years I searched for the phantom that caused my life; I hunted him as surely as I hunt my prey. And yet now that he is gone"— my voice quavered and I groped for the right words—"I thought I might go back to what I was before, when he died. But the change in me was too deep, too long-term; I will always be what I am. Max's death has freed me from many things, and one of these is the hope for a normal life. I have accepted that fact, I can live in that knowledge now. I can even accept the fact that I will meet my final death in the same manner. But I do not want that death to be at your hands."

"Deirdre," he protested, "I would never do that, I love you."

"And I loved Max," I replied. "Not the way I love you, it's true. But for many years he was my only friend, my only contact with what I thought was the human world. And yet I hated him," I blazed into anger. "Hated him enough to kill him. He changed me, in more ways than one; discovering that I was capable of murder, no matter what the circumstances, was terrifying. I can live with that, I have to, but I will not lead you, or anyone else, down the same dark paths I have had to follow." I could read pain in his eyes and the anger suddenly drained out of me. "Mitch," I pleaded with him, hoping he would understand, "I couldn't bear for you to hate me someday like that. Leaving, as hard as it is, and never seeing you again, is easier to bear."

He started to protest again, but I put my hand gently over his mouth. "Do you really want a life like mine? Never to walk in the sun, to exist in the night only. Is that what you want, Mitch?"

He met my eyes with a fervent glance. "I want you, Deirdre. And if this is the only way . . ." He struggled to rise from the couch and when he did, he put his arm around me and held me close to him. "Deirdre," he breathed into my hair. "Damn it, I don't know." There was uncertainty in his voice. "I haven't really thought it through, I guess. But the thoughts of losing you have made me half-crazy. I don't know what to do." He moved back to study my face. "Look, promise me you won't say no right now. So much has happened to both of us. Would it hurt to postpone the decision? That would give us both some time to think about it. Could you do that?"

I considered his words, his proposal. Over thirty years ago I would not have hesitated; he was the answer to my dreams at that time. Even with my newfound resolve, the prospect was beguiling. To share my endless years with him. . . . I sighed and he relentlessly pressed his case.

"Give it—oh, let's say—six months," he urged, "or a year at

the most. This would be different than what occurred with you and Max. I would do it willingly, and you could teach me, help me. We would have each other."

"No, Mitch," I began, shaking my head, but his eyes met mine, searching, pleading. I smiled at him finally, reluctantly, and gave in. "Oh, hell, Mitch, I have all the time in the world. Six months or sixty, it all means nothing to me. But I will not encourage you in this. The decision will be yours and yours alone. Do you understand?" His eyes lit again with hope; I looked away. "Now I have a plane to catch."

He pulled me to him again in a fierce embrace that made him wince in pain. "Oh, Deirdre," he said, "will you still leave? How can I let you go?"

"With love, Mitch." I kissed him a final time. He stroked my hair and cheek, then slowly began to walk away. "Mitch," I called to him and he turned. "I left something for you. It will be delivered to your apartment tomorrow." I thought of the parcel I had instructed my attorney to give him after my departure. He would appreciate its significance. He looked at me questioningly. "It's the Van Gogh," I explained. "The only sunshine you and I will ever share."

He gave me a quiet smile and I found that I had nothing left to say to him. Instead, I opened the door and watched as he limped down the hall to the elevators. The bell rang, and he got in. As the doors began to close, he stopped them with his hand and stepped out slightly for one last glance. He gave me one of his boyish, exuberant grins. "See you in six months," he said confidently. Then the doors shut and he was gone.

Smiling weakly, I covered my hair with a thick scarf, picked up my bag and turned out the lights. Taking one last look at the rooms, I closed the door. "I hope not, Mitch," I said to the empty hall. "I hope not."

Epilogue

The summer sun sets late in my new home. I have adjusted
to the life well, but my internal clock is still set to another time,
another place. I shower, dress and go down the stairs. The day's
mail lies strewn in front of the slot in the door. I pick it up and
glance through it, finding nothing of interest except for a small
envelope from that other place. The writing is bold and mascu-
line and my heart jumps at the return address. I have waited for
months to receive this letter. I open it with trembling hands. The
message is short; I can tell through the folded page that it is no
more than three lines. Before reading it I hold it to my heart,
not really knowing what I want to find. Then I carefully unfold
it; I can delay no longer.

"Deirdre," he writes, "I do love you, but you were right, after
all. There's no way I could live your life. I hope you can forgive
me." He has written nothing else except for his name; what more
could he say? A single tear drops on the signature; I wipe it away
and his name dissolves to a black blot on the white page. I fold
it gently and place it on top of the rest of the mail.

The streets of London are dark and shining. I raise my face
to the night sky and let the rain wash away the traces of that one
tear. Then, purposefully, I begin to walk, my footsteps echoing
off the weathered walls surrounding me. Five blocks away is the
pub at which I now work. It is a homey little place that serves
a decent port, and does a good business in the tourist trade.

Life goes on, I think to myself and quicken my steps. I can

hear the laughter, the singing, and as I near the bar, I can smell the scent of blood and flesh. The door swings open and I trade the darkness of the night temporarily for the lights of the pub.

Faces turn to greet me, some familiar, some strange. I make my choice for the evening and give him an encouraging smile as I make my way through the crowd to my position behind the bar. So life goes on.

BLOOD SECRETS was only the first chapter of Deirdre
Griffin's story. Now the Vampire Legacy continues in
BITTER BLOOD.

Please turn the page for an exciting sneak preview of
BITTER BLOOD.

I shook the cold rain from my heavy woolen cloak as I entered the pub. That the place was nearly empty was not surprising. Although the sun had been set for nearly half an hour, it was still early, too early, for most of our regulars and certainly too early for the tourists. Two men, hunched over their bitter ale, glanced at me from the bar. To my acknowledging nod, they gave a brief grunt of greeting and returned their full attention to the contents of their mugs.

Idly, I moved behind the bar, still groggy from my nightmare-interrupted sleep. I gave the counter a cursory sweep with the dishcloth, then poured myself a large glass of port. Sipping gratefully, I leaned back into the shadows, my eyes greedily searching the dark street outside for passers-by.

Business had been bad recently. And while I did not need the money, I did miss the tourists. The wine helped, but it would not be long before I had to feed, at any cost. The hunger possessed me fully, its grasp stronger, more savage each waking moment, seeming to grow proportionately with the intensity of the dream. Two years ago I had sought freedom from that grip to discover too late that there would be no deliverance for me, only a deeper traveling into the inhuman soul—mine or his, it made little difference.

A light touch on my arm drew me, shuddering, out of my thoughts and back to the present.

"Someone walking on your grave, Dottie?"

I looked up at the ruddy face of my one-time boss, now my
artner and smiled slightly. "I imagine so, Pete," I said, reaching
elow the bar to hand him a crumpled pack of Players. He
allowed the same routine every night before leaving the pub.
e would smoke one cigarette, drink a glass of stout and count
he money in the drawer, before making his way home, to wife
ad family.

I poured him a drink and handed it to him as he sat on his
ool, counting the day's take. The cigarette dangled from his
pper lip and he squinted up at me through the thick smoke.

"Thank you, darlin'. What did I ever do before you came?"

I laughed. "You lost money, just the same as we do now. How
as business today?"

"Could have been better, Dot. But you know how I'm not one
or complaining." He shut the cash drawer, stubbed out his ciga-
ette and reached for his coat on a hook behind the bar. "Now,
ou, I worry about. Tending this bloody place night after night—
's not right for a young thing like you. Close up early tonight,
ottie, and go out and have some fun. Get some roses back into
our cheeks."

I reached over and protectively pulled his lapels up closer to
is neck. "Pete, you are a dear, but I really enjoy the nights here,
vith no crowds, no pressure. And in any event, I don't know
nyone here well enough to go out with them."

He gave a brief, angelic smile, but the feigned expression of
nnocence did not fool me; try as he might, he could not disguise
he glint of mischief in his eyes.

"Now, and that reminds me," he started in his slow, matter-
f-fact way, "bless me if there wasn't a young chap in here a
ttle earlier, asking after you." He began to rummage through
is pockets, absently patting and prodding them. "Seems to me,
wrote his name and number down somewhere. A Yank, did I
ell you that? He said he knew you in the States. Awful anxious
e was. Now if only I could find that paper . . ."

I folded my arms and leaned against the bar, waiting for him
o complete his act as patiently as was possible. Pete, for all of

his sixty-plus years, was more of a child than I had ever bee
a lover of surprises and practical jokes. Finally he produced
wrinkled, grubby piece of paper with a flourish and I held m
hand out to receive it.

"Thank you, Pete. Have a nice evening."

"You, too, darlin'." With a wink he left, whistling an ol
music hall tune as he went through the door.

I shook my head and regarded the paper, folded and lying i
my trembling hand. There was only one person who knew m
current location. Two years had not been enough time to forge
him, or the taste and feel of him, yet those years had merel
reinforced my reasons for leaving.

Mitch was better off without me; I had believed it then and
believed it now. I was not the same woman I had been; I wa
changed and not, I thought, for the good. My desperate strik
for freedom had failed. I had not driven away the dark spiri
Instead, by giving him death, I had allowed him entrance to m
soul and will. Sometimes in my loneliest times, I held him close
savoring our shared passion and pain. We were one in his deatl
as we had never been in life—it was his whispering voice I hear
during the hunt, his cynical pleasure I felt when I fed.

I did not hear the door open—its cheerful little bell had no
announced a customer—but suddenly he was there, leanin
across the bar, one eyebrow raised and a sardonic smile on hi
face. "How lovely you look tonight, my dear. How about a drin
for an old friend?"

"Dammit, Max. Get the hell out of here."

His body wavered and shimmered, dissolving instantly int
the shape of one of our regulars, very surprised and slightl
belligerent. "All I want is a drink, Dot, then I'll leave yo
alone."

"Oh, God, I'm so sorry. I thought you were someone else."
gave him a bright smile and pushed a glass in his direction
"This one is on the house."

He took the drink and my apology good-naturedly. "Thanks
You don't seem too chipper tonight. You feeling all right?"

"I am fine, thank you. Just a little tired, that's all."

He shrugged and moved away from the bar to sit at a table, joined a few minutes later by a few of his friends. I shoved the note unread into my apron pocket and tended to the business of the pub.

Later that evening my long wait for tourists finally paid off. A group of six, loud and embarrassingly boisterous, arrived one hour before closing, quickly driving out the regulars. I singled out the likeliest candidate, tall and broad-shouldered, with a bold look in his eyes that caused my body to tighten in anticipation. I smiled at him as I took their orders and served their drinks, offering him a glass of port. When he questioned me, I leaned close to him. "For later," I whispered, "for endurance." He drank it in one gulp, shuddering slightly at its bitterness, and immediately asked for another.

"He's ours now, my little one," the cynical voice in my mind nodded. "Don't wait too long."

I did not. So desperate was I for this man that I issued last call almost immediately. My invitation to him to stay and help close up was met with unabashed approval from his friends and soon we were alone.

I locked the door, dimmed the lights and walked back across the room. He joined me behind the bar as I was counting the money in the register. "Aren't you afraid I might steal that?" he questioned with a crooked smile as he helped himself to another glass of port.

I laughed, low and sensually, as I put the night's profits in the safe. "There's not enough here to even be tempting." I gave him a warm, appraising glance. "And somehow I don't think that you're interested in my money."

"You sure are right about that, babe." He crossed over to me and put an arm around my waist. "When you're finished here let's go back to my place." He mentioned the name of his hotel and I nodded my agreement, leaning closer to him.

His grip tightened. "I don't think I caught your name . . ."

"Dorothy . . . ah, just Dorothy. And yours?"

"Oh, I get it. No last names, right? Then I'm Robert, Robbie to my friends."

"It's wonderful to meet you, Robbie. You'll never know how much."

"But I'll bet I can guess." He pulled me closer and kissed me; my teeth grazed his lip, drawing one intoxicating drop of blood. I savored it and probed with my tongue for more. My hands were wrapped about his waist. I slid my nails slowly up his spine and he shivered, took his mouth away from mine and looked down at me.

"God." He was breathing heavily and small beads of sweat appeared on his brow. "You really want this bad, don't you?"

I moaned in answer and his face grew fierce, full of passion. His hands grasped my waist and he lifted me onto the narrow counter behind the bar, pushing against me forcefully and insistently until I encircled his body with my legs.

He kissed me again and slid his hand down the back of my jeans, kneading the flesh of my lower back. His skin was so warm, so alive. I had to have him now.

"Wait," the voice inside urged. "Let's play a little first."

"I don't want to wait," I protested aloud and reached up to loosen his tie and unbutton his shirt.

"Neither do I." He lifted my sweater over my head and threw it on the floor. While he nuzzled my breasts, he struggled unsuccessfully to untie my apron. With an exasperated sigh, he spun it around on my waist and began to unfasten my jeans. I pulled his shirt off and he ground his groin into mine. Putting my tongue to his skin, I traced a delicate path to his neck and gently nibbled there, while he eased my pants down around my knees.

There was a pounding in my head and my gums tingled, signaling the growth of my canines. I was ready; it had been too long, entirely too long. The pounding increased, louder and more demanding.

Abruptly, he pulled away; I lost my balance and lurched up against him.

"What was that?" His voice was angry, suspicious.

"Nothing," I purred, wrapping my arms tightly around his neck. "Come back to me, make love to me."

"No way," he said, wresting himself away from me and putting his clothing back into order. "There's someone at the door."

"They'll go away. I need you, Robbie."

"Forget it."

I was trembling with my unsatisfied need. Quickly I fastened my jeans, put my sweater back on, and walked over to him where he was putting on his coat. Gently, I laid my hand on his arm, and rubbed my head on his sleeve. "Robbie, please, what's wrong? We can go somewhere else if you like, please . . . you can't leave me like *this*."

The knocking at the door continued, more urgent now.

"Nothing doing, babe. I've heard about this scam before. How much would it have taken to pay off that guy out there—the witness to your 'rape'—five hundred, maybe an even thousand? No thanks, you may be the sexiest bitch I've seen in this country, but you're still too rich for my blood." He pushed me away from him and opened the door. "She's all yours, pal," he said to the figure standing hesitantly in the doorway. "I barely touched her."

"Damn," I swore under my breath as the door slammed. The little bell jangled, discordant in my ears. I rubbed my hands along my jeans. "Well?" I addressed the man whose shadowed face was unrecognizable, even to me. "This had better be damned important."

"Deirdre?" The voice sounded embarrassed, and vaguely familiar. "What was that all about?" He stepped forward into the dim light of the room.

Instantly, I knew who he was—the mysterious Yank visitor that Pete had told me about, whose name and number were on a crumpled piece of paper in my apron pocket. And it was not Mitch. Disappointed at that realization, I understood that my dread at meeting him again would have been overruled by my strong desire to see him, hold him, make love to him one more time.

"Hello, Chris," I said to the man who had inherited Mitch's features and build. He had aged in two years, I thought; lines of worry creased his face and he looked like he hadn't slept in weeks.

"Deirdre, it is you, isn't it? I barely recognize you."

"Yes, it is I, in the flesh," I said with no trace of a smile. Were my changes so apparent, even in the darkness? My hair was still almost black, but I had let it grow to its original length. That could not have made much of a difference to him. And although I had not aged, I knew that my mirror revealed me to be harder, coarser, debased somehow by my inhuman instincts.

"Your eyes look funny, they're . . . well, they're almost glowing." I could hear fear in his voice, a reluctance that had never been there before.

"Don't be silly, Chris. The light in here is deceptive." I reached over and turned on one of the switches behind the bar. "There, now," I said reassuringly, squinting slightly against the glare, "is that better?"

"Yeah, I guess so." He paused for a moment and when he continued his tone was slightly sullen. "I hope I didn't interrupt something important. That guy sure shot out of here like a bullet. And do you always wear your apron backward?"

I reached down to my waist, twitching the apron around to its proper position, but ignored the unspoken questions about Robbie's presence. "Would you like a drink? On the house, of course." I smiled at him, but he refused to meet my eyes.

"Sure, why not? I'll have a beer."

I motioned him to a table. "Sit down," I said, opening two bottles of beer from the refrigerator, "and I'll join you."

He watched me intently as I walked out from behind the bar and sat down next to him. Without a word, he took the bottle from me and drank, quickly and furtively, as if to fortify himself against some dire event. His hands, I noticed with surprise were shaking. But then again, so were mine.

"Now, maybe you would like to tell me how you came to be here and how you knew where to find me. Did your father send you?" The emotion I tried to disguise in my voice was not just frustration over the interrupted feeding.

"No." His voice sounded choked, overhung with anger and grief. "No, he didn't send me. But I found your address while I was sorting through his papers and knew that I should come to see you. . . ."

My heart sank. He was dead. I could feel it. I could see it in Chris's face. Jesus, I wailed inside, Mitch is dead. He died and I could have stopped it, but I didn't. I had the power to keep him with me forever, and I did nothing.

"Mitch is dead." My voice, flat and toneless, did nothing to express the despair that the stating of those words caused.

"Oh, no," Chris was quick to protest. "It's not that, honest. It's just that, well, he's bad off, Deirdre. I don't know what's wrong, nobody does. But I think he's dying." He took one more drink of his beer then set the bottle back on the table softly. His eyes finally held mine and his voice, so much like Mitch's, fell gently on my ears.

"And I think that only you can save him. You must save him, Deirdre. Come back to him."

ABOUT THE AUTHOR

Always fascinated with the supernatural, Karen Taylor first conceived of writing a vampire novel while living across the street from a cemetery in Richmond, Virginia nearly 15 years ago. She enjoyed participating in theatrical productions during college as a Communication Arts major, but now readily admits that writing is better, since you cannot only write all the lines, you can also play all the parts.

Residing in Maryland with her husband, two children and the prerequisite number of pets (one dog and one cat), Karen is currently hard at work on *Blood of My Blood,* the fourth novel in the Vampire Legacy series.

Karen loves to hear from her readers and you may write to her c/o Pinnacle Books. Please include a self-addressed stamped envelope if you wish a response.

BOOK YOUR PLACE ON OUR WEBSITE AND MAKE THE READING CONNECTION!

We've created a customized website just for our very special readers, where you can get the inside scoop on everything that's going on with Zebra, Pinnacle and Kensington books.

When you come online, you'll have the exciting opportunity to:

- View covers of upcoming books
- Read sample chapters
- Learn about our future publishing schedule (listed by publication month *and author*)
- Find out when your favorite authors will be visiting a city near you
- Search for and order backlist books from our online catalog
- Check out author bios and background information
- Send e-mail to your favorite authors
- Meet the Kensington staff online
- Join us in weekly chats with authors, readers and other guests
- Get writing guidelines
- AND MUCH MORE!

**Visit our website at
http://www.pinnaclebooks.com**

ENTER THE WORLD OF KAREN E. TAYLOR'S
VAMPIRE LEGACY

BLOOD SECRETS (Book One)

Allow me to introduce myself. My name is Deirdre Griffin and I'm a vampire. Currently I'm living in Manhattan and I spend my evenings at the Ballroom of Romance, where I satisfy my blood lust with weekly feedings. Unlike other vampire's, I *never* drain my victims, but it seems there's another vampire on the loose, only this one *is* draining his victims—and pointing the finger of suspicion at me! What's a woman to do? If you're a vampire like me, you use your feminine wiles to hunt him down . . .

BITTER BLOOD (Book Two)

Remember me? Deirdre Griffin, *vampire?* After living in London for two years, I'm back in my favorite city. But life in New York's no picnic in the park. It seems that a group of vampires want revenge against me for killing their leader. What's worse, they're using my ex-lover, Detective Mitch Greer, as bait, and the only way I can save him is by converting him into a vampire like me . . .

BLOOD TIES (Book Three)

It's me again: Deirdre Griffin, *vampire.* When we last met, my lover, Mitch Greer, had finally become a vampire. Now we're back on the streets of New York, at the request of The Cadre, a secret society of ancient vampires, because another series of murders is taking place. It turns out this guy isn't just killing humans, he's also killing vampires . . .

BLOOD OF MY BLOOD
(Book Four—coming in October 2000)

I'm back. Deirdre Greer, vampire—formerly Deirdre Griffin. I've married Mitch, promising to love him for all eternity, but now he's vanished from our backwoods Maine cabin. As I embark on a search for my beloved, traveling to the French Quarter of New Orleans, I uncover a baffling trail—a trail supposedly left by me. Who is the shadowy, eerily familiar figure lurking on the fringes of my life? What does she want of me? And what has she done with Mitch?